JAMES HERBERT

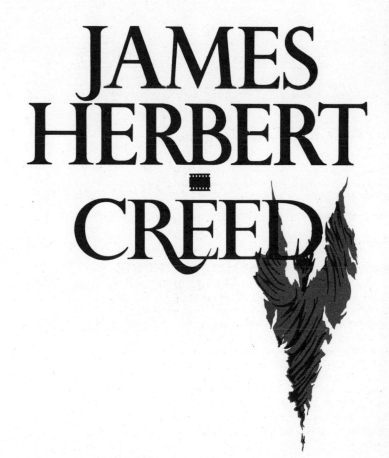

CREED

Hodder & Stoughton

LONDON SYDNEY AUCKLAND TORONTO

British Library Cataloguing in Publication Data

Herbert, James, *1943–*
  Creed.
  I, Title
  823.914 [F]

  ISBN 0-340-50909-0

Published by Hodder and Stoughton,
a division of Hodder and Stoughton Ltd,
Mill Road, Dunton Green, Sevenoaks, Kent TN13 2YA
Editorial Office: 47 Bedford Square, London WC1B 3DP

Photoset by Rowland Phototypesetting Ltd,
Bury St Edmunds, Suffolk

Printed in Great Britain by
Butler and Tanner Ltd, Frome, Somerset

My special thanks to Richard Young,
true paparazzo, but also true gentleman
(and certainly nothing like Joe Creed, the
dubious 'hero' of this novel). Richard's
help in research has been invaluable.
My thanks also to three other
photographers – David Benett for more
pap stories, Bob Knight for
technical advice and Dave Morse for
use of a certain mews house.

JAMES HERBERT
Sussex, 1990

Demons today are a shoddy lot . . .

1

The first thing you ought to know about Joseph Creed is that he's a sleaze of the First Order – maybe even of the *Grand* Order, considering his trade. The second is that he's our hero.

(Not by choice, incidentally, is he the latter – not by *his* choice, anyway. Let's just say circumstances and his own inglorious nature conspired to make him so.)

His trade? Taking candid snaps of the rich, the famous, or those who fall into that loose category of *celeb*. Ideally these snaps are of the kind the subject – or victim – would prefer not to be published (of course, the less preferred the higher their value on the media market). Creed, then, is a paparazzo (a scavenger lensman, some might say). Paparazzi is the plural, or 'reptiles' as their prey might refer to them. There are other descriptions: parasites, leeches, vultures. Scumbags is very popular. But lest we be too hard on them as a breed, it should be said at the outset that there are some exceedingly nice members of the paparazzi, some who even behave like gentlemen on occasion and yes, even those who are trustworthy. Unfortunately, Creed isn't one of these.

Sometimes – no, *often* – his own kind, fellow photographers, snappers, smudgers, monkeys, shunned him (although it should be said that envy played some part here, for Creed had an upsetting knack of capturing on film the almost impossible, of snapping the unsnappable). *They* thought *his* methods were despicable.

Something else that rankled with a few of the others in his male-dominated profession was his success with women (as a rule you have to be disliked in the first place for this to annoy others). His romances, to use an unfashionable term, seldom lasted long, but they *were* frequent and, three times out of five, his partners were definite lookers. He himself, you see, looked a little like Mickey Rourke, the actor (Mickey Rourke at his sleaziest, if you can imagine *that*) and when he smiled his knowing, almost mocking, smile, women knew, they just *knew*, he was trouble. And God help them, that was his allure, that was what intrigued the ladies. They sensed he was a shit and, it's true to say, he rarely let them down in that respect. Still they went for him, still they dipped in a toe and were upset, although not surprised, when they got scalded. Women aren't easy to understand.

He had other bad points. Joe Creed could be mean, selfish, disreputable. He was a moral cheat, both amoral and immoral – although, in his favour, not all the time. He could be tetchy, obstinate, cynical and, if he thought he could get away with it, belligerent. He had friends, but no *good* friends. And yet he was tolerated by establishments which would never entertain others of his professional ilk (another point of envy among his colleagues): he was allowed to drink in the bars of several 'in-place' restaurants and clubs when on duty, provided his cameras were kept out of sight, and doormen and bouncers of the trendiest and most élite London nightclubs would always tip him the wink if there was a worthy celeb inside. This was mainly because Creed himself was a 'known' face, having haunted these places for so many years now; his name, because it had appeared so often beneath photographs of the rich and glamorous, was also 'known'. He had, himself, become an integral part of the celeb circuit (or circus, if you prefer). As well as that, he knew how to grovel when the occasion demanded, and into whose hands to drop readies when required.

So that's our boy. A rough idea only, but you get the picture. He's sleazy, but good at his job; dislikable, yet interesting to certain women; accepted, although perhaps not respectable. You might like him, you might loathe him; maybe there'll be a balance between the two.

Unfortunately, the circumstances in which we first meet him aren't too endearing.

He's . . .

2

. . . pissing into the corner of a tomb, inside one of those big old
mausoleum affairs. A tomb, in fact, with a view, for it stands on a
small knoll in the grounds of an expansive and impressive cemetery,
surrounded by and slightly above others of its kind. As well as these
extravagant sepulchres, there are acres of headstones – crosses,
angels, obelisks and marble slabs, many of these crumbly and rotted
(but not as crumbly and rotted as what rests beneath them). Creed
zips up, shivering with the cold, damp, mouldy atmosphere, and
leans back against a tier on which a chipped stone coffin lies. He
continues to wait . . .

Creed sucked smoke from the thin brown roll-up dangling between
his lips, warming his lungs and neutralising the tomb's earthy smell.
He scratched his chin, fingernails loud against stubble within the
confines of the echoey granite chamber (Creed, incidentally, sported
stubble before and after it was designer, just as he wore clothes that

fitted badly before that, too, became fashionable). He looked at his wristwatch, angling its face towards the barred doorway through which cheerless light drooped. Not for the first time that morning he told himself there had to be better ways of making a living.

He stooped only slightly to check the Nikon's viewfinder, for the camera, with its 400mm lens, was mounted on a tall tripod. That lens was pointed down the hill towards an open grave, the mound of earth beside the excavation moist and dark. He imagined the long lens was a bazooka and mentally blasted the narrow foxhole to hell, whispering the missile's whooshing roar for sound effects. The earth explodes, bone shrapnel erupts from the pit, a thousand maggots feeding on the last of the flesh find the ability to fly . . . Creed closed his eyes.

Unhealthy, he told himself. Hanging around graveyards was definitely unhealthy. Skulking inside tombs was a degenerate pastime. And all for lousy shots of lousy people mourning a louse. Shit, Creed, Mother wanted better things for you.

He straightened, puffing smoke without removing the cigarette. Quit griping. You do it because you love it. The hours might be crazy, the conditions often lacklustre – he surveyed the stony décor – but you still get a buzz when *the* moment comes, when *the* shot's in the viewfinder, when your finger hits the shutter release at precisely *the* right time, and you know beyond doubt you've got *the* one, the perfect picture. Nothing quite like it, is there? Even the pay-cheque isn't as good as getting the shot. No, *the* moment is the thing, *the* moment rules. The ducking, the diving, the waiting, the scheming, they're all part of it – every bit of foreplay counts – but *the* moment is sheer ejaculation. And if you knew you'd got it, that supreme moment captured on film, the high lingered until it was in print. By then, with luck, you were already on to the next, and maybe planning the one after that, even though planning didn't come into it much because usually it all happened by chance (you just had to be ready for it). Gimme three big ones, Lord, was Creed's constant prayer. Prince Charles weeping for his lost friend on the Klosters ski-slope, John Lennon signing an autograph for his assassin-to-be, a burning Buddhist or two. Something *significant*, Lord, something for worldwide syndication, five-figure bids no less, front-page ratings. Gimme a classic like Jack Ruby gunning down Lee Harvey Oswald.

Or something like those Vietnamese kids fleeing naked from a napalm attack. Or even Joan Collins *sans* wig would do. Be good to me, God, time's running short.

He stubbed out the thin cigarette on the nearest coffin. They should be arriving soon, the bereaved and the vultures and those who *really* knew the deceased and wanted to make sure the old hag was properly nailed down.

Creed had never heard, never read, a single kind word about Lily Neverless, the actress (actress? She'd played the same part for nigh on sixty years, and that playing was easy because she had always played herself) who was about to be buried today in this rich man's boneyard. Neurotic, harpy bitch; that had been Lily in life and on stage and screen. Yet the public adored her *because* she was bad, real bad, larger-than-life *bad*. That was her trademark. Whereas Joan Crawford had battered her kids with coathangers, old Lil had bludgeoned her husbands (four in all) with public and eagerly greeted pronouncements on their individual shortcomings. They were mean-hearted and tight-fisted, they were miserably inadequate lovers, they were cheats, they were drunkards, they were pathetic, they were *pigs*. One of them, she proclaimed to help divorce proceedings along, was QUEE-AR – that's the way Lily enunciated the condition in her curious European-Americanised accent: QUEE-AR! This particular poor devil's lawsuit against her following the divorce never even scratched court: a cardiac arrest finished him on the day his brief was briefed. To add irony, it was he who had sired Lily's only child, although even this had now been called into doubt because of Lily's revelation. Another shared a similar fate healthwise, only this one's heart attack left him vegetabalised rather than finalised. In its way, this was even more cruel, for he was comparatively young, twenty years junior to old Lil, in fact (and this before toy-boys were common-place).

It took less than three months for Lily to unload the veg, and legend had it that mental cruelty on *his* part was cited in her petition for divorce. Maybe the slurpy sounds he made when he tried to communicate (apparently the best he could do with a tongue as flaccid as a spent penis) had a cutting edge of sarcasm to them that offended her sensitive nature; or perhaps the fact that he had to be spoon-fed by a full-time nurse at the frequent and lavish dinner parties that Lily threw, an embarrassing and conversation-stilting business no doubt, put too much of a strain on her endeavours to be the gay hostess. Whatever, she got her divorce.

Interestingly, her first husband had disappeared into the rainforests of Brazil never to be heard of again after only ten months of marriage. At the time he was a minor-league Hollywood star (who'd featured in more than one jungle movie, as it happens, although all had been shot on the Warner Bros' back lot) and Lily was fresh over from Europe where she'd been a minor queen bitch of the theatre. Only God, the actor, himself, and Lily knew what had prompted her husband to stomp off into the green like that, but the first two were incommunicado and the last one wasn't saying.

However, the real kicker was the way in which her fourth husband shed his shackles.

This poor old boy – he was older, much older, than Lil – decided to euthanise himself on his eighty-seventh birthday. Euthanise is the wrong word, actually, because the method he chose was far from painless; he was also, for his years, in a splendid state of health, and his mind was in reasonable order apart from an occasional meandering through all his yesterdays. So nobody understood why he had pulverised his favourite St Louis brandy glass in a food blender to make himself a butter and granule sandwich. Surely, they reasoned, there had to be easier ways to exit, particularly at that frail age. By all means use a brandy glass, but for God's sake, fill it to the brim with the finest brandy, use it to wash down as many sleeping pills or pain-killers as you can lay your hands on, and toast yourself to peace everlasting before pulling on a clingfilm balaclava. The note he had left explained nothing. 'Had enough,' it said in scrawly handwriting. Still, by then Lily had learned to wear black with considerable style, and her wakes (the invalid husband had been long dead and buried, and the jungle rover's undoubted death had been celebrated in his absence) were joyous affairs.

Now this was her own funeral and there must have been those present who, if not allowed to dance in the aisles, would surely have jiggled their buttocks to the requiem, for she'd made an awful lot of enemies in the business and just as many out of it. However, as mentioned, the public had adored her because, when all was said and done, Lily Neverless was a great actress when playing the

Woman-You-Love-to-Hate. It's believed that even Bette Davis had envied her splenetic image.

Creed stamped his feet, the big toe on either one numb with the cold. Bad circulation, he told himself, and smoking doesn't help. He reached into a top pocket of his combat jacket – the kind of loose, many pocketed thigh-length coat worn by the US infantry during the Second World War – and drew out a cigarette. He stuck it between his lips and squeezed by the tripod to press his face between the rusted struts of the barred door. His eyes swivelled left and right as his hand delved into another pocket for a lighter.

Action! Shiny black shapes gliding solemnly through the gravestone estate, the long hearse carrying Lily's dead body leading the way. About bloody time. What the hell they'd found to eulogise over beat him, but then, he supposed, showbiz was all to do with pretence and nothing to do with reality.

He moved back into the shadows as the cortège drew nearer, his cigarette remaining unlit. He checked the viewfinder once more, then stood poised, waiting.

Mourners appeared from the cars and trailed respectfully after the coffin-bearers; here and there handkerchiefs dabbed at cheeks. Maybe some of them loved you after all, Lil, mused Creed as he focused, searching the gathering for 'faces'. Ah, some reasonable ones. Gielgud was there, and Dame Whatsername – what *was* her name? Let the picture editor identify her from the contacts, that's what he was paid for. Attenborough? Looked like him. And Johnny Mills, yeah, that was certainly him. And that one – Christ, was *he* still alive? He hadn't made a movie in fifteen years, at least. Looking at him it was no wonder – senility had obviously set in.

A gaggle of old stars was in attendance, all of them no doubt wondering who was next to go. Now who was that one over there? From a different generation to Lily's. Maggie Smith? Looked like her, but then off-stage she looked like anybody. There was Judi Dench, looking nothing like a Dame. A sprinkling of well-known directors, an impresario or two.

Creed began pressing the shutter release, aiming, focusing, clicking, moving on. Okay, Sir John, is that a hint of a smile I see? Come on, don't be so bloody enigmatic, you're not on stage now. A little discreet grin is all I want. Gotcha. Thank you. Next.

That one. Yeah, I know that face. Character parts of distinction was this one's speciality. Something Elliot. Dennis, or – no, Denholm, that was it. Is that a smirk I see? Well, well. *Click*.

Creed continued snapping, perfectly happy in his work and no longer feeling the cold. He changed film and allowed the camera lens to roam here and there, the tripod holding it steady for each long shot, seeking out personalities among the general mill, mentally summoning up a story behind each cameo shot: the Minister for the Arts in deep conversation with a screen seductress of 'sixties' British comedies, whose penchant was for the ladies rather than the men; a huge-nosed chairman of the country's leading chain-stores, whose reputation had been considerably enhanced by the 'kiss and tell' revelations of his last bimbo but two; the television news-caster, whose recent payrise had elevated him way beyond his station (or any other station, his disgruntled rival newscasters pointed out). Creed's greatest hope was that an over-distraught person would leap on to the coffin as it was lowered into the ground, but common sense told him it just wouldn't happen, because no one would be *that* upset over Lily's departure (not even the accountants at Twentieth Century Fox, for she hadn't made a box-office hit for many a year now).

He swapped over to his other Nikon, this one fitted with a zoom lens, and took general crowd stuff, only occasionally homing in on individuals.

He shook his head in disappointment when the party finally began to break up. There had been a small chance that Lily Neverless' daughter, her only surviving kin as far as it was known, might have been allowed to attend. That could have brought some poignancy to the proceedings, especially with two white-coated orderlies by her side (all right, maybe they were more discreet nowadays, but that didn't stop Creed's imagination dramatising or picturising the scenario), but he guessed that whoever was in charge of her welfare nowadays had decided against letting her loose for the occasion. Pity.

When most of the crowd had drifted away, Creed moved further back into the tomb and lit the cigarette that had dangled cold from his lips throughout the session. The event was covered, he'd done his job; but where was *the* shot, where was the one that would make the other snappers, the rest of the pack that had been held at bay outside the cemetery gates along with the ghouls, sightseers and devoted fans, sick with envy?

He allowed himself a weary grin. That was the trouble with the young Turks nowadays – no balls. There were relatively few paparazzi left who took genuine risks or even *tried* to buck the system; they wanted it handed to them on a plate. True enough they'd kick, elbow and shove each other to get a clear shot, but cunning and *chutzpah* seemed to be in short supply. Creed, himself, had arrived at the upmarket boneyard just after six that morning – there's dedication for you – and had driven around the high walls until he'd found a quiet spot in a country lane far away from the main gates. He had parked opposite, beneath some trees, then crossed over and used a small aluminium stepladder (often essential equipment) to reach the top of the wall. His camera bag and tripod had been lowered to the other side by a length of nylon string with a hook at one end; the same had drawn up the ladder after him. Creed had dropped into the cemetery and waited, crouched against the wall, until it was light enough to search for an open grave; if it hadn't been dug the night before then he would have waited for the diggers to arrive and followed them to the spot. It was easier to find than he thought it would be, for there were virgin areas in the cemetery obviously reserved in advance for those who could afford the deposit (no pun intended). 'PLOT 1290 NEVERLESS' had been marked on a rough piece of board and planted atop the mound of damp earth beside the oblong pit.

Creed had almost yelped with delight when he scanned the locale and spied the grey mausoleum set on a low hillock not two hundred yards away. A perfect vantage point, provided some thoughtless bugger hadn't locked its barred door.

Again he was in luck for, although rust made the handle difficult to turn, the door wasn't locked. Why should it be? No one inside was going anywhere.

The horror-movie groan from the rarely used hinges was a little unsettling, and the unwholesome dank smell of the chamber itself hardly warmed the spirit, but Creed felt pleased with himself. He set up camp and began his vigil.

Four hours later it was all over, with nothing special to show. Decent enough crowd shots, a few close-ups of the faded and jaded, but nothing to set the juices flowing. Well, you couldn't win 'em all; in fact, the aces were rare. Always another day, though, another dollar. New opportunities were always around the next corner. Be ready, be there.

Had Creed been as philosophical as this about his work he wouldn't have screamed an expletive and kicked the coffin on the lowest tier. Stone and mould scraped off, leaving a scar as white as bone. Rather than apologise for the offence, Creed kicked the coffin again.

He turned back to the camera and tripod, one big toe no longer numbed by the cold but throbbing from the blow. Taking a last puff from the cigarette, he tossed it into a corner. His hand went to the small screw holding the Nikon to the tripod platform . . . and there it froze.

Not all the mourners had left yet, although even the diggers had finished their shovelling and wandered off. Someone was standing in the shadow of a tree.

Creed's eyes narrowed for better definition before he remembered he had the means of magnification at hand. He bent to the viewfinder and carefully altered the camera's angle.

Black shoes, dark trousers, grey raincoat – that's all our photographer could see through the lens. He tilted the Nikon further, but the lurker's head and shoulders were partly obscured by low foliage.

Now why was he hanging around after everyone else had left? And why was he hiding? – at least he seemed to be hiding. Was he a gatecrasher? Security would have been tight that morning and funeral liggers unwelcome. But then he himself had got in easily enough. Maybe he was just a hack covering the story.

Movement. The man was coming forward, ducking beneath the low branch. Grey gaberdine coat, scarf up around his face. Now he was pulling the scarf away. Christ, what a face! He was either very old, or had had a lot of worry. Certainly he was well past his sell-by date. He was looking around, making sure the coast was clear, strands of hair lying rigidly flat over his scalp as if welded there.

Creed exposed a single frame, then immediately wondered why. This guy was never going to be *the* shot: he was either an interloper, a journo, an acquaintance, or possibly an old flame of the deceased. Whatever, no way did he look or act like a *celeb*.

Creed straightened and watched the man stop before the freshly sealed grave. A pause for three or four seconds, then the man slowly walked around until he was facing the mausoleum once more. After which he repeated the circuit, this time going the other way, and all the time staring down solemnly at the swelling of earth as if expecting it to move.

He started the return trip, clockwise this time, but came to a halt with his back towards the hidden photographer. His shoulders began to shake, gently at first, a mild quivering; that quivering became a juddering, then a spasmodic twitching of his whole upper body.

The old boy's really upset, mused Creed, reaching for another loose cigarette. He fished one out – he'd had plenty of time that morning to build a batch of them – and stuck it between his lips. He lit up and the lighter lingered near his face when cracked laughter drifted up the incline into the tomb.

Creed stared down at the grey-coated figure in surprise. He wasn't bawling at all – the crazy was laughing! Creed capped the lighter: he was frowning, but his mouth curled its own smile. He shook his head slowly, wondering what old Lil had done to this one for her demise to cause such glee. Could be he was a relative or friend of one of her exes. Or maybe just someone she'd done wrong. Shame he wasn't familiar; a known face chortling over Lily Neverless' dead body would fetch a decent price.

No matter, it was something to finish up the roll with. Creed dragged smoke before stooping to the camera. Too close – head and shoulders only; he revolved the lens, pulling back as much as possible. Better. Right, you bugger, turn a little so we can see your mug.

The happy mourner ignored the request.

Creed shot film anyway. The shutter release refused on the third squeeze and he clicked his tongue in annoyance. He flicked ash on to the dusty floor and casually reached for the other camera resting on a coffin lid, his eyes never leaving the mystery figure outside. Before his hand touched the spare Nikon, something happened that startled him.

The man sank to his knees and began scraping at the hump of soft earth.

'Bloody hell,' Creed whispered as the man bent to his task. Unbelievable! The photographer's hand instinctively grasped the camera and he moved around the tripod for a clearer view. He quickly raised the Nikon and zoomed in; this time, because of the less powerful lens, the whole of the burrower was in the frame. First shot: good. Second shot: more of the same. Third shot: also. Fourth shot – the subject had stopped digging.

It was difficult to tell from that angle, but Creed thought the man was unbuttoning his raincoat. He was. He opened it out. He was taking something from an inside pocket. Hunching over again, he was –

Creed's eyes gleamed, and he muttered an oath. If only the crazy had been facing him . . .

What was he up to? Fumbling at his clothes again. He – oh no, he wouldn't. Creed raised the camera again. Shit, what a great shot it would have been if only the man had been facing the other way. Unusable, of course, no newspaper would use it. No British newspaper anyway. But certain European journals might love to have a picture of someone pissing on the great Lily Neverless' grave.

Wait a minute, that wasn't it . . . Oh no, not that. No one would do that in broad daylight, let alone in a graveyard! That was *obscene*! Creed almost grinned. *That* was bloody disgusting!

He raised the camera to eye-level again.

The man's head was bowed as though he were keen to witness his own self-abuse, and both shoulders were moving rhythmically. A two-hander. Creed allowed himself the grin. 'Who's a big boy then?' he whispered. He took a picture, then another. But not another.

Pretty boring, he told himself. Even a full-frontal would have been. Sick, but ultimately boring. Now if the man had had a female partner down there, and they were copulating on the grave, well that would be both interesting and saleable (although even the more salacious of the tabloids would have to do some heavy obscuring on the chosen print). Shame the pervert was a loner . . .

The man was becoming more agitated. And oddly (well, more oddly) he appeared to be talking as he beat. Wait, not talking: praying. Or maybe chanting. The words wafting up the rise seemed to have some cadence to them, like a monotone litany, a meaningless bunch of words that could be heard in churches on any Sunday. If this was some obscure religious sect's idea of a funeral ceremony, Creed wondered what a baptism would be like. Or a marriage. Could be the guy just liked music while he worked.

Creed began to hum 'Happy Days Are Here Again', his voice a low tuneless rumble rather than an aria to the other man's oratorio. But he quickly stopped – Creed, not the man down at the graveside.

This time the photographer's frown was intense, his eyes almost squared in concentration. Something else was happening by Lily Neverless' final resting place. The grass was waving.

The grass was waving? Creed grimaced. Stupid! There's a breeze out there, that's all. The grass was blowing in the wind. The sicko was still enjoying himsel – *wait, the breeze couldn't disturb the earth*!

Creed blinked. The ground couldn't move like that, it couldn't ripple . . . unless someone underneath didn't want to be there.

He squeezed his eyes tight, then opened them again.

At least the fresh mound of earth was still once more. Lily was obviously oblivious to the crazyman's incantations, invocations, whatever his bloody dirging was meant to be. It was the earth *around* the grave that was moving, the grass *beside* the mound that was dancing.

Yet the earth's movement was subtle, almost indiscernible, hardly a movement at all if you stared hard, really hard, the motion caught only in soft focus, in the periphery; but the grass was swaying, no illusion there, although a slight wind could be causing that, except the blades were shifting in different directions, one patch leaning into its neighbour, that neighbour fighting back, tangling with its bedfellow. None of it was logical.

The man's exertions were becoming wooden in their intensity, as if reaching their peak. His voice was still not loud, but somehow its resonance had increased.

Creed levelled the camera. The rippling ground could never be captured on a still and even if the definition was ultra-sharp, the grass would only reproduce as a confused mess; yet he felt compelled to get some record of this weird event, if only to prove to himself later that he hadn't been hallucinating (what a straight photograph would establish he wasn't quite sure, but it might be better than nothing at all).

He first focused on the area before the kneeling man, the ground that appeared to be agitated; then he aimed for the back of the man's head, using the thin tramlines of hair as a focusing point. That wasn't as easy, for the head refused to rest. The man was fast reaching gratification.

Creed's index finger tightened on the shutter release. He had to steady both hands, for they had suddenly trembled – not from any sexual excitement in himself, rather because unease had gripped him, a sensation that was not quite fear but closely akin to it. Incomprehension was the largest part of that unease.

The top of the man's skull offered itself to the camera as his neck arched backwards. Creed's finger began to press firmly. He held his breath. He kept his elbows tight against his ribs. He pressed down all the way and the shutter clicked . . .

. . . as the man looked over his shoulder directly at him . . .

Creed's own head jerked away from the camera as though a wasp had flown into the lens. He stared back at the man . . .

. . . whose mouth gaped, whose etched face darkened to red, whose whole body seemed to solidify.

For one brief but infinite second, photographer and crazy watched each other.

And in that brief but infinite second, Creed felt that the inside of his skull had been scoured, that whatever layers of consciousness protected the mind's inner core had been scraped away to leave it raw and bleeding.

He staggered away in shock, tripping over the camera stand behind him, falling to the floor with it, one elbow cracking hard against stone, the tripod clattering loudly in the hollowness of the tomb.

Creed grunted at the pain from his arm and rolled protectively against one of the tiers. He quickly turned and searched the shadows for the camera that had fallen with the tripod, the one he had been using instinctively clutched to his chest. He rose to his knees, bewildered by what had occurred, and drew the thin metal legs of the tripod towards him. The second Nikon, the one fitted with the telephoto lens, looked okay, but it would require closer inspection to see if it had been damaged; it had gone down with a smack, or had that been his elbow?

Creed hadn't forgotten the man outside; he just hadn't been the highest on his list of priorities. Now the photographer remembered those piercing, those *scraping*, eyes.

He hauled himself up, his right arm numbed from wrist to shoulder, and tottered towards the light, determined to brazen it out. After all, it was the sicko who had been caught in a compromising situation.

Nevertheless, Creed looked through the bars of the old door with some trepidation. But there was no one outside. The crazyman had gone. There was nothing out there now but the ornate, stone billboards of the dead.

3

S o, that's for starters.
        The burial of a famous but ancient actress, a madman (we
think, so far) committing an act of gross indecency at her graveside,
and our hero, Joe Creed, doing what he does best: thieving; stealing
moments of other people's lives.
   A mild enough beginning.

Creed trudged through the cemetery hugging stepladder, tripod and
camera bag, constantly glancing over his shoulder, this way and that,
half expecting to discover the sicko peeping at him from behind a
tree or headstone.
   There was a peculiar coldness at the back of his neck, the kind
you get when you hear a truly creepy story based on truth, or when
that odd noise downstairs wakes you in the hush of night. Being a
natural pragmatist, Creed endeavoured to shrug off the sensation;

that didn't work, though, for his disquiet had a lot to do with a feeling of being observed.

The dead love to tease, he told himself. You'll be fine when you're back among the living and the half-living. Anyway, it's not every day you see a loony jerking off over a corpse. Maybe the degenerate was a life-long admirer and this was the closest he could get to screwing the old bag. Better than a signed photo, at least.

But all that activity around the grave. Distraught grass, heaving earth. Maybe old Lil was getting her rocks off, too.

He shuddered, his dark humour not really working. Creed was *certain* he had seen the disturbances; however, the rational side of his nature, weighed down by the already mentioned pragmatism, not to mention his natural cynicism, convinced him otherwise. Everyone has these moments, fuckwit, he argued, times when things get unreal, when chemicals in the brain slosh around and create their own reality. *Déjà vu* was one of the effects, wasn't it? Or some people might just faint away, while others might see pink elephants coming out of the walls (how much *had* he drunk over the past few weeks? he asked himself).

Yeah, sure, he'd suffered a mental aberration – if that was the correct term for it – for a moment or two back there. Hell, he'd had an early start to the day, not like him at all. The old system hadn't coped too well, that was it. Nothing serious, nothing weighty. A good breakfast-cum-lunch, a couple of stiffeners, and the universe would be right again.

He continued to glance over his shoulder.

Reaching the perimeter wall at last – and with some relief – Creed used the stepladder to scale its moderate heights. He sat astride the uneven brickwork and pulled the equipment up after him. With the ladder still dangling halfway, he paused and looked back across the gentle-sloping acres. That moment of eye-contact between himself and the crazy was still vivid in his mind: the scouring – no, the *sandblasting* – sensation, followed by the raw, aching emptiness was still present, although now mellowed. And there had been no cleansing, no catharsis, following the invasion, only the dullness of after-pain. Creed shivered before his own scepticism galloped to the rescue like the Fighting 7th; it was the man's sheer grotesqueness which had turned him over, nothing more than that. So many lines and wrinkles, squalling around his sallow flesh like maelstroms charted on a weather map, the sunken cheeks, the staring, over-bright (the lustre of lust?) eyes, the thin black hair that seemed embedded in the scalp rather than growing upon it – Lily's visitor was enough to give anyone a bad turn.

Creed wondered if he were still out there, watching. Or had he been as shocked, albeit in a different way, as had Creed himself, and fled the scene? The dirty devil deserved to be embarrassed. Shit, he deserved to be shot!

Creed hauled up the ladder the rest of the way, cheered a little by his own indignation, then clambered down the other side of the wall, glad to be out of the cemetery.

He packed away his gear in the back of his poor man's Land-Rover, climbed into the driving seat, lit another cigarette, and headed back to the city.

First stop was Blackfriars where he dropped off three rolls of film at one of the few remaining daily newspapers close to the once (in)fam-ous street of shame, Fleet Street. To protect the not-so-innocent we'll call the tabloid *The Daily Dispatch* (although *The Daily Rumour, Gup,* or *Gospel* might be as appropriate). Creed wasn't a staff photographer, but he was on a loose kind of retainer, which meant his choicest snaps were exclusive to this particular journal and its Sunday sister (not forgetting colour supp.). Two of the rolls he handed in covered last night's work, the third part of that morning's. He chatted briefly with the picture editor and picked up two assign-ments for the day, the first at the Old Vic where yet another biography on the late Olivier was being launched, and the other that evening at Hamiltons, Mayfair, where Benson & Hedges were presenting their annual Gold Awards to the advertising industry. Boring stuff, but you never knew: someone might disgrace him- or herself.

Next he went along to see the resident gossip page columnist, Antony Blythe, a dapper, bald-headed prat (in Creed's considered opinion) who treated his team of four researchers with equal amounts of scathing contempt and gushing endearments. Today appeared to be a 'contempt' day – the youngest team member, her name Prunella, had apparently mislaid recent clippings of a well-known rock singer's divorce celebrations – so Creed felt little inclination to linger. He didn't feel up to bad-hearted banter with Blythe that morning; you see, the paparazzi were generally considered the lowest of the low by this particular scribe ('hypocrisy' is a Pickwickian word to some journalists – imaginary, therefore meaningless). Joseph Creed was considered to be lower than the lowest of the low by Blythe.

He listened to Blythe berating Prunella for a while, interrupted to say film of Lily Neverless' funeral was at that moment being devved up (developed), asked if there was anything special to be covered later on, was curtly told to sniff out his own muck, picked up a Celebrity Bulletin (which announced which particular international celebs would be in town that week, with flight arrival times and, if possible, where they would be staying), and beat a retreat.

He had his hearty breakfast/lunch – he *hated* the word 'brunch' – in a café nearby, then returned to the Suzuki which was parked half on the pavement in the narrow lane that ran alongside the newspaper offices. Peeling the parking ticket from the windscreen and tossing it into the rear of the Japanese jumped-up jeep, he went to Fix Features, a photo-agency in Hatton Garden with which he was also on a retainer. It was from here that his photographs were syndicated worldwide. He delivered three rolls of used film, helped a production editor mark transparencies of a movie mogul's weekend-long party he had covered, collected new film, black-and-white and colour (for which he had to pay, although only at cost), then drove across the river to the Old Vic.

A dreary hour there, abetted by dreary canapés and wine, and not helped by actors and reviewers and publishing people all enthusing about the book which they were well aware would just about recoup the cost of the dreary canapés and wine and the dreary author's advance in hardback sales. Creed took the odd snap of a Dame, a Knight, a couple of MBEs, old Thespians and theatre people (funny how none were keen to discuss Lily Neverless' funeral, as if it would be unlucky to do so) but got nothing to excite a picture editor. Creed neglected to shoot the author, whom he'd never heard of anyway.

From there a trip across town to San Lorenzo's where he sat in the bar nursing a whisky sour, cameras stashed away in the cloakroom. The Royal Di, everybody's favourite princess (but *never* call her Di to her face), often lunched or dined there; but not today. Disappointingly, there were no VIPs present, no minor celebs, nor even any long-legged models or pampered pussies (rich men's mistresses) to spend a little time with. Dismal, a goddamn dismal day. Maybe the night would bring more. (Oh Creed, if you only knew.)

He went home.

Home was in Hesper Mews, just off the Earl's Court Road, a small, cobblestone street that looked like a cul-de-sac but which, in fact, wasn't: it turned a corner at the far end, although you'd never know viewing it from the top. The mews branched off midway into what really was a cul-de-sac, and it was on the corner here that Creed's house stood. It was a modest enough pit, but on the current market its value would have been astronomical. He'd bought the property eight years before when London prices were merely ridiculous and not insanely ridiculous. The ground floor was mainly garage, with a small office to the side. A short staircase led to the first floor – there was no basement – which provided living room, kitchen/diner, bedroom and bathroom, all small but, as any eager estate agent would enthuse, 'compact and practical'. Rising from the kitchen was an iron spiral staircase painted an impractical white and giving access to a loft which Creed had boarded, decorated, and turned into a tiny drawing room. A sofa-bed and coffee table was the only furniture apart from two low bookshelves.

Next door to this was his darkroom where, time and inclination permitting, he developed his own film.

He parked the soft-top jeep in the garage, closed the up-and-over door from inside, and went through to the office. There were no messages on the answerphone and only junk mail on the hall carpet. Grin was waiting for him at the top of the stairs.

'Caught any today?' Creed asked the cat as he climbed.

The cat stared.

'I told you – no mice, no meals.'

Grin refused to give way and its master was forced to step over her. He had no idea how old Grin was or where she had come from; the animal had sauntered into the garage one winter's morning three years before and had decided to stay. She was a dirty grey-black, one of her ears was chewed away, and parts of her tail were fur-less. She wasn't at all pleasing to look at, but she did appear to grin a lot, so life couldn't have been all bad.

'You gotta work for a living, same as the rest of us,' Creed called over his shoulder as he dumped the camera bag and switched on the kettle. 'I know they're here, you know they're here.' He opened the larder cupboard. 'I'll even show you what one looks like.' He crouched to pick up the trap. He waved the mouse, skull crushed by the trap's spring-bar, tiny limbs akimbo in frozen surprise, at the cat who sauntered forward with haughty interest. She sniffed at the little corpse, and looked up at Creed.

'You think it's funny?' Creed prodded the cat's nose with the dead mouse. 'How about I chop it up and put it in your dinner bowl? Think you can go back to basics?' He lifted the bar and shook the mouse into the pedal bin. 'Maybe it's time I invested in a dog.'

Grin jumped up on the table and sat on her haunches, watching Creed as he ran water over a mug in the sink, then shovelled in two large spoonfuls of instant. As he poured boiling water, the photographer told the cat, 'One last chance. Tonight, when those little bastards come out to play, you go to work on 'em. You get a bounty on every stiff I find in the morning, okay?'

Grin grinned.

'It's your career, pal,' Creed warned as he hoisted the camera bag and, with the coffee mug in the other hand, wound his way up the spiral staircase. Taking the still-loaded camera with him, he went through to the darkroom, switching on the light and closing the door. He checked the temperatures of the processing chemicals before turning off the light again. In total darkness, he opened the camera and lifted out the cassette of film.

Although there were still several unexposed frames left, Creed was curious about what he had shot that morning. Normally he would hand over all used film to either the newspaper or the agency, having extra prints made or taking spare colour transparencies for himself later, but now and again he devved up personally, usually when there was no rush or there was something in particular he wanted to keep for his own files. Besides, nobody would be using those last shots of the funeral, particularly if he explained exactly what the kneeling man had been up to at the graveside.

He forced off the cassette's top and tipped out the roll of film; it felt slippery in his hand.

In the darkness he remembered those pale but piercing eyes staring back at him from the grave. Had they been pale? He hadn't noticed at the time. Nor had he noticed the myriad tiny red veins that made the whites of his eyeballs look like bloodshot porcelain. How could he have seen that? The distance between them had been too great, even with the Nikon's zoom lens. He was imagining, his mind had gone into overdrive. The bloody pervert had spooked him!

The film began to uncurl in his hand.

'Shit,' he muttered, fumbling in the dark to contain the roll. It slipped from his grasp like an oiled eel and he managed to control its escape only by cupping the whole film in both hands.

'That shouldn't have happened,' he told himself unnecessarily. Films don't unroll themselves. Wait, wait – it didn't. It slipped over the edge, and its own weight did the rest.

He felt on the bench for scissors, clutching the untidy roll to his chest with one hand and hoping the emulsion hadn't become too grimy. Feeling for, then clipping, the thinner feed end of the film, he coaxed it into a spiral with no further problem (even though its edges did feel peculiarly waxy), then placed it in a round tank. He capped the tank and poured in the chemical mix through a hole in the top. Only then did he turn on the light.

When he had inserted the agitator rod and given the spiral a couple of twirls, he set the timer-clock and sipped his coffee. His hand was shaking.

Loosen up, Creed, he silently admonished. Graveyards don't usually have this effect on you.

Coffee slurped over the side of the mug when the darkroom's wall-phone rang. He wiped a hand on his jeans before grabbing the receiver.

'Bastard,' a woman's voice said at the other end.

'This is he,' Creed replied.

'You know what you've done, don't you?' said the voice. 'Or what you didn't do, I should say.'

He sighed. 'Tell me, Evelyn.'

'You didn't pick him up again. And you promised him faithfully this time, you shit.'

'Oh, n . . . Evelyn, I'm sorry. Honest. It slipped my mind.'

'You tell that to Samuel. He was looking forward to the car race – not that I wanted him to go. Cars smashing each other up is just the juvenile sort of thing you would encourage him to enjoy.'

'Stock cars. They're meant to smash each other up. Listen, is Sammy there –'

'He's at school, where he's supposed to be, you fool. And it's *Samuel.*'

'For fuck's sake, he's only ten years old. Look, I had an assignment yesterday; I couldn't cancel it.'

'That's your story. There was a time when I'd've believed it. More likely your son was the last thing on your mind. How is your sex life these days, Joe – still bedding dogs?'

Not like the one I used to, Creed thought. 'Will you tell him I'm sorry, Evelyn?' he asked his ex-wife. 'I'll make it up to him next weekend.'

'You don't get him next weekend. Every fortnight, that's it. And that's too much. My God, I could have told the court some things about you . . .'

'You did, Evelyn. Get Sam to ring me when he gets home, will you?'

'No.'

'You're still a princess.' A Jewish princess who should never have married a goy.

'Fuck you, too.'

'Rather than you,' he muttered.

'What?'

'I said okay, I'll phone him.'

'He's not talking to you.'

'An apology could be tricky, then.'

'That's your problem.'

'Always a delight to talk, Evelyn.'

The phone went dead.

Creed agitated the developer a little more briskly than necessary, cursing himself for having forgotten the day of access to his son – it would give the little shit more excuse for sulks. The truth was that he had covered an all-day Sunday party at the mansion home of a computer tycoon, a deadly drab businessman who bought (as opposed to brought) some semblance of glamour into his otherwise uninteresting life with lavish parties to which he invited the A division of the glitzies. Paparazzi and gossip columnists were natural appendages to such celebrations, for the computer genius wanted the world to know he was a fun-loving guy as well as being mega-brained. The beautiful people, who thrived on freebies, disguised the fact that they thought him a boring, supercilious drip without difficulty, and the rest of the world really wasn't that interested. Nevertheless, his jollies filled a few column inches and the photographs used up a bit more space, so the mutual parasitism more or less evened out. Not much of a reason for missing a day out with your son, Creed reflected, but better than reluctance alone.

When the timer belled, he emptied the tank and poured in the stop, repeating the process with the fix. He made a couple of phone calls from the darkroom, then washed and squeegeed the negative strip, leaving it in the drying cabinet while he went through his engagement book on the sofa in the next room.

He yawned more than once, not just because of the list of events ahead of him that week, but because of that morning's early rise. Creed liked to think of himself as a night creature.

Within minutes the night creature had dozed off.

Someone was leaning on him. Someone was pinning him to the sofa.

He could smell their horribly foul breath. He could feel their warmth.

In his sleep he was afraid; in his rising consciousness he was terrified. But that something, that huge weight on his chest, didn't want him to open his eyes, wanted him blind and defenceless.

Creed struggled, not with the weight, but with his own will. He *had* to open his eyes. He had to confront whatever held him there. His eyelids felt like lead slabs.

Breathing was not easy. The rise of his chest was inhibited by the weight. The weight wanted to crush him.

Had to fight it. Had to leave the sleep. Had to wake. Had to open his eyes, had to . . .

His eyes stuttered open.

'*Get outa here!*'

Creed twisted and heaved at the same time and Grin skidded across the room, her claws digging into the single rug which travelled along with it over the polished boards.

Creed sat up and threw a cushion after the cat. Grin yowled and headed for the staircase.

'*Judas Christ!*' the photographer yelled after her. '*You coulda given me a heart attack!*'

He massaged his chest, encouraging the beating to continue, loud though it was. It took a full two minutes for his nerves to settle.

'Oh . . .' He looked at his wristwatch, remembering the negs in the drier. He'd been out for twenty minutes at least.

Creed tottered to the darkroom and whisked the glossy strip from the cabinet. 'Dry as a grasshopper's tit,' he mumbled to himself, yawning at the same time. No harm done though.

After cutting the negs into six strips and marking them with a rapidograph, he closed the door and switched on the amber light. Yawning again, he laid them on bromide paper, pressing them flat with a glass plate. He exposed them for five seconds without bothering to do a test strip (he rarely did), then put the bromide through the developer dishes.

With the full light on, he examined the resulting contact sheet. There was the kneeling figure, its back to the camera. And a white blob that was the man's turned head – nothing clearer than that. Why the fascination? Why such interest in this loony? Instinct, he answered himself. Years of sniffing and catching the scent. There was something more to this and he was curious to find out what.

He placed the neg in the enlarger's frame carrier, laying down another sheet of bromide under the masking frame below. Normally after focusing he would have used a card to shield parts of the film paper from the light, progressively moving it across the surface in a striped pattern of varying exposures; this time, however, he went for a straight twenty-second exposure.

Something was wrong with the negative image, but he couldn't figure out what.

Killing the enlarger light, he lifted the frame and slid the photographic paper into the developer tray. Within a few seconds shapes began to form.

Gently rocking the tray to create a smooth back-and-forth current, he waited for the emerging greys and blacks to make sense.

The crazy appeared as if gliding from a mist – the soles of his shoes aimed at the camera, his raincoat, with creases in the material picked out in fine detail, the slight twist of his torso. Around him the grass, static and hued orange by the darkroom's light, headstones and trees in the distance. The man's shoulders, arms stretched forward out of sight. His head, turned, a three-quarters profile, peering towards the hidden lens, the lines, the swirls, ingrained in his features, appearing as though meticulously drawn with a fine nib.

Creed's mouth slowly opened as he stared down at the face.

He remembered the eyes. So clear, so penetrating. So . . . fucking scary.

But not present here.

He bent forward, distrusting his own sight. Where the man's eyes should have been, there was only blackness.

Just two black smudges. That quickly spread and joined together. Rushing now to obscure the whole ravaged face.

4

Well weren't they the trendiest of trendies, the yuppiest of yuppies? The men in unstructured suits, hair gleamed back, some with tiny tight pigtails, shirt collars buttoned, not many with ties. The women, mainly in black, skirts generally as short and thigh-hugging as the legs would bear, or wearing floppy trousers that a hippo would be comfortable in. The conversation buzz was low-key, cool, and ego-bristling.

Creed descended the steps into the frothy pool of advertising piranhas, scanning the faces for anyone snap-worthy, a Saatchi or two, a Tim Bell, any personality who transcended the junk-sell world to the real one, someone whose status or troubled personal life might be of interest to the punters. A tall, pale-faced teenager with gel-spiked hair gawked at Creed's camera and went stiff, his eyes wide and expectant behind small round glasses. The photographer pushed by without acknowledging the youth's jerky nod. The kid, whose clothes were as ill-fitting but not as expensive as those worn by the pros he rubbed shoulders with, was no doubt a student up for one of the Gold Awards that Benson & Hedges doled out every

year to the advertising industry to show it was into commercial
aestheticism as much as lung cancer. Creed almost *felt* the boy's
hopes take a dive as the camera passed him by.

The photographer lifted a white wine from a travelling tray and
continued through the scrum until he reached an empty corner
(corners aren't the place for advertising folk) where he dumped his
bag on the floor. Sipping the wine, Nikon standing proud over his
navel like a stubby and misplaced phallus, Creed examined the crowd
in more detail. He spotted George Melly in his usual chalk-striped
double-breasted and Fedora and prayed the old jazzman was there
to hand out prizes and not to sing – the day had been too long for
such a climax. There were a few other familiar faces, but not one
that merited a single frame of black-and-white, let alone colour.
Across the gallery two raised television screens ran a looped tape of
nominated commercials, illustrations and photographic stills. They
all looked pretty classy to Creed; pretty expensive, too, apart from
the student stuff. But how many would really sell the goods they
advertised? And who gave a shit anyway? Big budgets and grand
locations seemed to be the order of the day; the copywriter or art
director's *next* agency was the important thing, not the product.
Even the clients who paid for it all didn't seem to mind helping the
creative teams' career moves (but then, it was all tax-deductible,
wasn't it?).

'Wonderful work, isn't it?'

The voice was soft and friendly.

Creed turned to the girl and smiled his Mickey Rourke smile.
'Wonderful,' he said.

She was as tall as he, and close to being beautiful; an ideal mate
for any hero. Maybe a little too good for Creed, though.

'You're Joe Creed, aren't you?'

He nodded. 'We've never met before.'

'No. But I've seen you around.'

'And you've been dying to introduce yourself.'

She hadn't smiled yet, nor did she then. 'I couldn't hold back any
longer. Goodbye.'

He straightened from the wall he'd been leaning against as she
turned away. 'Hey, wait. Can we start again?'

The girl paused. 'Will it be an improvement?'

'Could it be any worse?'

At last a smidgen of a smile appeared. 'I came over because you looked thoroughly bored.'

'That obvious?'

The smidgen bloomed to a full smile. 'You're not part of this scene. But don't be put off by what you see around you. Most of these people have incredible talent, and they work fast and hard in a business that's as cut-throat as you can get.'

'It couldn't be that you're also in the business?'

She laughed, a small cough of a sound. 'Guilty. But I needn't defend myself or them.' She flicked her head towards those behind her.

'How did you know my name?'

'I asked one of the gallery's girls before I came over. You have a reputation, you know, and a dubious one at that.'

Creed looked genuinely aggrieved.

'Am I stopping you from working?' she asked then, quickly stepping aside as if apologising for blocking his view.

'Are you kidding? Unless old George throws a wobbly there's nothing here to brighten the breakfast table. You want a drink, you want to tell me your name?'

'No to the drink and my name's Cally.'

'As in . . . ?'

'As in Cally.'

'Oh.'

Creed pretended to survey the white-walled, picture-hung room again, but when she too looked around as if to help him find someone interesting to shoot, he quickly and surreptitiously eyed her up and down.

The girl caught his sneaky appraisal, but pretended she hadn't. 'I wonder if I could ask you a favour,' she said.

It was disappointing to realise it hadn't been his charisma nor that she had really wanted to relieve his boredom that had brought her over. 'My body's sacred,' he said lest she see his disappointment.

'It's quite safe, too. The favour isn't really for me – it's for a friend of mine. Well, my boss, actually.'

Creed had already lost interest. He drained the rest of his wine and waggled the empty glass at a nearby waiter. The young man, whose uniform was loose black trousers and equally loose white shirt (buttoned at the throat, of course, with no tie), quickly came over and offered his tray of drinks. Creed took a claret without returning a thank-you.

The girl, Cally, waited patiently for his attention.

'I work for a production company,' she said, realising after a while he wouldn't prompt her. 'Page Lidtrap. We make TV and cinema commercials, prestige shorts for big-name companies, management films – all kinds of things really.' She was aware she hadn't caught his attention. 'We're just putting together our first feature movie. It's a major step for us.'

'Parker and the Scott brothers are way ahead of you.'

'We'd like to catch them up.' She didn't like the mocking in his eyes, but she persisted. 'The thing is, we need some media attention. We've got a certain amount of financial backing, but we need more, and you know how a recognisable name helps on that score.'

'Nope, I don't know. It's not my field.'

'Take my word for it then. It definitely opens a few doors even if you're soon kicked out again.'

If she hadn't been such a looker, Creed would have told her to get lost there and then; but her body was appetising and the more you studied her face, the more beautiful it became. He liked her hair too – darkish blonde, medium length, swept back. 'You think I can make you famous?'

'Not me. Our director, Daniel Lidtrap. And it hasn't got anything to do with making him famous – I know that isn't possible. But if his face started showing up in the gossip columns and the glossies, well, that might just help the process.'

The request wasn't unusual. It wasn't unusual at all. Most celebs and pseudo-celebs went out of their way, even begged, to get their names and pics in print; it was only when they reached superstar status that they pretended otherwise. Creed scarcely knew of any big name who didn't secretly – or overtly – love, even crave, the attention, for publicity was like a drug and there was nothing that the famous loathed more than cold turkey. On the scandal side, too, many so-called 'clandestine' affairs had been carried on at the most popular restaurants and nightclubs for the paparazzi and gossip columnists to suffer guilt over the exposure. What this girl obviously failed to understand, though, was that he, Creed, had no influence at all as to what appeared on the page. He merely supplied the shots and the picture editor and writer decided what should be used. The fact that this guy – what was his name? Traplid? – was a total unknown as far as the rest of the world was concerned meant he hadn't a chance in hell of making an item.

His smile was warm. 'Well, I might be able to do something . . .'

Her face brightened and he noticed that her front teeth were slightly crooked, a tiny flaw that strangely enhanced her attractiveness. If Creed had thought harder about it he would have realised that this was because that small imperfection somehow made the girl more accessible; it held her beauty to realistic terms, rendered it more natural, less sublimely classic.

'But a favour for a favour,' he told her.

Her expression became guarded, but still she smiled.

'We have dinner, you pay.'

'Daniel is over there.' She pointed to a spot beneath one of the television screens. 'The tall man. The one with curls next to the man with the beard.'

Creed hated him on sight. He was too tall, too handsome. His clothes were no doubt Armani or whoever the in-vogue designer happened to be at that moment in time, and his 'natural' curls had been persuaded to sweep back over his ears and hang in hi-lited ringlets around his shirt collar. He and Cally made the perfect couple, and Creed wondered about that.

'A commercial of his has been nominated for an award tonight,' she told him.

Wouldn't you know it, thought Creed, not altogether impressed. 'I'll catch a snap before I leave,' he promised the girl, 'but you'll have to get him into more interesting places than this. We can discuss that over dinner.'

She hesitated only for a moment. 'That'd be great. But not tonight. We've already arranged to go on somewhere after the awards ceremony.'

'That's okay. Look, here's my number.' He took a dog-eared card from his camera bag and handed it to her. 'Give me a bell when you get a chance, okay?'

'I don't know how to . . .'

Creed's usual smile was not unlike a leer, so the girl couldn't be sure. At least he was shrewd enough not to give an obvious response. 'Don't worry about it,' he said.

She held up the card as if it were a prize ticket. 'I'll call you.'

He nodded and she weaved her way back into the crowd which had now become wall-to-wall, more bodies still drifting down the stairway from the street.

Possibilities, he thought, staring after her. Definite possibilities . . .

Creed strolled the length of the long bar at Langan's until he was behind the stairs and out of sight from the main restaurant area, winking at one of the black-waistcoated barmen as he went. The barman followed him down.

To anyone knowing no better, the paparazzo could have been a patron of the restaurant, despite his general dishevelment, for he had left his camera bag in the jeep parked opposite the *brasserie*. He leaned against the bar and kept his voice low. 'He's in?'

'Twenty minutes ago,' the barman confirmed. 'He's still on the first course.'

'Anjelica with him?'

'I'm not sure.'

'What d'you mean, you're not sure? She either is or she isn't.'

'He's with a lady, but she looks different. Maybe she's changed her hairstyle, I don't know.' The barman shrugged.

Creed looked around, tapping the bar top thoughtfully. 'Anyone else?'

His informant shook his head. 'No one worthwhile. You having a drink?'

'Coffee. Let me have an Irish with it.'

'Straight?'

'Yeah, and no ice. I've been cold all day.'

The call had reached Creed while he was still at the gallery – he always made sure his answering service knew where he would be at set times during the day or night. The word was that Jack Nicholson was in town and had reserved a table for five at Langan's Brasserie for that evening. It was the same barman who now served the photographer his coffee and whiskey who had given him the tip-off.

Creed had wasted only a little more time at the gallery, taking a couple of frames of Cally's curly-mop boss on the way out. At least the girl looked grateful, so the moderate effort might pay dividends later on. Traplid or Pratlid had looked suitably bored by the intrusion, but Creed noticed that the director offered the obviously preferred side of his face to the lens, his jawbone tensed to make his chin appear even firmer.

The whiskey enlivened Creed's gullet and he quickly gulped coffee to tone it down. The barman had moved on to serve another customer, leaving the photographer to ponder his plan of action. It was important to discover if the woman Nicholson was with really was Anjelica Huston. These two, both respected stars in their own right, had been carrying on an on-and-off relationship for years now, but the story was that John Huston, the renowned film director and father to Anjelica, had, on his deathbed, made Nicholson promise to make an honest woman of his daughter (the story was untrue, incidentally, but it was the kind of legend the media loved to promote). Hence the actor and the actress had apparently put their last exceedingly stormy break-up behind them and were back on line again.

So, this was the shot: the couple *had* to be shown together, a reunified unit. The plain evidence of the physical link would help the newspaper diarist confirm the story. That might seem a somewhat flimsy connection to someone outside the profession, but to a paparazzo or newsman, it represented rock-solid proof.

The problem was that Nicholson was a 'devil' and of course, a multi-million-dollar joker, and he loved playing games with newshounds and snappers. He liked to tease. The only vulnerable moment would be when the two walked out of the *brasserie* door together. Once outside, Creed knew they would separate, if only for the fun of it.

A hand brushed his shoulder and he glanced round to see two paparazzi heavyweights, Richard Young and David Benett, saunter past into the inner sanctum beyond the bar area. They sat at a small round table, a discreet position from where the main door could be observed but sufficiently tucked away so that their presence would scarcely be noticed.

Creed groaned inwardly. The word was out. Other paps, the

underprivileged who were not allowed to set foot on the premises, would soon be gathering like buzzards outside on the pavement. The mere fact that Creed, Young, and Benett were loitering inside meant something was going down and the cowboys would want some of the action. There was bound to be a skirmish outside when they all jostled for position as the targets left. Shit!

To make matters worse, Bluto had just appeared and was chatting to the girl on duty by the reservations podium.

Now not many in the business were too fond of Creed, but they all *detested* Bluto.

He was a thickset oaf of a man who always dressed in black. Not tall, but very broad – very. His chin was set into a short fat neck, this itself grimed by a dark wiry beard. His nose was stubby, thick black eyebrows meeting at the bridge, with but an inch (or so it seemed) of forehead above. His hair was as short and wiry as his beard. He resembled Popeye's old adversary (although his vocabulary was less extensive than the cartoon character's), hence the nickname. He looked Japanese, a Sumo-wrestler type, and his real name was quite unpronounceable.

He spied Creed at the bar and glared. The pair of them had crossed swords on too many occasions for there to be any civility between them. Creed lifted his glass towards the foe and it took a skill not given to everyone to make it a gesture of contempt rather than greeting.

Bluto disappeared through the swingdoors and the place brightened up considerably.

Creed had plenty of time to think while the movie stars and their companions enjoyed their meal and, where normally he would mentally run through the next day's list of events or locations, this time he brooded on what had happened that afternoon: namely, the blackening image in the developer tray. No matter how he tried with other bromides, he could not stop that curiously spreading shadow; even a fresh developer mix failed to halt the process. All he was left with each time was a totally black sheet of glossy paper. It was inexplicable. And bloody irritating.

Only when he tried another negative did he achieve a result.

He did another. Fine, no problem. Another. Fine again. Then he went back to the original. As before, the blemish refused to be contained: it expanded like an ink stain until it reached the very edges of the paper.

He randomly chose one of the others again. It printed correctly.

Only then did Creed realise something that was completely absurd, but which was somehow relevant: the shot that constantly failed to print properly was the only one in which the subject was looking directly into the lens. The one that had been taken at the precise moment Creed's cover had been blown.

Did that make any sense? Naturally, not.

So what the hell was going on?

'They're on their coffees.'

Creed looked up in surprise.

'They're on their coffees,' the barman murmured again. He drifted away, looking busy but doing nothing in particular.

Creed's mind was immediately back on the job. He rose from the bar stool, noting that his two colleagues (rivals might be more appropriate – colleague wasn't a comfortable word in their trade) had already departed. Although he appeared casual enough, Creed's stomach muscles were beginning to knot. No matter how many years in the business, every paparazzo or news photographer changed up a gear when the big moment approached. It was too easy to get it wrong, you see, too easy to miss that vital moment. And if you did, it meant that all that waiting had been for nothing, all the planning down the tube. A missed opportunity didn't help your own self-esteem either.

At the same time, this tension was undeniably heady, for adrenaline began to pump, the nerve-ends began to tingle. The body was getting itself ready.

The experienced along with the inexperienced, the old hands along with the young Turks, became nervous at this point, although they would never mention it to each other. A successful snap was all they asked for; a momentously candid classic was what they *prayed* for. And one other thing: that the camera was loaded (you think *that* never happens to pros?).

Creed headed for the door and quickly scoured the huge L-shaped dining room. As usual, it was packed to capacity, but he found his target. Nicholson was about halfway down; even the back of his head was recognisable. And there, across the table from him, was his lady, Anjelica. Her hair was different, more orange than brunette, but that handsome face was unmistakable. The tension in his belly took the next flight up to his chest.

Ignoring the disdainful glare from the *maître d'*, who had just finished his farewells to a valued customer (it was a mutual dislike between Creed and the other man, but fortunately the *maître d'* appreciated the kudos of a mention in the gossip columns), he stepped out into the night. Most of the paparazzi had gathered on the opposite side of the street and were chatting and grumbling to one another, telling stories but no secrets. Creed went straight to his Suzuki, unlocked the passenger door, and reached in for his camera bag. After checking exposure settings (he rarely used anything other than F8 at a 60th of a second on 400 ASA which, as far as he was concerned, covered most eventualities) and recharging flashes, Creed hung both Nikons around his neck. Then he joined the herd.

Bluto was on his own, skulking like some disconsolate troll in a shadowy doorway, his silver Celica Coupé parked nearby.

Creed was greeted by the others without much enthusiasm; in truth, he had only made his way over to ascertain who was there. As usual, a rough mixture of cowboys and pros. The younger ones were quicker and more physical, but less artful (in the sense of cunning) than the older members of the click clan. They also hadn't the instinct for the right moment, not in photographic terms, but in 'caption' terms. Help the picture editor, that was the idea; get the pic that had a storyline, no matter how slight or meaningless that line might be. It was this lack of judgement that often loused things up for the veteran snappers. For instance, the kids – and that was anyone under thirty to Creed – wouldn't understand that the shot had to be Nicholson and Anjelica together, preferably arm-in-arm; half this bunch would be popping as soon as the first person in Nicholson's party hit the street. It was important for Creed to be at the front of the scrum, with no arms, shoulders and heads blocking his view. He exchanged banter, then strolled away, keeping an eye on the restaurant as he went.

Benett was leaning against his red Porsche talking quietly to Young. These two knew the score – they'd make sure they were at the front too. Bluto snorted the contents of his nose as Creed passed by.

It was another twenty minutes before the paparazzi became agitated and suddenly dashed across the street in an over-excited and disorderly gaggle, with just one objective in mind: to preserve the next few moments for posterity (or, to be less fanciful, to make the next buck). But Creed was way – no, just – ahead of them.

He had positioned himself at an angle to the long windows of the *brasserie,* which gave him a perfect view of the target, and had thus witnessed the actor rise from the table. Still he'd waited until the last moment before walking swiftly to the restaurant's entrance (to have moved too soon would have alerted the others) to take his place squarely in front and barely five feet away from the door. His camera was already raised, his finger poised on the shutter release.

He steadied himself as the pack hit him from behind, all jostling to stake their claim on a suitable piece of pavement.

One half of the swingdoors was opening. Somebody was emerging.

A non-face. Nobody recognisable. But the actress was with him. And not with Nicholson!

Anjelica barely smiled at the cameramen as the man who had preceded her took her by the arm and guided her to a vehicle parked further along the street while flashes flared and shutters clicked in a peculiarly hushed cacophony. And only when they were at some distance did Jack Nicholson appear on the doorstep, grinning that sardonic grin of his.

Bastard! He'd done it on purpose. He'd sent his lover out ahead of him!

'Take it easy, boys,' he drawled, showing his teeth.

His presence sent the pap back into a frenzy. White sheet lightning was almost continuous, the cries of *'This way Jack over here Jack another smile Jack'* almost a screeched litany. The 'boys' were claiming their scalp.

All except one, that is. Joe Creed was sprawled on hands and knees on the hard stone.

Someone – and he knew precisely who – had cracked an elbow against the side of his head at the exact moment the actor stepped from the entrance.

Spitting curses, he hauled himself up as the mob followed Nicholson along the pavement – followed him from the front, that is, for they hobbled backwards, snapping all the while, tripping over each other, but never losing their feet. Creed scrambled after them, then dodged between two parked cars, guessing the actor's intention. Nicholson abruptly stepped off the kerb and, to the amazement of everybody, crossed the street. The diners watched the fuss from the large windows with equal amounts of disgust and amusement.

There were no vehicles parked on the other side, so the photographers couldn't understand what he was up to. Nevertheless, the change of direction allowed Creed to reel off some choice shots unhindered by the other lensmen.

The pack swarmed after the star, but Creed hung back. He'd seen this trick of Nicholson's a few years before.

A car engine started up behind Creed. A Ford Scorpio began to move away from the kerbside. The photographer backed away from it as someone in the passenger seat leaned over and, with some difficulty, pushed open the rear door on the road side.

Suddenly the movie star was hurtling across the street, his body aimed at the slow-moving car.

Creed got shots of Nicholson running, then diving full length on to the backseat of the moving vehicle. It was a magnificent manoeuvre which left the photographers gawping.

The Scorpio sped away leaving the pack mesmerised. A good few seconds went by before they scattered for their own transport.

The idea had been to prevent the paparazzi from following and discovering which hotel he was staying in, and the ruse appeared to have worked, for the Scorpio's rear lights were already disappearing round the corner of Stratton Street.

Normally, Creed would have taken up the challenge; even if he lost the Scorpio, he could have whizzed around the top hotels in the locale in the hope of catching the car parked outside or nearby. Tonight, though, he felt he'd had enough. It'd been a long day and there were still other things to do before he could hit the sack. Maybe he was getting old. Maybe the thrill was beginning to fade. Maybe he didn't give a fuck.

Creed dropped that night's film off at the *Dispatch*'s processing lab and called it a night.

Well, he *thought* he'd called it a night.

5

Creed, his sleep disturbed, snuggled up closer to the pillow, pressing his face into its softness. A child might do the same with a teddy bear or favourite doll; in Creed's case, the pillow substituted for the cushiony flesh of a woman. Occasionally he liked to sleep alone (and of late he'd had little choice), but generally he favoured the warmth of a female body next to him. He mumbled something that might have been quite rational in the dream he was still half involved in, then twisted in the bed, taking the pillow with him.

His eyes flickered open.

Light from a streetlamp further down the mews came in through the window, but it wasn't much and certainly not enough to make sense of the objects in the room. The chair over which he'd hung his coat resembled one of the gravestones he'd so recently wandered among. A navy-blue dressing gown hanging on the open door could have been a figure watching over him. The tall wardrobe in one corner could well have been the entrance to a tomb. The ornaments on the mantel –

He blinked twice, rapidly.

His dressing gown lay over his feet on top of the duvet (his feet got cold at night in the winter when there wasn't another body present to steal heat from). He lay on his back and looked towards the door without moving his head.

He'd been mistaken: there was nothing there at all.

He allowed his head to follow the movement of his eyes. He frowned in the dark. He was sure there had been . . . *Dickhead.* Obviously the dream hadn't let go quickly enough, an image had lingered. Creed turned on to his side, bristle on his cheek scratching against the pillow's fabric. That was all he needed, a frigging bad night. Just can't settle into a steady sleep, keep stirring, waking for a second or two, drifting off again. Mind's not settling down, that's the problem. Maybe a smoke would soothe the old think-box. No, too tired to get one. Need to rest, heavy day tomorrow. Count sheep? Deep breathing would be better. Six seconds in, eight out, from the stomach, not the chest, fill every corner, then expel every last bit of puff. One, two, three . . .

He yawned with the fourth breath, spoiling the rhythm. Start again.

Up to five when a noise from somewhere brought air to a halt halfway up his throat.

What was it? What the fuck was that?

He stared at the ceiling. Grin mooching around. Had to be. Cats were born to be night moochers. But Grin was too lazy even for that. She rarely woke up even when he arrived home at two or three o'clock in the morning. Still, tonight might be the exception. She might even be on the prowl for mice, God help us! Maybe the cat had more sense than he'd given it credit for and had actually heeded his warning. Don't let me down, Grin, go get the little buggers. It's better than exile.

But the next noise was too heavy to have been made by the soft paws of a prowling cat. It sounded like a footstep.

And there was another.

Creed stiffened. Judas, there was someone in the house. He swallowed spit. He listened again. Nothing now.

Could've been creaking floorboards, old timbers. Yeah, yeah, that was it.

But *that* wasn't a floorboard shrinking, nor was it a footstep!

'Oh Christ,' Creed whispered as he sat up, still clutching the pillow. *Somebody was rummaging around upstairs.* He listened intently and prayed there wouldn't be another sound.

There was though.

Creed groaned inwardly. What the hell was he supposed to do? Go up there, confront the burglar? No bloody way. Ring the police? Whoever it was would hear. What then? Get out fast, he answered himself. Leave them to it, it was only property, after all; flesh and bones were more sacred.

And our hero would have done just that had it not been for one thing. The sounds had come from directly overhead and directly overhead was his photographic room. Creed's livelihood was up there. Files, records, cameras, film stock, equipment. Shit, his *history* was there! The accumulation of his years as a photographer, shots he'd taken for himself, 'overs' he'd kept from numerous jobs, transparencies, black-and-whites. All the best from twelve long years of working his butt off. Okay, pal, you're in trouble; *nobody* was taking away any of that stuff. Only over my dead bod – Get serious, Creed. Equipment and stock could always be replaced, new shots could always be taken. This guy might be dangerous.

Didn't the police always maintain, though, that in most burglaries, the burglar was more frightened than the victim? With his luck, he'd get the villain who was fearless. Creed's grip tightened on the pillow.

Only the inescapable fact that there was precious else that he could do finally drove him from the bed. He tugged on his dressing gown – nothing like nakedness to make you feel utterly vulnerable – before peeking through the open doorway. Again he held his breath and listened, realising he hadn't heard another sound for a while now.

Could be, he tried to reassure himself, could be it really was only mice. Rats, even. He shuddered. It was possible. Yeah, it was likely. Those bastards could make a hell of a noise, and in the dead of night sounds were amplified anyway. Anything might sound like footsteps once the imagination got itself into a tizz. Sure, and rats could easily get in through the rafters of these old buildings. Didn't he read somewhere that rats were taking over the city? Good idea for a book there. Somebody ought to do it. So where was Grin? Why wasn't she up there sorting them out?

He could see across the hallway into the kitchen, but that didn't help at all. The question was, should he make the climb up the spiral staircase to chase the vermin away? *If* it was vermin, of course.

It'd been quiet up there for some time now. What if an intruder was waiting for him to put his head through the round hole in the floor? But there was an alternative to sticking his neck out, so to speak, and it would probably deal with either burglar or beast.

He grasped the key in the bedroom door, ready to slam it shut and keep it that way.

'*Okay, I know you're up there, I've rung the police, you better get out now while you've got the chance!*'

He'd shouted loud enough to wake the dead, and the near-hysteria hadn't shown. They might get cocksure, villain or vermin, if they thought he was afraid.

Nothing scuttled, nothing panicked. Nobody returned his call.

He tried again. '*You've got about four minutes to get out, the police are pretty quick round here, go now and we'll say no more about it!*'

Nothing at all.

Creed waited a while longer before reaching out and switching on the hall light. Christ, Creed, you're like a bloody maiden aunt, he scolded, feeling just a trifle braver with the light on. No one was up there. No one. He'd been mistaken.

Nevertheless, he crept into the kitchen with considerable caution and took out a long carving knife from a drawer just in case. He stood at the foot of the circular staircase and peered into the dark hole over his head. Gotta check it out, Creed. You'll spend the rest of the night listening if you don't.

He put one foot on the bottom step, paused, made it to the second.

The hell with it. He continued the climb, bare feet quiet but not soundless, his eyes soon drawing level with the next floor. He took his time looking over the rim.

It felt as if his heart had thickened into a heavy, glutinous lump inside his chest when he looked across the loft room.

The lightswitch was near, but it couldn't be reached from his position. Not that it mattered, for there was another light source: the amber light from the open darkroom spread softly towards him.

And in the darkroom, its bald skull like a dull setting sun in the orange glow, was a crooked figure. It stood sideways to Creed, holding a strip of film to the light with fingers that appeared extraordinarily long, like talons. But its awful face was turned towards the round pit from which Creed's head protruded, as though it had been waiting for him to appear.

Not a sound came from Creed, but his mind babbled, *Oh shit oh God oh Christ* . . .

Then he was running backwards, not taking time to about-face, descending the circular staircase in a flurry of limbs, scrabbling at the rail and the centre-post for balance, shins scraping against the metal steps.

Choosing not to linger in the kitchen, he finally turned to face the direction in which he was fleeing and ran into the hallway, virtually leaping down the stairwell leading to the frontdoor.

Unfortunately Grin was making her way up those same stairs at that precise moment, her purpose being to investigate the ruckus caused by her master. She was a mere shadow in the darkness, but an extremely loud one when Creed's foot landed on her back.

She screeched and Creed fell.

He grabbed air and found it insubstantial; Creed tumbled, headfirst, then over, then headfirst again. The streetdoor at the bottom of the stairs shook in its frame as he hit it.

Moaning, he rolled over, consciousness sinking fast but not yet quite gone. Eyes barely open, he looked back up at the shadowy hallway to the top of the stairs.

He muttered something before fading completely, and that partial word came from extreme shock.

'Nos . . .' he said quietly, and that was all he could manage. His eyes closed as though he were falling asleep and his head lolled to one side, a hand slipping from his lap on to the floor, fingers uncurling.

6

Envelopes dropping on to his head were the first thing to disturb him. He opened bleary eyes with difficulty and noted that three of those envelopes lying on his chest were brown, the kind that contain bills. He drifted off again.

It was an hour later – although Creed wasn't aware of the time lapse – that pounding from the other side of the door roused him again.

He groaned, he moaned. He barely moved.

Pounding again, matching the pounding inside his head. Somebody was putting hearty force behind the knocker. Creed attempted to push himself upright, but the effort of doing that seemed to hurt his head more than anything else. More cautiously, he tried again.

'Mr Creed.'

The letterbox flap above him had sprung open as if it were a mouth. The voice was female. 'Mr Creed?' it came again, the caller not realising just how close he was.

'Okay . . .'

'Mr Creed!' Louder knocking this time, too.

'*Okay*, for f——!'

He sat, the top of his head only inches below the letterbox.

The voice was much quieter. 'Mr Creed, is that *you*?'

He strained his neck to look round and upwards and saw a pair of eyes gazing down at him. Even without the rest of the face they looked astonished.

'Are you all right?' he was asked. 'It's me, Mr Creed, Cally. We met last night – at Hamiltons gallery, remember? What are you doing down there?'

He made it to his knees and rested there, knuckles digging into the carpet. 'A minute,' he begged. 'Just wait a minute. Oh Judas . . .' He gingerly touched a hand to his forehead and groaned aloud once more when he felt the fresh contour. He pressed against the swelling to see if it would go down and instantly regretted the attempt.

'Mr Creed . . .'

'*All right, all right!*' That hurt too.

Drawing in a breath, Creed dragged himself to his feet, clinging to the doorcatch for support. The door scarcely budged when he released the catch and pulled; he remembered the bolt and bent to slide it back. That hurt even more.

The girl's face was full of concern when he opened the door six inches. 'What happened to you?' she said. 'You look as if you're growing another head.'

It was then that it all came back to him. He staggered for a moment and quickly sat down on the stairs behind him; he stared ahead blankly, without realising the girl had stepped inside and was kneeling before him, looking earnestly into his eyes.

'You look terrible,' she said. 'Shall I call for an ambulance?'

He was too occupied with his own thoughts to reply.

'Let me get you something,' he heard her say without understanding what she meant. 'Where do you – never mind.' She glanced into the room off the hall, then climbed over him to go upstairs.

Still he stared ahead, oblivious to the chill breeze coming through the open door. Soon there were footsteps behind him and a blue-denimed leg slid over his shoulder.

'Here, drink this.' Cally put a glass to his lips and tilted it towards him.

He choked, then spluttered as she patted his back. 'What . . . what the . . . brandy? Brandy this time of the morning?'

'It'll bring you out of shock.'

'I'm not in shock.'

'I told you so. Come on, take another sip.'

He did, a small one, and had to admit it helped some.

'Do you want to go to a hospital?'

He shook his head and wished he hadn't.

He shivered, not because of the brandy, but because he was almost naked. He quickly drew the dressing gown around himself.

Cally pretended she hadn't noticed anything. 'Let's get you somewhere comfortable. D'you think anything's broken?'

'Yeah, my skull.'

With her help, Creed rose to his feet, suddenly not sure whether he was shivery or shaky. They slowly climbed the stairs, Cally helping him all the way, and found the cat waiting for them at the top.

'Move, pussy,' Cally said. 'Let's get by.' She could have sworn the thing was grinning.

The cat studied the girl, and then Creed.

'You –' her master began to say, but the sharpness of his own voice made his head hurt even more. 'She was the one who tripped me,' he complained to the girl.

'Ah, I see. You fell over the cat. My God, I thought you'd been attacked.'

He froze, remembering again what had happened the night before, this time more vividly. 'That's not poss . . .' His words trailed off.

'Hey, steady. Let's sit you down. I'll make you tea or something.'

Cally guided him into the room where she'd found the brandy bottle. She lowered the photographer on to a sofa and again knelt down in front of him. 'Are you sure you don't want me to ring for a doctor?' She peered intently at him. 'You look terribly pale.'

He looked beyond her, eyes unfocused. His mouth opened and it seemed he was about to say something; instead he struggled to his feet and dashed past her, almost sending her sprawling. Cally picked herself up and followed.

His naked legs were disappearing up a spiral staircase when she reached the kitchen and she, too, began the circular climb. She found him in a small room – obviously a photographer's darkroom – staring around in dismay at the mess.

Film was scattered everywhere: sheet film, rolls of negatives, transparencies. The floor was awash with liquid from upturned chemical dishes. The drawers of a tall filing cabinet were open, its contents in disarray, many of the buff-coloured files soaking on the floor. Creed was standing in the midst of all this looking stunned. He kept shaking his head as if to say, 'No, this hasn't happened at all, this is only me dreaming.'

'Shall I call the police?' Cally said, stepping up behind him and touching his shoulder.

He looked at her as though disbelieving her presence too. 'Uh . . . yeah. Yeah, call the police,' he said at last, some sense beginning to creep back into his expression. 'Wait, though, wait. Just give me a minute.'

He stared around again, then briefly closed his eyes. 'They won't believe me,' he said.

'Sorry?'

'The police won't believe what I saw last night. They're gonna think I'm crazy.'

'You saw who did this?'

He nodded slowly. 'At least, I think so. It couldn't have been a dream. Could it?'

Cally didn't have the answer to that.

He shuddered. 'Let's go downstairs. I've got to think.'

They left the darkroom and Cally led the way down to the kitchen, twisting her body as she descended as if to catch him should he stumble. Creed pulled out a chair and sat, elbows on the kitchen table, hands over his face, while she switched on the kettle and dropped a teabag into a cup. She sat opposite him while the water boiled.

'You want me to try the police?' she asked again, quietly.

Creed took his hands away from his face. 'It must have been part of a nightmare. Maybe I didn't see anyone at all, maybe I just think I did. The bump on the head, y'know? Maybe I'm remembering wrong.'

'You've had an intruder, there's no question of that. Unless you caused all that mess upstairs.'

'No, I mean what I think I saw. I imagined something, or I dreamed it. I honestly don't know.'

'Tell me what you – what you *thought* – you saw.'

'Got a cigarette?'

She shook her head.

'Hand me that tin then, will you?' He pointed to the dresser.

Cally brought the tin to him and watched as he fumbled it open. He reached in for a brown pre-rolled cigarette and stuck it in the corner of his mouth. He searched around, not leaving the chair, and the girl spotted the matches for him. She brought them over and lit the cigarette, wondering if it were a joint. The first unpleasant billow of smoke confirmed that it was straight.

'D'you like old movies?' he asked her.

Surprised, she said, 'What?'

'Old films. Really old ones – silents, black-and-white. You know the stuff.'

'It isn't really important right now, is it? Your place has been ransacked and you've been hurt. Tell me what you saw, who made that mess upstairs.'

'That's what I'm trying to get to.' He drew in on the cigarette and released the smoke in small coughs. He gave a shake of his head. 'I had to be dreaming.'

She reached across the table and touched his wrist, a hint of impatience creeping into her tone. 'Just say it.'

'D'you like vampire movies?'

She let go and straightened in her chair. Her mouth had dropped open.

Embarrassed, Creed cleared his throat before going on. 'My favourite was always the first. I think it was made in the early 'twenties. The . . . uh, the person I saw last night . . .'

The kettle began to boil noisily, steam rolling from its spout. The *click* as it turned itself off was like a gun hammer on an empty chamber in the stillness of the room.

'Oh shit,' said Creed, as if coming to a decision. 'I saw Nosferatu last night.'

Cally's mouth opened a little more.

'I saw the first bloody vampire.'

He puckered his face, as if the words, soft-spoken though they were, had hurt.

7

You know, some people will refuse to believe what their own eyes have told them. Usually it's because they don't want to believe. Put it down to ignorance, prejudice, or blindness to the realities and the enigmas of life itself. It can also have a lot to do with being unable to deal with the unpleasantnesses of the world we live in. This doesn't just occur in the individual; it's probably more common with the masses, and often more prevalent with certain peoples (although we won't give any particular nation a hard time here, because none of us have copyright on the blind-eye). Lest we get too deep – and too depressed – let's stick to Joe Creed.

Now, you can't really blame him for disbelieving what his eyes had told him that night (disbelieving *after* the event, of course); rationale tends to rear its pushy head in the cold light of dawn. And besides, if *you* thought you'd caught sight of a vampire, or *vampyre*, especially if it wasn't in the darkly suave guise of Christopher Lee or Louis Jourdan, nor the comically pasty-faced version of Bela Lugosi, then you'd probably want to reason sensibly with yourself and come to an accommodation that might just prevent a nervous breakdown.

You see, the original Nosferatu/Dracula was the *scary* one. Visually created by the German director Friedrich Wilhelm Murnau for his film *Nosferatu, eine Symphonie des Grauens* (Nosferatu, A Symphony of Horrors) made in 1922 and unofficially adapted from Bram Stoker's *Dracula*, the vampire was portrayed as a rat-like creature, with an enlarged bald head, permanent long thin fangs in the middle of his mouth (as opposed to the magically blooming incisors of later movies) and cruel curling fingernails that resembled talons. To complete the flesh-crawling image, our man was humpbacked and supported by spindly, crooked legs. The real McCoy, this one, the kind of guy you'd sincerely hope never to meet in a crowded supermarket let alone on your own in the dead of night.

A vision of total unloveliness, and a one-off (unless you know someone just like him).

So Creed wasn't too much at fault for assuming (or deceiving himself into believing) it was a bad dream. The robbery itself was real enough, and that *was* baffling, for nothing much had been taken. No valuables, no cash, no photographic, hi-fi, or video equipment. Just rolls of used film and a few prints. If he was slower than you in guessing the motive, then again, it was hardly his fault; it's usually much easier to see the answers when you're on the outside looking in.

Nevertheless, it didn't take him too long to realise the reason for the burglary. By that time the police had come and gone, informing him that he'd been lucky in one respect because he'd disturbed the intruder before anything of value could be stolen, and even luckier in another respect because he hadn't been physically assaulted. They'd found the garage door open and the lock of the door leading off from it forced, so that was how the thief had gained access and why the frontdoor was still bolted on the inside. When asked by the boys in blue to describe the intruder, Creed had become some-what coy for, by this time being fully dressed and with people around, daylight flooding through the windows, and three cups of tea inside him, plus the original brandy, and five cigarettes smoked, normality had overruled the memory. 'A thin guy with a bald head,' he told them. 'And oh yeah, he had a humpback.' 'Not a lot we can do, sir, but get a strong lock on your garage and the connecting door. A decent alarm system wouldn't go amiss, either. If you find anything else has gone missing, anything *important*, that is, give us a call at the station.' Standard response from the police in cases where no real harm has been done and there wasn't a hope in hell of catching the culprit anyway.

It was only when they and the girl, Cally, had gone that it dawned on him just what the break-in was all about.

He went up to the darkroom to check again and nodded at his own conclusion. All the previous day's funeral shots were missing. Someone – and it was obvious who – hadn't wanted his picture taken.

Judging by what the man had been up to at the cemetery, Creed could understand why. But was evidence of gross indecency (of course, the shots he'd taken had shown nothing of the sort, but this kinky mourner wouldn't know that) with necrophilic overtones reason enough to break into someone's home? Certainly, if the perpetrator was important enough for his whole life to be upset by the disgrace. For the first time that morning, Creed smiled.

More puzzling though was how the loony had found out who Creed was and where he lived. The coverage of Lily Neverless' funeral wouldn't have appeared until this morning's edition of the *Dispatch* – if it appeared at all. He had a deal with the newspaper that his name usually appeared beneath his pictures, but the question was still the same: How had the thief known where to come last night?

He could be wrong, but Creed felt a tiny prickling in his gut and that usually indicated that he was on to something hot, a story worth following up. Besides, his personal territory had been invaded and, hypocrite that he was, Creed didn't like that at all. Not one bit.

The thing to do was find out just who the dirty old man was. Surely someone in the business would be able to recognise him from his mug shot if he truly were anyone of note. But the negs and prints, even those totally black sheets of shiny paper which he'd kept out of curiosity, were gone.

Creed smiled a second time. Oh no they weren't.

The wall-phone *brurrped* at that point.

'Yeah?' he asked into it, irritably.

'It's me – Cally. I've just got to my office and I wanted to make sure you were all right.'

'Yeah, I'm great. Thanks for calling, 'bye.'

'Hey wait. Didn't you wonder why I came over this morning?'

'I hadn't given it a lot of thought.'

'I had a schedule of Daniel's movements this week to give you – you know, social events, film locations, that kind of thing. I got into the office early to type it up for you.'

'Daniel? Who's Daniel?'

'My boss, Daniel Lidtrap. Don't you remember our conversation last night? You were going to try and get him some mentions in the diary column. For publicity, remember?'

'Uh – oh yeah, that's right. Slipped my mind.'

'I'm not surprised. How's your bump?'

'Rich in colour. Thanks for this morning, Cally – d'you have a phone number and last name, by the way?'

'It's on the list I put on the hall window-ledge before I left. My other name's McNally.'

'Cally Mc*Nally*?'

'Sorry, not my fault.'

'Well it's got a rhythm to it. Look, I gotta get going. Can I call you later, talk about those publicity shots for Giltrap?'

'Lidtrap. That'd be fine. Don't forget, the number's by the frontdoor. Hope your headache soon goes away.'

'It's going already. Talk later, okay?'

'Sure . . .'

The phone was back on the hook without catching her goodbye. Creed was smiling again. The buzz was on.

He drove straight to the *Dispatch*, grabbing a copy of that morning's edition from the reception desk as he passed, opening it up as much as he could with elbows pressed to his sides in the crowded lift.

There it was, page five. He pushed against his fellow travellers on either side, making room to open the newspaper wider. Big picture, across five columns. A wide view of the burial scene, an attempt to show how beloved(?) and respected old Lily Neverless had been, the mourners spread across the page in various shades of grey. The caption mentioned many of the bigger names, but not one of the faces was recognisable. Creed scanned the blurs, looking for one person in particular, even though it would be impossible to discern him.

The lift doors opened and he was flushed out along with most of the other passengers. He paused in the corridor to give the dot-image closer scrutiny. Impossible . . . impossible to tell . . . unless . . . could that be the guy, behind everyone else, beneath the tree there? It was pointless squinting: the picture was never going to sharpen. But it could just . . . be . . . him . . . right there at the back. Some of the other shots would be more promising.

Creed headed for the newspaper's photographic department. Once there he knocked on the darkroom door and a voice on the other side said, 'Half a sec.'

He placed his camera bag on a chair and nodded to a staff photographer, Wally Cole, who was sitting at a bench nursing an oversized mug of coffee. The staffy, a veteran, who'd been with the newspaper long enough to consider Creed a young upstart, gave him a grudging nod in return and went back to studying that day's racing form. He wheezed a cough before dragging on an untipped cigarette. 'Fuckin' cripples,' he said to himself as his rheumy eyes ran down the list of horses. For consolation he tipped a little more Scotch from a dulled chrome hip-flask into the coffee.

Creed ignored him and went to the darkroom door again. 'Come on, Denny, I –'

The door opened before he could finish and a youth in his early twenties grinned at him as he pushed by carrying three sets of freshly developed negatives. He clipped them in a drier and closed the metal door. His close-cropped hair made him look as if he were prematurely balding.

'Can you let me have the stuff I gave you yesterday?' Creed asked him.

'What was that?'

'The funeral.' He showed him the photograph in the newspaper.

'Oh yeah.' Denny indicated a shelf with his thumb. 'Somewhere in that lot. Hasn't been filed away yet.'

Creed delved into the semi-transparent envelopes, quickly reading the magic-markered inscriptions. He soon found the one he was looking for.

'Got no time to devv anything up for you, Joe,' Denny quickly told

him, heading over-briskly towards the darkroom to emphasise the
point.

'Do it myself.'

'Sure, but can you do it later? We're flat out in there.'

'Couple of minutes, that's all I need.' He added, 'It's important.'

'Aren't they all.'

'All of 'em and none of 'em,' grumbled the staffy, sipping on the
whiskied coffee.

'Think of it as a career decision,' Creed said to the youth.

'You call this a career? Okay, two minutes. We're really fucked in
there, Joe.'

'Bless you, my son.' Creed slipped into the darkroom.

Ten minutes later he was out again, closing the door on the
moaning that came from inside. Clutching three wet blow-ups in his
hand, camera bag over his shoulder, he strode down the corridor to
the newsroom.

A voice stopped him on the way to the picture editor's desk.

'What have you got on today?'

He turned to see Blythe, the skinhead diarist (to be fair, Blythe
had an abundance of silver hair, fringing that gleaming pink bald pate),
gliding through the newsroom towards him.

'Uh, I'm not sure . . .'

'Right. Get over to Claridge's. I've just had word Woody Allen and
his whole brood are staying there.'

'*All* the kids?' Creed remembered there were seven or eight at
the last count, some of them Mia Farrow's from previous marriages,
others adopted, and one at least from the loins of the comedian
himself.

'He's dragging them around Europe for some reason that he and
God alone know. How eccentric can you get? A horde of petulant
infants with just Mia and a nanny to control them. He's totally doolally,
of course.'

Creed, being Creed, found it difficult to disagree. Sammy could be
murder just on his own; imagine a whole posse of snotnoses hanging
on to the backseat of your pants. Christ, that was beyond common
reason.

'You know I'll never get past the hotel's frontdoor,' he said.

'Then you'll have to hang around outside in the cold, won't you?'

Blythe replied with some pleasure. 'That is your job, isn't it? Hanging around street corners.'

'At least I keep out of the gutter.'

'Oh, *my*, do you now? Well that is news.'

The diarist waggled his head and Creed felt like smacking it. Instead he turned away.

Blythe's icy voice stopped him again. 'I assume you'll be covering Lady Coventry's little soirée at the Grosvenor this evening?'

He'd forgotten all about that one. 'I haven't forgotten,' he said.

'I'd like something other than guests arriving and leaving, thank you.'

'You know how difficult it is to get into one of her bashes. She's one of the few socialites who detests publicity.'

'Can't get into Claridge's, can't get into the Grosvenor. Is our boy losing his touch?'

Several of the journalists nearby were looking up from their word processors with interest.

'I've never been beaten yet,' Creed said coolly, aware that one of the journos who knew him better than most had cupped a hand to his mouth, his snigger sounding like a small sneeze.

'Well then, let's see how you do, shall we?' said Blythe, obviously pleased that the paparazzo had risen to the bait. 'My sources tell me that the Duchess of York will be attending tonight, gallivanting, no doubt, while her husband roams the oceans. I also have it on good authority that the diet has gone to pot again, so how about a nice one of that gorgeous pouting bottom? I have the caption in mind already: "Fergie's fast fails to last". How does that grab you?'

'Very pithy. You want me to get a shot of her arse?'

'With her face at least in profile, dear boy. Otherwise it could be *any*body's rear end, couldn't it?'

'That might be difficult. You see, arse and face are at different ends and on different sides of the body.'

A snigger from nearby again, but the diarist was enjoying himself too much to notice.

'Then we'll find out how good you really are, won't we? I mean, it might just be possible to *understand* Jack without Anjelica, even though they'd been dining together all evening and even left the restaurant at the same time. One of Jack leaping headfirst into a car might be exciting, but hardly provides a story to hang on it. But now you have two subjects inescapably joined at the waist to capture in the one frame. It doesn't sound too difficult to me. And to show how much we all admire your efforts at the *Dispatch*, I'll award you a nice magnum of champagne when you bring me the shot.' Smiling airily, he looked around the newsroom as if for witnesses, then back at Creed. 'How does that sound to you?'

Creed clenched his fist; oh yes, he was sorely tempted to throw me. But then the newspaper's editor valued this creep's services more than he did Creed's. Paparazzi were ten-a-penny, even the good ones, whereas gossip columnists were rated on their high society and celebrity contacts; Blythe, fuck him, had the best. He decided that today, *just* today, he wouldn't pop the diarist.

Blythe was already walking away, too superior even to smirk, and the journalists became absorbed in their screens once more.

'Will you have a look at these?' Creed said quickly, bringing the other man to a halt once more. He held the damp prints aloft and Blythe pulled a face, waiting for the paparazzo to join him rather than walk back.

Creed obliged. 'I wondered if you might recognise him.' He handed the photographs to the diarist, who peered at the three blurred images of the crazy Creed had snapped the day before.

Blythe's lips pursed and his nose wrinkled as though he had just been served wine of the wrong vintage and temperature. 'I can't say your focusing has improved these days,' he remarked.

'I had to blow them up quite a bit. He was in the crowd at Lily Neverless' funeral.'

'He looks a nasty enough piece of work, even without definition. Why so interested in him?'

'No special reason.' It hadn't sounded convincing and Blythe's arched eyebrow indicated so. 'He, uh, he looked vaguely familiar and I wondered if he were someone from old Lil's past.'

'Dear boy, I'd imagine almost everybody there was someone from Lily Neverless' past – why else would they bother?'

'Do you recognise him?'

Blythe gave the photographs back. 'As a matter of fact, I don't. Though I might think about it a little more if you were to tell me why you're so intrigued to know.'

It was Creed's turn to walk away. 'Don't let it bother you,' he said over his shoulder.

The picture editor was on the telephone when Creed reached his desk, and he motioned with a pencil for the photographer to take a seat. Creed did so, lighting up a cigarette, distracted by the run-in he'd just had with the gossip columnist. How the hell was he going to get a shot like *that* of Sarah Ferguson? The staff at the Grosvenor – or at least, the ones that counted – knew him too well to allow him in uninvited. The best he could hope for was pics of the Duchess arriving or leaving. Maybe she'd trip over the kerb as she left her car. *Maybe Salman Rushdie would appear on* Wheel of Fortune. Shit, there was nothing Creed hated more than a challenge.

'How you doing, Joe?'

He looked up to see the picture editor, Freddy Squires, another veteran who had known Fleet Street before the exodus, peering over the top of his glasses at him. 'Life could be kinder,' Creed replied.

'So I see. What famous personality landed you one last night? Or was it one of your girlfriend's again?'

Creed reflexively touched his forehead and winced at the move. 'Fell down the stairs.'

Squires regarded him sceptically.

'It's true. I took a dive, from top to bottom. My cat tried to kill me.' He didn't feel in the mood for going into the whole story. Christ, what would the old man think if he mentioned he'd been paid a visit by Count Dracula last night? The bars around the office would be merry that lunchtime.

'I didn't think you were the sort to keep pets.' The picture editor began sifting through papers on his desk, the photographer's condition no longer of any interest. 'Got anything for us?' he asked. Squires' voice was gruff, his manner direct, but he was one of a minority who genuinely looked upon Creed with warm regard. The fact that the photographer had provided him with some of the best celebrity snaps of the past five years in terms of newsworthiness and amusement value had something to do with it; the other side was that Squires enjoyed originals, and to his mind, Creed, no matter what else he was, was certainly that.

'It's a bit early in the day, Fred.'

The picture editor grinned at the photographer's pained expression. He pulled a sheet of paper free from the rest and offered it across the desk. 'A list of events for you to cover the rest of this week. Film première, charity auction, nothing thrilling, but reasonable fodder. Good funeral stuff yesterday, by the way.'

'Thanks. That's what I wanted to talk to you about.' Creed exchanged the photographs for Squires' list. 'D'you recognise this guy? He was there, at the funeral. I thought he might be an acquaintance of Lily's.'

'Hm.' Squires shuffled the pictures, studying each one for a few seconds. 'Why d'you want to know, Joe?'

'Uh . . . I caught him up to something after they'd laid the old girl to rest, when everyone else had left. Something a bit naughty.'

Squires stared across the desk at him. 'You've got some other shots?'

'Not exactly.'

'Come on, son, don't waste my time.'

'Bear with me, Fred. Just tell me if you know who he is for now.'

The picture editor's eyes went back to the photographs. He was silent for a while, then slowly shook his head. 'Can't say that I do. Looks vaguely familiar, though.' He held up two together, looking from one to the other. 'Nope, no good. Can't place him. How important is it?'

'I'm not sure at the moment.'

'Tell you what, I'll keep one and pass it around. We've still got a few of this character's generation about the place. Shame it's such a grainy shot. Are these really all you've got?'

'They're the best of the batch.' He still felt disinclined to go into details.

Squires put the other two photographs into an envelope and pushed it across the desk. 'Right. You know Woody Allen's over at Claridge's, don't you?'

'I've been informed.' Creed tucked the events list and envelope into a pocket of the camera bag and stood, cigarette dangling from the corner of his mouth.

'You don't look good, Joe,' the picture editor told him. 'Have you had that bump seen to? You could suffer concussion, you know.'

'Nah, I'm okay. Bit of a headache, that's all. You'll let me know about that shot?'

'Sure. Oh, and Joe . . .'

About to turn away, Creed paused.

'Grab a shave before you go over to the hotel. You know what they're like having scruffs hanging around their frontdoor.'

'Go suck on your granny's tit,' Creed answered amiably.

'I've sucked on worse. Mind how you go.' Smiling, the picture editor went back to work.

But ten minutes after Joe Creed had left, he picked up the photograph again. His brow wrinkled. He tapped a pencil against his teeth.

Yeees . . . he thought, the word drawn out in his mind. *I know that face from somewhere. Now where was it? When the hell was it?*

Either someone had opened a window somewhere or something long-forgotten suddenly chilled him.

8

As always, driving through the West End was a bitch, which lightened his mood not at all. Stop-go-crawl-curse-stop, not necessarily in that order. One day the whole city was going to collapse in on itself and for all Creed cared it could happen there and then.

His head pounded and there was a sour taste in his mouth. He cut in on a Volvo and raised a stiff middle finger in response to the vehicle's abusive horn. There was bright sunlight out on the streets, but that made the littered gutters no more attractive. Most of the people on the pavements looked as depressed as he felt; those crossing the streets merely looked apprehensive.

Now someone in a Ford Sierra cut in on him and Creed became outraged, thumping his horn and wishing it was the road hog's snout. He desisted when he noticed the width of the other driver's shoulders and the thickness of his neck through the Sierra's rear window.

Our hero's mind was no longer on the incident of the night before – that had become just a bit too unreal for him in broad daylight. A vampire in his loft? Forget it. He'd seen something, all right, *someone*, but obviously not what he'd thought. Right now he wasn't sure if it had been imagination – after all, he *had* just woken up, and he *was* scared shitless – or if he misremembered. The way he figured it, his head had taken a pretty hard knock, so maybe his memory was scrambled. Besides, the tangible day-world of snarled-up traffic, bitchy gossip columnists, thumping headaches and impossible assignments imposed a reality that was perversely comforting when considering the alternative.

Claridge's was just ahead. Creed pulled over on to a double-yellow, far enough away from the hotel's entrance not to be obtrusive, but close enough to keep an eye on it should a traffic-nazi (warden) wander by. Another monkey (journalese for photographer, and a term not always used endearingly) was hanging around outside and Creed wondered whether he was loitering with or without intent. There was always a chance with high-class hotels like Claridge's that somebody famous or infamous would walk out the door during the course of any day, so if nothing better was on offer, it never hurt to linger for an hour or so.

He locked the jeep and strolled towards the waiting paparazzo who, on observing Creed's approach, looked dismal. Creed saw it was Terry Roche, a pro who'd been in the business twice as long as he.

'Anybody in?' Creed asked without a greeting.

'Cut the crap, Joe,' Terry replied.

So, they both knew the score.

'He enjoys taking the kids to the park, doesn't he?' said Creed, taking one of the Nikons from his bag and slipping the strap around his neck.

'Yeah, I've had a quiet word . . .' Creed understood the 'quiet word' probably would have been with the doorman, '. . . and he hasn't set foot outside this morning.'

'It's a bright day. Shouldn't be too long. Any idea why he's over?'

Terry shrugged. 'Looking for European locations, I heard.'

'Don't tell me he's had enough of New York.' As Creed spoke he was looking over the other snapper's shoulder through the glass revolving door into the hotel lobby. His movement was unhurried when he took off the Nikon's lens cap and tucked it into a pocket, at the same time making a quick check on the camera setting. Bit of luck, he thought to himself, saying nothing to his companion. A couple of good ones and I'll be on my way.

The sudden heightening of tension on such occasions has already been mentioned, and it's palpable enough to be sensed by professionals of Terry Roche's ilk.

'Is he coming out?' he asked Creed, not looking round to see for himself.

'Will be. Don't move – he can't see my camera through you.'

'Kids with him?'

Creed nodded.

'Mia Farrow?'

He couldn't be sure. 'If it's her, she looks different from her pictures.'

'Yeah, I've seen her on the street before. She doesn't dress up.'

'You're telling me. Let's move to the side, give 'em a chance to clear the door.'

Their attempt at nonchalance as they did a kind of sideways shuffle along the pavement wasn't very convincing, but fortunately their prey had a handful or two of youngsters to organise which required his full attention.

Once out of sight of the lobby, Creed and Roche raised their cameras and stood poised, like big game hunters, ready to shoot.

They waited, both tingling tense.

And waited.

And waited some more.

But nobody emerged from Claridge's revolving door because, as everybody knows, Woody Allen is a lot smarter than he looks. He'd taken his brood out the back way.

The rest of the day wasn't much better for Creed, either. With no specific mission in mind he toured the 'in' restaurants without finding any really worthwhile targets, although he caught two male Members of Parliament, one Labour, the other Liberal Democrat, who were having a 'jolly' affair (if the combination had been Labour and Conservative, then a snap would have been worthwhile), leaving Rue St Jacques, arm-in-arm, and Jane Seymour, all sugar-coated gorgeousness, offering a two-finger salutation to the camera on her way out of Joe Allen's, and Jeffrey Archer tripping over the kerb outside Le Caprice but, as ever, landing squarely on his feet. By late afternoon, Creed's headache was as bad as a headache can get without becoming a migraine and he drove home, fit only for one thing. Stripping off completely, he did that only one thing and crawled beneath his duvet, pulling it over his head to close out the rest of the world. He was soon asleep.

The dream he had wasn't good, but for the life of him, he couldn't remember what it had been about when he woke; all he knew was that although the pain in his head had subsided, there was an unease fidgeting in his gut. The house was in darkness.

He rubbed his eyelids to get them operating, and when he opened them he saw the black figure watching him from the door; only this time – and it took several heart-stopping seconds to realise it – this time it really was his dressing gown hanging there from a hook. 'Christ,' he muttered, and switched on a bedside lamp.

6.48, the clock said. For a moment he panicked. Morning or evening? He surely couldn't have slept the night away.

He hadn't. There was no morning chill and the atmospherics were all wrong for the beginning of a new day. He lay back in the bed, an arm like a lover's around the pillow at his side. Gotta go to work, he told himself. Nightshift. What was it tonight?

He remembered the challenge and groaned. Why the hell hadn't he told Blythe into which sunless region he could shove his little assignment? There was a time when Creed would have been turned on by the prospect of a night's ducking and diving, but nowadays it all seemed like too much bloody bother. No, that wasn't quite true: the spark hadn't fizzled out, it was just that it spluttered occasionally. This was a time of spluttering.

He showered, he even shaved (if he got inside the Grosvenor, he'd have to look halfway decent); he spent ten minutes sitting on the loo reading the next two pages of Hawking's *A Brief History of Time* to blank his mind completely. He burned a French Bread Pizza, drank three cups of coffee and smoked four cigarettes, checked his cameras were loaded, opened a tin of food for Grin, who seemed to be keeping well out of the way, either because of guilt (the cat had nearly killed him on those stairs) or from common sense.

The doorbell rang around 8.15.

For reasons he wouldn't care to admit even to himself, Creed opened the bedroom window and stuck his head out rather than go downstairs.

'Yeah?' he called, unable to recognise the figure down there in the poor light.

'Hello, it's me, Cally,' the figure called back.

'Yeah?'

'Oh.' A short pause. 'Can I see you for a moment?'

He remembered how good she looked. 'Down in a sec.'

She was growing on him fast, he realised when he opened the frontdoor, for that little quirk in her features – the slightly crooked front teeth – now seemed in perfect harmony with the rest of the picture. Her hair was different tonight, parted on one side and falling in a loose-curled bob. He gave her the Mickey Rourke, forgetting for a while that night's mission impossible.

'The swelling's gone down,' she observed as he stepped aside and waved her into the hallway. He plucked the list she had left that morning from the windowsill and held it behind his back.

'Hardly hurts at all,' he said. 'I've got to go out soon, but if you'd like a quick drink . . . ?'

'I won't keep you. I know how busy you are and you were a bit involved in other things earlier, but I wondered if you'd had a chance to glance at the list of Daniel's activities for the rest of the week.'

'Of course I did – I know it's important to you. I might be able to get along to something.'

'I thought the zoo would be a good one.'

'Yeah, I thought so, too.' What could Lidmap be doing at a zoo?

'They used to bring the chimps to the studio to shoot the commercial. With this new campaign they're taking the teabags to them – at the zoo. You know, chimps watching a chimps' tea-party?'

'Ah. How about that drink?'

'I don't want to hold you up.'

You could be worth it, he thought. 'I could skip the arrivals – I'm supposed to be covering a charity bash at the Grosvenor. Things won't get cracking 'til well after ten. Come on up.'

He let her lead the way, mainly for the view, but also so that he could tuck the notepaper containing her list into a pocket.

'Did the police get back to you?' she asked over her shoulder.

'Are you kidding? Do you know exactly how many break-ins there are in the London area in any twenty-four-hour period?'

'No, how many?'

He gave a shake of his head. 'A lot. The police won't be getting back to me. Turn left,' he directed.

She went through to the sitting room and Creed stood in the doorway. 'What would you like?' he asked.

'White wine? Dry, if you have it.'

She looked around while he went off to fetch the wine. The room was untidy, but there wasn't enough in it to make a mess. Over the mantelpiece were two Henri Cartier-Bresson prints, both black-and-white, one depicting a man leaping over a large, seemingly fathomless puddle (and obviously not going to make it), the other of a small kid proudly carrying home two bottles of wine.

On the wall opposite was another chrome-framed photograph, this one, according to the 12-point type beneath, by Elliott Erwitt. It showed a dog lying lazily beneath a car, the wheel threateningly resting against its head. All three photographs seemed sombre with their harsh shadows and grainy greys; yet each one was warm in subtle humour. A television with a fourteen-inch screen was on a stand in one corner and on the lower deck was a small hi-fi system with cassettes, some without their plastic cases, scattered before it. On the mantelshelf were several opened envelopes, their messages peeking out as if returned once read, a carriage clock showing the wrong time, a box of matches, and a red candle in an ornate silver holder.

A glass-topped coffee table littered with magazines stood between a sofa and an armchair, neither of which matched, although their loose cushions were of the same design and colour. She sank into the sofa and continued her inspection of the room.

There was no ceiling light, but lamps were in opposite corners, their glows (he'd switched them on before leaving the room) subdued by plain shades. One rested upon a waist-high yew bookcase which, instead of books, was filled with old, if not antique, cameras. A rubber plant whose leaves were brown around the edges shared space with a full ashtray on a tiny square table by the sofa.

Nothing matched apart from the cushions, not even the carpet and curtains: the former was a bland, patternless beige, and the latter a kind of dark yellow ochre that might not have been so dull in daylight. Most of what was there looked as though it had been acquired for function rather than for any design congruity.

The sound of a cupboard being opened, glasses clinking, came from the kitchen across the hall. A cat, the weird one that looked as though it was permanently grinning, looked round the open door at her. It studied her for a few moments, refusing to venture further in despite her soft encouragement; it disappeared, not in the least bit interested in her.

A thump as though someone had stumbled, and then Creed came through carrying two glasses and a bottle of Vouvray. 'I'll kill that cat,' he muttered.

'Are you sure I'm not holding you up?' she said, taking one of the glasses from him.

'I've got plenty of time. Besides, I need something to get me through the night.'

'Why, what are you up to?'

'You don't want to know.' He touched her glass with his own and slumped into the armchair. 'Have you got a thing going with Milchip?' he asked, and from the tone you'd have thought the question was completely without guile.

Her shoulders jerked. 'With who?'

'Your boss, the director.'

'Daniel Lidtrap? What makes you ask that?'

He shrugged. 'You're so keen to make him a big name.'

'He already is in advertising circles.'

'Small stuff. You wouldn't be pressing me if that meant anything in the real world.'

'Yes, you're probably right. But wrong on the other count. Daniel isn't into women.'

Creed smiled and sipped wine.

'Are you – were you – married, Joe?'

'Was. She took most of my worldly possessions, including my kid.'

'You must miss him.'

'Not much. Most of the time he's a snotty little brat.'

She hid her surprise behind her glass. 'Do you see him at all?'

'I do my duty once a fortnight. At least, I try.' He proceeded with the ritual of sounding each other out. 'What about you, Cally? If you're not involved with your boss, how about others?'

'Nothing significant. My job's more important than –'

Somewhere outside the room a phone had begun to ring. Creed murmured something under his breath and put his glass down.

'Won't be a minute. Help yourself to another while I'm gone.' He moved the bottle closer to her on the coffee table, nudging magazines aside. A brown ten-by-seven envelope that had been lying on top slid to the floor.

When he had left the room, Cally finished her wine but didn't help herself to another glass. Instead she retrieved the envelope from the carpet.

There was no hesitation when she looked inside, and very little reaction when she drew out the two different photographs of the same ravaged face.

9

Time to interrupt for a very sketchy rundown on our hero's career before the plot (such as it is so far) begins to thicken.

Joseph Creed had seen a lot and experienced a lot, and so he fancied himself as something of a world-weary cynic; which, to give him his due, he was, and the fact that he played up to the image to the point of boorishness didn't make it any less so.

Part of that cynicism came with the territory, so to speak. As a photo-journalist, to give his trade a more respectable title, he'd ambushed the private moments of the eminent and not-so-eminent, often exposing situations that the party concerned would rather have kept discreet. When scandal was in the air, Creed and his kind – no apologies to the boys for saying this – were like vultures waiting for their prey to stagger and fall so that the pickings would be easier; and fall they generally did. At its most innocuous, Creed's job was merely to catch the celeb wearing a goofy expression, with his or her latest fling, or maybe even taking a swing at the camera; if the subject were female, then a shot of over-exposed thigh or cleavage was always a favourite. But, working for so many years with the maxim that 'good news is no news', it had become natural to look for the darker or seedier side of human nature and the shot that might bring that into focus. In a way it was a shame that Creed was rarely disappointed in his searches.

He'd spent his late teens and early twenties bumming around America, working where he could, moving on the moment it felt like routine, making his way from the East Coast to the West, from New York to L.A., stopping to catch breath and earn bread at various points along the way – Charleston, Knoxville, Nashville, Salt Lake City, and quite a few places you might never have heard of. The route wasn't direct and the stayovers never planned: a conversation with a pretty girl at a bus station, a casual beer with a local who would, after the fourth or fifth, become a bosom buddy, a HELP WANTED sign in a store window – any interesting 'connection' was good enough.

Sometimes it was circumstances rather than desire that kept him in these places, other times it could be the reverse (a ripe female body was always worth lingering over). Often he was requested to move on rather than taking the initiative himself.

In Los Angeles he worked for a time in a recording studio – more as a gofer than an arranger – then hustled his way back across the States after an incident involving a black session vocalist, her equally black-tempered boyfriend, a damaged tape deck, and a wrecked Plymouth Fury (the latter due to Creed's hasty and careless departure). It took him under a month to get back to New York where a job as a messenger for a fashion magazine got him interested in photography. He picked up what he could from the mag's staff photographers and freelancers, but ended that particular career (which could have been promising, who knows?) when one day he borrowed a Leica from the studio to do some freelance work of his own and someone he didn't know on the street 'borrowed' the camera from him. He wasn't such an accomplished liar in those days, so he was collared soon enough.

Around the same time the authorities became interested in his activities, wondering why Joseph Creed didn't appear to exist on any of their lists, particularly on those appertaining to work permits. The decision that he should return to England wasn't his alone.

Within three months of his being home, his mother died miserably of a slow-failing heart (his father was long gone, but with a secretary, not an ailment) and with the small inheritance left to him, Creed bought himself the mews house which proved to be the wisest, not to say the only, investment he'd ever made. He had just enough left over to buy a few sticks of furniture and basic photographic equipment (like a camera and two rolls of film).

He took to life as a paparazzo like a duck to water or a pig to slime, finding he had an aptitude for the right moment, the right shot, in a profession where bravado was all and the photo-thief was king. A few lucky snaps got him under way and he soon established a certain reputation for himself with one or two pieces of derring-do. He took chances, he trod where devils feared to tread. He inveigled, he lied, he cheated. He gave his word and broke it. He had no regard for anybody's – *anybody's* – privacy. He was a pro. And so help him, he loved the smell of sleaze.

But lately – oh lately – something was lacking. One assignment seemed like the one before and the one after. They all had variations, of course, but essentially it was the same routine: hanging around, bored out of your skull, a sudden dramatic rush of adrenaline, the thrill lasting a couple of minutes at most, then waiting for the next fix, kicking your heels, wasting your time, married to your camera, cursing it when it let you down, loving it when it did all you asked; and you, yourself, scorned and courted in equal amounts – no, be real: scorned more than courted – cruising the streets when most good people were tucked up in bed, shrugging off indignities (Robert Redford had clipped Creed's ear once), labelled a parasite by a society which, itself, fed off you.

These thoughts, and others, meandered through Creed's mind during the down periods; at other times, when he was on a high, he had the greatest job in the world. Trouble was, the downs were exceeding the highs these days.

However.

Here he is, driving along Park Lane towards the Grosvenor House Hotel, his mood already beginning to lift. He'd checked it out earlier, had been thrown out the rear entrance, the staff entrance, the goods entrance (security being extra tight because of the visiting Royal) and had finally reached the conclusion that no way was he going to enter. Meanwhile, possibilities elsewhere could be pursued – the phone call earlier was from a publicist whose client, a fast-fading comedian of late-middle years, was celebrating his birthday with the latest bimbo in a BIG way at Annabel's that evening (any publicity *was* good publicity when you were on the slide). Creed had covered that, particularly enjoying the moment when the estranged wife, along with the estranged daughter (who looked like a bimbo herself), doused the comedian's girlfriend with their piña coladas. After that, and considerably cheered, he'd completed a tour of duty, knowing that nothing would be happening at the Grosvenor until after midnight. He could have caught the Duchess of York going in, but the best time was coming *out*, when one or two glasses had been consumed and spirits were frisky (and Fergie was renowned for her friskiness). In a good mood, she wasn't averse to obliging the cameramen, although right now, Creed seriously doubts she'll pose for the particular shot he has in mind.

But, he's going to get *something* tonight, and it'll be more than a cheery wave. As he drives he wipes the back of his hand across his lips, which have become moist. Oh yeah, no way is he leaving without *something* . . .

Creed slowed down when he neared the Grosvenor's Park Lane entrance, noting the line of waiting chauffeur-driven stretch-limos and Rollers waiting alongside the kerb. No space had been left unoccupied adjacent to the Great Room's revolving doors, and that made him suspicious. The pack was gathered outside, along with the usual sightseers who gathered anywhere they saw waiting cameramen. He drove on.

The hotel's other entrance, this one leading directly into the reception lobby, was round the other side in a cul-de-sac off Park Street, a road parallel to Park Lane. Creed made his way to it and parked the jeep in a mews directly opposite the cul-de-sac. Hoisting the camera bag on to his shoulder, he locked up and walked back towards the main road. He paused when he recognised a familiar vehicle tucked in among others along the mews.

He smiled, remembering the crack on the head he'd taken outside Langan's the night before. It was nothing to the crack he'd received tumbling down the stairs, but at least there might be some retribution for this one.

Creed lowered the bag to the ground and knelt beside it, popping the fastener to one of the small side pockets. He took out a tiny tube.

He joined the other paparazzi – the more canny ones these – a few minutes later and in time to see his old chum, Bluto, arguing with hotel security inside the lobby. Oh wonderful. In his bid to pose as a regular guest, Bluto had left his cameras inside his car and was obviously packing a miniature. No doubt he'd been sussed two seconds after getting through the hotel doors. He was lucky they'd tabbed him for what he was and not a goddamn terrorist, which was what he looked like.

The thickest paparazzi knew better than to argue unnecessarily once the game was up, and he left grouchily, ignoring the welcoming cheers of his compatriots outside.

He managed a sneer for Creed as he lumbered by, then looked twice at Creed's I-know-something-you-don't grin. He passed on, crossing the road and heading for his parked Celica, no doubt to fetch his grown-up cameras.

'Any action?' Creed asked the closest photographer.

'You just saw it. Other than that, nothing. Fergie's inside though, and a few others worth getting.'

Creed slipped his cameras around his neck, charging the batteries on both as he peered back into the lobby. He noticed the pool of royal snappers waiting in there, a permanent circle of privileged photographers who had special access to such events, known as the Royal Ratpack. Anyone else in the profession was an outsider and had to make their own opportunities. Creed, and the small group of (canny) snappers around him had guessed correctly: the Duchess of York would be leaving the charity ball through the main lobby and out these doors. The giveaway, and what the cowboys around the other side had been too dumb to spot, was the fact that no space had been left at the kerbside for the royal vehicle to pull into. No way would Fergie's bodyguards allow her to walk out into the road.

He checked his watch. Five-to-midnight. Plenty of time to grab a smoke or two. Hopefully, she had a full engagement list tomorrow, so she wouldn't stay too late. Hopefully . . .

He began to light up, but dropped the match instantly. Something was happening inside. Guests were stopping, the royal snappers were moving forward, raising their cameras. She was on her way out.

Even though there were only five members of the paparazzi present outside, the jostling began, each of them trying to manoeuvre into the best position. A doorman immediately hurried forward to move them back.

Meanwhile, in the mews opposite, Bluto was frantically struggling with his car door. For some reason the key wouldn't turn in the lock. And when he tried to withdraw the key so that he could use the other door, it wouldn't come out. He slapped the roof of the Celica hard as though it were being obstructive deliberately, and rattled the doorcatch as if wrath alone would do the trick. He leaned forward to examine the lock and when he touched the smeared chrome, the tips of his fingers almost stuck to it. He cursed loudly, stood back and kicked a tyre. He heard the commotion across the road, saw the first camera flashes.

He remembered Joe Creed's mocking grin.

'Bastard!' he hissed.

Unlike his colleagues, Creed bided his time, seeing no sense in wasting good film on pictures of the Duchess of York's famous red hair bobbing into view over the heads and shoulders of those around her. He was now resigned to settling for less than he wanted, that he would have to eat shit when he delivered the goods to the *Dispatch*'s gloating diarist, but that was the way of it sometimes. Win some, lose some. There was nothing he could do about it. He'd get something though, even if it was only one of those loony-toon expressions of hers. A Daimler drew up to the entrance, forcing the paparazzi to move around it for a clear view. The doorman who had ushered them away before opened the rear door.

Here it comes, flouncing out the door, bodyguard ahead. Come on, babe, pull me a face, give me *something* . . .

He heard the roar coming up from behind and turned just in time to see a great black shape pushing aside anyone in its path and bearing down on him.

Creed ducked reflexively and Bluto piled into him, arms swinging, his incoherent roar startling if not terrifying everyone in the vicinity.

They both sprawled on the pavement, but Bluto's impetus carried him further so that he was virtually prostrate at Lady Sarah's feet. At once, two burly individuals had hurtled themselves on top of him, one being the Duchess' bodyguard, the other a plain-clothes policeman who had been keeping an eye on the gathering outside. A tall, distinguished-looking gentleman in a dinner suit, materialised from inside the lobby and quickly led the Royal by the arm around the scrimmage, to the waiting car. She bent down to climb in.

Creed, by then on his knees, had watched the proceedings in astonishment. Somehow he felt disembodied from the action, as though it were all taking place on a screen before him – and in slow motion at that. It didn't take long to realise who had tried to attack him though and, of course, to understand why. But the bloody fool had spoilt any chance of his getting a decent shot of . . .

He saw her from the rear, leaning forward to duck into the Daimler, and his whole body – his whole *psyche* – snapped to attention. Oh thank you God, thank you . . .

'*Look out, I think he's got a gun!*' Creed shouted.

Screams then, shouts, smacking sounds coming from the scrum only two or three feet away from him. And best of all, *best of all*, the Duchess of York, still bending forward to climb into the car, craning her head round, a look of alarm on her face.

Creed didn't have to think further: his index finger did it for him. *Click*-flash. Simultaneously.

He was on his feet instantly for a better angle. *Click*-flash. Simultaneously.

Then the tall escort was bundling into the Daimler behind his charge, pulling the door closed behind him with a solid *clumph*. A last glimpse of wide eyes in a suddenly pale face beneath lush red hair before the car sped away, burning rubber as it made the tight turn.

Trying not to smile too broadly, Creed took a quick, almost contemptuous, snap of the three men rolling around at his feet before slipping away.

He carefully eased the Suzuki into the narrow garage, flicking a lightswitch on the wall as he passed. The garage was L-shaped, so that once inside there was plenty of room to climb out from the jeep's passenger side. It was here that Creed stored odd pieces of junk and machinery; there were shelves filled with tins of paint, most of them half-full or near-empty, brushes, tools, a box containing nuts, screws, nails, several outdated telephone directories and a car battery re-charger. He also kept there, when they were not in the back of the jeep, his camera tripod and small aluminium stepladder, as well as two tungsten lamps and three rolls of coloured backdrops for occasional (very occasional) studio shots.

He turned off the headlights and engine and waited until a yawn had been fully expelled before climbing out and sliding back through the narrow gap between the rear end of the Suzuki and the garage wall to close the garage door. His head was throbbing again, although his fingers told him the swelling on his forehead was almost gone. Despite the headache, he chuckled to himself – and not for the first time over the last hour or so – wondering where Bluto was right now. Locked up, or still ringing round for a 24-hour motor mechanic who knew how to pull a car door-lock without doing too much damage?

Creed had developed that night's take himself at the *Dispatch* and had been delighted with the results. He did a ten-eight of the Fergie snap (actually she'd looked pretty good that night, trim and vivacious, but at the angle he'd caught her and wearing a ballgown that billowed from the waist down, the result was inevitable) and put it on Blythe's desk in an envelope with the message 'Make it a Krug – I earned it!' pentelled on the flap. The deputy picture editor was more interested in the bundle of arms and legs on the pavement, and Creed had given him the full details over a plastic beaker of whisky from a bottle kept close at hand in a filing cabinet.

Creed was tired, hurting some, but content as he unlocked the door leading from the garage area to the ground floor office. He locked up behind him, mindful that the intruder had come through this way (as there was no obvious damage, the police thought he'd forgotten to secure both office and garage doors the night before).

He turned to see the red light on the answerphone glowing from the shadows.

Creed was in two minds whether or not to play back the messages; all he was in the mood for was a drink, a cigarette, and bed. But when you live alone it's hard not to be curious about messages from the outside world.

He switched on a desk lamp and pressed PLAYBACK on the machine. There was only one message:

'Er, Freddy, Freddy Squires here, Joe. I ran a check on that photograph you gave me today, you know – the nutter at the funeral? I think I said he looked familiar, and Wally Cole thought the same when I showed it to him. As Wally's been snapping longer than anyone else on this earth I thought he might recollect something. Trouble is, it can't be who we thought it was, although he's a dead ringer. Talk to you tomorrow about it.'

The tape stopped, then rewound itself.

Creed flicked through a square leather-covered book on the desk and found the picture editor's home number. He tapped out the digits and lit a smoke while he waited for the phone to be answered. Eventually it was, and the voice that growled down the line wasn't happy.

'Who is it?'

'Fred, it's me, Joe Creed.'

'Are you kid—? D'you know what bloody time it is?'

'Some of us are still working.'

'Some of us have a bloody day job. What the fuck d'you want – and it'd better be good, son.'

'You said the guy at Lily Neverless' funeral looked like someone you know.'

'*What?* I don't believe it! You're ringing at this time of . . . Joe, take a hike, will you?'

'Come on, Fred, you're awake now. It's important.'

'No it fucking isn't, it isn't important at all. We were wrong, it can't be who we thought it was.'

'Why? How d'you know?'

'Because I took the trouble to search through our old files. Bloody hell, I wish I hadn't bothered if this is what I get for my pains. He's a dead ringer, all right, but the person Wally and I thought it was is long gone. He was hanged fifty-odd years ago.'

Click.

10

<C> reed felt shaky after he replaced the receiver, as if the news Squires had just imparted had some shocking significance. Which was ridiculous, of course. The man he'd photographed in the cemetery resembled someone who had been hanged over fifty-odd years ago. So what? He himself had a friend who was the spitting image of the Yorkshire Ripper. The deputy manager at his local Barclays could have doubled for Heinrich Himmler (their personalities were not dissimilar either). Everyone has his or her Doppelgänger, they say. And anyway, fifty years was a long time: a person would change considerably.

Creed shrugged. What the hell was he on about? There couldn't possibly be any connection, unless. . . unless, of course, the crazyman was related to the hanged man. Now *that* might make an interesting angle. Then again, he, Creed, was a photographer, not a journalist: such stories weren't really his department. Still, it was curious, no matter which way you hacked it. Why the obscene act over Lily Neverless' remains – an act that had been almost like a ritual with its twice-around-the-grave routine? Weird, very, very weird.

Creed climbed the stairs and Grin joined him in the kitchen as he filled the kettle.

'I hope you've been busy,' said Creed grimly as the cat perched itself on the table and watched. 'You've got a lot to make up for, pal.' He leaned forward to show the cat the discoloration on his forehead.

The cat seemed pleased.

'Okay, enough sarcasm. Go get mice.' He swept Grin off the table with a firm hand, and the cat disappeared through the kitchen door with a flick of her tail.

Although tired, Creed was still on a slight high from that night's main event. It's a condition that goes with the job, usually when a 'result' has been achieved; entertainers and sportsmen have the same problem of bringing themselves down after a performance. Freddy Squires' titbit was still bothering him, too.

Where had he put those shots of the loony? He glanced around the kitchen. No, he was sure he'd dropped the envelope on the coffee table in the lounge when he'd returned that afternoon.

But he didn't find it there and nor was it anywhere else in the room. He checked the office downstairs and even searched the back of the jeep. He tried the two rooms at the top of the house. Not there. The envelope seemed to have vanished.

Creed descended the spiral staircase, both puzzled and agitated at the same time. The photographs couldn't have just disappeared. And he was sure that he'd brought them back after leaving one with the picture editor. What was going on here?

He brewed tea and poured himself a stiff brandy as well. Sitting at the table he started rolling some cigarettes, dipping into his 'shag' tin and sprinkling tobacco on to the thin brown papers while he pondered. His fingers trembled as he worked, his thoughts far from the labour.

Somebody had got inside the house again. That was the only conclusion he could draw. He took a swallow of brandy, a sip of hot tea, then lit the first cigarette. But how? There were no signs of forced entry anywhere and he'd had to unlock both garage and office doors to get in a short while ago. It hit him with a jolt.

The girl, Cally. He had left her alone in the sitting room when he'd gone to get some wine, then again a little later when the phone had rung. The photographs had been in an envelope on the coffee table

in front of her while he was downstairs in the office taking the call –
Fix Features had been on the line wanting to arrange a shoot three
weeks ahead. He'd been there for at least ten or fifteen minutes.
Cally hadn't stayed long after that, much to his disappointment, but
he himself had had to get over to Grosvenor House. Christ, she
could have easily slipped the envelope into her bag. No, no, that
couldn't be right. Why the hell would *she* take them?

He drank too much brandy this time and closed his eyes as the
liquid burned a path through his chest. What reason could she have
for stealing them? It didn't make sense. She was a stranger . . .
she *was* . . . a . . . stranger. Exactly. What the hell did he know
about her? And when he thought about it, her reason for getting
to know him was just a mite flimsy. Sure, would-be celebs and
starlets often used him to promote themselves, giving him advance
information on where they were going to be at such-and-such a
time, inviting him to parties and other social events in the hope
that they would be featured in the next day's Diary or even
news columns, but her approach was perhaps the most blatant
he'd ever experienced. And because she was a looker, because
she'd stirred his dick, he'd been suckered. Who *was* she, *what* was
she?

He puffed at the cigarette, more mystified than angry. The thinking
seemed to be making his headache worse.

Tomorrow he'd call her, find out what she was playing at. But
what if he were wrong? What if she really was only interested in
promoting her boss, this Daniel what-was-his-name? Then he'd feel
a jerk, that was all. And not for the first time in his life. But the
question still begged: Who *had* taken the photographs and why? The
person who'd broken in last night? Maybe he had got in again, maybe
he'd found a spare frontdoor key that time and used it tonight. It still
didn't explain why, though.

Know that feeling of being watched, of eyes boring into the back
of your neck? It could be in a bar, on a train, or in a crowded room –
you just sense someone's thoughts and gaze are directed at you and
you alone. Creed had that feeling right then.

He'd taken another gulp of brandy and the glass was just leaving
his lips, about two inches away, when his hand froze. For a moment
he felt numbed. Smoke from the cigarette held in his other hand

drifted up in a lazy stream creating a thin mist before him. It took a long time for him to turn and look towards the window.

Some of the brandy sprayed from his mouth, while the rest somehow lodged in his throat. He wheezed, coughed, did a half-retch. The chair he was sitting on flew backwards as he jumped up; he gripped the edges of the table to steady himself.

He didn't want to look round at the window again, he didn't want to see the terrible, cadaverous face that had been watching him from outside, but he forced himself to, because he knew it was beyond logic, that there really couldn't be anyone out there, for the kitchen was above the garage and office, and nobody could look through the window at that height, and if they had a ladder he would have heard it scraping the wall or bumping the window-sill, so there couldn't possibly be anyone out there, couldn't possibly . . .

He *forced* himself to look again.

And there wasn't anybody there at all. No thin and pitted, skull-like face, no glaring eyeballs set in the dark sunken sockets watching him. No one there at all.

He was suddenly aware that his feet were becoming wet and warm. His cup had been knocked over and spilt tea was trickling from the table in a steady stream. Quickly he righted the cup, then grabbed a dishcloth to mop up the spreading brown liquid. Only when that was done – and reluctantly at that – did he venture over to the window.

The cobblestone street below was empty, as you might expect at that time of night/morning. Plenty of shadows, though, plenty of places to hide. But no way could someone reach this floor. No way . . .

His headache had shifted, no longer pressuring his temples and the area just above the bridge of his nose; instead it seemed to be occupying a space high at the back of his head. Creed touched himself there, fingers probing his hair as though attempting to move the pain around. It wouldn't budge. Delayed concussion? Was that the problem? Maybe he should have had a doctor examine him after all. Could concussion cause hallucinations? He had no idea.

He returned to the table and finished the last of the brandy. The face he'd seen – *imagined* he'd seen – at the window belonged to last night's intruder, Mr Nosferatu. He shivered. A vampire could crawl up walls, couldn't it?

Now basically – and you may already have gathered this – Creed was a down-to-earth non-believing feet-on-the-ground world-weary practising cynic. His firmest belief was that he, himself, existed, and he accepted that only because it required no act of faith on his part. He could sense, he could feel, he could see, he could hear, he could taste. He could even think. All this was irrefutable. As for anything else, then he really wasn't that interested in the question, let alone the philosophy behind it. Was reality no more than an illusion of the mind? Was existence nothing more than an elaborate dream? Did an individual exist only because others perceived he or she to *be*? Creed really didn't give a shit. *I fornicate, therefore I am,* was his credo. So, because his imagination had grown lazy with regard to such intangibles, it was obvious to him that the crack on the head that morning was playing silly buggers with his brain.

And maybe he was right.

Taking the half-smoked cigarette from the ashtray, he made the short trip down the hall to the bathroom. There he opened the medicine cabinet and reached in for a carton of paracetamols. He swallowed four, washing them down with water from the cold tap. The visage that stared back at him from the bathroom mirror was not encouraging. The eyes were red-rimmed and bloodshot, the skin was almost sallow in complexion, and the bruise on the forehead was a mushy kind of purple. He stuck out his tongue and at least that looked healthy enough.

Creed unzipped his fly and stood over the toilet, cigarette back where it belonged, drooping from the corner of his mouth. He watched the flow of urine, not with interest, merely to make sure it hit the target. Water in the bowl bubbled under the fall.

His hand touched the wall by his side to steady himself, for he had felt his body sway. He blinked, then felt his body move again. Christ, he'd be pissing on the floor at this rate. He steadied himself mentally this time and exerted muscle pressure to vacate his bladder more speedily.

Movement again, but this time he realised it wasn't him. This time it had come from the toilet itself. The porcelain sides where the water lapped had seemed to move inwards for a fraction of a second.

'Boy, you're in trouble,' Creed muttered to himself. He needed to lie down, to crawl into his pit and pull the cover over his head so that he could sleep this thing off. Oh Christ, there it goes again. The toilet bowl was moving, as though the sides themselves were flexing, contracting – *breathing*. The flow from his bladder was easing, becoming a trickle, and Creed tried to help it along. A spurt, nearly done. Thank –

Oh God, that wasn't right. Something more was happening down there. The sides at the water's edge appeared to be breaking out. The cigarette fell from his lips into the well with a plop and a fizz as the shiny-smooth rectangle beneath him shaped itself into a loose jagged oval. It flexed once more, became even more of an oval, its jagged edges forming into what . . . looked . . . like . . . oh shit . . . *teeth* . . .

He was looking down into a porcelain mouth!

Creed felt himself go weak at the knees.

But he jerked upright in absolute shock and stepped back when that tooth-edged, pissed-on mouth suddenly shot from the bottom of the toilet, glazed sides stretching as though elastic, and gnashed at the air where he had been standing a split-second before.

He screamed as water mixed with his own urine drenched him, and he fell backwards. The mouth reared over him on its long dripping neck, the snapping of its porcelain teeth loud and sharp in the tiled confines of the bathroom, before it abruptly disappeared back to where it belonged.

In a flurry of kicking legs, Creed pushed himself to the far end of the bathroom (which wasn't very far at all) and lay there gawking and trembling, not comprehending what had happened, yet believing it implicitly. His clothing was soaked and his penis had shrivelled (understandably) into insignificance somewhere inside his trousers.

Oh dear God, what was happening to him? This was insane, a nightmare, like a bad acid trip. Things like this couldn't happen, they couldn't be real. It was his head, it was all inside his head. He needed a doctor, he needed one very badly.

He forced himself on to one knee, eyes never leaving the toilet that stood impassive – impassive but *waiting* – at the other end of the bathroom. Using the edge of the bath for support, Creed reluctantly (knowing what had just happened couldn't have happened at all) slid himself back towards the seat. He had hallucinated, he knew that; yet he had to be sure, he had to make certain, that nothing really lurked down there, no mouth, no teeth, nothing. That the whole thing had been a mind-joke.

He crept nearer, scarcely daring to breathe. Levering himself up into a shaky half-crouched position, he peered over the rim. There was only still water, slightly greenish, a cigarette butt floating on the surface, at the bottom.

Nevertheless he slammed down the toilet lid.

Creed sprawled on the floor for a while, trying to bring his senses together, his breathing now ragged. He didn't feel well at all.

Gradually, reason infringed upon lunacy, as it usually, or at least, eventually, tends to do with the perfectly sane when something ridiculously illogical has happened. He should have had the bump seen to; it was as simple as that. Nobody could walk away from such a fall without suffering worse after-effects than a nasty headache. Brain cells had been jiggled, and this was the result. Probably, drinking alcohol that night hadn't helped any. Moaning more from self-pity than pain, Creed crawled to the door and used the handle to pull himself erect.

His clothes were wet, but that didn't surprise him: as far as he was concerned it was just another part of the illusion. Guided by the lights from the kitchen and the bathroom behind him, Creed lurched along the short hall and all but fell into the bedroom. A rest, he told himself. All I need is to get my head down for a few hours. Too late – too *early* – to call a doctor in. What would he tell me anyway? Take a couple of aspirins, that's what he'd say. A good night's sleep will do wonders. See me in surgery hours. Thanks a lot, Doc. Maybe I should call an ambulance. Yeah, maybe that's the thing to do. Just . . . just rest for a moment, though. Just a little sleep . . .

Kneeling on the bed, Creed began to shed his clothes, handling them carefully because they were damp and smelled of pee. Only they didn't, did they? No, Creed, it's in your mind, only the result of upset brain chemicals. Shaken and definitely stirred. Christ, what a mess.

Jacket and shirt were gone. He sat, kicked off his shoes, then pulled at his trousers and underpants. Getting his socks off was the most difficult.

Naked, he flopped back on to the duvet. He didn't mean to, but he couldn't help it: he giggled. Crazy. A mouth jumping out of the toilet, snapping at his pecker. Oh Jesus, Judas . . . crazy . . . Before tiredness overtook him completely, he managed to slide beneath the duvet cover, pulling it up to his neck, relishing and *needing* its comfort. He lay there spreadeagled and bare, and oddly enough, the beginning of his dream was fairly pleasant.

But his awakening wasn't pleasant at all.

He'd been on a beach to begin with, the sun high and warming his stomach. The sea sounds were soothing, gulls circled overhead. Relaxing . . . restful. Sand trickling over his chest. More. Beginning to cover him. His belly, his crutch, his thighs. Squinting into the sun, a shadow suddenly blocking the glare. That you, Sammy? Burying your old man, huh? It's all right, kid. Enjoy yourself. Make a castle on my chest. Keep the sand away from the kisser though, son, grit in the teeth isn't nice. Come on, now, take it easy, that's too much. I'm not dead yet, boy. I told you, Sammy, keep it away from the face . . .

The sun had faded. It hadn't disappeared behind a cloud – it had just faded, gone, shrivelled away. And he wasn't on a beach any more. There were stone monuments all around, some leaning over perilously, most of them decaying, lichen-covered and cracked, slabs of stone, their legends hard to determine. Gravestones.

The sand wasn't sand any more; it was great clods of earth, thick and damp, smelly and clinging. Cut it out, Sam. Enough's enough.

But not just the locale had changed: Sammy was different too.

His face had aged, become lined, weary. His eyes were staring. He'd grown gaunt, all puppy-fat gone. He looked like someone else . . .

Dirt stifled Creed's next cry. He choked, spat it out. He tried to move, but earth was packed around him, pressing against his chest, making it difficult to stir, let alone shout . . . let alone scream . . . He was being buried alive, but it was someone else, someone familiar . . . but not familiar, no one he knew, a stranger, a thin man in a grey gaberdine raincoat . . . digging dirt, chuckling while he shovelled the soil . . . piling it on to Creed . . . covering his whole body . . . his arms . . . his legs . . . his belly and chest . . . his – oh God no – his face.

He awoke and the dream was gone almost immediately.

He felt cold, even though the duvet was still up around his neck. He wondered what he had been dreaming of. Something not very nice, he was sure. Something about graveyards. Yeah, wouldn't you know it?

He raised his head from the pillow and looked towards the end of the bed. Moonlight through the open window revealed his bare feet. That's why he was so cold. They were like blocks of ice and his big toes were completely numb. Wriggling them hardly improved the circulation. He rested on one elbow and reached out with his other hand to push the cover back down, but something black and scurrying caught his eye. It had sped from the edge of the mattress, as though having climbed from the floor, and disappeared beneath the duvet.

Before Creed could kick out with his feet, he became aware of other movement in the bed with him and he felt a prickling sensation that was not unlike goose-bumps rising on chilled flesh.

Then he saw another little black thing hurry over the bottom of the mattress and race into the shelter of the duvet.

Creed leapt from the bed, almost tripping over his discarded clothes lying in a heap on the floor. He stumbled into the door and his hand scrambled against the wall for the lightswitch. He found it and smacked it down.

He immediately clapped a hand over his eyes, shielding them from the sudden glare, lifting his palm cautiously after a while like a traveller staring into the sun towards the horizon. Nothing was on the floor around the bed apart from the jumble of clothes. Had he honestly seen a spider – two spiders – disappear under the duvet? Or had it merely been the tail-end of his dream? Whatever, he had no taste for creepy-crawlies, but they certainly didn't frighten him. Not much, anyway.

After a few more blinks he scanned the rest of the room to make sure he really was alone. His gaze returned to the bed.

The duvet was rumpled, a corner turned over where he had scrambled out.

He wiped the back of his neck with a hand, twisting his head to relieve a stiffness there. Again Creed looked over at the bed.

There was nothing peculiar about it. Yet something was not quite right.

He watched the cover as if expecting it to move and, of course, it didn't.

So why was he reluctant to get back into bed? Be sensible, he told himself. Lie down and think of nice things.

He was tired, very, very tired; but part of him was extremely alert. Something wasn't quite right, but he didn't the hell know what. Creed approached the bed cautiously, in the way a hunter might approach a downed tiger, knowing it was lifeless but still taking no chances.

Creed, naked, stood over the bed. Reaching out he gripped the turned-over corner of the duvet. He paused for just one moment, then swept back the cover so that half of it tumbled on to the floor.

He meant to scream, but couldn't quite work the parts that allowed it. He wanted to back away, but those parts wouldn't function either. The bit that did work was his bladder; fortunately it was only a brief squirt of urine that wet his thigh, more like a nocturnal emission than anything else.

All he could really do was to stare. And stare, and stare.

They were small, yet somehow bulky, their hairy little bodies bulbous and seeming too heavy for their tiny legs. They were mostly black, although the tops of their swellings were hued a deep red, as if liquid inside was pressing to be released. And they came in a variety of shapes, some long like caterpillars (many of these were wormishly hairless, though), others round and energetic, while still more were but minute grubs grubbing around in packs. The one thing they all had in common was that they looked bloated. Glutted, you might say.

And Creed had already made the connection before he looked down at himself and saw the pinpricks and smears of blood all over his own body.

These busy creatures had feasted on him while he slept. They were obese (in their small way) with his blood.

Creed cried out as much in revulsion as in fear.

He staggered backwards towards the door, never taking his eyes off these revolting, detestable creatures that had invaded his bed, hundreds of them it seemed, all moving in a madness of direction, the bedsheet beneath them splodged red as though flicked with ink.

His hands fumbled with the doorknob behind him and it was awkward to twist, but not once did Creed consider turning his back on those blood-gorged mites occupying his bed. At last the lock sprang and he pulled at the door, jarring it against his bare heel as he did so. Only then did he face away from the bed and hurry into the hall, slamming the door shut once outside. For several seconds he held on to the doorknob, irrationally making sure those crawly things couldn't follow him, his breath drawn in sharp and shallow gasps.

His next idea (this one perhaps more rational) was to run downstairs, grab an overcoat from the rack, and get out of the house. But when he looked down towards the frontdoor, he saw that someone was there, someone lurking in the shadows, someone whose domed, bald head caught the faint light shining through from the kitchen upstairs.

That skull-like head shifted, tilting backwards so that whoever it was there in the dark could look upwards, upwards at Creed. The eyeballs were so big set in that dreadfully thin (and now familiar) face, they appeared almost round. The pointed front teeth were dulled in the poor light.

Creed fainted.

11

He stirred. Then he shivered.

His belly was warm, but the rest of him was freezing. He had no feet: they'd gone away. Another shiver – no, more violent than that: this time it was a shudder. Creed moaned and hunched himself around the warmth at his stomach. He turned over on to it.

A screech and frantic scrabbling beneath him brought Creed to his senses. He shot up as the cat flew away from what had been a comfortable nest in its master's lap and disappeared into the kitchen. Grin leapt on to the table and turned to glare back through the open doorway at the naked man who was pushing himself against the hall wall, a wild-eyed look on his face.

Creed's vision did some dips and curves before settling. He gazed back at the bristle-furred cat on the kitchen table uncomprehendingly, then down at his own bare legs with pretty much the same expression. His feet were totally numb with the cold, but at least they weren't actually missing.

The night's events began to come back to him, just bits and pieces like a poorly edited trailer for a horror movie (a B horror, at that).

A swift examination of his private parts brought him some relief. But what was he doing out here in the hallway? He concentrated very hard to bring some order to the jumbled images and instantly regretted the effort when he saw in his mind's eye those . . . those . . . *things* . . . he had shared his bed with. My God, they'd been drinking my blood! Creed struggled to his feet as if to make himself less accessible.

A further inspection of himself denied the memory: his flesh was unmarked apart from one or two fresh scratches from the squashed cat. He touched the bedroom doorhandle very tentatively and it took some courage to turn it. He swung the door open a few inches, listened, peered through the crack, then swung it wider. He looked round the door towards the bed.

The duvet cover was turned back and the rumpled sheet over the mattress looked pure enough. Creed ventured in, scrutinising every step of the way before taking it, scarcely feeling the carpet beneath his frozen feet. The bed really was empty of bugs as far as he could see, and when he hauled back the duvet further – again, hesitatingly – there was nothing lurking beneath the folds.

He pulled the cover off completely and wrapped it around his shoulders; he stood there afraid and alone and wondering what was happening to him.

There had been nightmares before, lots of them – Christ, everyone had nightmares at some time or other – but nothing so real, *nothing so bloody awful*! He shuddered again and this time continued to do so. Only the deadly chill forced him into some kind of action, otherwise he might well have stayed there dwelling upon the nightmare for the rest of the morning. He went over to a chest of drawers and took out a pair of socks.

Sitting on the corner of the bed he pulled them on, then reached for a pair of jeans lying over the back of a nearby chair, the duvet still around his shoulders like a quilted shawl. The Wranglers were only halfway up his legs when the thought of those hairy, blood-swollen creatures busying themselves on his naked flesh while he slept slipped into even sharper focus and his stomach contracted and flipped and chose to rid itself of any contents.

He hobbled to the bathroom, tugging at the jeans on the way, shawl falling to the floor, dignity and poise having little value to him at that point in time. Past the stairway he hurried, one hand momentarily gripping the rail there to steady himself. He made it in time, but stopped, his throat and cheeks filling as he looked down at the toilet, with its closed lid and biding attitude.

Creed turned aside and let loose into the bathtub, sinking to his knees with the second wave, leaning his chest against the rim. It was unpleasant – in fact, it was disgusting – but no way was he going to open that toilet lid, nightmare or no nightmare; he really wasn't ready for that just yet.

The nausea passed, along with all he'd eaten that month, he figured, and his stomach felt raw and hollow. Still resting against the bath, head and neck hanging over as if waiting for a falling axe, Creed reached out blindly for the taps. His shaking fingers found one head and twisted it to its fullest extent, then crossed to its companion. He swirled the water with the same hand, rounding up the slimy pieces and directing them towards the drain. Repellent though it was, the activity had some small therapeutic value.

He only stopped when his thoughts finally acknowledged what his eyes had noticed lying in the hallway only a few moments before.

He crawled to the bathroom door, his hand leaving damp patches on the tiled floor. It was there, exceedingly white on the beige hall carpet, lying quite near the top of the stairs. He watched it for a little while.

Creed slowly rose to his feet, hoisted up his jeans and buttoned them at the waist, wiped his mouth with the back of his hand, then went forward, hand trailing along the rail overlooking the stairway.

He didn't pick up the envelope immediately; instead he took time to wonder how it had got there. His hand gripped the top of the rail post when he remembered what had been at the bottom of the stairs last night.

His mind did tumbles when he pictured that *creature* climbing up towards him, placing the envelope on the floor beside him, or . . . or even *on* him. Had he, Creed, dislodged it when he'd woken from the nightmare? Nightmare? Which was the nightmare and which was the reality? His body was unscathed, there were no bugs in the bed, yet here, lying at his feet, was material evidence of that *thing's* presence! Creed lowered himself to his knees, hand still clinging to the post. Oh God, God, God, was he really so vulnerable? Could strangers enter and leave his castle whenever they wanted?

He touched the envelope as if expecting a reaction from it. There was none (but if toilets could develop teeth, there just *might* have been), so he picked it up and held it before his eyes. The flap was not sealed.

Finger and thumb slipped inside and pulled out the single sheet of folded paper. The note had been typed in caps and in two neat lines. It read:

```
YOU WILL BRING THE FILM TO US
   YOU WILL NOT SPEAK OF IT
```

That's all it said.

12

The motorist in front mistakenly imagined that the parking space just about to be vacated was his: Creed had other ideas. He pulled up close behind, pretending he hadn't noticed the other car's reverse lights, nor the indicator winking the intent.

The driver of the parked vehicle shook her head in despair as she was forced to ease her way around the rear of the Suzuki, and Creed ignored her clearly mouthed obscenity as she finally drove by. He reversed the jeep, swinging a hard right, having to go forward again to avoid scraping the Peugeot next to the empty parking space. Meanwhile the driver whose meter he was stealing let his resentment be known by way of his Mercedes' horn. Creed ignored this too, going forward once more so that he was correctly aligned.

What was difficult to ignore, though, was the supremely ugly face (that is, what could be seen of it above the wiry, matted whiskers and equally wiry, matted hairline) that appeared at the side window.

'Oi'll see y'all roight, sor,' came a muffled voice that was as grizzled as the man's features. Life-wearied, bloodshot eyes blinked at him from the other side of the glass.

The old lag waved his arms in the no-nonsense manner of an airport marshaller docking a 747, his fairly useless instructions liberally aided by shouts of 'Sor!' In the meantime, Mercedes Man had gone off in search of fresh pastures, albeit after having let Creed know what his life expectancy would be should they ever meet again. The rear wheels of the jeep nudged the kerb and Creed switched off the engine.

He had parked in Soho Square, using one of the rarely unoccupied bays fringing the tiny gardens there, all the vehicles positioned front- or rear-on so they resembled multicoloured metal petals around a giant sunflower's centre. He touched his temples with stretched thumb and fingers and squeezed gently; neither the vociferous expressions of hostility, nor the filthy old buffoon out there still waving his arms and issuing instructions had helped his headache one bit. He felt hungover, but if pleasure had preceded it, then Creed wouldn't have minded so much. He wondered if he'd suffered permanent damage in the fall downstairs the night before last. Brain damage, maybe. No, couldn't be. He could think, see, smell. Nothing was impaired. The problem was, he was seeing *too much*.

Taking his hand away, he found the worn old face peering at him through the window again, a nightmare itself with its red-veined cheeks and nose, shiny wet lower lip, and yellowy eyes. A rag as grease-stained as the tramp's ankle-length raincoat appeared on the windscreen and began a wildly exaggerated circular motion that left smears rather than clear patches.

Creed opened the sidedoor three inches and said, 'Piss off,' in a matter-of-fact way.

'Be done in a minute, sor,' was the unoffended reply. 'Sparkly clean it'll be.'

Creed sighed and dipped into a top pocket of his combat jacket for a smoke. He'd had to take time to roll fresh ones before leaving the house that morning, using the work as a kind of therapy, something to do while he pondered on bad dreams and the very real message left on the carpet at the top of the stairs. Unfortunately the physical occupation hadn't helped the thinking and vice versa: his fingers had been incredibly clumsy so that the cigarettes themselves were malformed and loose. He should have followed his normal habit of rolling a few the night before; but of course, he'd been a little shaky then as well, if he remembered correctly. In his possession he'd had a photograph of someone who was a dead ringer for a man hanged over fifty years ago. Nothing really unnerving about that. He could have been a relative – a son, a nephew – or just a guy with a similar face. So what?

Somebody wanted the photos and the negs, and they were going to unusual means to get them, that was so what.

Those prints were already gone, and although he could be wrong, it might have been Cally who had taken them.

The old sot outside spat on the windscreen and, to show that he honestly hadn't aimed at the photographer's face, he rubbed furiously at the spittle with his grubby rag. 'Sparkly clean in a jif, sor, don't you worry about that.'

Creed lit up, inhaled smoke, removed flakes of tobacco from his lower lip, and stepped down from the jeep.

'Will I look after it f'yer, sor?' The ancient watery eyes showed happiness at the prospect. One hand still held the rag to the windscreen, while the other was free to accept any coin proffered.

'I told you to piss off,' said Creed, this time not as friendly.

The tramp snorted and spat a very off-colour missile at the car next to the jeep. The blob of runny phlegm did nothing for the shiny red bodywork.

'On the other hand,' said Creed, digging for a silver piece, 'have a nice day.'

He gave the tenpence to the square's permanent but unofficial parking attendant, dropping it from a height of an inch or so above the vagrant's outstretched hand rather than make actual contact. Creed turned away to feed the meter.

'It's a saint, y'are,' the old man proclaimed, even though his natural good humour had been slightly dented. A finger touched his forelock in salute and Creed wasn't entirely oblivious to the irony contained therein.

It was a fine day – cold, true enough, but the sun was shining and there wasn't an umbrella in sight – and Creed gulped deep draughts of air as he made his way around the square, heading towards Carlisle and then Dean Street. Soho was never seedy at this time of day, only somewhat dishevelled. It was rarely too busy, either; that came with the lunchtime rush and continued through the afternoon and evening until night-time when it took on a distinctly different 'other' life.

Once in Dean Street, Creed began scrutinising street numbers, walking towards Old Compton, certain the place he was searching for would be in that direction. He passed restaurants, pubs, film companies and offices as well as piles of rubbish and cardboard boxes dumped in doorways and gutters. He came to a halt when he reached what appeared to be a rather exclusive shop, its huge plate-glass window and door framed by deep olive-green wood, with terracotta tiles rising to knee level below the window. On display was a very large Regency doll's-house painted white, its interior lit by tiny chandeliers and wall lights; furniture and furnishings could be glimpsed through the windows, and he saw there were tiny, costumed figures lounging in chairs or standing around, one ballgowned young lady seated at a miniature grand piano. Belowstairs there was even a rotund cook and a lean scullery-maid.

If Creed hadn't had other matters on his mind, he would have taken a snap of the whole thing. (Our boy *always* carried a camera on him outside the house, even if he was only putting out the trash can, for you never knew when a great, or at least important, or at least reasonable, shot would present itself. Missed opportunities from earlier days when he'd known no better still came back to haunt him. If he didn't have his camera bag with him, then a Nikon was always hung around his neck or, like today, stuffed inside one of the voluminous pockets of his combat jacket.)

Beyond the shop window was a receptionist's desk, all dark leather and chrome, and a receptionist, all dusky-skinned and fine-boned. She was at that moment speaking into a red slimline phone that matched her glossy lipstick perfectly, and unaware – or, if not, pretending to be – of the scruffily dressed window-shopper. Averting his attention, Creed read the stylised gold script discreetly positioned at the bottom left-hand corner of the window: *Page Lidtrap*.

'Lidtrap,' Creed reminded himself. He said it again: 'Lidtrap.'

Tossing what was left of the cigarette into the gutter, he pushed open the glass door and crossed the grey carpet to the desk. The girl still refused to notice him. Downcast though he felt, Creed managed to relish her dark beauty while he waited for her to finish with the phone. Her hair, naturally uncrinkled, was tightly pulled back over her scalp to rise up on top of her head like a braided hard-on. He speculated on how the effect was achieved until he saw she was watching him watching her.

She bade goodbye to the thin phone and set it in its cradle. 'Can I help you?' Her voice was as good and as dark as her looks.

'I'd like to see Cally McNally.'

Large, exquisite brown eyes stared at him. 'Excuse me?'

'Cally McNally.'

'Is this a joke?'

'No. Cally. She works here.'

'I think you must have the wrong company.'

The street door behind him opened and a tall girl with long blonde hair and short skirt that exaggerated legs whose length hardly needed exaggeration entered carrying a portfolio tucked under one arm.

'Take a seat, Mandy, be with you in a moment,' the receptionist said, before returning her glacial gaze to Creed.

'She really is here,' he insisted. 'McNally – assistant to Mildrip.'

'Mildrip?'

He looked desperately at the window. 'Uh, Libprat.'

'Mr Lidtrap? Sorry, you're mistaken. We have no Cally – *McNally*? – here.' Her voice was polite, but her eyes were telling him to get lost.

'Let me talk to Lidtrap.'

'I'm sorry, but unless you have an appointment . . .'

'It really is important.'

The girl wasn't impressed by the Rourke smile, but then Creed really was well below par that day. 'Mr Lidtrap is extremely busy at the moment . . .' Again she left the sentence open-ended as though the refusal was implicit in the trailing space.

'Two minutes of his time, that's all it'll take.' In desperation, Creed produced his Press card and held it up like an arrest warrant. She seemed even less impressed by that than by his smile. But at that point someone came through from a room at the far end of the reception area.

'Harry, is Daniel in his office?' the girl asked, looking around Creed as a bearded man strode by.

Harry stopped at the street door, one hand resting on its diagonal bar. He winked at the waiting model before replying. 'He's upstairs in editing.' He regarded Creed who, as mentioned, was not looking his best, with less enthusiasm than he had the waiting girl. 'Can I help?'

'You were at Hamiltons the other evening,' Creed said. 'There was a girl with you called Cally.'

Harry shook his head. 'Don't remember her. Have a word with Daniel.' With that he swung open the door and called back to the receptionist before stepping outside: 'Meeting at Vickers, Suzi, then lunch, back around four.'

Suzi made a note in a book lying open on her leather desk, then shrugged at Creed. She pointed her pen at a stairway in the corner. 'Keep going to the top. Editing room is on your left. I'll let Mr Lidtrap know you're on your way.'

Like many of the buildings along Dean Street, the Page Lidtrap production house was long, narrow and high. By the time Creed reached the top floor he was very short of breath and his thighs were complaining. The man, the too-handsome one with 'natural' curls he'd seen with Cally at the gallery, poked his head around a door on the landing. His manner was brusque.

'I can give you half a minute,' he grumbled before disappearing back inside the room.

'Thanks a lot,' muttered Creed, making it to the last step with some effort. He followed Lidtrap into the cutting room.

A bench worktop interrupted a lower editing table at one end. Above the benches and desk were film racks loaded with silver cans, all of which were labelled in heavy pentel. Any open wall space was filled with film posters, and a small coffee machine burped and gurgled in a far corner; a pic-sync, splicers, spools and reels used up most of the available space on the worktops themselves. Lidtrap, a slim, yellow-haired Adonis in loose white denim shirt and tight faded blue jeans, was leaning over the desk's raised viewing screen and murmuring to an editor seated at a typist's chair next to him. Film whirred through the machine until the director said crisply, 'Right there.' Only when satisfied did he straighten and turn towards Creed enquiringly.

The photographer leaned against the doorjamb, catching his breath.

'Yes?' Lidtrap wasn't one to hide his impatience.

'I need . . .' a breath '. . . I need to speak to Cally.'

Lidtrap looked at him as though Creed were insane. 'What on earth are you talking about?'

'The girl who was with you at the awards the other evening. She told me she worked for you.'

'Really? In what capacity?'

'Your assistant?'

Lidtrap gave a cold smile. 'Someone's been having you on. We don't have anyone here by that name.'

'But she was with you, you were talking to her.'

The other man frowned in thought. 'Yes . . . yes, I do remember a rather attractive girl introducing herself to us that night. Tall, slim, blondish hair?'

Creed nodded and reached into his pocket for a cigarette.

'Not in here, man,' Lidtrap admonished when Creed put the thin brown weed in his mouth.

The photographer removed the cigarette and tucked it back out of sight.

'I can't remember the girl mentioning her name, but I believe she worked for one or other of the big agencies. She kept mentioning a big film project that was coming up, otherwise I wouldn't have wasted time with her.'

No, I bet you wouldn't, thought Creed. 'She told me she worked for you.'

Lidtrap looked perplexed. 'I can't understand why. What's this all about, er . . .'

'Creed.'

'Creed, yes. I've seen you around, haven't I? A photographer of sorts, aren't you? Yes, you photographed me at Hamiltons.' The sneer was in his tone rather than his expression.

'She gave me a list of your engagements for this week.' He rummaged in another pocket for the slip of paper Cally had left him. 'You're shooting a commercial at a zoo this week, right?'

'A zoo?' Lidtrap reached for the folded schedule, a mixture of incredulity and amusement on his face.

'With chimps.'

'With chimps.' Said flatly, this. 'Somebody really has been pulling your plonker, old chum.' He frowned at the list. 'Dear God, I'd have to be some kind of wunderkind to get through this lot in a week.'

'I thought you were busy,' Creed offered limply.

'Busy, but not masochistic.'

'It's got your company name and address at the top.'

'Typed, not printed. Anyone could make this up.'

Creed was beginning to feel foolish. 'But she was with you at the gallery.'

'She spent some time talking to me and my partner, I'll grant you that. But that doesn't mean she's one of us.' Although his eyes remained on Creed, Lidtrap half turned away. 'Now if you'll excuse me, I've got better things to do than answer questions about people I don't even know.'

Creed nudged himself off the doorjamb and began the long climb down.

His mood didn't lighten when he got back to the jeep to find a spiderweb crack in the passenger side of the windscreen. Somebody had either thrown a stone or smacked the glass with something small and hard. As he drove off, he caught sight of the old lag shaking a fist at him from one of the square's offshoots, but Creed had neither the energy nor inclination to give chase.

'Where the bloody hell have you been all morning?' was the welcome he received from Freddy Squires at the *Dispatch* offices.

'Fred, this character you thought – '

'And as for phoning me in the middle of the – Christ, what's happened to you?'

'Uh?'

'You look like the lost weekend. What the hell've you been up to?'

'Bad night.'

'You and me both. It took me ages to get back to sleep again after your bloody call. You ever do that to me again, Joe, you'll be in such deep shit you'll have hearing problems. Understood?'

Creed dumped his camera bag on the floor and dragged over a spare chair. 'Freddy, tell me about this guy who was hanged.'

The picture editor reached for his pipe and matches, then appraised the photographer. He shook his head as if in sadness before lighting up. 'The state of you . . .'

'Freddy . . .'

Squires sucked the pipe until he had a burn, then contemplated Creed again. 'Why the interest?'

Creed sighed. 'I think . . . I might . . . it's possible I've got something . . . well, something weird going.'

'So tell me.'

YOU WILL NOT SPEAK OF IT

The words were there, brightly lit on the screen wall at the back of his forehead, typed in caps, differing only from the note in that these were white on black.

'Not just yet,' Creed replied. 'You got a cigarette, Tony?' he said to a reporter at a nearby desk.

'You're kidding.' The reporter carried on typing, pausing briefly to flick ash from the cigarette he was smoking into an ashtray.

Creed fumbled for one of his own, the badly rolled brown paper only just together, tobacco flakes littering his lap.

'You might well have something weird going, my old son,' Squires was saying, 'but I've got something a bit more current than ancient look-alikes. That's why I've been trying to get hold of you this morning.'

Creed barely showed interest. The end of his cigarette flared when he lit it.

'Remember the Pamella Bordes scandal at the House of Commons some time back,' the picture editor went on. 'The, er, "exotic" lady employed as a certain Tory MP's researcher. She was given a special pass so she could come and go as she pleased, even had a Division Bell in her own bedchamber?' Squires smiled at the memory. 'Then they discovered who some of her alleged "clients" were – and some of their political connections.'

Creed had already nodded, extra details unnecessary for him to remember the scandal.

'Well we've dug up a new one. Male this time, no more than a kid. And this time it's the Opposition who's embarrassed. A Labour MP is involved.'

Creed still couldn't summon up the interest. 'Nothing exceptional about that,' he remarked. And there wasn't. Quite a few of the

so-called parliamentary researchers were nothing more than individual member's girlfriends or boyfriends, taken on to the public payroll
supposedly to supply their employers with facts and figures concern-
ing anything from the price of rivets in Solihull to the USSR's capital
expenditure on agricultural machinery for any given year. True
enough, this particular type of research assistant (the majority are
genuine – well, a good many are) usually does just enough to
legitimise their existence in the halls of power, enough that is for
their masters not to be overly embarrassed by their presence. See,
the problem in the House is that politicians by their very self-seeking
and self-gratifying natures (there are one or two exceptions, of
course) have always been vulnerable to scandal, so the domino factor
is invariably a risk when an individual member's misconduct has been
exposed: knock down one and others will surely topple. And beware
those who *do* jump up and down with pious outrage over such
allegations against their colleagues, for a politician's hypocrisy knows
no bounds (never – *never* – underestimate a politician's hypocrisy).
So endeth the lesson.

'Nothing *unusual*, anyway,' Squires had replied to Creed's comment. 'This one, though, this laddie, was moonlighting as a rent-boy.
And one of his more illustrious clients just happens to be . . .' At
this point the picture editor mentioned the name of a prominent Irish
stage actor whose staunch support of the IRA was well-known in
government circles, but little known to the public. Call him O'Leary
for want of a better – or real – name.

'They never learn, do they?' It was the best Creed could offer.
Then: 'You don't need me for this. You can use a staffy.'

'We already have. But O'Leary's gone to ground and I think you're
the man to flush him out.'

'Ahh, c'mon, Fred. That's investigative journalism – it's not my
line.'

'It's digging the pictorial dirt, and you're one of the best at that.
If I wanted something on my wife and her lover – should she ever
be so lucky – you're the man I'd employ to get the photo evidence.'

'Thanks, I'm flattered. What exactly d'you expect me to do?'

'Check out the haunts, the gay bars – you know 'em all. One of
the actor and the rent-boy together could earn you a lot of extra
shekels, you know.'

'Even they wouldn't be stupid enough to be seen together now. There isn't a hope in hell.'

'Joe, for a paparazzo you're in a privileged position. This newspaper retains you for a lot of dough and for it, we sometimes expect you to excel. Quit giving me a hard time and go excel. Oh, and something that might help a little . . .' He dipped into a desk drawer and produced a folded sheet of paper. Leaning forward, he handed it to Creed.

Creed looked back at him questioningly.

'An address,' said Squires. 'Take it.'

Creed took it. 'The hanged man, Freddy. Who was he?'

Squires had already lifted the phone, his mind occupied with other things. 'Nicholas Mallik,' he said as he dialled. 'The Beast of Belgravia. I think that's how they described him. Hanged in the late 'thirties. Look him up in files. George? Freddy here. What's the update on the Khashoggi story? I've got a beautiful picture here that requires some words . . .'

Creed had checked the address and was rising to his feet when he spotted one of Antony Blythe's hackettes coming towards him bearing a champagne bottle. Prunella was wearing a Sloaneish green jumper, shirt-blouse collar folded over the neck, a long, check skirt, and dark stockings with sensible brown walking brogues. She was pretty in a pallid and lank-haired sort of way, although her small tight mouth tended to make her look more prim than she actually was.

'Present from the prick,' she said, straight-arming the bottle to him as if it were some kind of award.

'The deal was for Krug, not Moët,' said Creed, nevertheless tucking the piece of paper away and accepting the bottle.

'It would have been if we'd used the picture.'

'You're kidding me.' Creed snatched a copy of that morning's *Dispatch* from the picture editor's desk. He flicked through to page nineteen and opened it out. The picture was large, his name was beneath it. But it wasn't of the Duchess of York bending forward to climb into the limo while looking back over her shoulder at the same time. Instead it showed a group of dark-suited men rolling around on the pavement outside the Grosvenor House Hotel, a bundle of arms and legs really with Bluto's bulging frame melding into those of the two men trying to pin him to the concrete. The caption read: A RIGHT ROYAL SCRUM.

Creed groaned and looked at Prunella, who shrugged and said, 'Sorry.' She blinked twice and stared at him curiously. 'You look awful. Did you get involved in this fracas, too?' She made it sound like frac*arse*.

'Not likely. Why didn't Blythe use the one of Fergie? It was what he wanted, for Chrissake.'

'Oh, this one was much more fun. It might have made the front page if the MP and the rent-boy scandal hadn't broken. Actually, Antony asked me to find out if you had any juicy shots of Jamie O'Leary – at his most camp, he said.'

'There's some over at the agency, none here though. And all old stuff from O'Leary's barnstorming days. Anyway, it seems my task today is to get something fresh on him.'

'You will let Antony have first sight, won't you?'

'Fuck Antony. This is more than just a gossip column item.'

Prunella looked momentarily disconsolate. No doubt she would be the butt of Blythe's bitchy wrath if the diarist failed to lead with the news on O'Leary. After all, this was showbiz, politics and sex all rolled up into one gloriously sleazy ball. What columnist could ask for more?

'Tell you what,' Creed said, taking the girl by the arm and leading her over to a quiet filing cabinet. 'I need something from files, information on a man named, er . . . Mallik, Nicholas Mallik, hanged by the neck . . .' she cringed ' . . . over fifty years ago for some dastardly deed or other. You dig out the info on him for me and I'll slip you the contacts of anything I get on O'Leary before anyone else gets a look-in. Blythe can deal with the news editor if he finds anything he wants. What d'you say?' Of course, he had no intention of letting Blythe have first sight, and anyone who knew Creed, or of the mutual dislike between the photographer and the diarist, would have realised that. Prunella, however, was neither perceptive nor devious in thought. Creed smiled encouragingly, despite the dull throbbing inside his head. He raised his eyebrows, still smiling.

'All right,' she said. 'I'll do it in my lunch break. Mallik, you said?'

He nodded. 'Nicholas Mallik. Maybe we'll share the champagne later.'

'That would be lovely. Will you be around this afternoon?'

'I'll call in.' He just stopped himself reaching round and cupping her bottom with his hand. You never knew with these Sloane types and he wouldn't want to upset her before she had done the favour; besides, his aching head, along with the thought of snapping toilets, had considerably undermined his libido. He watched her walk away, any impure thoughts he had merely transitory and derived from habit rather than yearning.

He checked the address Freddy Squires had given him again and groaned. It meant an hour's journey. And no doubt a lot of hanging around.

'Fuck it,' he said to himself, and picked up his camera bag.

13

◼

Joe Creed doing what he does best. Sneaking around, being unobtrusive, waiting. And waiting, and waiting. Whether it's outside a nightclub, an eaterie, a private home, or hotel, he is the Master of Waiting. That doesn't mean he likes it – he doesn't, he hates it. He's just very good at it. What's more, he has the ability to leap straight into action at a split-second's notice, despite the lethargy or the stiffness that invariably creeps in after the first hour. In some ways, if he'd had the discipline, he would have made a perfect guardsman. Hard to imagine him in sharp red tunic and bearskin hat, it's true, but one thing's for sure, he'd be instantly alert the moment an intruder set a foot wrong. The fact that he'd probably throw down his gun and run off in the opposite direction is another matter: the point is, he's good at spending a long time doing nothing, then becoming zealously active in the blink of an eye.

This ability, acquired over the years as a professional paparazzo, came into call after he'd located the address supplied to him by the *Dispatch*'s picture editor, Freddy Squires, had done a little recce of the immediate area, and settled down to wait in his jeep, which was discreetly parked behind a screen of trees.

The first hour went by slowly enough, the second even more slowly. But just into the third there was movement around the target area.

The location was in one of those narrow little lanes that cross-hatch the English countryside, the kind usually only frequented by motorists who know the area well, or who are lost and off the beaten track. Not too far outside London, this place, but well beyond suburbia and fairly deep into lush greenery. A slate-roofed nest called Rose Cottage. In the right season there would be roses creeping up around the door. There was a small front garden with weed-filled flowerbeds on either side of the cracked centre path. Rickety grey picket fence, low gate ajar. Pretty in a rundown sort of way.

Creed had just leaned forward, his nose almost pressed against the windscreen so that he could peep through a break in the trees, when he saw the cottage door begin to open. In a flash, Creed was out of the jeep and creeping past foliage and tree-trunks towards the beginning of the picket fence. One Nikon was in his hands, the other, containing colour film, hanging around his neck.

He stopped to watch for a moment, quietly moving foliage for a sneaky view. Someone was on the cottage doorstep.

'Oh boy,' he breathed to himself. This was luck beyond the realms of fancy. It could only be him, the target! Judas Christ, it was. Creed recognised him from the picture on the front page of that morning's *Dispatch*, poor quality though it had been. Kevin Plaskett, the baby-face researcher, the cherubic rent-boy. He wouldn't have believed it if he wasn't bearing witness with his own eyes! The actor, O'Leary, was deliciously stupid, he really was! To have the kid – he looked no more than twenty, twenty-two – actually staying in his less (now) than secret hideaway! But the all-important, crucial, and God-please-be-kind-and-let-it-be-so, question was: Was O'Leary there too? Could the actor really be *that* stupid, with the scandal breaking that morning and all? Maybe he didn't know it was all over the news. Maybe he didn't listen to the radio or read the dailies when he was locked away in his charming retreat. Maybe he was too arrogant to care. Never one to ponder too much on life's little mysteries, particularly when there was a job at hand, Creed quickly double-checked his camera. Everything was fine. Yet, eager though he was, he paused to consider.

He needed the right shot, the right moment. A good one of young Kevin on his own would have been okay, but it wouldn't have meant that much. It wouldn't have been *the* shot. But one of the 'researcher' and the subversive actor together would be supreme. Arm-in-arm would be perfect. But was O'Leary there? Was he, could he possibly be, that insane?

Creed decided to take a chance. It would have been so easy to snatch a picture with his zoom lens of the young man on the doorstep – any newspaper's picture editor would have been pleased with that – but our hero wanted something more. It was a risk, he could easily blow the whole thing, but if the gamble paid off, the shot would be priceless (for a day or two, anyway). If the actor was in there, then Creed wanted to flush him out.

He straightened, swung the camera over his shoulder so that it now hung out of sight down his back, set the other Nikon's focus range at six feet and slid it into the roomy side pocket of his coat. Then, bold as brass, one hand still resting on the camera in his pocket as a gunslinger's hand might rest on the butt of his pistol, he strode through the gate.

''Lo, there,' he called out to the startled cherub as he breezily walked up the path. ''Fraid I'm a bit lost, wondered if you could give me some directions.'

The other man backed into the shadows of the doorway.

'Trying to get to the A22, lost my bearings a bit in these country lanes,' Creed continued without a break. His smile was ingenuous (from a distance).

The man at the door hesitated before poking his head out, his feet remaining firmly inside.

Creed pointed back over his shoulder with a thumb, taking care not to twist his body. 'I got to the end of the lane and didn't know which way to go at the junction. Head's useless at direction, could do with a compass. What would it be, left or right?'

He came to a halt several yards from the frontdoor, a subliminal invitation for the young man to come out.

Foolishly (maybe he found Creed attractive – Lord knows, some did) the 'researcher' did step out. He appeared even younger in full light, his tight curls tinted reddish, his cheeks not fat but just pink and full enough to give him that cherubic look.

'I'm not quite sure, but I could find out for you.'

It's unfortunate perhaps, but some people you meet just *are* stereotypes. His voice was soft, though not quite soft enough to be rated girlish, and his walk, while not exactly mincing, had a feline kind of fluency to it. He brushed a curl that wasn't really there away from his forehead, his brow flicking across his fingertips rather than the other way round.

Creed became even more alert, if that were possible. Plaskett had just implied that he was not alone in the cottage. Creed shifted the camera in his pocket in the manner of that same gunfighter loosening the pistol in its holster.

'It'd be great if you could,' he said. 'Late for an appointment, you see. Got to get on my way.'

The cherub turned towards the doorway. 'Jay, need your help for a mo,' he called out.

There was a short silence which was broken by an almighty roar. *'You stupid bloody fool!'*

A raging figure followed the raging voice.

O'Leary was a big man – barrel-chested, black-bearded, and bad-tempered – 'a brough of a boy' – whose voice alone exuded machismo. The critics held him in high esteem as an actor, and the fans adored him for his outrageous and boozy personality. He appeared before the public as an endearingly forthright man of the people, but one whose Thespian talent elevated him above other mortals. A lovable hellraiser, a kind of latter-day Richard Burton in some ways. Even his occasional (and, superb actor that he was, very moving) cries of support for a united Ireland did little harm to his public image. But what was not generally known was just how strong were his ties with the Provisional IRA, and how much of his own earnings he freely donated to the cause. Also not generally known by the doting fans was their idol's ambiguous sexuality. It was a tribute to O'Leary's PR people that his penchant for boys, the younger the better, had been kept under wraps for so long. It wasn't that it mattered so much which way he swung in this day and age, it was just that he looked so goddamn beer-swilling *masculine*. The

disappointment to his adoring fans – and we have to be honest here
– would have been immense.

So here he was, this bear of a man, all bristle-bearded and
bristle-tempered, storming from the cottage, a look of sheer murder
in those dark Irish eyes. Even a hero would have cowered, and
Creed was no hero.

He was already shuffling backwards along the path when O'Leary
made his first mistake. Instead of going straight for the photographer,
the actor paused to grab the cherub by the shoulder and snarl, 'Get
back inside, y'bloody eedjit! Can't y'see what he is!'

Young Kevin's eyes rounded in fear. 'I didn't . . .' he began to say
before O'Leary flung him back towards the cottage door.

Creed, the gunslinger, had been faster, though. The camera was
out of its holster – sorry, pocket – at that very point when the actor
made contact with his young friend. Three shots whirred off before
O'Leary advanced again with a roar of, *'Gimme that bloody thing!'*

Creed did a backwards shuffle, snapping off more shots as he
went, not bothering with the viewfinder now. O'Leary came on in a
rush.

Time to depart, Creed concluded as Kevin disappeared inside the
cottage. He turned and ran for the garden gate. Footsteps – very
heavy footsteps – pounded after him.

He was almost at the gate when something caught at his throat,
causing him to squawk like a crow as he was jerked to a halt. He
could easily have gone down had not self-preservation been one of
his strongest points (perhaps *the* strongest): instead he twisted so
that the camera strap (O'Leary had managed to grasp the Nikon
bumping against Creed's back) snapped and released him.

He was through the low gate in a trice, a hand that worked by
instinct alone reaching down and yanking it shut behind him. Big,
blundering O'Leary, mouthing oaths that even his deep rich baritone
could not render glorious, made his second mistake by continu-
ing pursuit. His legs hit the gate, which jarred against its latch,
becoming an immovable object. The actor tumbled over it to land flat
on his back in the lane outside where he quivered and flapped like a
hairy beached whale.

Creed took time only to pick up the Nikon that had fallen from the
actor's grasp before scooting for the jeep. He jumped in, turned the

key that was already in the ignition, and gunned the engine. The jeep dug dirt as it leapt forward.

He gave the actor, who by now was on his knees and shaking a hefty fist, a finger-and-thumb circle of 'okay' as he sped by. If he hadn't thought it would have been wasted, he'd have managed a wink too.

'Pretty smart, Freddy.'

The picture editor looked up questioningly from his desk. 'Just about to leave, Joe. You got a problem?' He stood and shrugged on the jacket that had spent the day hung over the back of his chair and which was as crinkled and worn as the editor himself.

'No problem at all. O'Leary and his boyfriend are being devved up as we speak.'

Squires grinned. 'You got them together.' This said as a statement, with no surprise.

'Yup, practically holding hands. O'Leary wasn't pleased.'

'I'll bet.' Squires sat down again. 'So what's on your mind, Joe?'

'Nothing really. Just wondered where you got the address from.'

'Passed on to me by our lords and masters. I didn't ask, didn't want to know. You look a bit better than when you went out of here.'

Wearied, Creed drew finger and thumb down his cheeks, stretching the skin. 'Yeah, I feel like a million lire. So the powers-that-be used our proprietor, who used our noble editor, who used you, who used me.'

'It's the way of things. Like I said – what's your problem?'

Creed settled on a corner of the picture editor's desk. He shook his head. 'Just tired, Freddy, nothing more than that. I got some good shots, so I'm not complaining.' He smiled to show that he really wasn't. 'O'Leary was the one they were after, right? They wanted to smear him, discredit him a little in the eyes of the public.'

'It isn't hard to figure out, is it? Call it an opportunity seized rather than a well-planned strategy, though. After all the stick the Tories took from the Opposition over that bloody ridiculous Bordes affair, someone in government circles obviously saw the chance to get their own back. A Labour politician involved in a homosexual scandal, plus

– and what a plus – a terrorist connection. It was all there on a plate.'

'But they decided to take it one step further.'

'Two birds with one stone, old son. Not only could they expose the Opposition for stupid misdemeanours that could have harmed national security, but they could also damage Jamie O'Leary's credibility at the same time. How could they resist it?'

'Does it really work that way? I mean, just because O'Leary's not straight . . . ?'

Squires grinned again. 'It's more subtle than that. Not only do O'Leary's fans discover their idol is as bent as two pins, but they also learn over the next few days that his involvement with the Irish problem is a bit more sinister than he lets on. He might have survived the exposé of one of his little "quirks", but both at the same time? Anyway, at least you have the satisfaction of knowing they chose you to get evidence on the sexual angle. It's a compliment of sorts.'

'I still don't get it. Why just me, why not others? You know, the more the merrier?'

'Think about it. If hordes of snappers and journos had descended upon the place, then O'Leary and his pal would have drawn the curtains and waited it out. Or more probably, they'd have laid low and pretended the cottage was empty when the first cars pulled up outside. And a mob would have given the game away, it would have been too obvious that the Press had been directed towards the actor and his hideaway. No, much wiser to send a pro down there on his own, make it look like a good piece of single-handed rooting out.'

'I'm supposed to feel honoured?'

'Yeah, as a matter of fact you are. Don't tell me you're getting a touch of conscience in your old age. You did your job, you showed life as it really is and not how those with vested interests want it presented.'

'Shit, they've *all* got vested interests, they *all* want it presented the way *they* see it.'

'Spare me the indignation, Joe. We've both been at this too long for that crap.' Squires gripped the arms of his chair and levered himself to his feet once more. 'Tell you what, I'll let you tell me about your mid-life crisis over a stiff one. Marty' – he pointed to the overweight deputy picture editor, who was ambling towards them down an aisle between desks carrying a plastic beaker of coffee, his shirtsleeves rolled to the elbows, tie at half-mast – 'can take care of the snaps.'

A large Scotch and ice was exactly what Creed needed, followed by another, and then another after that. However, he declined. 'Got things to do, Freddy. Did Prunella what's-her-name leave anything for me?'

'Not that I know of. Sure you won't change your mind? A good blast'll restore your cynicism.'

'No, I'll see what the pics are like, then be on my way. I get a name under as usual?' He meant acknowledgment beneath the picture of O'Leary and Plaskett which no doubt would appear on the front page of tomorrow's edition.

'Naturally. Unless you're so pissed off you don't want a mention.'

'See you tomorrow, Freddy.' Creed hoisted his camera bag and headed for the processing room.

Squires called after him, 'Stay home tonight, Joe, leave the glitzies in peace for once. You look better, but you still don't look good.'

The contact sheet of that day's shoot was ready by the time Creed reached the photographic department and he studied each frame through a magnifier, making small crosses against his personal choices with a white chinagraph, although it would be the picture editor or his deputy who would make the final decision. He was pleased with the results, but somehow couldn't work up the enthusiasm to be delighted. You're tired, he told himself. Tired, mystified, and . . . he had to admit it . . . scared. It was difficult to feel delighted about anything in that condition. Today's assignment had kept him busy, kept his mind concentrated on more mundane – mundane and (relatively speaking) *natural* – things. But now it was dark outside and he had to go back alone to the house and he had to sit down and consider what to do about the note and the negs and whether to call in the police and how the fuck did you explain what had happened to the boys in blue who would probably want to search his place for drugs the moment he mentioned the toilet bowl had tried to bite off his pecker and the night before he'd met Nosferatu the thinking man's fucking Dracula and last night bugs had tried to eat him alive in his bed although they'd left no marks on his body and the police would ask him how he got the bump on his head and he'd tell them he'd fallen downstairs the day before and yes he realised concussion could lead to all kinds of complications and even hallucinations . . .

He stopped, having wandered into a corridor outside the processing room, and leaned against the wall. Concussion? Had he jolted something inside his head, was something swelling, blood clotting, something pressing against certain cells . . . touching certain nerves . . . pressuring tissue . . . oh God, was that it?

He moaned softly.

Wait. That didn't explain the note. It didn't explain Cally. Both were real enough. Neither one was a figment of his imagination. Were they?

He reached into his trouser pocket and pulled out the piece of paper.

```
     YOU WILL BRING THE FILM TO US
      YOU WILL NOT SPEAK OF IT
```

It was real enough.

And so was Cally. He'd spoken to her, given her wine. He'd lusted after her, for Chrissake! She was no figment of the imagination. Dipstick – *Lidtrap* – remembered her, even though she'd lied about working for him. So you're not cracking up, Creed. Not yet, anyway.

He left the corridor and went through the newsroom to the features department next door. In a far corner there were four desks pushed together, these combining to make up the Diary desk. Not one position around the assemblage was occupied. Creed scanned the untidy working tops, looking for a folder or package among the jumble of papers and cuttings that might bear his name.

'Is this what you're looking for?'

He looked up to see Antony Blythe, without jacket but still immaculate in blue pin-stripe shirt with white collar, pink silk tie and lethally creased grey slacks, standing in the doorway of the glass-partitioned cubby-hole he called an office. He held a fifteen-by-ten manila envelope in his hand.

'Has it got my name on it?' asked Creed.

Blythe waggled the prize at him.

Creed walked over to the diarist and reached out for the envelope. Childishly, Blythe held it tight against his chest.

'You were supposed to deliver some photographs to me,' he said tartly.

'They haven't been processed yet,' Creed lied, snatching the package from the other man's grasp. 'You can go down and help yourself when they're ready.' For all the good it'll do you, he thought. No way would the story be allocated to the gossip column alone. He noticed the envelope flap was open. 'Have you been into this?'

'Prunella is my assistant. Any research she does comes to me first.'

'She gave it to you?'

'She works for me.'

Yeah, and you picked it up from her desk and stuck your nose inside even though it had my name on the front.

'Why the desperate interest in this foul person Mallik?' Blythe had no shame.

Creed had had enough for one day. He turned away, waving a weary hand at the bald-headed diarist as if to dismiss him.

'I asked you a question.'

'It's none of your business,' Creed replied, already walking away.

'I can make it my business, you know,' Blythe called after him.

The photographer's response wasn't very clear, but the diarist was sure it had something to do with his own head and a bucket of shit.

All Creed wanted to do now was sleep.

It'd been a long day and the preceding nights had been nightmarish – literally. It was catching up on him. Maybe tomorrow he'd see a doctor about the bump on his head, maybe even take the day off, phone in sick. The newspaper didn't own him, neither did the photo agency; ultimately he was his own boss, even if he did have contracts with them both. Sleep away the tiredness and the dull ache inside his head, that was the thing to do. Hell, when was the last time he took a day off? He couldn't remember. When he got home he'd have a stiff drink and a long bath, followed by another stiff drink. The booze would help him sleep better.

The traffic, even at that time of evening, wasn't good, but at least it was moving freely. He kept his speed low, too tired to do battle with others on the road.

Stopped at traffic lights, he glanced down at the envelope lying in the shadows on the front passenger seat. The right thing to do would be to turn the whole lot over to the police first thing in the morning and let them get on with it. He had the photographs of the funeral, the warning note, and now whatever information Prunella had dug up on this character Mallik. Let them make of it what they will. If he were in some kind of danger, then it was their job to protect him (but would they, *could* they?). He needn't mention the hallucinations, and they already knew about the intruder. Let them figure out the connection between the nutter at the funeral and the man who was hanged all those years ago.

He snatched a look at the envelope again. For some reason it made him nervous just lying there in the shifting light.

Eventually he turned off the main drag into the sidestreets and from there it was only minutes before he reached Hesper Mews. He left the jeep idling on the cobblestones outside his garage while he opened the doors; he climbed back aboard and drove in, then closed the doors again, making sure they were firmly locked. He used another key to get into his office and locked it after him. He left the office and locked that door too. Then he stood at the foot of the stairs and wondered why a light was shining from the landing above.

Creed scrabbled blindly for the frontdoor latch behind him as footsteps approached the top of the stairs.

14

'Lo, Dad.'

Creed's hand stayed on the door lock. 'Uhhh . . .' was all he could find to say.

His small but portly son stepped down one step, light from behind throwing his face into shadow.

'Sam . . . Sammy?'

No reply from the boy.

Creed moved away from the door, his hand reaching out and clutching the stair-post for support. 'What . . .' rage crept in '. . . what the f – the hell are you doing here?'

The first sniffle broke from the boy. A knuckle lifted to his face.

'Okay, okay, take it easy.' Still shaking from the shock he'd had, Creed began to climb, one hand outstretched to pacify the boy before the floodgates opened. Sammy stared down at him, his shoulders drooped. He was still wearing his school uniform, Creed noticed.

When they were at eye level, Creed three steps from the top, he paused. 'What's going on, Sammy?' he said as gently as he could, restraining himself from grabbing his son's shoulders and shouting into his face for scaring him half-to-death.

'She doesn't want me,' came the reply that was more petulant than sorry. Another sniffle followed.

'Who? Your mother? Christ, 'course she wants you, Sammy. Your mother loves you.'

'She doesn't!' The boy turned and stomped away from him into the kitchen.

'Hey, wait a min—' Creed ran a hand through his already dishevelled hair. This was all he needed. Usually Evelyn and Samuel teamed up against *him* – God knows what poison she'd fed him over the years – but now it seemed the ranks had split. So what was he supposed to do with the kid?

'Sammy . . .' He followed the boy into the kitchen and found him sitting at the table, a loaf of bread in front of him, jam and sugar spread on the slice he was just cramming into his mouth. 'I've got plates in the house, Sam. And you don't need a carving knife to spread jam.'

The boy regarded him sullenly, his jaw steadily working on the mulched bread.

'Your mother will be worried sick. Does she know you came here?'

Samuel nodded, then licked jam off a finger.

'You rang her?'

A shake of his head with another sniffle.

'Then how does she know?' Creed pulled out a chair and sat down opposite his son. 'Will you stop feeding your face for a minute and answer me? How does she know you're here?'

'She sent me.'

Creed leaned forward, arms on the table. 'She sent you here?'

The boy nodded again.

'Sam, I'm gonna give you five seconds to explain yourself. If I'm no wiser after that you're in serious trouble.'

Samuel considered him for four of those seconds. 'Mum put me in a taxi and told the driver where to take me. She gave me the key to get in in case you were out.'

'She's got a key?'

Sam shook his head. 'No, I've got it.' He dipped into his blazer pocket and put a Yale key on the table between them.

The crafty bitch, Creed thought. How long has she had that? Another reason to change the locks. 'I don't believe you, Sammy. She wouldn't send you here.'

The boy shrugged and resumed eating.

'I'm gonna call her,' the father warned.

No reaction at all this time.

'Okay, kid, you asked for it.' Creed rose and went to the phone. He dialled and watched the boy eating as he waited for an answer.

'Hello?'

'Evelyn, it's Joe.'

The voice at the other end dropped a tone or two. 'Enjoying your son? You see what I have to put up with?'

'What's this all about, Evelyn? Did you send him here?'

'Of course I did. You are its father, aren't you? Perhaps you'd like to take on that responsibility for a while.'

'Evelyn, you know it's not that easy – '

'*You think it's been easy for me all these years?* Bringing up that brat on my own, acting as mother, father, and God knows what else, teaching him things his father is supposed to teach him, laying down the law when he's difficult – which is *most* of the time – feeding him, clothing him, nursing him. Running myself ragged for the ungrateful little . . . little . . .' Tears now. 'You don't know what it's been like, you have no idea. While you've been having fun I've had to work and worry and take care of everything myself . . .'

'Evelyn . . .'

'And what do you care, what have you ever done for him? Well enough is enough, *you* can see what it's like for a while, no, not for a while, for good, permanently, you –'

'Evelyn!'

The outflow stopped momentarily. Her words were icy, not a tear in them, when she resumed. 'It's your turn, Joe. It's about time you were a father to him, so here's your chance. See how you like it for a few days.'

'A few days? You know I can't do that. Christ, I've got a job that keeps me busy at all hours. And I can tell you this – *now*, right *now*, isn't the time to have him with me.'

'There's never a good time for you. You're just going to have to cope.'

'Look, Evelyn . . .' wheedling ' . . . have a talk with Sammy –

Samuel. You know, he's missing you already.' Creed watched the boy sprinkling sugar on a fresh slice of bread and jam. 'He's really upset, Evelyn.'

'The little shit!'

'Hey, c'mon. What's he done to upset you like this?'

'Ask him, why don't you? Ask your son the thief.'

'He's been stealing?'

'Ask him! Money from my purse, money from the other children at school. Did you know he was a bully, too? He's been taking – not stealing, *taking* – money and sweets from the smaller boys. The headmaster called me in today. I had to go to the school and be told my son – *your* son – was a thief and a bully and if he didn't change his ways pretty smartish the headmaster would have no choice but to expel him. Can you imagine how I felt? How small, how low, how . . . how degraded! And do you know what excuse Samuel gave me when I got him home? When I asked him why he'd done such a terrible thing? And by then, of course, I'd realised what I'd only suspected before, that he'd been helping himself to money from my purse for months now. Do you know what excuse he gave me?'

'No, I don't know, Evelyn.'

'*None at all!* Doesn't that make you want to hang your head in shame, you bastard?'

'Me?'

'*You.* You're its father. And God, doesn't it show! Well, now it's time for *you* to show it some discipline. Let's see how you handle it.'

'I've told you, I can't – '

'*You've got no bloody choice!*'

The phone went dead. Creed stared at it and then at the boy. 'Your mother's missing you already,' he said.

The jam around Samuel's mouth was like a big cheery grin, but his eyes remained sullen. Wearily, Creed went over to the table and leaned against the back of a chair. 'Right, let me get us both a drink, then we'll talk. You want milk, lemonade, orange juice?'

'Diet Pepsi.'

'Lemonade coming up. You don't mind if I have something stronger?'

'Whiskey? Mum says you always drink whiskey.' The boy seemed genuinely interested.

'Not all the time, Sam. But tonight I think I need it. You want me to fix you something proper to eat? Some beans or something?'

'Fish fingers and mashed potatoes with gravy.'

'Uh, I'm out of fish fingers and I think – I can check though – I think I'm out of potatoes. Hey, how about a burger? I could nip round the corner and bring some back for us both. I'll get you a milkshake, too.'

'I'm not allowed.'

'You're only ten, for Chrissake. You're supposed to have those things.'

'Mum says I've got to cut down.'

'Well, yeah, you can have too much of a good thing, but let's make tonight an exception. Sam, the other kids at school been calling you names?'

The boy looked down at his bread as if he'd found something interesting crawling in the jam. If he had, it was soon devoured.

Creed regarded his son with a feeling that was dangerously close to compassion. Since Sammy had turned six a rift had opened up between them – not that the link before had been too wonderful in terms of father-son relationships. Evelyn was right: Creed had always been too busy, his working hours irregular, for his natural parental duties and obligations to be effective. And for sure, as every parent knows, there's more to bringing up children than duties and obligations. Apart from the obvious loving and caring, there is what might best be termed 'free time'. That's the hours, even the minutes (they're all crucial), you give over to just being available, whether it's to play, tell stories, instruct, or enter into debate. This time is equal to the other two in importance (some might say more so) and that was the biggest problem as far as Creed and Samuel were concerned. Finding time for fun wasn't easy for this particular working man, but worse than this, when there *was* time, Creed's boredom level was very, very low. Playing with his son was okay for brief periods, say five, ten minutes or so, but after that his attention invariably wandered, 'important' things he had to do suddenly occurred to him; his patience ran out. It's a problem the selfish have. To be fair to the father, though, the son wasn't exactly a bundle of joy either.

Samuel was overweight by the age of two and, while on some

infants 'baby-fat' can be cute, on Creed's son it was undoubtedly obese – no other way to describe it. His face, with its mop of curly brown hair above it, would have been almost pretty had not his swollen cheeks and forehead recessed his eyes to such a degree that he appeared to be wearing a permanent frown. That, you might remark, was hardly the boy's fault especially if his parents indulged him so; but Samuel did have the tendency (and the cunning) to create the most God-awful fuss if he were hungry and sustenance wasn't immediately forthcoming. Burdened with the difficulties of an already rocky marriage, Evelyn was inclined to appease Samuel rather than endure his ear-bashing tantrums; also, lost affection for her husband was increasingly redirected towards her son (so much so, in fact, that Creed eventually realised that mother and son had formed some kind of tacit alliance against him). And Samuel wasn't dumb: from an early age he was adept at using mother-love against father's wrath. The final and irrevocable break-up of the marriage hadn't helped the kid's personality any, and naturally enough parental guilt was fully taken advantage of. Creed wasn't at all surprised to learn that his son had developed into a thief and a bully, for on those odd days or weekends they did manage to get together he had found Samuel not just sulky (unless things were going entirely his own way) but also a little sly and a whole lot spoilt. In truth – and a terrible thing for any father to admit – Creed found his son somewhat obnoxious.

Now he gazed down on the boy who, when all was said and done, was only ten years old, and felt an unfamiliar lump in his throat. The boy might be a bit overweight, he might be a mother's boy (albeit not quite at that particular moment), he might have an attitude problem, *but he was his son*!

Creed swallowed. 'So listen, why don't you hang out with me for a coupla days? Forget about school, that's always gonna be there. You like horror movies? I've got some tapes. You could watch them while I'm out working. Maybe, uh, maybe you could even come along with me in the morning, give you a chance to see how the old man works. What d'you think?'

'Do you smoke marianna?'

'Marijuana? Christ no. What makes you ask that?'

'Mum says you do.'

And what else has she told you? 'Look, Sammy, your mother and

I don't get along, you know that. That's why we're not married any more. She may say things about me from time to time that aren't necessarily true just to get back at me, you know? Women are like that.'

Samuel nodded, but he didn't look convinced. 'Can I have a Big Mac?' he said.

'Sure. And a double helping of fries. What kind of milkshake would you like – strawberry, banana . . . ?'

'Kiwi.'

'You got it. Make yourself at home – you know where the television is – and I'll be back in ten minutes.'

'Dad?'

'Yeah?'

'I didn't mean to steal anything. I mean . . . I did, but I didn't want to.' He looked helpless sitting there, a ten-year-old in dark red school blazer, grey shirt unbuttoned at the neck, tie halfway down his chest, hair unkempt, jam-grin and sad eyes set in his face. An overweight kid who'd just been passed from one parent to the other, at that moment not really wanted by either. Creed could have been looking at himself twenty-odd years ago, except he hadn't had a weight problem and his abandonment had been more radical and eventually more permanent.

He walked around the table to his son, leaned down, and hugged him. Sammy resisted only for a moment.

He hurried through the shady moonlit streets carrying the carton of Big Macs, french fries and strawberry milkshake ('Kiwi? What's Kiwi? We don't do Kiwi') tight against his chest as if a precious gift, perhaps for a prince. Well, Sammy was no prince, but he was his offspring and he was hungry. Creed was also hungry, the realisation that he hadn't eaten a thing all day surprising him. It wasn't like him at all. While never a big eater, he did tend to snack it through the day and night. Today, however, he just hadn't felt hungry. Now he was ravenous and didn't much fancy tepid food. Hence the haste.

Earl's Court is a thriving thoroughfare at any time of the day and usually well into the night, but the backstreets are something else.

Full of elegant terraced houses, garden squares, hotels and bedsits, it's both seedy and select, a not uncommon paradox in the big city. These streets and squares are quiet though, and not particularly well-lit. The mews are even quieter and even less well-lit.

Creed's attention was so engaged on the problem of what the hell he was going to do with his son until Evelyn got over her sudden attack of child-phobia that he failed to notice the figure lurking in a shadowy doorway ahead. Only when a throaty growling sallied forth from those shadows did he stop dead in his tracks, the toughened carton he was holding caving in under his fierce grip. The figure revealed itself, although not completely; it clung to the darkness as though umbilically linked.

'*Yerrulabobof.*' An arm extended towards the frightened Creed. '*Cerrlabobuv.*' The voice sounded curiously strangled, as though there was a furious struggle going on between his throat and mouth to form the words. By the time the old down-and-out managed '*Coupla bob, guv*' Creed was long gone.

In fact, Creed didn't stop running until he was safely back in his own mews, where he slowed to a trot and eventually a breathless quick-march when he was almost at his frontdoor. Once inside, the door securely locked behind him, he leaned back and fought to calm himself. Music drifted down from upstairs.

He dumped the battered box on a lower step and bent almost double, one hand on his hip, the other resting over the stair-post; he sucked air like an athlete after a four-minute mile. Can't let Sammy see him like this, don't want to scare the boy. Why now, why did the bitch have to unload him *now*? Judas, he had enough things to worry about without having Sammy to look out for as well.

What had that character shouted at him? Something foul, something nasty, he was sure of that. The beard and wild hair, the dirty smelly clothes – hadn't he seen that same person only that morning? The old sot in Soho Square, the one he suspected had cracked the jeep's windscreen – had it been that very same tramp? No, no, couldn't have been. He was getting paranoid. There were hundreds, *thousands*, of these old reprobates shuffling around the streets of London, sleeping in cardboard boxes or dosshouses, begging and scrambling their brains with cheap booze and meths. *Millions* of them. And they all looked alike. Scruffy old lice-bags, reeking of madness and filth. Couldn't have been the same one. No way.

He was perfectly correct, of course – an unfortunate coincidence, given his dreadful state of anxiety at that time – but Creed couldn't be completely sure, and his rightly reasoned explanation to himself cut little ice with his not-so-irrational fears.

'Dad?'

He looked up to see Sammy peering down at him.

'Did you get me a Big Mac, Dad?'

Creed had lost his appetite again by the time they settled down to eat, but that was okay: Sammy managed to tuck away everything his father couldn't. Creed began to understand why Evelyn had imposed a diet.

The gurgling as Samuel drained every last drop of milkshake from the beaker through a coloured straw had started to grate on the photographer's already frayed nerves. 'I think it's all gone, Sammy,' he advised.

A few more strained gurgles and the boy stopped. 'You got a phone call while you were out,' he said after withdrawing the straw and licking its length.

Creed realised he'd forgotten to switch on the answerphone that morning. Who could blame him for that? he wondered sourly. 'Did you take a message?' he asked.

'Two. You got two calls. From' – he pulled a *yukky* face – 'GIRLS.'

'You'll learn to live with them one day.' Or maybe not, Creed thought. 'So? Did you take messages?'

The boy nodded as he prised off the beaker's lid and looked inside. He poked in his tongue as far as it would go to swab round the edges.

Creed kept his voice even. 'Will you leave that alone. You must be busting by now.'

His son's expression assured him he was not, that he could easily manage the whole thing again, Creed's share as well. 'One' – that grimace again – 'girl said something about champagne. I forget her name.'

'Prunella?'

'Think so. Something soppy-sounding. The other one didn't say who she was. She asked me who I was, though. I said you'd be back soon.'

'What was her name, Sammy?'

'I told you, I don't know. She didn't tell me. She said she'd call later. I think.'

Creed wondered. Could it have been her, Cally? It might have been any number of girls, so why her? 'Did she say when she'd call back?'

Sammy shook his head. 'Just said later. I think.'

And she did ring later, and it was her, Cally.

'Sam,' Creed, a hand over the mouthpiece, called to his son who was back in front of the television set in the living room. 'Get yourself ready for bed now. Climb into mine for tonight.' He put the receiver to his ear again and lowered his voice, making it mean. 'What the hell are you playing at? Who are you? Your name isn't really Cally, is it?'

'Yes, it is. But that doesn't matter. You must listen to me.'

'Okay, but it's not McNally, is it?'

'Yes, it is. Will you *please* listen to me? You're in trouble.'

'No, *you're* in trouble.'

'Oh for God's sake. Look, you have to give him the film – or films if you took more than one roll. Prints, negatives – everything.'

'Give them to who? Who wants them? The freak who broke in the other night? Christ – last night, too.'

'It doesn't matter who he is. Just let him have them. I mean it, you'll be in terrible danger if you don't.'

That worried Creed considerably. For the moment though, bluster prevailed. 'It's got something to do with Nicholas Mallik, hasn't it?' It was an old journo's trick: throw in a name, wait for a reaction.

The reaction was silence.

'You there? I was right, wasn't I? It's got something to do with this guy Mallik.'

He waited, then heard her say: 'You bloody fool. Why couldn't you leave things alone?'

Now *he* decided to stay silent.

After a few agonisingly long seconds, she said, 'Please do as I ask. It may not be too late.'

'Maybe we can do a deal.' Creed allowed himself a smile, although it was a grim one. If he couldn't syndicate these sicko pictures, there might at least be another way of earning a few bucks from them.

'What?' Her tone was very cold.

'As you seem to value the pictures so highly, I wouldn't be disinclined to sell them to you.'

'Creed, don't do this. It isn't worth it, please believe me. Just . . . just don't get involved. Let us have the prints and the negatives, and then you can forget all about this.'

He liked the nervousness that had crept into her voice. A tiny surge of power swelled his chest. 'Two – uh, three grand. That's what I'd want for them.'

'Don't be ridiculous!'

'Two-and-a-half, and that's it. They're probably worth a lot more than that, seeing the trouble you've taken to get them. Or maybe I can convince my newspaper they're worth a bonus. Who knows what a good news team could dig up?'

'Joe . . .'

Ah, back to Joe, was it? Now she was really anxious. 'That's the deal, Cally – if that *is* your name. I'll hand over everything I have on this weirdo who likes doing unpleasant things in graveyards, and that'll be the end of it. I'll forget about what I saw, about the shots of him. I'll even wipe you from my mind.' He couldn't help adding, more from smooth-talking habit than anything else, 'If you want me to, that is.'

'Oh, you bloody idiot. Can you bring them to me tonight?'

'Sure, if it's a deal. But why don't you come over here and collect them?'

'No, better that we meet somewhere . . . neutral.'

'Like where?'

'The park. Kensington Gardens. It's not too far from you.'

'Are you kidding? At this time of night? It'll be closed.'

'So much the better. Do you know where the Round Pond is?'

'The place'll be locked up.'

'It's easy to get in. You want the money, don't you?' She took his silence (quite rightly) for a definite 'yes'. 'You know where the Round Pond is?' she repeated.

'Yeah, it's opposite Kensington Palace.' He wasn't happy and still wasn't sure he'd agree.

'There's a small bandstand close by. You can't miss it.'

'In the dark?'

'Look out your window – there's a bright moon. Can you meet me in the park in an hour's time?'

'I don't know . . .'

'You've got to trust me on this. I promise you, it's your only way out.'

'What're you talking about? Are you threatening me?'

'God, no. I'm trying to help you, believe it or not. Just be there, Creed.' She hung up.

Just be there. Oh yeah, just be there and get your legs broken. Or worse. He put down the phone and scratched his chin. So what could they do? Murder him? For some photographs? Nah, his imagination was running away with him. They'd given him a couple of scares, but that was all. No violence. He touched the bump on his forehead; an accident, his own fault really. They'd made him see things that were not possible – how, God only knew – but they hadn't actually harmed him. Hallucinations, that was all, nothing worse than a bad trip –

Wait a minute. Wait . . . a . . . minute . . . Hallucinations. The night of the blood-sucking bedbugs, and the toothsome toilet – Cally had been with him earlier. That had to be it! Christ, yes. She'd somehow managed to drop something into his drink. What *had* he drunk last night? Coffee, brandy? Whatever, she must have got to it. But wouldn't it have tasted odd? In brandy, though? Probably not. Anyway, she could have used something that was tasteless. Acid, maybe? That had to be it, didn't it? Yeah . . .

Then he remembered the strange, the illogical, earth movement around Lily Neverless' grave two days before. The ground had seemed to ripple . . .

An optical illusion. Like the shimmering effect of a road's surface on a hot day. But it had been a cold day . . . An illusion anyway. Drizzle playing tricks. Shape up, Creed. Too many old horror flicks for too many years. They've crept into the old brain-box, settled themselves in, made themselves at home. Bound to have had some effect sooner or later.

Bravado banter still running through his head, he went through to the living room and found Sammy still pigged out in front of the television.

'Come on, Sam,' he said without much patience. 'Time for bed. Forget about washing if you want, but get yourself in. Did your mother pack pyjamas? Okay, sleep in your vest, we'll sort you something out tomorrow. Move it.' The boy rose and trudged to the door, his eyes never leaving the television screen. Creed noticed he'd been watching one of his videos, *The Tingler*, no less. 'You can see the rest tomorrow, okay? Listen, I may have to go out in a little while – will you be all right on your own? I shouldn't be gone too long.' Hell, these were old men he was dealing with. Both of them – the one in the cemetery and the bald codger he'd found in the house – looked as if a sudden fart would deck them. What could they do to *him*? Glare him to death?

Sammy stopped in the doorway and shrugged. 'Doesn't matter,' he said.

'Well, I don't have to if you don't want me to . . .'

The boy shrugged again, then went into the hall. Creed heard the bathroom door open and close. 'I'll be there to say goodnight in a minute,' he called after him. He turned off the television and recorder and returned to the kitchen.

Creed sat at the table and opened the large brown envelope he'd brought back with him from the newspaper offices, while Grin sat on a chair opposite and watched.

15

■

He looked nonchalant enough as he strolled along the Bayswater Road, but inwardly Creed was a mess of nerves. A part of that condition was due to professional excitement, the *buzz*; another part, perhaps the largest, was due to fear; the final proportion had much to do with curiosity. He lingered, looked around. Traffic was halted momentarily at the lights further down the broad main road, too far away for the drivers and passengers to observe a lone figure standing by the brick and iron barrier that bordered the northern edge of the park. Creed had left his own vehicle in one of the many sidestreets opposite.

'Now or never,' he mumbled to himself. It had taken a good fifteen minutes to find a reasonable gap between traffic and pedestrians, even at that late hour, so he couldn't afford to hesitate too long. In no more than three seconds he was perched on the horizontal bar of the railings mounted on the low wall, one foot resting between the spikes. He balanced there for barely another second before leaping into the blackness beyond.

He landed heavily, but years of jumping into forbidden territory had taught him the trick of collapsing his legs and rolling forward on one shoulder. Quickly he pushed himself back against the thick hedge on the inner side of the railings; he rested there, waiting to find out whether or not he'd been seen. His breaths came sharp and heavy, and for a few brief but almost enjoyable moments he imagined himself an escapee in one of those venerable prisoner-of-war films.

That fancy soon passed when he recalled why he was there.

He could be, he might *just* conceivably be, on to something BIG, the revivification of a story that had involved sex, scandal, obsession, suspicion and ultimately, mutilation and murder. Juicy stuff.

Prunella had done a good job: inside the envelope she'd left for him he had found Xerox copies of an old newspaper story, one that had made front-page headlines in its day, a story whose principal ingredients were sex, scandal, etc, etc . . . The editorial comments and features had been full of indignant outrage, an obvious reflection of the public's views.

Nicholas Mallik apparently had been one of those enigmatic figures who, while generally unknown to the public at large, moved in high social circles: there were photographs (unfortunately somewhat bleached by the photocopying process) of him alongside members of government, industrial tycoons, a fair glittering of movie and stage stars, and the occasional high-ranking church elder. Judging by the company he kept, Mallik's wealth must have been considerable, yet nowhere amongst the cuttings was there a hint of where it came from. Nor was there any certainty as to his origins, although one story suggested that Hungary might have been his birthplace, while another decided upon Russia, for Nicholas obviously – to the journalist writing the piece, at any rate – had been altered from Nikolai. Mallik, according to others, could have been the shortened version of a dozen or more foreign names. Wherever he came from, however, Nicholas Mallik wasn't saying; but his accent and aristocratic manner continued to fuel the speculation.

Still, that little conundrum was not what had excited the masses: no, it was the man's nefarious activities that had done that. Many of the stories about Mallik referred to him as a colleague or cohort of Aleister Crowley – Aleister Crowley, later to be dubbed 'the wicked-est man in the world', whose motto was, 'Do what thou wilt shall be the whole of the Law'. A satanist, black magician, mountebank, dope fiend, womaniser and sexual pervert, Crowley appeared to be an all-round hateable guy but an interesting person to knock around with. Both of them, along with the likes of Algernon Blackwood and the poet, W. B. Yeats, belonged to a dubious mystic society known as the Order of the Golden Dawn. It appeared that this infamous pair, Mallik and Crowley, had finally fallen out over an incident in Paris. Nothing Creed read indicated the cause.

Anyway, that was all background gen. The real meat was this: Nicholas Mallik, later dubbed 'Count Nikolai' by the Press, was something of a roué (this despite a rather gaunt and ravaged appearance which even the contrasty photocopies could not disguise) and his list of 'conquests' (the early *Dispatch*, incidentally, was careful not to use such a term but any fool could have read between the lines) was pretty impressive. Interestingly – and this is where Creed had become very excited – Mallik had had a fairly long-standing relationship with Lily Neverless who was, at that time, married to a businessman named Edgar Buchanan (this was the husband who, when finally divorced and on the point of suing Lily for slander, had brought proceedings to an abrupt halt by way of his own heart attack). That had been during the 1920s and there was no suggestion that the relationship had continued beyond that decade.

As Creed had sifted through the sensational newspaper stories, he came to realise that there were very few hard facts about Mallik himself, or his activities; most of the journalists dwelt upon his associations with others, particularly certain dignitaries of the day. Implied rather than stated were his numerous relationships with other men's wives. One solid fact that was known about him, though, was that he owned an elegant Regency house in Eaton Place and another large but far less select abode in Camberwell, South London.

The beginning of the end, for Mallik, came in the form of a striking young socialite (unmarried, this one), by the name of Lavinia Nesbit, who developed, as had many females before her, an unwholesome and obsessive passion for the 'Count'. Age difference appeared not to matter as far as the girl was concerned and, according to later evidence, it wasn't long before she was completely under Mallik's domination. The relationship lasted for almost three months; then Lavinia vanished without trace. Only the dogged efforts of her father, an aircraft manufacturer whose fortune had been made when he joined forces with a number of other private airline companies to form the government-subsidised Imperial Airlines, had led to the discovery of her body.

To add further to patriarchal distress, the body was found in several pieces.

Now comes the *really* bad part.

The girl's father, who had powerful friends of his own, was able to bully, inveigle, or shame (probably all three) the police into making a snap search of Nicholas Mallik's two homes. It was the one in Camberwell that provided the blood-curdling surprise, for not only did the police find the various parts of the missing girl there (the head had been pickled in an iron bucket in the cellar), but they also discovered odd bits and pieces of other human bodies. Most of these appeared to be of children.

Although the 'Count' never admitted to such, it was the prosecution's submission that the defendant held a propensity for cannibalism. It was further alleged that illegal and diabolic rituals had taken place inside the Camberwell house, but no one had stepped forward to verify the fact (for obvious reasons, Nicholas Mallik had become *persona non grata* as far as his wide circle of 'friends' was concerned. They claimed they knew him only on a casual basis, in fact, hardly at all; if truth be known, they had met him once perhaps at a social gathering, and what was that name again?), and Mallik himself wasn't saying. Nor did any of his staff, which he undoubtedly must have had to run such large homes, present themselves as witnesses. Creed assumed these people had flown as soon as the soft stuff had hit the fan.

Reading between the lines, it looked to him as though much of what had taken place at Mallik's Camberwell home had been hushed up, and because of that he wondered what else had been discovered inside that house of slaughter. The fact that two refrigerators which had been found stacked full of old and fresh foetuses was mentioned almost as a footnote indicated that some editorial censorship had been invoked, and if that *was* the case, then why? To protect the public sensibility from more gruesome revelations? Or to protect certain parties who had been involved in some way?

Since Mallik would say not one word in his own defence nor offer any explanation, and since none of the other victims could be properly identified (although files on several missing children were closed around this time), Nicholas Mallik, nicknamed 'Count Nikolai' and latterly 'The Beast of Belgravia', was hanged (by the Home Office's top executioner no less) only for the murder of Lavinia Nesbit.

Creed had been puzzled as to why the awful story was not more widely known to the public of today – after all, such murderers as Crippin, innocuous by comparison, had become part of criminal folklore. The answer came to him when he noticed other headlines and then checked the date of Mallik's execution: 25 August 1939. The week before the outbreak of the Second World War. The outrage had been overshadowed by the greater tragedy of world events. And naturally, after the horrors of global devastation whereby millions upon millions had been killed or suffered the most dreadful tortures and deprivations, who would care to be reminded of atrocities that had happened before the great conflict, a period that must have seemed like a lifetime away to the shell-shocked masses? The story – and, apparently, the memory – had been smothered by greater horrors.

Creed had smiled to himself as he had slid the Xerox copies back into the envelope. Perhaps it was time for a revival.

Now, crouching against the rough hedge, he considered the possibilities. The lunatic he'd photographed in the cemetery was no doubt a relative of Nicholas Mallik's, for their likeness, despite the poor quality of photocopies from old newsprint, was undeniable. Mallik's son? A nephew? The Press had estimated Mallik himself to be somewhere in his forties when he was executed, although no evidence of his birth date had been discovered. That was fifty-odd years ago. The graveyard crazy, judging by his line-etched features, might have been about seventy (Christ, was it possible to practise self-abuse at that age? Creed made a mental note to find out for himself nearer the time), so he could easily have been this monster's offspring. No mention of Mallik's son in the newspapers though, nor of any relatives; but then there had been hardly any background information at all.

He could easily understand the man's desire not to have his father's(?) grisly past resurrected, but to go to such lengths? There *had* to be much more to it than just family shame. And why the graveyard desecration? The question Creed asked himself was this: To blackmail (and make a quick financial killing) or to indulge in a little piece of investigative journalism (which could lead to glory and perhaps an even higher financial reward)? *No* question really. Two birds in a bush was *always* better than one in the hand as far as Creed was concerned. Fame *as well* as money was what he was after.

He stashed the Nikon back inside his coat and rose to his feet, brushing damp mud from his jeans as he did so. A smoke right now would have been terrific.

He looked around, this way and that. Silver light rendered the grass flat and the trees black; shadowy bushes could have hidden anything.

To his right was a children's playground, a surreal landscape of climbing frames and unmoving swings. To his left was a broad tarmac path, a road really, that, like the yellow brick one, led to the unknown. He shook his head in disgust at his own overwrought imagination.

In the distance he could make out Kensington Palace looming in the night like some huge sinister tomb. *Shut up, Creed. Christ!* He was giving himself the shakes. Okay, the pond, the Round Pond, should be somewhere to the left. Thing to do was cross the road – the strip they called the Broad Walk, he now remembered – and head south. That way he had to run smack into it. Wet feet would tell him when he was there. Not funny. In fact, nothing about this was funny.

For just a few moments he debated on whether or not to get the hell out of the park – after all, he really didn't know what he was getting into – but inevitably the call of greed and glory prevailed.

He crossed over the road to where cover was better and trudged towards the big pond, using odd trees here and there to screen himself from the main highway, constantly on the lookout for any patrolling police cars, vans or whatever else they made their rounds in. Better to keep well away from Kensington Palace, he advised himself; it was bound to be guarded at night. Soon he saw the broad expanse of water, moonlight giving its surface an unearthly sheen.

He crouched when he spotted headlights in the distance, the vehicle obviously somewhere near the Serpentine, the park's great lake. There was no chance of his being seen from that far away, but Creed stayed where he was until the lights faded completely. He tried to remember where the park's police station was located, not because he was afraid of being caught, but because it might be the place to head for if he got into trouble. He groaned when he realised how far away it was. Not only that, but the lake also cut him off from it. There was the bridge, of course, the one that divided the Serpentine and the Long Water, but even that was some distance.

Nothing's going to happen, he reassured himself. You'll meet the girl, find out a bit more about the necrophilic nut, then renege on the deal, saying you'll only hand over the film to the man himself. For added incentive, snap off a few frames of Cally so that she'll also be on record. And if it turns out that the man, himself, is there waiting for collection, well so much the better. Deal with the top dog, that was the thing. Ask him some questions, put it to him straight that he, Creed, knew he was a descendant of Nicholas Mallik no less, wait for a reaction. Then reel off a few more shots before the crazy had a chance to cover his face. When that was done, shift like shit out of there. The guy was over the hill – he'd never catch him. Yeah. Right. Easy.

Creed's mouth felt very dry.

He got to his feet, did a 365-degree scan, and moved on.

The pond – almost but not quite a lake – looked particularly uninviting when he reached its edge. In the moonlight it appeared more like a great slab of concrete than a refuge for ducks. There wasn't a ripple on its surface.

His gaze travelled across the still water towards a tall shape on the far side, a light structure that was all but lost in the dark backdrop of trees. That was it, that was the bandstand where he was supposed to meet Cally.

Creed dipped a hand into his pocket and set the switch that would charge the Nikon's flash. Which way round the pond should he go? Left or right? Or should he just turn round and head back in the direction he'd come from? Might be the sensible thing to do, all things considered. He could always arrange to meet her some place else, somewhere where there were people and lights and sounds. This was too creepy.

Come on, Creed. You're almost there. You might blow the deal completely if you back off now. She sounded pretty serious on the phone.

'What the fuck,' he mumbled to himself as he turned to the left and began the journey around the water's edge.

The bandstand was set by itself in a clear, grassy area, its tall white posts rising dully from a high black-painted base to support an umbrella-like canopy. Spear railings surrounded the narrow and rather delicate pavilion.

Creed's approach was not direct: he left the curve of the pond at a tangent, treading a path that was a hundred yards or so away from the bandstand, with the intention of skirting the perimeter to get a good look from all angles. If there was more than one person skulking there, then he wanted to know about it. Unfortunately, because of the high base, it proved difficult to judge; anyone wearing dark clothes would have blended in nicely.

Once on the side that fully caught the moon's rays, he was able to make out a stairway rising to the rostrum. As far as he could tell, the place was deserted.

Creed walked towards the bandstand with only slightly less trepidation than before. When he was ten or twelve feet away he stopped. He held his breath. He listened.

He heard the creaking of a floorboard.

Creed took one involuntary step backwards, then checked himself. His eyes narrowed as he peered into the darkness beyond the iron railings.

'Cally.' He cleared his throat, embarrassed by the shake in his voice.

He heard more movement.

'Cally, it's Joe Creed.' He added, somewhat unnecessarily: 'I'm here.'

Something caught his eye. Something up there on the bandstand.

That's not possible, he thought. He'd checked it out as he'd walked round. The rostrum had been empty, he was sure.

A figure moved forward from the shadow cast by the canopy. It was him, the person Creed had photographed in the cemetery. He was wearing the same long raincoat and the same scarf masked the lower half of his face. Creed was certain it was him.

The man stood there quietly looking down at the photographer.

'Cold night,' Creed said by way of conversation. Cold as the grave, he thought.

The figure didn't move.

'We should talk, right?' Creed leaned forward a little, whether to encourage a response or to get a better look, he wasn't sure himself. He cleared his throat again. 'Seems I've got something you want.'

Instead of replying, the figure moved to the top of the stairway and began to descend. Creed resisted the urge to back off more. He wasn't going to show this fruitcake he was nervous. No way.

'Maybe you oughta stay where you are,' he suggested.

The man ignored the suggestion. He reached the bottom step and stood behind the gate in the railing, his eyes on Creed all the time. He swung the gate open, slowly.

'I'm glad you're here,' he said, advancing no further.

Creed shivered. He couldn't help it. The man's voice was gravelly and tight, as if squeezed from the larynx. He either had a bad cold or a disease of the throat. But it wasn't just the sound of the voice that caused his anxiety – there was something more, something he couldn't define. Some people exuded vitality when they spoke; this one exuded whatever the opposite was. A doctor informing you that you had cancer might induce the same reaction. Creed felt suddenly nauseous.

'Where . . .' he said, as if to assert himself '. . . where's the girl? Where's Cally?'

The man lowered his scarf, tucking it below his chin, causing Creed to flinch at the sight of the ravaged face now caught in the shine of the moon. Even though he'd become used to studying those same features on film over the past couple of days, they still came as a shock in the flesh. Strange how the soft light emphasised each corrugation, presenting the deep-etched lines so definitely they could have been rubbed in with soot; the moonlight, like the poor Xerox copies, should have washed his face to blandness.

That awful, dread-making voice again. 'She isn't necessary, Mr Creed. I'm the one you have to deal with.'

It sounded so ominous, the way he said it, and Creed began to wonder if he really had made a mistake in coming. Maybe he should have turned the whole thing over to his editor and let the *Dispatch* get on with the story – if there really *was* a story. A good idea might be to take the money and run, give the creep what he wanted and forget about the Journalist of the Year Award, which wasn't his line anyway, he was a snapper, for Chrissake, not a journo . . .

Creed became aware that he was mentally gibbering and, with an effort of will, desisted. 'Look,' he ventured, 'I don't know who you are, but could be I've made –' He was going to say, 'made a mistake', but the other man interrupted.

'Give me the film.' It was a command that brooked no dissension.

'*I haven't got it with me.*' Creed's response was rapid, blurted out with no thought behind it. He stood there like a weak-kneed schoolboy who'd impulsively confessed to stealing the headmaster's wallet. He felt badly in need of a lie-down.

The man was silent again. Was there rage building up inside him, was he disappointed in what he'd just heard? Creed couldn't tell.

'You're a very foolish man,' the tortured voice announced.

But this time – and the photographer couldn't understand why – the words had less effect. Perhaps it was the weariness in them that weakened their impact, their power. This guy was *antiquated*, Creed told himself, a little of his usual belligerence slowly – very slowly, it must be admitted – beginning to crawl to the surface. What was he worried about? An old wrinkly who didn't look strong enough to spit against the wind? He looked scary enough – he *sounded* scary enough – but think about it logically: What could he actually *do*? Nothing, that was what. Creed's smile was forced, but he hoped the old boy could see it.

'Yeah,' he admitted, 'I'm very foolish. But then, you're not so smart yourself. You know, there's a law against the kind of thing you were doing at Lily Neverless' funeral.'

Creed became even more emboldened (although not as much as he pretended) when he saw the dark-coated figure grip a railing to steady himself. Somewhere outside the park a motorist tooted his horn, the anger muted by distance.

'And listen,' Creed continued, 'I don't appreciate anyone breaking into my home. D'you really think that freak you sent frightened me? Christ, I've seen worse in the mirror after a heavy night. Just who the fuck are you anyway?' He was beginning to work up a steam. 'The son of Nicholas Mallik, is that who you are? Oh yeah, I know all about him. Ashamed of your old man, want the whole gruesome mess to rest in peace? You shouldn't have done nasty things at Lily's funeral, if that's the case. So let's have some answers, and then we'll consider where we go from there. You understand me?'

A bravura performance, you might say, even though he did get just a little carried away.

'I said, do you understand me?' Creed repeated, impressed by his own impudence.

If he did understand him, the raincoat man wasn't saying. Instead he stepped to one side of the gate, then turned to something behind him.

The blackness of the bandstand's base was not as total as Creed had first thought, for now there was an even greater darkness spreading within it. He stared in dismay, then realised that what he was actually witnessing was the opening of a door; the bandstand itself was obviously built over a chamber of some kind, probably where odd bits of equipment and park deckchairs were stored. The deeper black grew no more.

The bald dome of a head emerged first, cast by the moonlight as dull ivory. Creed remembered the intruder in his house had been stoop-backed. The freak came out from the shelter and now its hands, with their extraordinary long fingers and nails, were visible; white and skeletal, they were nasty-looking things. Its huge eyes were almost luminous, as though moonrays reflected on something behind them, giving off an inner gleam; their pupils were like jet-black dots. Its mouth opened and the two long, jagged teeth that touched its lower lip did nothing to enhance the grin.

As it came out into the open, its thin limbs like sticks, their movement brittle yet weaving, Creed could not help thinking of a giant spider emerging from its hole. The analogy was hardly calming.

'*Ohfuckinhell,*' said Creed in a hushed voice.

The 'thing' loitered in the gateway.

'You really are an extremely loathsome person,' the man from the cemetery told Creed, and this time his words had a wintry sharpness to them, all weariness apparently shed.

The photographer was lost for riposte, obvious though it should have been; instead he turned to run. At least his mind did. In fact, his mind had already scooted down the Broad Walk and was clambering over the railings at the end, whereas his body had remained rooted to the spot. With some effort he looked down at his feet as if to reprimand them. They refused to take notice. His attention shot back to the two figures by the bandstand.

'Let's negotiate,' he suggested, and wondered if they'd understood him. The words had sounded garbled even to him. 'I can easily get the film and the prints for you, it'd be no problem at all.'

A tickling around his ankle caused him to glance down again.

At first he could see nothing amiss, but as something tightened over his foot, he bent slowly to take a closer look. Something else snaked around his other ankle and he examined that one, too.

He murmured something too agonised to be understood.

Where he stood the grass was growing at an amazing rate; it slipped over his shoes and up into his trousers. He could feel the tendrils curling around his legs. Creed stepped back in fright – or tried to.

The grass blades tore, but their initial resistance sent him stumbling backwards. He fell, landing heavily on his butt, then flattening out on to his back. He pushed himself up almost immediately and as he sat there, stunned by the impossibility of his fall rather than the fall itself, the grass began to weave through his outstretched fingers.

His cry was less contained this time. He tugged his hands free and scrambled to his knees; but even then he could feel the long tendrils of grass wrapping themselves around his calves. Creed jumped to his feet, snapping the blades as he did so, then hopped a peculiar kind of dance in the moonlight, afraid that if he stood still too long he would be (literally this time) rooted to the spot. That frantic jig at least had one positive effect: it released him from the fear that had gripped him so tightly.

The stooped, bald-domed figure was making its way towards him again, one hand outstretched, a long bony finger pointed at Creed as if singling him out in a crowd. The 'thing' still hadn't spoken, nor made a sound of any kind.

The stench of its breath reached Creed well before the emaciated creature itself did, and it was foul, the odour of sewers filled with excrement and dead things, enough in itself to overwhelm the most stalwart of us.

'Keep away from me, you fucker,' our hero warned, raising a fist above his right shoulder and taking the stance – and resisting the urge to retch.

That almost fleshless digit, with its gnarled and twisted fingernail, stretched even further forward and sank into the material of Creed's buttoned coat. *Literally* sank in, raising steam as it went. Creed screeched when he felt it piercing his chest.

He found himself running, the moment of deciding to pull himself free of that impaling finger and run like buggery completely lost to his thoughts because it was never registered as a conscious decision in the first place. There was no pain, although he clutched at the hole in his chest to stem the blood that must surely flow, and the speed of his flight was something to behold despite the clumsiness of his stride.

There were trees ahead of him, a dark brooding clump of them, and he knew that beyond was the Albert Memorial, and beyond that the lovely, busy Kensington Gore, where there would be cars and people and maybe even *(oh please Mother of Christ)* policemen.

His pace slowed, his rhythm became even more awkward. His legs became uncoordinated. He ran in the jerky fashion of Jerry Lewis in his prime, stopping, starting, slowing . . . There was something wrong with those trees ahead. He stopped running altogether.

There was *definitely* something wrong with those trees ahead.

Because they were getting closer . . .

He was standing still.

And they were getting closer . . .

Creed could barely shake his head in disbelief. The clump of trees was moving towards him like a black-shrouded army, their leafless tops swaying as if caught by a wind, their trunks *seeping* – that was the only word to describe the slow but fluid shadow mass – forward.

Creed was soon running back in the direction he'd come from, back towards the bandstand and the two figures that waited for him there, one of them – the stooped one – standing in a clear and glittering patch of grass, thin arms outstretched to welcome him home.

Creed skirted around the Nosferatu clone and tasted the foul air that soured the breeze. As he ran he imagined one of those taloned hands reaching after him. His footsteps suddenly became sluggish, as if he'd hit an invisible boundary where the atmosphere was congealed, dragging at the body, rendering each movement an exaggeration of effort. It was the stuff of nightmares, that frustrating feeling of helplessness, when limbs are leaden and the slow stalking beast is catching up. A battle of wills, no less, between pursuer and prey.

Creed tripped over something lying in the grass and even his head-over-heels tumble seemed lazy and unreal. The jolt when he struck dirt, however, was realistically painful. But it did him some good. His thoughts and his tempo became brisk once more, as though whatever mental link existed between himself and the plodding oddity had been broken. Terror was the key, of course, for there's a fine line between paralysing dread and galvanising fright. Adrenaline rushed with full force again and Creed lifted the collapsed deckchair he'd fallen over and hurled it at the stoop-back, who was now only yards away.

A wooden corner hit the pursuer in the bony face and Creed was relieved to observe it stagger. At least the freak was normal in that respect.

The low mewling sound it made indicated its displeasure; those long, clawed fingers rubbed the bridge of its nose. Creed didn't linger to find out if blood – whatever colour – was going to flow. He fled, his stride no longer hindered by treacly air.

He looked over his shoulder and moaned aloud on seeing he was being followed again. And furthermore, just glancing back had somehow re-established the sensory link. His legs began to feel heavy once more.

'Oh shit,' he groaned.

The great expanse of pond was ahead, still solid and unrippled under the deblemishing moonlight. For one brief and hysterical instant he considered running across its surface to escape – it certainly looked firm enough – but then another thought crossed his mind (this one equally hysterical). He knew from all the horror movies he'd seen and all the junk books he'd read that vampires would not, could not, cross water (the fact that it's *running* water that these things weren't supposed to traverse was a detail Creed didn't care to remember right then, and that was not unreasonable given his excitable state).

He staggered across the wide path that bordered the pond and plunged into the water.

Its shocking coldness was almost equal to the shock of his visions by the bandstand – the grasping grass, the approaching trees, *et al.*

– in its heart-clutching intensity. The sensation served to slap his consciousness into better shape.

The water reached his knees and then his thighs in no time at all, and he turned to face the chaser, taking care not to slip on the pond's greasy bed.

Nosferatu's double had come to a halt on the grass before the concrete pathway and was watching him. Creed fancied it looked perplexed, but at that distance and with the moon behind it really was impossible to tell.

'That's fucked you, you bastard!' he called back, elated at having outwitted the beast. 'A little cold water's bad for the complexion, right? It'll shrivel you to nothing.' (At this stage of the game, Creed honestly believed he'd been chased by a vampire.)

He chuckled then. Creed actually chuckled. But the chuckle eroded to a dry moan when the 'thing' scuttled across the path – and now its movement was *fast*, undoubtedly like the swift rush of a spider (a huge, spindly spider) when it closes the final ground between itself and the ensnared fly – and entered the water.

At this point Creed's professionalism, the learned and earned instinct that had become second nature, came to his rescue. He remembered the Nikon inside his coat pocket.

His first thought was to save it from the water. The second was to get a shot of this fabulous (in the nastiest sense) creature. His *third* thought – and they were all in rapid succession, each triggered by the preceding one – was inspired by the Hitchcock film, the one where the leg-in-plastered James Stewart uses his camera flash to temporarily blind a wife-murderer who has come to his apartment to silence the only witness to the crime (Mr Stewart, himself), giving the police, who'd already been alerted, a little bit of extra time to get there and save him. (The thought obviously occurred much quicker than it takes to explain it.)

He reached into his pocket and offered a silent prayer that the Nikon hadn't become waterlogged. He held the camera chest-high and aimed.

The 'thing' was already up to its skinny knees in the pond.

16

Y ou've just suffered a dramatic pause.
       This was to emphasise that dreadful heart-stopping second or so before Creed pressed the shutter release without knowing whether or not the water had ruined his equipment. At such a time, the apprehension can be quite unbearable, so much so that a certain reluctance to discover the truth of the situation may hinder the action – in this case, the movement of a finger – for longer than is necessary, and sometimes, in the most dire circumstances, completely.

Fortunately, Creed was too motivated by self-preservation to mull over the situation, although he definitely paused and it was dramatic.

He closed his eyes and pressed the release.

The flare on the other side of his eyelids informed him everything was working normally.

He opened up immediately and was delighted to see the thin one standing before him as if transfixed. Those big marble-like eyes were not closed, but were staring directly at Creed; yet, their expression was blank and unseeing. The creature seemed to be in a state of suspended animation.

The photographer did it again, and this time the flash of white light sent the 'thing' tottering backwards until it fell with a plop rather than a splash into the water. It sprawled, its domed head, from chin to ridged skull, above the waterline, for all the world looking like a Hallowe'en buoy floating on the surface. The eyes continued to stare sightlessly, yet somehow balefully, at Creed.

Its mouth opened wide in what might have been a snarl, although no sound emerged. Strings of spittle hanging from pointed teeth to lower lip reflected moonshine as the cadaverous head arched skywards.

That vision, in all the starkness of the silvery night, leaden water encasing the rest of the creature so that the head appeared disembodied, an entity in itself, was the most heart-wrenching sight it had been Creed's misfortune to witness thus far.

And when the vampire 'thing' shot from the water as if propelled by some great force beneath, so that water spouted with it like a hot-spring geyser, Creed's legs gave way and he, himself, fell backwards.

Instinct saved the Nikon once more, for he held it aloft as he collapsed; he also pressed the button by accident, flooding the area with light again. Thoroughly soaked and spluttering brackish water, he struggled to regain his feet and was halfway up when he saw the stoop-back bearing down on him as if arriving from the night sky itself.

Creed yelped and threw himself aside, almost going under this time, the 'thing' diving into empty water, the whole of its body, bald head and all, submerging. It was up in an instant and capering after its prey like an aquatic grasshopper. Creed was practising his own hopping, moving away from the madman, trying to get to the edge of the pond, but tripping and drenching himself every step of the way, the pair of them presenting a frenzied kind of moonlight ballet.

Claws snagged on the photographer's clothing, but he managed to wrench himself away. And then he was down on his hand (the other one clutching the camera to his chest) and knees only a foot or two from the path around the pond, with the freak drooping over him, the stench of its foul breath rotting the air Creed was so earnestly inhaling. Flesh-skimped fingers entwined themselves in his hair and Creed cried out as his head was jerked back.

Above him, two pointed teeth gleamed.

'*Ahhhhgnhhh,*' Creed said.

'*Hhhhhssssuh,*' came the whispered reply.

The teeth began to descend, to come closer and closer, and to Creed it was as if they came on their own without benefit of jaw and face, for his concentration was upon them, them and them alone. He could feel those fangs sinking into his flesh long before they reached him.

Suddenly he did become aware of the features around the two teeth, for ivory flesh had turned pale yellow.

The 'thing' looked away from him, showing an inverted profile. Brighter yellow sparkled in one bulbous eye.

Creed's neck snapped forward as his hair was released, and his nose dipped into the water so that he snorted bubbles.

Nosferatu's double was clambering up the gentle slope of the pond's edge, twiggy legs rising high in comic fashion to tread over the water. Creed saw the glaring headlights approaching through the park and was puzzled for only a second or so, for it quickly dawned on him that lightning flashes in a supposedly deserted park on a perfectly clear night had obviously aroused the interest of a patrolling cop car.

'Oh thank Christ,' he moaned to himself, then he, too, was scrambling towards the concrete bank, desperate to get away from there, too panicked to stay and explain himself to the nice policemen, too damned scared to stay in that Twilight Zone one second longer.

The fleeing figure had been picked out by the headlights, its shadow thrown incredibly long and fantastically weird across the grassland. It was making for the bandstand and the vehicle had left the roadway to head it off.

Unseen, Creed dragged himself from the water and loped off in his own direction, back the way he'd come, crouching low as if that would make a difference and endeavouring to merge into the darkness of friendly (hopefully) trees. Not once did he look back.

Very soon he was at the perimeter fence and clambering over, not caring if he were seen on the other side. Three young men of Mediterranean cast, who were either waiters on their way home after a hard night's work, or tourists in search of some action, turned in surprise as the bedraggled figure dropped to the pavement almost in their midst. They avoided him, at first astonished, but then pointing and laughing, walking on and turning to point again, cackling some more. Glad that he'd made their night, Creed sploshed across the road, looking for the street in which the Suzuki was parked.

As he drippingly hurried along, he clutched a hand to his chest and wondered if the freak's homicidal finger had done permanent damage. At least there was no pain – yet – and when he took his hand away there was no blood. He paused beneath a sodium light and looked down at his damp chest, picking at the material of his coat, holding up segments for inspection. The coat wasn't even torn.

Squelching onwards, oblivious to the curious stares and comments he evoked from people he passed – one youngish lady of nocturnal trade declared he was the wettest dream she'd ever seen – Creed found his way to the jeep and climbed in with feverish relief.

He switched on the interior light and examined himself again. Not a rent, nor a drop of blood. What the hell was going on? He hauled off the coat and inspected his shirt. Judas, he really was all right. But he'd seen the smoke or steam rising from the cloth, *felt* that wicked, bony finger sink into his flesh. Yet . . . yet he hadn't felt any *real* pain, had he? No, he hadn't. *The fuckers had played games with his mind.* That was it, that *had* to be it! They'd messed with his head, tonight and last night! It'd all been illusions. He hadn't seen what he thought he'd seen. No rippling grave, no hovering head at the window, no bedtime bloodsuckers, no walking trees – and *no* finger burrowing into his chest! The bastards were trying to scare him to death! And they were succeeding!

Creed shivered. He was cold, but he was more frightened than cold. He switched off the light and sat there in the dark, watching the street, nervous that *they* might have followed him.

No, right now the park pigs would be questioning them. One of them, anyway – the stick insect couldn't have escaped. But they might visit him later back at the mews. Oh Jesus. Enough is enough. Time to turn the story over to the news editor; let the newshounds, the 'insighters', the investigative journos – the penheads – look into it. He could give them enough to get going. And why not call in the police again? After all, he *had* been attacked, and that cadaverous creep had broken into his home. (He wondered how the freak was explaining himself to the cops at that moment in the park. That it had a fetish for ice-cold, moonlight dips? With luck they'd put it in a cell for the night. With greater luck they'd lock it up for good on the indictment that it was too grotesque to roam free.) Hell, let the *Dispatch* decide; the ed would know how to play it.

He switched on the engine and the headlights, but remained there thinking. The seat was wet through, his feet felt as though they were wrapped in soggy rags, and when he delved into the breast pocket of his coat for a cigarette, his fingers touched soaked mush. He swore. Loudly.

He reached for the cloth he always kept on the backseat, then pulled out the Nikon from the coat pocket he'd shoved it into when fleeing from the park. As he dried it off he prayed that the camera had survived the ducking.

The drive back to Earl's Court was wretchedly uncomfortable, not even his new-found outrage managing to warm him. They'll get it, the bastards, he promised himself. They'll get what's coming to them. You don't screw with the Press and get away with it, no sir. He grinned maliciously. So you wanted to keep out of the public eye, did you? Just wait and see what happens when your ugly wrinkled mug appears in the paper, page one, no less, across three columns at least! Nobody pisses on Joe Creed. *Nobody.*

He swung into the mews, the jeep's beams highlighting the bumpy cobblestones, and came to a halt in front of his garage doors, parking tight, sideways on. He was too cold, tired and shaky to garage the Suzuki. Besides, it wasn't the first time it'd had to spend a night in the open – a few beers seemed to narrow the garage's entrance too much for precision parking.

Picking up the cloth-wrapped camera, Creed slid over to the passenger door and stepped out. He walked around the corner to his frontdoor, key pointed like a homing device.

But the door was already open.

He gawped and became aware of the banshee-like wailing, a sound that a child in agonising pain might make.

'*Sammy!*'

The stark cry was left ringing in empty air as Creed dashed into the house and up the stairway. Dread on arriving at his own home had become an almost familiar sensation by now, but he didn't pause to dwell upon the fact. Lights shone from the kitchen and lounge, but both rooms were empty. So was the bedroom. And so was the bathroom.

He realised that the terrible wailing was coming from the floor above.

'Sam?' This time his voice was hushed. 'Sammy?' Louder, but not much.

He entered the kitchen and looked up into the vortex that was the spiral staircase, the dark circle at the top tinged orange. He trod the metal steps warily at first, but his ascent gathered momentum when the wailing over his head rose in pitch to an awful squawking screech.

There was no light on in the room directly above, but amber glowed from the darkroom doorway. Something hung there in the opening, silhouetted as it swung and twisted from side to side.

'No, no, no . . .' Creed muttered as he approached, incredulity as well as fear intoned in the word. Who would do something like that? You'd have to be . . . you'd have to be inhuman . . .

He turned on the room's light and stood there as if receiving an electric shock, his trembling fingers still gripping the switch. The thought occurred to him that he'd have to search the garage area for a hammer.

He'd need that to prise out the nail that pinned his cat over the door.

17

Life is full of crises, we all know that. It's how we learn, how we grow. They help form character, mould the man (or woman), as it were. As an opposite to good times, they even help us appreciate life a little more; and a person without strife is a person without passion, for trauma both tests and strengthens moral fibre, becomes a measure of human depth. There is no adversity on this earth that cannot be overcome by fortitude and positive will. Or so we're led to believe.

Now, to be chased through a park in the dead of night by an emaciated ghoul and a herd of trees, to play cat-and-mouse in freezing pond water, to be stabbed but not stabbed by a dagger-like finger, then to return home and find your pet cat nailed to a doorframe and your only son missing is not, mercifully, a common experience to us all, but it is one that would sorely test the stoutest of spirits. Creed, as we know, does not possess the stoutest of spirits.

He didn't go to pieces – at least, not right away. First he found a hammer, then he wrapped his coat around Grin to stop the poor animal scratching his arms and face to shreds. After that he levered the long nail from the wood and the cat's tail, while holding on to the squealing creature beneath the coat with one arm. Once free, Grin didn't bother with thanks: she shot from Creed's arm in a blur of furry speed and disappeared down the well of the spiral staircase. Where she went after that the photographer had no idea, and he made no effort to find out; his prime concern was the whereabouts of his son.

The folded piece of paper, coloured orange by the darkroom light, lay on the floor in the doorway as if the cat had been used as a pointer to it. Creed picked it up, his fingers smearing blood on to its surface. He opened it and read:

HE'LL DIE IF YOU TELL

That's when he went to pieces.

So an hour later we find Creed ruminating in the kitchen, the bottle of Bushmills in front of him down to its last quarter, the room itself thick with fug, the ashtray on the table piled high with brown cigarette stubs.

'Bastards,' he murmurs to himself, not for the first time in that long, hysterical, then lachrymal, then guilt-ridden hour. How could he have been so stupid? he asks himself. What the fuck was he going to do? How was he going to get Sammy back? *What* was he going to tell Evelyn?

Oh God, oh God, oh God.

He drains the whiskey in the tumbler and pours another. Before drinking he fumbles with a cigarette paper, overloading it with tobacco, scattering flakes across the table, into the booze. It takes two hands to hold the match steady. What a night!

The liquid no longer hurts his throat when he swallows; neither does it revive his spirits. *I'm dead*, he groans inwardly. *Evelyn will kill me. If she doesn't, they might!*

His head sags, nods once, jerks up again. It sags again, stupor at last beginning to dull everything. His eyelids are too heavy, they start to close.

Footsteps on the stairs . . .

'The door was open,' she said quietly.

He eyed Cally with disbelief, amazed (and wide awake again) that she had the nerve to confront him. Her hair tonight was tied into a bunched tail at the back, leaving her face exposed, somehow guileless. Beneath her beige raincoat she wore a soft black polo-neck that emphasised the clean curve of her jaw. She looked good and he hated himself for noticing.

'You . . .' he said, the word accusing.

'I've closed it behind me. You're quite safe.'

'I'm . . . safe?' He may have been wide awake now, but his thoughts were not yet together.

'For the moment,' she added, but not for assurance. 'Can I have some of that Scotch?' She nodded towards the bottle.

'Irish,' he corrected. 'It's Irish.'

She came all the way into the room and he couldn't make up his mind if it was sympathy or disgust he saw in her eyes. He straightened in his chair, palms flat on the table, cigarette jutting from his mouth. Cally looked around for another glass, walking over to a wall cupboard and looking inside.

'Below,' he told her.

She knelt and took out a tumbler that matched his, then brought it to the table and poured herself a drink. She swallowed half before saying anything else. 'You don't look so good,' she commented.

Creed leaned back in his chair and managed a crooked smile. 'I don't look so good? Really? You know what? *I don't feel so fucking good!*'

He was on his feet, the chair toppling over behind him, his face livid, his knuckles white-ridged and aimed at her.

Cally took two steps back, her glass nearly slipping through her fingers. He came around the table towards her and she backed away, pulling out a chair and positioning it between them.

'Joe, please calm down. Please calm down.'

He drew some satisfaction from the light of fear in her eyes.

'You want me to calm down, you fucking bitch? You kidnap my son and you want me to calm down?' He grabbed the back of the chair and tossed it aside. Cally retreated around the corner of the kitchen table and held out a hand to ward him off.

'You've got to listen to me, Joe. You mustn't blame me for this, I'm trying to help you. If you don't want Samuel to be hurt you must listen to me.'

He stopped, dearly wanting to throttle the life out of her, but not quite sure if he had the strength right at that moment. His anger had not dissipated, but concern for his son and his own weariness dimmed it. 'You drugged me the other night, didn't you? You dropped something into my drink that made me see things that weren't there.'

Perhaps in some perverse way she thought the truth might help him trust her a little. 'I mixed something in your tobacco, Joe. Not enough for you to notice, but enough to have an effect. Can we sit down and talk?'

'Not until you tell me why you did it?' His voice was low and his fingers flexing.

'To frighten you.'

'Shit – *why*?' He took a step towards her and she backed away again. Creed managed to restrain himself, but only just.

'To soften you up, to scare you. It was a mild hallucinogen – no lasting effects. It helped them put thoughts – *bad* thoughts – into your mind.'

'Jesus, I guessed it was something like that!' He shook his head tiredly. 'For a while there I thought I was going nuts. I . . . I've got to sit down.' He did so, shakily, using the chair he'd just thrown aside. He stretched across the table for his drink and gulped it back.

If she was afraid, Cally no longer showed it, although her movement as she took the seat opposite him was steady, wary.

He watched her for a little while and when she picked up the cigarette that had been burning the table since falling from his lips earlier, and offered it to him, he regarded it suspiciously.

'It's okay,' she promised. 'The tobacco's clean. Your tin was emptied, the tobacco replaced. Look at all those others you've smoked tonight.'

He took the cigarette and revived it with short drags. 'Where is he?' he asked finally, forcing calmness upon himself.

'Safe. For the moment.'

He lunged across the table (so much for forced calmness), his hands reaching round the back of her neck to pull her towards him. Their faces were only inches from each other as he all but spat the question at her again: *'Where is he?'*

Cally tried to pull his wrist away, but he merely tightened his grip. 'You're hurting me,' she said without pleading.

'*Answer me.*'

'If you harm me they'll kill him.'

His fingers loosened as if in reflex, although he continued to hold her there against the table. 'Who're they? The two freaks in the park couldn't have taken him – they wouldn't have had time to get back before me. Besides, they're probably in the slammer by now.'

'No, they're not.'

'They got out of the park?' He let go of her neck completely, but she pulled off only an inch or so.

'Joe, you don't know who you're dealing with. These people aren't . . .' She paused, as if searching for an appropriate word. 'Ordinary,' she finished limply, as though the description were inadequate.

'Sure. One's a vampire, right?'

She said nothing.

He lounged back in his chair and drew on the cigarette. 'So who did take Sammy? You?'

'I came so he wouldn't be too frightened.'

'That was the idea – get me out of the way, then snatch him. You knew he was here because you'd spoken to him on the phone.'

'If you had handed over the film this wouldn't have happened.'

'But you didn't know I wasn't going to.'

'Not until you got to the park, no.'

'So you kidnapped my son for insurance, just in case I didn't deliver.'

She straightened and picked up her glass. She closed her eyes when she drank.

'They can have the negs and prints,' he told her. 'They can have whatever they like – anything. I'll guarantee never to mention any of this to anyone. I haven't got much money, but I'll scrape up whatever I can. They can have that too. All I want is Sammy returned and for me to be left alone.'

'They don't trust you.'

'Then what's the alternative? There's nothing more I can do.'

'They'll have to talk to you before they decide.'

'Maybe I should just go to the Law.' He said it as if thinking aloud.

Cally slammed down her glass, spilling whiskey. 'Don't even think of doing that! Oh God, you mustn't even consider it.'

He blinked, taken aback by the vigour of her outburst. 'Then you'd better tell me who these people are and what they are and why that crazy bastard wants his wrinkled kisser kept out of the newspapers. I mean, I can understand his shame at the family connection – if there is one – but he can hardly be blamed for what Mallik did before the last World War. What the hell is the big deal?'

'For your own sake it's better that you don't know anything about them. They want to be left alone.'

'So did Garbo, but things don't always work out that way. What are they up to? Look, at least tell me if the man is related to old Nick. Nicholas Mallik,' he added on seeing her confusion.

'Yes,' she admitted reluctantly. 'They're related. But that's as much as I can tell you.'

'It's something. What do I do now?'

'I've told you – you give them what they want. After they've talked to you.'

'Why can't I just hand it over to you right here and now?'

'Believe me when I say I wish you could. Unfortunately you have to do it their way.'

'And if it's a set-up? They'll have me as well as my son.'

'You've no choice. You did before, but now you haven't. I'll stay with you tonight.'

'To help me make up my mind?'

She shook her head. 'I keep telling you – you have no choice. I'm just here to make sure you do nothing rash.'

'How could you stop me?'

'Perhaps I couldn't. But this way we'll know.'

Not if I beat the shit out of you first, then call the police, he thought. 'Have you got a weapon of some kind on you?' It would have been silly to put the question casually, so he didn't even try.

'Forget about attacking me, Joe. You're too tired for that. Anger helped you before, but most of that's gone, hasn't it? You're exhausted.'

'It's been a long day.' And he realised the earlier weariness had returned.

'You're very tired, Joe.'

'What're you – a hypnotist?' His glass felt peculiarly heavy when he lifted it. The whiskey tasted sour.

'It's just that I can see how exhausted you are. It must be hard to think straight in your state.'

'I can handle it.'

'Your clothes are damp, did you realise that? Were you too tired to notice?'

The glass was too much of a burden, so he put it down. 'Who are you, Cally? What's your part in all this?'

She may have given him an answer – he definitely heard her say something – but his brain was closing down. It *had* been a long day. Sweet Judas, it had been a long *life*. 'What'd you say?' he asked, attempting to straighten his shoulders.

'It's all right to sleep, Joe.'

'No. You said something else . . .'

'I said I'm Lily Neverless' granddaughter.'

'. . . Yeah . . . that's what I thought you said . . .'

His head rested against his arms on the table. Creed slept.

18

She had left the note on the table, close to where he slumbered. It was the first thing he saw when he woke.

He groaned and ran a hand through his tangled hair. His clothes stank. His *body* stank.

Why were they always leaving him notes? he wondered as he unfolded the small sheet of paper. Why couldn't they just tell him things face-to-face? It was an address. He assumed he was supposed to go there, although nothing was mentioned to that effect.

Creed eyed the dregs of his whiskey, a dismal and solitary sight in the cold light of morning. He noticed her glass was no longer on the table. In the sink and washed of fingerprints, he mused. He examined the address again. Handwritten, in capital letters. Was he really supposed to go there?

He jerked upright when the phone rang.

Blood drained from his head when he stood too quickly and he swayed there by the table for a moment or so, one hand resting there for support. The telephone insisted and he made his unsteady way over to it. Anger and fear were bubbling by the time he snatched the receiver from its hook.

'You'd better listen to –' he began to say.

'How is he, Joe?' interrupted Evelyn's voice. 'Has he had his All-Bran?'

'Evelyn?'

'Samuel has another mother?' The phone seemed hot with her impatience. 'Did he sleep all right?'

'Evelyn, do you know what time it is?'

'Yes, it's four minutes to ten. What's the matter with you?'

He glanced at his wristwatch, but cheap doesn't buy waterproof. The hands had stopped at forty-three minutes past midnight. Nevertheless the clock on the mantel swore truth to his wife's words.

'He's, uh, yeah, he's fine,' he said into the mouthpiece.

'Does he want to talk to me? Put him on, Joe.'

'No,' he replied too quickly. 'He's gone out for a walk. To get me a newspaper. He wanted some chocolate.'

'He's not allowed chocolate. Dear God, didn't he tell you that? Do you want him to balloon up again? What on earth are you thinking of?'

'He can't get much, I didn't give him a lot of money.'

She was only partially placated. 'Probably off his diet because of stress. Is he missing me, Joseph? Did he say he wants to come home? He must be miserable.'

'He's okay. Quite chirpy really.'

'What?'

'Uh, you know, putting on a brave face. I think the break might be doing him some good, giving him time to think about things. You know what they say – absence breaks the heart but cures the head.' His own head was hurting with the pretence. Christ, he needed to lie down.

'Who says that?'

'It's just a saying.'

'Hmn,' she mused, 'it's one I haven't heard. Well, maybe the punishment is a little harsh. He's a sensitive boy, he needs his mother.'

'To tell you the truth, Evelyn, he was only saying last night that a man has to stand on his own two feet occasionally, to get away from hearth and home to get a proper measure of himself.'

'Samuel said that?'

'It made me smile, I gotta admit. He looked so serious, as though he'd taken on a couple of years.'

'I've never heard him speak like that before. Hearth and home?'

'Yeah, well, they weren't actually his words, but that was the gist of it. In fact, he said it would be fun to stay with his dad for a while.'

'Oh did he now?' The temperature of her voice had dropped considerably. 'I don't think it'll be long before he changes his mind about that. Oh no, not when he starts to miss his creature comforts. Things like a freshly made bed, regular meals, someone to dote on him like a bloody fool! We'll see how long it takes him to get fed up with dear Daddy and his slummy ways. Wait 'til he wants a nice clean shirt to wear, or something other than junk food to eat. Then we'll see what his' – she parodied the words – '*proper measure* is.'

Creed's attitude was very reasonable. 'I think it's only fair to let him –'

'Fair? What do you know about fair? Fair to you is when everything goes the Joseph Creed way. My, my, wait 'til you find out what it's like to be responsible for another human being twenty-four hours a day, seven days a week. It'll soon put a damper on your usual fun and games having to look after your son. Let's see how you cope, let's see how *you* take care of him.'

Oh bitch, if only you knew. 'We'll make out just fine,' he said, all bravado. 'Don't you worry about us.'

'I won't. I'm going to have the time of my life, believe me. For once I'll be free to enjoy *my*self, to do what *I* want to do. This is the first time in I-don't-know-how-many-years I can just please myself! I can't tell you what a good time I'm going to have! If he needs more hankies I'll put them in the post.' With that, the line shut down.

He breathed out, a long sigh of a breath. Tomorrow she'd want Sammy back home. He had to do something about the situation by then.

Creed can stew in his own juices for a bit while our attention is turned to someone else who figures (albeit peripherally for the moment) in the story. Antony James Barnabas Blythe was a man who was easy to despise. Born of fading gentry, schooled at Marlborough, stiffened by a brief spell in the Household Cavalry, he had armed himself against the common *rigueurs* of everyday life with the right connections before embarking on an uncloistered career. (The same connections had counterbalanced a lamentable lack of funds earlier on, for the economic realities of the 'seventies had taken their toll on the family wealth and, furthermore, his father had been inconsiderate enough to join the angels when a socialist government was in power and death duties were at their meanest.) His entrée into journalism was as a stringer to an established diarist, feeding through and often inventing tittle-tattle gained from his own society contacts, until eventually to take on the prime role himself after one costly libel case too many against the newspaper had tugged the rug from under the incumbent columnist.

Because of certain effete affectations, his prim lips, and acute sense of dress (nothing unstructured about *his* Savile Rows) plus a suspicious sensitivity regarding his own private life, it was generally assumed that Blythe was homosexual. That assumption was not quite correct for, whilst there had in the past been 'dalliances' with others of his own sex, particularly in the Guards, and he had accumulated an inordinate amount of Cinderella friends over the years, genuine lack of desire and haemorrhoids had long ago cooled any inclinations he might have had in that direction. In truth, and in practice (or non-practice, as it were), Antony Blythe was asexual. It's a condition that precludes many problems in life.

Like Joe Creed, he was not well-loved by his peers but, unlike the photographer, neither was he respected. After all, who really likes gossips beyond a superficial level? Not only do you automatically know they can't be trusted, but they also make you feel guilty for listening. Besides which you can never be sure you won't be the next target. It was a bitchy profession, and Blythe was more bitchy than most.

He was good at his job, though. He had a nose for scandal, an ear for hearsay, and an eye for spying. Unfortunately, the fast-growing popularity of litigation had tamed his and other gossip columns somewhat in recent years, although occasionally, just occasionally, his Diary reports were *so* scandalous they merited front- or second-page features. Those were the ones that Blythe loved best, for ultimately these were his *raison d'être*. You see, he was someone who liked to damage, to sneer rather than praise, to hurt rather than help. It's a common enough qualification for his particular trade, but one that was developed to its highest (or lowest, whichever way you look at it) degree in Blythe. The pocket-book Freud might say it had something to do with the individual's own sense of inadequacy, a need to drag others down to his or her own level, or possibly below it. Antony Blythe was full of insecurities, although to look at him you'd never know it; in fact, he hardly knew it himself, so arrogant was his nature. He looked up to no one, and constantly endeavoured to prove to himself that there was no one to look up to. A real sad case (something else he himself wasn't aware of).

If he was more irascible than usual this morning (and he was usually pretty irascible at any time of day) it was because the contents of the envelope that Prunella had left for Joe Creed had nagged at him most of the night. Creed, whom he seemed to loathe a little more than almost anyone else, was on to something and Blythe wanted to know what. Something (instinct? His nose for dirt?) told him it was newsworthy, and his own eyes had told him it had to do with a mourner at Lily Neverless' funeral who looked like a murderer (he remembered the photograph Creed had shown him) hanged half a century ago. Creed wouldn't waste his time on a story that wasn't going to earn for him. But he was only a snapper, for God's sake. His job was to take pictures. Real stories were best left to the pros, to those who really knew how to dig deep, to those who had the right contacts. Professionals like, well, like Blythe himself.

From his cubby-hole office, he spotted Prunella making her way to her shared desk. He caught her eye and beckoned, curling his finger in the manner of a schoolmaster summoning the class clown.

He started pleasantly enough. 'You are exceedingly happy in your chosen profession, aren't you, my dear?'

His affability made her nervous. 'Of course, I –'

'That warms me, Prunella. Sometimes one becomes concerned for one's employees. You do work for me, don't you?'

Prunella, her small mouth contracting even tighter, her pallid skin blanching even paler, regarded the diarist with doleful eyes. What had she done wrong this time? She hated Blythe when he was in this sarcastic mood, which was most of the time, for it always seemed to be her who took the brunt of it. Just because she was the junior on the Diary team, it didn't mean that he could constantly bully her. Someday she'd tell him exactly what he could do with his job and his waspish remarks. Not today, though. 'Of course I work for you, Antony.'

'Aha. Yes, that's what *I* believed. Foolish of me to suppose otherwise.' He rested his elbows on the desk, supporting his chin with fingertips. 'Then why, I wonder, are you moonlighting for someone else? You do know what moonlighting is, don't you, Prunella?'

'I do, but I don't know what you're insinuating,' she replied resignedly.

'I'm referring to your extracurricular activities for Mr Scumbag.'

'Mr . . . ?'

'Joe Creed, Prunella. The grubby little person you left an envelope for yesterday.' His voice had ascended a scale or two as if astonished at the gravity of her misdemeanour. 'It was full of old newspaper stories about some vile creature who had a penchant for chopping people up and preserving their parts. Is it coming back to you, my dear? It seems so odd that when I request a teensy piece of research of you it requires such an effort and generally takes you most of the day, yet when our friend Creed – excuse me, I should say, *your* friend Creed – asks for the same you have no difficulty at all in providing envelopes absolutely *loaded* with details and photocopies and everything he could possibly need.'

'Oh, Antony, it took me twenty minutes or so, and I did it in my lunch break.'

'I don't care *when* you did it. What matters to me is that you did it at all. You . . .' he pointed a finger to make sure there was no mistaking whom he meant '. . . are here to serve me. Just me. No one else. Your duty is not to God, nor to our proprietor; not even to our dearly beloved editor. On these premises you are mine, my sweet. Is that perfectly clear, I wonder . . . ?'

'It wasn't that import—'

He placed a finger before pursed lips to hush her. 'I wonder why Creed wanted such information on this particular *nasty* excuse for a human being.'

'Why did you open the envelope I left for Joe?'

He sighed. 'Spare me the indignation. This is a newspaper office

– our very function is to pry. Besides, anything you do during working hours comes under my jurisdiction. Nothing you do with your job can be private from me, Prunella.'

She opened her mouth, about to reply, then thought better of it. The creep was going to win whatever she said in her defence.

'So will you please answer my question: Why did Creed want information on Nicholas Mallik, and what *is* the connection with the man he photographed at Lily Neverless' funeral?'

'I honestly don't know. Joe didn't tell me anything.'

He eyed her coldly. 'I see. You're not willing to say.'

'No, it isn't like that. I really don't know.'

'Hmn, perhaps you don't. After all, why should he confide in you? Use you, yes, but take you into his confidence? I doubt he'd be so foolish.'

He wagged his finger at her, and Prunella fought back the urge to smack it away. 'Fortunately you have a chance to redeem yourself,' he said. 'Find out what Creed is up to and let me know. In the meantime, I'll make some enquiries of my own.'

Blythe tapped out a name on the small electronic organiser he'd taken from a desk drawer, then picked up the telephone. Receiver in one hand, he looked up at her as if wondering why she still stood before him. His other hand dismissed her with an airy wave.

19

The building was in one of those rising streets close to where Billingsgate fish market stood before property developers, those infidels of tradition, set their greedy beady eyes on the site. Creed drove by, slowing down and scrutinising the open doorway before finding somewhere to park. It was an old building, narrow and made of coppery red bricks, wedged incongruously between later styles; entering was like walking into a large dank cave, the hollow smell and the cold echoes of his footsteps chilling his thoughts as well as his flesh.

On a wall inside was a rubber-ridged noticeboard on which were pressed incomplete company names, the black spaces as unsightly as gaps in teeth. However, the name he was looking for was there in its entirety. LIABLE & CO. He checked the address in his hand. No mistake. Seventh floor. He hoped the lift was working.

It was one of those ancient affairs with contracting iron doors and metal latticework caging the shaft itself. He pressed a button and somewhere high above machinery clunked into life. The lift heralded its own approach with regular heavy thumps and groans, and while he waited Creed looked round at the high-ceilinged and municipal-tiled hallway. He suddenly had a yearning for sunshine and people.

The building appeared to be unoccupied, the only noise apart from the complaining elevator to be heard coming from somewhere outside; the muted sounds of drilling and crashing masonry somehow were reassuring. There was only one door in the hallway, this made up of two sections so that the top half could be swung back on its own. He assumed that a porter or janitor was usually stationed there to be on call or to answer enquiries. Creed went over and rapped on the top section, but there was no answer. He was about to try again when a final metallic groan announced the arrival of the lift.

He returned and pulled back the iron door with some effort; the matching door to the car itself was a little easier. Creed stepped inside and closed both doors again, feeling as if he'd just voluntarily shut himself up in a cell.

The buttons for each floor were round and prominent, like discoloured eyeballs, with serif numbers as pupils. He pressed 7. After a moment's consideration, the elevator rose with a shudder, then proceeded smoothly enough (although the *clunk-thunk* it made as it passed the floors was somewhat disconcerting: it was as though the shaft itself had shrunk over the years and the car had to squeeze past each level). The higher he went the gloomier the corridors outside became.

What was he doing? This had to be crazy! These people weren't normal. Nobody sane would kidnap a boy just to get back photographs of themselves. They – *he* – could have had them anyway. All they had to do was ask nicely. Or even just ask.

Machinery above whined and the elevator jolted to a halt, causing him to shift footing. He peered through the bars of the gates into the corridor beyond. Light from a grimy window at the far end barely had a say in the gloaming, and the urge to press the G button was powerful. You've got no choice, he reminded himself. You can't fail Sammy now. His very life might depend on it. Talk to them, agree to turn over everything, and then you could all go home. But would it really be that simple? In his heart he knew it wouldn't. Not now . . .

Creed yanked back the lift door and then the outer one. No more thinking, he told himself. Just get the fuck on with it. Action was what was needed here, and thinking only diminished resolve. He hummed to himself as he left the elevator, something from *The King and I*, but even he didn't know what it was. There were four doors in the corridor, two on either side, and he strode resolutely to the first. Faded gold lettering told him this wasn't the one he was looking for, but he tried the handle anyway. It was locked.

Crossing the corridor to the next, he struck out again: also locked.

The third door, further along, had no title on its dusty speckled glass, but it opened at his touch. He poked his head in first.

It wasn't much brighter than the corridor in there, for blinds were drawn on the two windows. He could hear the faint drone of traffic rising from the street seven flights below as well as distant sounds of building works, but the office itself was as morbidly quiet as a tomb.

'Anyone home?' he called out.

There was no reply and he wasn't too disappointed. He opened the door wider and hesitantly stepped across the threshold. It was difficult to make out the room's contents, so poor was the light. Bookshelves, a filing cabinet, a couch against one wall, a desk – he could just about identify those. Oh, and one other thing – a figure sitting behind the desk.

'Close the door,' a low – a *very* low – voice said.

'It's dark in here.' Creed refused to move far from the doorway. 'Let's have some light.' He half turned, looking for a switch.

'Wait.' The figure at the desk rose, an indiscernible shape among the shadows, and Creed took a step backwards, tensed to run. The voice was not that of the man he'd met in the park the night before, and perhaps it was curiosity as well as fear for his son that prevented him from bolting. It had a certain roughness to it, like the other man's and it was just as deep-pitched; but it was . . . different. He realised how different when slatted blinds snapped open and daylight filtered through (the windows were filthy with grime).

The woman was almost in silhouette, the day's greyness outlining long dark hair, her shoulders, the swell of a hip. It flashed through his mind that it was Cally standing there before the window, but of course the voice wasn't the same, the hair was dark . . .

'Close the door.'

It was a command he still felt no inclination to obey. 'I'd rather not,' he said.

He thought he heard her laugh – no, a smaller sound, a snigger? She may have just coughed.

'Very well. Will you at least take a seat?' She moved back to her own chair. 'Or will you continue to be difficult? I think we have the advantage, you know.'

He'd been wrong: there was no roughness to her voice, just a deep huskiness that made it, well, seductive. *Judas*, he said to himself, *what was he thinking here*?

'I want to know about my son.'

'We'll discuss your son when you're seated.'

What the hell could she do? She was only a woman. But was she alone? He inspected the office, grim daylight at least throwing some relief. Just him and her, although across the room there was another door which obviously led to an adjoining office. Could the two freaks be lurking in there?

'The couch,' the woman said.

Creed shrugged. No big deal. Anyway, the couch was close to the open door if he wanted to get out fast. It smelled of age rather than leather when he lowered himself on to it, rising dust spoiling the air, the material itself creaking dryly. It finally dawned on him that the building and its offices were not really in use at all; the whole place was probably waiting its turn for the demolition squad.

'What've you done with Sammy – with my son?' he asked mildly enough. Inside he was scared, he was seething, he was distraught.

'The boy is unharmed.'

A sudden flare and her countenance was lit up. The end of her cigarette glowed and the lighter flicked off. Smoke caught the light as it rose from the shadow of her face.

Creed continued to stare as though he could still see that face.

It was beautiful.

Full, blood-coloured lips; a nose that was strong but not dominant; sweeping hair that framed her cheeks to curl against the jawline. The eyes had been downcast, eyelashes thick and long, but before she had snuffed the flame they had looked up at him; they must have been a deep brown, but they seemed softly black. Her glance was languidly sexual. Then the light was gone.

Creed cleared his throat.

'Don't you like the darkness, Joe?' The tone was as sexual as the glance she'd given him. 'Don't you find it . . . restful? It veils so much ugliness, while light only serves to shatter illusions.'

'I want my son back.'

Although he couldn't see her eyes now, he underwent a similar sensation to the one in the cemetery when his own eyes had met the crazyman's, a feeling that his skull was being invaded. This time, though, it was a softer exploration, a delicate probing of his thoughts rather than a scouring. He shivered suddenly, and even that was not unpleasant. The skin of his back seemed to be dilating, stretching, causing an agreeable crawling tingling that almost made him squirm. And . . . *oh Judas Christ, not that, not now* . . . a muscle twitched between his legs.

Her cigarette glowed again and she appeared to be smiling.

'Of course you want the boy back,' she agreed soothingly. 'But you've been very troublesome to us, Joe. That isn't easy to forgive.'

He saw her shoulders rise, watched her as she came round to his side of the desk. Oh boy, she was tall, five-ten at least. She made Sigourney Weaver look frail and positively dowdy. She leaned back against the desk, one arm folded across her stomach and holding the elbow of the other, cigarette poised inches away from her face.

'I've got the negs, the prints – everything you want. Just give me Sammy.' He was tempted to go over and grab her by the shoulders, maybe shake her some to let her know she shouldn't mess with him. The temptation wasn't very strong.

'I'm not sure if it isn't too late,' she said.

'What?' For a moment he was stunned. 'You haven't –'

'I told you the boy is safe. No, I didn't mean anything like that, although . . .' She let the sentence hang. 'You see, you've already stirred up interest in something that would best have been left alone.'

'That isn't true. I'm the only one that knows about the connection with this character Nicholas Mallik and even I don't understand what it is.'

He thought he heard her sigh, although she might merely have been exhaling cigarette smoke.

'You know about Nicholas.' She said it as a wife admitting she had a lover might.

'I, well, I . . . no.'

'A pity.'

A pity he *did* know, was the implication.

'But then, perhaps not.'

He wondered at that.

'Would you mind . . .' he said, ever so politely. '. . . would you mind telling me who you are?'

'Do you really want to get in deeper?'

'Uh, no, it's not important. Look, I've got what you want right here.' He drew out a large envelope from inside his buttoned coat. 'It's all there, everything you – he – wanted.' He proffered it towards her.

'You can call me Laura, Joe. Yes, I'd like you to call me that.'

She came towards him and he thought it was to take the envelope. She ignored it.

He could see her more clearly now and at any other time he'd have approved. She was not quite slim, but her body looked firm and her curves were gentle. Her perfume was odd, a musk of some kind, a fragrance that had an underlying bitterness; it was strangely erotic. Her face really was beautiful in that half-light.

The envelope slipped through his fingers when she kneeled before him and said, 'Let me breathe you, Joe.'

20

It wasn't a proper reception desk; nor was it a proper reception hall. It was an old and somewhat tired-looking oak table with ornately carved legs situated in a marble-floored hallway opposite the home's main doors. The woman seated there – a very rotund lady with the puckered yet dainty face of a gorged twelve-year-old – looked up at Antony Blythe in surprise. She put down her copy of *Elle*.

'Can I help you?' Her voice was somehow distant, as though having lost much of its strength in the struggle through all those layers of flesh.

In her pale blue uniform, over which she wore a fluffy pale pink cardigan, she reminded Blythe of a pastel blimp. 'My name's Wingate,' he told her. 'From Birchenough, Mibbs and Burroughs,' he added, as if confident that would explain everything.

She blinked at him with eyes narrowed by the fat around them.

'My secretary rang yesterday to make the appointment.'

The woman, who could have been aged anywhere between mid-twenties and early-forties so heavily did her weight disguise her, blinked again. 'I'm afraid she didn't, Mr . . .'

'Wingate. Well someone here accepted the appointment,' Blythe blithely lied. 'I'm here to see Ms Buchanan – Grace Buchanan. It concerns her late mother's estate.'

'Her mother . . . ?'

Blythe showed only a little of his usual impatience. 'Lily Neverless. The actress. You might recall she died very recently. I've come a long way and my time is short . . .'

'I'm sorry but Grace isn't allowed visitors.'

'And I'm sorry but you really can't deny me access. This is a matter of importance.'

'I'm afraid she isn't well enough . . .'

'That's as may be, but not altogether relevant,' the diarist prattled. 'It's a point of law that I see her whether she understands what I say or not. In some ways it's like serving a writ, only in this circumstance it's entirely beneficial to the recipient. Will you please make the arrangements as quickly as possible so that I'm not further delayed.'

Those piggy little eyes stared at him blankly. 'Would you wait for a moment?' She rose from the table like a mountain from the sea and moved surprisingly swiftly and lightly down the hallway to disappear with one last glance back at him through a door at the far end.

Blythe considered what to do should whoever was in charge of this high-class institution refuse his request to see Lily Neverless' mad daughter. Insist? What if they demanded to see some form of identification? Beat a hasty retreat, that was what he would do. It was a reasonable ploy, pretending to be an executor of Lily's will, but one that would be impossible to brazen out.

He glanced around, curious about this place called the Mountjoy Retreat. It didn't look like a lunatic asylum, despite the walled grounds, nor was it billed as one. A retreat for the elderly, the infirm, or the emotionally exhausted? he wondered. He hadn't seen any yet. The only person he'd met so far was the fat receptionist. How old would Lily's daughter be now? Late-fifties/sixties? Had to be something like that. She'd been incarcerated for thirty years or so, poor imbecile.

Blythe's original aim had been to discover the connection between the Beast of Belgravia and Lily Neverless (there *had* to be a reason for Mallik's offspring to visit her grave), but the few calls he'd made to some of Lily's friends had yielded nothing initially (older Thespians these, in the main, who would trade a confidence without conscience for a mention in the tabloids). No, they couldn't recall Lily associating with someone called Nicholas Mallik – *'Wasn't he a notorious spy during the war, dear?'* one not-quite senile actress enquired of Blythe – but then she'd 'associated' with so many men in her life, hadn't she? Possibly the one person who would know, advised a financier who had indeed had an 'association' with Lily some time in the long-gone past, was Lily's daughter, but then she was probably too loopy to give him a sensible answer. Where was she now? God knows, old boy. The fact that her one and only child was twopence short of a shilling wasn't something the old ham wished to be generally known. Never heard her talk about the lassie, let alone where she was kept locked up.

Naturally that had merely increased Blythe's curiosity, for the public, hence journalists, loved skeletons in cupboards. They loved those old bones to be dragged out and cast to the ground where they could be read like runes. A madness in the family was wonderful stuff, if the family was famous (a madness in the Royal Family was even better, but virtually impossible to get into print).

So who would know where Lily's dippy daughter was being kept?

Simple, really. Lily Neverless' solicitors would know. He checked with the newspaper's own legal office, who provided the answer within ten minutes (the actress had had occasion to sue the *Dispatch* some years ago for publishing a 'malicious and untrue' story about herself; apologies and money had passed hands and the litigation had been dropped). Blythe rang the company of Birchenough, Mibbs and Burroughs and enquired if Lily Neverless' will had been read yet and, making no pretence as to his own identity (solicitors are well-used to such enquiries from journalists), who were the main beneficiaries? The solicitor, who had every right to withhold the information, even though it would eventually be a matter of public record, was surprisingly helpful and informed him that the *sole* beneficiary of Lily Neverless' last will and testament was the Mountjoy Retreat, an arrangement made years before and swiftly expedited on her death. But did she leave her daughter nothing? Blythe had asked. Grace Buchanan had been well provided for, came the reply, and the insinuation was plain to see. So the old girl had left everything to the home or asylum or retreat or whatever tasteful term they used to describe the funny farm that cared for her daughter. She must have had a lot of faith in the people who ran the place.

Tracing the Mountjoy Retreat had been relatively easy; locating it on the map had been difficult.

But eventually, by travelling to the area and searching country backroads, he managed to find the place. He wondered why it was not even listed in the telephone directory. He also wondered if they would allow him to see Grace Buchanan.

The pale blue dumpling appeared at the end of the corridor and swept back towards him, her pudgy face expressionless.

'That will be fine,' she squeaked.

'I can see her?'

'Yes, not for long though. Would you like to follow me?'

He did, lengthening his stride to keep up with her (how *did* she manage to glide like that?). Up one flight of stairs, along a bright, white corridor, then up another flight. My God, where do they keep her? In the loft? He wrinkled his nose at the sickly stale smell that pervaded the air, an unpleasant sweetness that was not unakin to baby's vomit or old people's body vapours. A door on his right opened an inch or so as he passed by and he caught a glimpse of a solitary eye that was so yellow-stained and damp, the skin around it so sagging and cracked, that it could have belonged to some leprous creature locked away because of its own hideousness. Allow me to die before I get old, Blythe silently pleaded. His obese guide stopped dead in her tracks, perhaps alerted by the worse stench that had filled the corridor like a jet of polluted steam. She turned back and yanked shut the door from where the offending smell came. The diarist thought he heard a feeble moan from the other side.

The fat woman resumed the journey without so much as a glance his way, leading him *down* a short flight of stairs and along yet another corridor. This one was much narrower and would not have allowed Blythe to walk alongside the woman even if he had wanted to. He imagined that vast bottom ahead of him bouncing from side to side like a giant fleshy pinball and the thought filled him with loathing rather than humour.

Another staircase (up, this time) which wound round and round as if it were in some kind of turret (Blythe had noticed two from the outside) until it reached a small dingy landing. Only one door led off from there.

The receptionist stood to one side. 'Grace Buchanan,' she announced as if that were the name of the door itself.

He stood on the landing and raised his eyebrows at the fat woman.

'You can go right in,' she said, and smiled.

And right then he didn't want to go in. Suddenly he wanted to climb back down those stairs, find his way along the confusing corridors, get to the main hall, run through the large doors there, jump into his Rover, and drive back immediately to the warm world of scandal and calumny that he knew and loved so well.

Unfortunately for him, it was but a fleeting and indeterminate moment, a swiftly suppressed intuition that had no real influence over the opportunity for a good and meaty story. He was about to catch sight of a famous star's crazy daughter, someone who had been locked away for the past thirty-odd years, a prisoner of her own mother's shame. The princess in the tower, the loon in the attic! It was irresistible.

He gripped the doorhandle, looked once at the fat woman (was there just a glint of mockery behind those beady little eyes?) and opened the door.

Again he was revolted by the stench that greeted him, although this was slightly different – perhaps more sour – than that of the corridors below.

He stepped inside the darkened room and faced the most peculiar individual he had ever seen in his life (alas, a life that was to be all too short).

21

Breathe him she did.

    Creed was perplexed. What the hell was she playing at?

The woman called Laura nuzzled his neck, taking in short sharp breaths, first through her nose, then her mouth, capturing the air around him – *capturing his smell!* – drawing it into herself. She moved over his chest, pushing his coat aside, her nose and lips almost touching his sweatshirt. Up again, under his chin, now lightly brushing his mouth.

He couldn't help but *breathe* her, *taste* her redolence, that bitter muskiness that was so much stronger now she was so close. Her thick black hair tickled his nose and he angled his head away, looking up at the ceiling as if appealing to the Almighty beyond.

'Uh, listen . . .' he began to say, but she was descending once more, past his chest to his stomach. Her hands tugged at his sweatshirt so that his flesh was bare. She breathed it.

'Oh no . . .' he muttered as the animal at his groin stirred again. He put a hand on her shoulder, but his pressure was not insistent. Without raising her head, she lifted the hand away.

She went down to his thighs, moved to and lingered over his crotch, inhaling all the time, those breaths becoming stronger, a little more urgent.

He moaned inwardly as he felt himself swell.

With some effort, he said, 'I'm here for Sammy, not . . . not this . . .'

She paused only to look up at him, ducking her head once more almost immediately to resume her curious exercise. Her shoulders rose and fell in quickening shudders.

Creed squirmed in the seat.

Her hands touched the buttons at the neck of her dress and so deft was the movement they seemed to open of their own accord. Her fingers travelled down them and still she did not stop inhaling him, her lips parted, their redness moistened.

Oh shit, he said to himself, *oh shit oh . . . not this. Christ, not now . . .*

She pulled at her dress and it slipped from her shoulders.

Her skin was white, so very white. Even in the gloom he could tell it was as white and pure as ivory; but soft, so soft, demanding to be touched . . .

We know Creed wasn't the strongest of men when it came to morals – in fact, he wouldn't even have regarded sex with a proper stranger *as* immoral – but the thought of the danger his son might be in did put something of a downer on the situation. He struggled to sit upright (for he had sunk low into the couch, the nape of his neck almost on the headrest).

'Quit it!' he said, and there was an element of desperation in his voice. 'I'm here to get my boy, that's all, that's it, that's what I'm here for. Let's cut this crap and get down to business. Who the fuck are you, anyway?'

She paused to smile at him.

'I told you, you can call me Laura.'

'Laura who, Laura what? What have you got to do with all this? I came here to see the pervert who kidnapped my son, not some fucking nympho who gets her rocks off snorting body odour. You better start talking before I get *really* mad.'

Her broader smile barely showed her teeth. Her dark-rimmed eyes watched him intently, yet there was a vacuity there, a kind of distant emptiness, that was disconcerting, not to say downright eerie.

He felt that probing again, gentle exploring fingers inside his mind, sensuous as they touched certain nerves, certain thoughts. And those thoughts were suddenly *bad*. They were of her. They were of her and *him*. No, no, not *now*! He thought he heard her laugh, but her lips had not moved, they still smiled, and the sound was too far away, too hollow, as if coming from a locked attic. She hadn't laughed; but the laughter had come from her.

She touched her dress again and it opened further, almost to the waist. The material appeared to be sheer, as if having metamorphosed into gossamer, and he could see the curves of her breasts against the hardened dark tinges of her nipples. She drew the dress to one side and he groaned at the pleasure of her body's full, soft whiteness.

He attempted to speak again, tried to resist, but he was only human and what's more, he was only Creed. He had to caress that exposed flesh.

She stayed his hand.

Then reached into him with her other hand. The zip of his jeans opened in the same magical way as her dress buttons, almost without being touched (or, more realistically, her touch was so expertly light it seemed as if the undoing was of its own accord). Her fingers were cool and soft as they delved further. She brought him out into the open.

Creed shifted, unsure if he should join her on the floor, or if she should join him on the couch. Laura placed her hands on his thighs to still him.

Creed glimpsed himself and marvelled at his own erection; it had been quite a while since he'd been aroused to such eminence. It was worthy of a snap.

He wanted this strange woman very badly. So badly that Sammy had become no more than a shadowy thought somewhere at the back of his mind, there, not forgotten, but not in the reckoning at that precise moment. If Creed felt guilt, it was easily overwhelmed by lust.

'Come on . . . ' he urged her dryly, but she smiled and kept him there, the pressure on his legs firm and uncompromising. She released him only so that she could feel her own naked breast. Her eyes half closed as she fondled the nipple, and her smile became more inward. She freed her other breast, cupping both in her hands, stroking them, arousing herself and arousing Creed even more. He tried to reach for her again, but she warded him off, swaying back on her haunches, not allowing him to touch.

She remained leaning back, her legs apart, and slid the skirt up to uncover stretched, milky thighs, the most erotic thighs Creed had ever looked upon, thighs so beautifully rounded, so wonderfully taut in their posture of openness, the dark valley between so enticing . . .

He moaned aloud when she drew the hem higher and he saw the deeper darkness there, the unclothed hair like some large jet arrowhead pointing in the direction he wished to travel.

Too much. It was too much for Creed. He sank to the floor so that he was kneeling before her, his knees outside hers and touching, his back against the edge of the couch. She had not tried to stop him.

She dipped her hand into herself and shuddered, her eyes closing completely for a moment. Her fingers came away and she smeared his lips with her own wetness. A tiny stab of repulsion jarred him, but it was soon overcome. Creed licked his lips.

Laura dipped again, and this time his hugely erect penis took the wetness and it mingled with his own seeping juices. She spread the mixture down his full length.

Her moistened hand left him and she ran her fingers along her own thighs, teasing herself, up and down, reaching higher with each stroke until finally she plunged into the shadowy recess with both hands, arching her body backwards so that her vulva was thrust at his face. She gasped repeatedly and Creed, goggle-eyed and slack-jawed, panted in time with her gasping.

Around them, the room darkened.

He could bear no more. He flung himself at her, springing the top button of his jeans and jerking them down as he did so.

She let out a cry as they fell together, her legs straightening, one kicking the couch so that it banged against the wall and released a shower of dust.

His right of passage was hindered by her hands, for she still covered herself, she still caressed herself, her movement at once hard, and then soft, hard and then soft, the tips of her fingers more and more lost from view. Creed grabbed her wrists to pull her hands away and briefly she allowed him access. He was in – fast, forever the opportunist – and the exquisiteness of sinking deep into the damp yielding opening made him yell and slaver and grip her waist beneath the flimsy dress so that he could be inside her to the very limits and he thrust and thrust until the fluids roiled and began to erupt . . .

But Laura spasmed her body and tossed him from her as his liquid gushed; it spilt itself over her thighs, over her dress, sputtering more as he fell away, to plop in milky drops across the carpetless floor.

The room sank darker still.

Her breasts rising and falling in heavy shudders, she rested on one elbow and watched him.

For his part, Creed was confused. Discharged, but confused. And disappointed. But intoxicated, too. And not entirely satiated.

She began to laugh, a giggle at first, proceeding to a chuckle. He grinned inanely back at her, the grin wavering when she let loose a graceless snort, followed by an inelegant bellow of laughter.

It ceased abruptly and her gaze left his to wander down his body, stopping only to rest upon his nakedness. She studied his dripping penis and Creed felt its ugly head rear again in a small flicker of excitement. He moaned yet again, thinking this was not possible, not so soon after, that although not fully satisfied, he was certainly fully spent. But no, his wayward member twitched once more, started to stiffen with free-willed resolve.

Laura smiled and a shadow, like a veil, shifted over her face.

In a languid movement, she dipped her fingers into one of the white pools left by him on her thigh and touched the moisture first to her lips and then – the movement tantalising in its slowness – to her vagina.

Something rose from that second orifice, curling in the air, some-thing nebulous, ill-defined, but nevertheless a shape; it ascended to the darkness above her, more than just a wispy vapour, for something moved within it, a form inside a formless sac.

More protoplasmic tendrils began to rise from other semen pools on her legs and the cloth of her dress. A minute shape floated like steam from a mother-of-pearl speckle on the floor between Creed and the woman.

She watched them climb into the air with a rapturous expression, as a child might gaze at a release of bright balloons.

Creed felt cold, a sensation so immediate and acute that he shivered violently. 'What are they?' he asked in a slow, quavery voice.

She didn't answer right away, but continued to watch as the cloud-forms smoothed out against the ceiling, spreading so that their ragged edges began to join.

'Phantoms,' she answered after a while, still without looking at him. 'The phantoms of emissions.'

'. . . the fuck . . . ?' he said.

'Weanlings,' she added, as though that would explain all. She sighed in regret. 'They won't amount to much.'

Creed fumbled with his clothing, deciding he'd had enough. He tried to scramble to his feet with jeans and underpants still gathered around his knees, and lost his balance, collapsing on to the couch.

Laura calmly turned to him. 'You're not leaving, you know.'

'Like hell I'm not!' he yelled back at her, tugging at his trousers and attempting to rise at the same time.

'But we haven't finished.' Pleasantly said, a gentle coaxing.

She rose and stepped out of her dress to stand naked before him, tall and long-limbed, shadowed interestingly by the insubstantial light, her legs firmly apart, her arms stretched towards him. The forms on the ceiling floated down and prowled around her. In one Creed thought he saw a tiny pain-racked face, a gaping hole for a mouth, dark smudges for eyes; stumps that might have been Lilliputian arms appeared straining at the mist-like sac in which it was imprisoned. He noticed another such form, then another. Soon, several.

They circled her, gathering speed, looping between her legs, some disappearing into her, emerging a split second later through her open mouth.

Creed headed for the door.

It was shut. *How did it get shut? It shouldn't have been shut! He hadn't seen anyone shut it!* Worse, he couldn't open it.

Clasping his jeans to his waist with both hands, he turned to face her.

OhmyGodherheadwastouchingtheceiling!

And her head had changed also, her face had extended! She had a snout! She looked like a fur-less fox – no, a vixen! A naked, grinning vixen! And her breasts were long, drooping udders. And the hair between her legs was like a beard, trailing on the floor. And her legs were pipe-thin, and they were knobbled and scaly and her toes were long and splayed and curling at the ends . . .

He blinked, unable to believe his own eyes, and then it was the same woman standing there, bare and beautiful, skin unblemished and not in the least distorted. He blinked again and the creature had returned, and there were grotesque faces spinning around it, weaving patterns in the air. Small ill-formed voices derided him. He could hear Laura's laughter.

He turned away and he heard her say, 'Wait.'

She was a woman again, standing in the centre of the room, alluring once more, tempting still, even though he was so bare-arsed scared. 'I promise not to do that any more,' she assured him.

The vaporous shapes had gone, too.

'How . . . ?'

'Just fun,' she soothed. 'Just a silly game. I promise I'll behave. If you stay . . .'

He shook his head, to clear it more than as a rejection to her invitation. 'You're fucking with my brain,' he said with angry resentment.

'Of course,' she said. 'Of course.'

She smiled sweetly and her skin began to expand.

'Oh Christ . . .' he complained.

This time Laura did not elongate herself so much as stretch herself into a kind of thin phlegmy mess. She retained a head of sorts, although her cheeks attenuated until they became transparent and then holes, holes that joined with her grinning mouth to become one hugely spacious wound in which a pale-glistening tongue squirmed like a mother maggot (if such things existed). Her eyes had drooped forward because the skin around them had become too squishy to contain them, and her nose seeped to become one large dewdrop. Her hair still looked good though.

The skin between her outstretched arms and body became webs so fine that he could see grey light from the window behind shining through. Her breasts had diminished completely into her elasticated torso and her pubic hair now brushed the floor between feet that were no more than spreading puddles.

He was barely aware of the woolly shapes – his own seed demons (although he wasn't cognisant of that particular fact right at that moment) – that skimmed around the darkened room, dainty wan faces within them, some grinning, some tormented, all of them absurd.

The quivering tacky mass before him reared up, began to fold over at the top like an ocean wave, more gapes peeling open in the flesh (could it still be called flesh?) as it stretched condom-thin. Creed stood stock-still, mesmerised, petrified and even scandalised (it was so *disgusting*!). A small voice inside his head instructed him to flee, but another small voice argued that the door behind him was locked. Creed paid attention to neither one for he was too shocked by the thing – the *apparition* – which was looming over him, spreading like an oozing, tattered blanket with a grotesque parody of a head near the top and weird appendages at various corners.

It dropped. This great spread of runny mucus dropped on to him like a net over a paralysed animal, draping itself over him, smothering, clogging his mouth, his eyes, his nostrils, sliming over his skin, filling his cracks. His scream was muffled, the tensile substance thinning over his yawning mouth so that air from his lungs ballooned it like bubble-gum. The stuff was heavy, but not heavy enough to drag him down. It was smelly, acidy, like seminal fluid. And its velvety touch was perversely sensuous although, fortunately for Creed, not quite enough to gain his favour.

He punched his way through, tearing an opening in what must have been the thing's gut (for sinuous tubes were visible there, coils of transparent rubber that could only have been intestines). Viscous lumps and strands clung to his arms as he pushed himself forward, but they broke away easily, having no unity, no texture to bind them. He stepped through to the other side, not cleanly, not as though through a paper hoop, but messily, bits going with him, sticking to his skin and clothes. He stumbled further, ever-thinning strands stretching with him. He came to a halt and brushed frantically at himself, clawing at his face, his eyes, spitting gob-like bits from his mouth.

The thing had collapsed to the floor as if punctured, and was lying in a dishevelled heap, a large part of it, a part that might have been shoulders, heaving as though drawing breath, regaining strength. It began to form into a proper shape again.

Creed ran to the other door, the one he had assumed earlier led to an adjoining office, left hand gripping his jeans, right hand reaching for the doorhandle.

Please God don't let it be locked, he pleaded.

It wasn't.

Thankyouthankyouthank—

He staggered back as if pushed.

Someone was standing on the other side of the doorway. Just standing there, not moving. Not smiling. Not scowling, either. Just standing there.

The raincoat man just looked at him.

Creed backed away until he was in the middle of the room. The peculiar thing was (in this day – in this *week* – of peculiar things) that the office in which the graveyard crazy stood was totally and utterly black, as if he were in a void, a place without light, a place of absence. There was nothing there except the man himself.

With a strangulated whimper, Creed ran for the other door, hopping over the rising slimy mound that was forming limbs again, a woman's shape again, although it still oozed and curdled tendrils still sucked at the floor. Arms folded across his head, Creed smashed into the frosted glass of the door's upper half.

The aged brittle glass shattered easily enough and he tumbled through, his hips catching against the lower wooden section so that his feet lifted and the rest of his body toppled over. He landed headfirst in the corridor outside, rolling forward so that his heels chipped the wall opposite. Winded and fearing he'd been mortally wounded by glass shards, he nevertheless lurched to his feet and tottered away, gathering pace as he fled, having no idea in which direction he was headed, but not caring either, simply wanting to be far away from that horrible room.

The corridor ran out, but there was a door tucked away in an alcove to the left, an exit door with a bar-lock across its middle.

He crashed into it and the door gave way. Creed was blinded by stunning white light. And suddenly he was falling.

22

He hung there from the bar-lock, yelling and kicking, seven floors of space between him and the rubbled earth below. Had it not been for the cacophony of pneumatic drills and bulldozers the workmen down there might have heard his cries for help. His jeans had gathered below his knees, but that didn't embarrass Creed at all; he wanted to be saved, and not only from a nasty fall.

'*Help meeeeeee . . .!*'

He was losing his grip in more ways than one. His fingers were beginning to uncurl, his own weight dragging him down. God, if his hands weren't so damp he might have had a better chance. He was slipping, the door he clung to was swaying, and the debris below was anticipating. Even the winter sun that should have been vapid conspired to sting his eyes.

Half-mast clothing prevented him from swinging a leg up to gain some kind of purchase. He attempted several bar-lifts, the muscles of his arms throbbing with the effort; he managed to hook his chin over the iron rod and he stayed that way for a while, letting his neck take some of the strain. It was useless though: his jaw began to tremble; then it began to tilt. It slid off the bar like a boat from a ramp and once more he was relying on his increasingly weakening hands. He started to go . . .

. . . when a hand above him grabbed at the bar, a gorgeous, pink, slender hand, one that he would have kissed right there and then had he the strength to reach it. The door began to swing inwards, but painfully slowly, his weight and the strong breeze hindering its progress. All he could do was remain still (according to the voice that shouted in his ear) and so he concentrated on not letting go, that single consideration driving any others – like the notion that it might be the freaky Laura who was hauling him in – from his mind. He realised he wasn't going to make it; the rescue process was too ponderous, the guardian angel pulling at the bar not strong enough. His lower lip quivered at the thought of what awaited him. He clung by his fingertips.

But then he was sandwiched between the door and the floor level, concrete lip digging into the small of his back. Hands were beneath his shoulders, hauling him up, and he helped as best as he could, using his last reserves of strength to hoist himself.

The edge of the concrete scraped his butt as he was dragged in, and then he was sprawled inside the corridor, gasping for breath, tears of fright and relief streaking his dirtied face.

'Thank you,' he tried to say, but it emerged as a blubbery burble.

Cally was on her knees beside him, looking anxiously into his eyes.

Between broken breaths he said, 'You . . . ?'

Her tone was sharp. 'We've got to get away from here.' She tugged at his arms and, after a moment's hesitation, Creed rose with her. He was unsteady, but he managed to hitch up his jeans and zip them. That, at least, improved his morale. The girl attempted to lead him along the corridor, but he resisted.

'I'm not going back there.'

'It's the only way out. We've got to move, Joe.'

'*They're* down there. I'm not going.'

'It's all right – trust me. We've got to move fast, though.'

He tried to shrug her off, but Cally held on to him.

'There's no alternative,' she insisted.

'There never is with you.'

'Joe, I'm going to leave you. You can either come with me, or you can stay here 'til they're ready to come after you again.'

He looked at her quizzically.

'She's gathering her strength. I don't know what you did to her, but you've damaged her in some way. She'll soon get over it.'

'Laura?'

'If that's what she called herself. Now *shift*!'

Creed went with her, albeit reluctantly, his feet dragging. 'What about *him*?' he whined.

'He won't touch you. Not yet. Please, Joe, hurry.'

As they neared the door with its broken glass window, Creed pushed himself against the opposite wall, sliding his back along it, never taking his eyes off the jagged hole. Inside there was the same utter blackness he'd witnessed earlier, as though the darkness of the adjoining office had snuck out and swallowed its neighbour. Inch by inch he crept along the wall, Cally gripping his wrist and drawing him forward as if against a fast-flowing current.

'Come *on*!' she urged, and the desperation in her voice almost did the trick. Creed jerked himself off the wall and adopted the sprinter's start; he was locked into that pose by a roaring that came from the black hole opposite.

It was as if the room had belched.

The wind caught Creed and the girl and slammed them back against the corridor wall. Objects came crashing through – empty file books, pens, a shower of hornet-like paper clips, a waste bin – smallish objects that hit them like shrapnel, cutting and punching them, forcing them to protect their faces with their arms. The roar ceased, leaving them cowering against tattered wallpaper.

At first it seemed there was no noise; then they became aware of what sounded like a repeated sighing.

'I think they've exhausted themselves,' Cally said in a quiet voice.

The second roar came as abruptly as the first, but it was a thousand times louder and a thousand times worse. It was a brutal hurricane that spat its wrath at them, tearing at their skin, distorting their features, ripping at their clothes. An old Adler typewriter crashed against the wall only inches from Cally's head. Creed looked up to see the room's large desk appear from the black and jam against the doorframe with such a jolt that old plaster fell away from either side and the frame itself cracked and splintered. The door buckled when something else struck its base.

He closed his eyes against the wind and dust; hands tugged at him once more.

Cally's voice was feeble against the storm: '*. . . move, move, move . . .*'

Bent double, they staggered away from the heart of the mael-strom, the gale howling round the corridor after them, its intensity diffused a little. They choked on the dirt gathered by the tempest, wiping it from their eyes as they ran. Lengths of wallpaper, skinned from the walls, waved comic-strip arms at them as they passed.

The iron folding gate of the lift was open and they both fell through as though the cage itself might provide refuge from inclement weather. And it did. The storm stayed outside, whirlpooling round the liftshaft, dust motes and junk sailing in the currents. Cally slammed the outer door shut, then did the same with the inner door. Miraculously, with the closing of the doors, the wind outside abated.

All became quiet once more. Dust, abandoned by the wind, began to settle.

'Let's get the fuck out of here,' Creed suggested shakily. He sagged against the sturdy grillework of the cage.

Her voice was almost as unnerved as his. 'They're used up. We're going to be all right.'

'Yeah, you said that last time. D'you mind if we get while the going's good?'

She nodded and her finger was trembling when she pressed the G button.

The elevator dropped like a stone.

Creed wailed as he clutched at the bars behind him, his body lifting of its own accord so that he was on tiptoe, his stomach somewhere under his chin, his head, it seemed, left up there on the seventh floor. Cally was just as panicked: she threw her arms around his neck and clung to him as though he might provide some comfort. It flashed through his mind that her added weight would do him no good at all when they landed, but pushing her away meant letting go of the cage wall (how holding on to the bars would help him when the lift hit bottom he hadn't quite worked out). It further occurred to him (very fast, these thoughts, practically instant) that he should jump into the air a moment before the elevator touched ground; that way only his legs might get broken. But when to jump, how would he know? How many *clunks* had he heard so far as the cage bumped through each level? It was no good, he'd lost count, this was really it. *Oh Mother* . . .

The lift slowed, lurched, plummeted again, this time less hastily; machinery groaned and whined. It squ*eeee*led.

Creed and the girl collapsed to the floor as the elevator droned to an awkward but mercifully gradual stop. They had reached the ground floor.

Cally raised her head first. She looked around and saw daylight shining from the end of the hallway.

'Creed – Joe, we're safe. We're okay.' She shook his shoulder.

Creed took his hands away from his face and looked up. He gazed around him. 'We're on the ground,' he said.

'Yes. But come on, let's get out of here.'

'We're on the ground,' he said again, his mouth remaining open as if in awe.

'Come *on*,' she persisted. She got to her feet, then helped him up; they leaned against one another on rubbery legs. He had to assist her in opening the gates, but that was no problem; his instinct for survival was re-establishing itself by the second.

'We've got to get out of here,' he told her as if the idea was fresh.

She shook her head in despair, but said nothing.

Creed shot out of the lift and Cally raced after him. She had to chase him all the way back to his jeep.

23

As you might imagine, by now Joe Creed had had enough. If he'd passed a policeman on the way back to the jeep he'd have blurted out everything that had happened thus far, with no embellishment (hardly any needed), no lies, no underplaying and no exaggeration – the whole truth and nothing but. However, as the adage goes, there's never one around when you want one, and maybe that's as well in this instance: he'd have probably been locked up and put under sedation until a vacancy in the nearest mental hospital could be found. His appearance wouldn't have helped his case either: his clothes were filthy and unkempt (more unkempt than usual) and his hands and forehead were bleeding where glass had cut him.

On the whole, not a respectable sight, and gibberings about a sex-craved woman who could reshape her body into all manner of bizarre and fantastical things and rooms that were nothingness voids and an ugly man who'd kidnapped his ten-year-old son and a lift that had dropped like a stone but slowed at the last moment and another man who looked like Count Dracula, *no* not Christopher Lee but Nosferatu, you know, the vampire from the original German movie, and they'd nailed his cat over the door and . . . well, you can see, the police wouldn't have taken him too seriously. And, of course, it was doubtful whether the girl would back him up.

Cally rapped on the Suzuki's passenger window and he thought twice about leaning across and unlocking the door.

'You need me!' she shouted through the glass. Passers-by looked at her pityingly; one matronly lady told her not to waste her life on the 'shit-bag' (and this stranger didn't even *know* Creed).

He let Cally in. 'Joe, where are you going?' she asked immediately.

'To the nearest nick, where d'you think? I've had enough of this.'

'Don't do that. Drive home and let me talk to you. If you want to involve the police after that, I won't stop you.'

'You couldn't.'

'All right, I couldn't. All I ask is that you hear me out.'

'It's the same old line with you. Look where it's got me.'

'This one last time. Think of your son.'

'I am thinking of him. But what more can I do? I brought the shots, I gave them to that . . . that thing, that woman. Isn't that enough? What the hell do they want from me?'

'Drive home, Joe, and I'll do my best to explain. Any other way and you're going to lose.'

For at least half a minute he looked deep into her blue eyes. She seemed anxious, and more than a little scared. Was it for him though, was she really concerned for him and Sammy? As yet he had still not found out her role in all this. *As yet he'd found out nothing at all.*

'You'll tell me what's going on?'

'As much as I can.' She turned away from him. 'It's up to you whether or not you believe me.'

He frowned, but switched on the engine. 'It'd better make some kind of sense, Cally, otherwise I'm bringing in the police, the newspaper, the fucking Pope in Rome – anyone I can think of who might do some good. And if I think you're stringing me along, I'm turning you over to the Law. I'll tell 'em you were the one who took Sammy.' He tried to make all this sound mean and moody, but the bubbling hysteria just behind the words was hard to suppress. The strange thing was, Cally looked genuinely sorry for him.

She held his wrist for a moment. 'I'll do what I can,' she said. 'I promise you that.'

Creed turned the jeep out into the midday traffic and headed west.

Grin stood at the top of the stairway and let out a piteous yowl. Holding out a friendly hand towards the cat, Creed carefully climbed the stairs, muscles all over his body hurting with the effort.

'Hey, Grin, you okay, feller? It's been a rough coupla days for both of us. Let's have a look at you.'

The cat backed away several steps.

'Come on, it's me. I'll get the bastards who nailed your tail, don't worry. Nobody fucks with us, right?'

Grin came forward and took cautious sniffs at Creed's hand. The photographer sat down on the top step and settled the cat in his lap so that he could examine her injured tail. It was caked with dried blood and seemed to have developed a peculiar kink. 'I think you're okay, pal. You were never the handsomest of mogs anyway, so this won't make a whole lot of difference.' He stroked her fur and when Cally joined him on the stairs she noticed his eyes were watery.

'If they've done anything to Sam . . .' he said fiercely.

Grin left him, sensing his anger.

'I'll get you a drink,' Cally said.

'I could use one.' His rage was suddenly spent; his body sagged.

She stepped over him, going through to the kitchen and opening the booze cupboard. She poured him a large brandy. He followed and sat at the table. 'Seems like I've been through this scene already,' he said tonelessly.

She gave him the drink. 'Let's go into the bathroom where I can clean you up a bit.'

'I want you to talk.'

'I'll do that while I clean you.'

He took a sip of brandy. 'I need a cigarette,' he said. 'Not one of your doctored ones though.' Reaching into his breast pocket, he drew out a crushed roll-up. With difficulty he smoothed it into a smokable shape. He lit it and rose from the table, shrugging off his coat and taking the brandy glass with him into the hallway. Cally followed him into the bathroom.

'D'you mind? I gotta take a leak first.' He closed the door on her.

The cat watched her from the kitchen doorway and she returned its stare. Grin ducked back out of sight. Cally heard the toilet flush and the bathroom door opened again.

'I look a mess,' said Creed.

Cally nodded. 'No real harm done though.'

'You wanna bet.' He let her in, sitting down on the edge of the bath so that she could get to the basin.

She looked into the mirror and scowled at herself. 'I don't look too good myself.'

'Only dirt. I'm the walking wounded.'

She ran water over a flannel, then wiped his face. 'I think you'd better try yourself. You're filthy.' She filled the basin with warm water and offered him the soap. Creed dumped his half-smoked cigarette into the toilet bowl and took off his sweatshirt. He washed himself, then ran cold water over his face, holding the flannel against his eyes and forehead for long seconds.

'Do you have any iodine?' she asked.

He shook his head and winced as she touched one of the cuts with a dry towel. 'Probably some TCP in the cabinet there. Take it easy, will you?'

'Cotton wool?'

'No.'

'We'll make do with this.'

While Creed pulled on his sweatshirt again, Cally took the disinfectant from the bathroom cabinet and dampened a small section of towel with it. She dabbed at his cuts. 'Hold still, don't be such a baby,' she scolded.

He mumbled something she didn't catch and shifted his position on the bath as though uncomfortable. None of the wounds were deep, nor were there any glass fragments embedded. 'You'll live,' she assured him.

'I suppose I should be grateful you pulled me back from the brink.' He didn't look at all grateful. 'It was a long drop.'

'I'm glad I got there in time.'

His mouth was tight with resentment. 'I said I *suppose* I should be grateful. The fact is, you're involved in this. I don't know what you're up to, what you are to those weirdos, but I figure it's time to find out.' He held her arms, their bodies close in the narrow bathroom.

'I can only tell you some of it, Joe.'

'No, I want to know everything.'

She pulled away and walked from the room.

Creed caught up with her in the hallway and grabbed her by the shoulder, spinning her round. He clenched his fist and held it only inches from her face, the muscles of his arm quivering with tension. She appraised him coolly.

'Not the macho bit again,' she said.

He felt utterly drained once more, his spirits as well as his strength taking a sudden dive, his body sagging so that he almost collapsed against her. 'Please, Cally,' he said in a low, miserable voice. 'Help me. Please . . .'

She held on to him, her arms encircling his waist and hugging him close. He could smell her hair, feel the softness of her body against his own; he could sense her regret.

Cally took him by the hand and led him into the lounge. 'Sit down, Joe, and listen. Try not to interrupt . . .'

He opened his mouth to say something, but she put a hand to his lips. 'Just listen.'

Creed sat, feeling old and beaten, his anger still there, but contained by hopelessness. There was nothing more he could do: Sammy's life was in their hands. He watched Cally walk over to the window.

She gazed out, but saw nothing. How much could she tell him, how much would he believe? Did he accept what he'd witnessed that day, or did he believe he'd hallucinated, been drugged, been hypnotised – been duped? The cold light of day invariably produced its own logic. How to begin?

'You've upset them, Joe.'

'I think you told me that before. Who have I upset?' There wasn't much energy in his words.

'A certain group of people. One of them is the man you photographed at the cemetery.'

'The creep who looks like Nicholas Mallik?'

She continued to look out the window. 'He *is* Nicholas Mallik.'

'You know, I was afraid you were going to say that. I need the rest of that brandy.'

Now she turned. 'I'll get it for you.'

He waited there, too exhausted to move anyway. He ached in odd parts and his cuts stung with the disinfectant Cally had used. Even the bruise on his forehead, the one he'd got falling downstairs days ago, was throbbing again. But the worst was the confused state of his mind; that was the most wearying thing of all.

Cally returned and handed him the glass, which Creed held up to the light before taking a sip.

'It isn't laced with anything,' she promised.

He shrugged. 'At this stage, I don't give a monkey's. For all I know, you've had me dosed up for a coupla days. How else could what I've seen be explained?' He lifted the glass again and took a deeper swallow. 'Go ahead,' he insisted. 'I won't interrupt.'

'You believe me – about Mallik?'

'I said I won't interrupt.'

She sat on the edge of the sofa, at the opposite end to him. 'Nobody must know he's still alive.'

'Yeah, that's understandable. After all, he was supposed to have been hanged half a century ago. So what happened – they topped the wrong guy?'

She shook her head just once.

'Ah shit . . . I'm calling the police, Cally. I've had enough of this runaround.' He made as if to rise from the sofa, but she leaned across and placed a restraining hand on his arm.

'You said you'd listen.'

'You said you'd explain.'

'I'm trying to. It isn't easy.'

'Damn right. Try the truth.'

'Whatever I say you won't believe me.'

'That's possible. I don't like being taken for a fool.' He jerked his arm away from her. 'If I didn't need you to get Sammy back I'd kick the hell out of you right here and now. I want you to tell me who these people are and what they want from me.'

Hesitation, a closing of her eyes, a decision made. She looked straight at him. 'They call themselves the Fallen . . .'

'Oh Christ, I knew it!' He banged the sofa with his hand. 'Some crazy religious sect! What are they? Devil-worshippers? Scientologists? Seventh-Day Adventists? Moonies? Trekkies? Tell me what they are?'

'The Fallen Angels.'

'The Fallen . . . ? Don't *do* this to me.' He drained the glass and banged it down on the coffee table in front of him. 'I knew this guy

Mallik was involved with that devil-loving maniac Aleister Crowley when he was alive, but Fallen Angels? What'd he do – start a new cult when he fell out with Crowley? Is it still going strong, is . . . my God, they mutilated children! Sammy –'

'Calm down, Joe,' Cally snapped. 'Just calm down and listen to me. Your son is okay. These people are old –'

'That woman I saw today wasn't old.'

'Laura?' Cally offered no other comment. Instead she reached over and touched Creed's forehead. 'You're so tired, Joe.'

He slapped her hand away and leapt to his feet. 'Don't start with that. You knocked me out last night with that shit, so don't try it again.'

'You were exhausted.'

'Yeah, you convinced me of that.' He backed away to the other side of the room. 'No more of it, don't even look at me! All I want you to do is tell me about these Fallen fucking Angels.'

'All right.' She raised a placating hand. 'But to understand what I'm about to tell you, you have to accept what *they* believe.'

'And what exactly is that?'

'The interrelation of all things spiritual and physical.' She paused, waiting for a reaction. Creed didn't oblige, but she proceeded as if he had raised an objection. 'Look, our normal senses don't permit us to perceive certain things, certain forces. We can't see ultra-violet light, for instance, but we now have instruments that reveal it to us. It's the same with extreme sound frequencies. Just because we don't see or hear these things, it doesn't mean they don't exist. Unfortunately, we don't have the scientific means to prove different levels of existence at present.' She leaned even further forward in the seat as though to emphasise the point. 'Yet millions believe in a Supreme but incorporeal Being they call their God.'

He could hardly disagree with that.

'So why not spiritual sub-beings?'

He raised his eyebrows.

'Demons,' she said.

A low groan from Creed.

'Hear me out,' she said quickly. 'Open your mind and listen to me. Remember what I told you – this is what *they* believe.'

He made a resigned gesture for her to continue.

'There are all kinds of such beings – demons, devils, evil spirits, call them what you will. Some are nothing more than ethereal vapours, others are more powerful, more evident. And there are many, *many* divisions, but I won't go into that – I know I'm straining credibility enough as far as you're concerned. But I will say these divisions are based on the hierarchies of angels; or to be more specific, the hierarchies of the Fallen Angels.'

It was at that point that Creed returned to his seat.

'The mediaeval and Renaissance Europeans developed the conjuring of demons to a fine art – probably because they assumed the Church itself would bail them out if they got in too deep, or the powers they unleashed got beyond their control. Unfortunately, the Church of those times tended to be as corrupt as they were themselves and left them helpless; what followed was famine, pestilence, disease, wars. In a word, destruction.'

The phone outside the room rang, but Creed made no move to answer it; another two rings, then the answerphone in the office downstairs picked it up.

'Nicholas Mallik knew how to control those unearthly powers,' Cally went on. 'It was a secret that he revealed to Aleister Crowley in Paris in the 1920s.'

At last Creed spoke. 'Is that when they fell out?'

'You know about that?'

'I know they fell out.'

'It was a little more than that. Crowley and Mallik took over a small hotel on the Left Bank for a weekend. They emptied a large room at the top of the building of furniture, ornaments, anything that could be moved, and locked themselves in. MacAleister, Crowley's son and principal disciple, was with them, while the others of their cult remained downstairs, forbidden to enter the room until the following day, no matter what they heard.

'They heard plenty, but obeyed their orders. When morning came, nobody in that room upstairs would answer their calls, so they were forced to break in. They found Crowley's son dead, but with no external marks on his body, and Crowley himself a gibbering wreck lying naked on the floor. There was no sign of Nicholas Mallik.

'Aleister Crowley spent four months in an asylum after that and he was never the same man again. And he always refused to speak of what had happened that night.'

'And Mallik? What happened to him?'

'He turned up in London a year later. He and Crowley never met again, and Mallik also declined to tell anyone what had happened in Paris.'

The phone rang and once more Creed left it to the answerphone.

'As you were aware of his association with Aleister Crowley, can I also assume you know something of Mallik's activities in London?'

'I know he and his happy little troupe murdered and dismembered people – mostly kids. I also know he was caught and hanged in 1939. But now you're telling me different, you're telling me he wasn't hanged at all, that he's still walking around as large as life and twice as ugly. What d'you take me for, Cally? A complete fool?' He gave a snort of disgust. 'Even if he did by some miracle escape the gallows and the newspapers at the time were persuaded to print lies, or had been duped themselves, even if the wrong man had been arrested – a double who didn't even speak up with a noose around his neck – even if any of those things were true, Mallik would be too old to wipe his own arse by now, let alone commit indecent acts in cemeteries or run around parks in the dead of night. The man I saw wasn't that old.'

'Oh, but he is. And he had friends in high places in those days.'

'High enough to prevent his execution? Even the King couldn't have arranged the release of the Beast of Belgravia. You must think I'm stupid.'

'You have to believe me – he and his kind have incredible powers.'

'They're great illusionists.'

There, Creed's own logic was already suggesting he hadn't seen what he'd seen.

'They're much more than that. They can change shape, Joe. They can become grotesque things, they can grow in size, they can shrink themselves. They can create phantoms from menstrual blood, or from semen . . .'

She appeared not to notice that Creed had suddenly paled (paled even more, that is).

'. . . These people can sap your will, weaken your spirit, by drawing off your aura . . .'

Breathing, Creed realised. *Breathing his aura, weakening his spirit. That was what the woman, Laura, had been doing.* Wait a minute! He was falling for it. Like some bloody simpleton he was being drawn in. But the room and the black nothingness that had been inside it . . . the wind that had torn through the doorway like a gale force, strong enough to lift a desk . . . the lift that had plummeted and stopped as though it had a mind of its own . . . Incredible, but it had happened. It *had* happened, hadn't it?

'. . . They're old, Joe, and not so strong any more. Now you've roused them, and I think they're suddenly enjoying themselves once again. After so much time, so many years, they're starting to revive . . . But they'll grow weary of it soon, and then perhaps frustration will make them even more dangerous.'

'Was Lily Neverless one of them?' Creed gripped the edge of the armchair. 'Was she part of the cult? Is that what this is all about? Are they frightened I'm going to expose them as some satanic group who go about performing obscene ceremonies over the graves of their departed? If it hadn't got out of hand, it would be laughable. You hear me, Cally? A bloody big fat joke!' Something nagged at the back of his mind. 'What are they? A hyped-up bunch of extremist Freemasons? Or are they *really* devil-worshippers who dance naked around fires in the dead of night, calling on Old Nick to do their dirty deeds for them? You know, you nearly had me . . . wait, what was it you said last night just before I crashed out?' It came back to him in a rush. 'You told me you were Lily's granddaughter! Oh boy, that's it, that's the connection.'

Her voice was steady, unlike his. 'You mustn't meddle any more.'

The doorbell sounded and Cally quickly stood. 'Who is it?' she said.

'How the hell should I know? Ignore it – they'll soon go away.'

Someone pounded on the door. The bell rang again. A familiar voice called Samuel's name from the street below.

'Oh no . . .' said Creed.

'Who is it?' Cally repeated.

Creed closed his eyes for a moment. 'It's my ex-wife the hellhag. Sammy's mother.'

24

■

E nter Evelyn.
Creed's plan was to stay quiet until his ex grew tired of
ringing the bell and beating the knocker and stormed off to terrorise
some other poor sap. But life is never that accommodating, is it?

He heard a key turning in the latch downstairs, heard the door
opening, footsteps inside. Then: '*Saammuell!*'

The door slammed shut and those footsteps stomped the stairs.

Creed clasped a hand to his eyes as though a migraine had struck.
Evelyn had *two* spare keys, one she'd given to Sammy, the other
she'd kept for herself – no, probably, she had half-a-dozen to hand
out to friends and relations.

Cally was alarmed.

He pushed himself up and went to the door in time to meet Evelyn
as she arrived at the top of the stairs. She looked harassed, a little
strained around the eyes and the neck but, he had to admit to himself
– and despite himself – she still looked pretty good. If it wasn't for
her acid tongue and sour nature she'd still be eminently humpable.

'Where is he?' she demanded without pausing to catch her breath.

'Who?' It was the best he could do.

She raised her eyes heavenwards and pushed by him. She came to a halt when she saw Cally in the lounge; before turning back to Creed she gave her a cool, hard once-over. 'Sorry to interrupt your bimbo-time, but I've come to take Samuel home. I don't know what I was thinking of letting him come here in the first place. God knows what he's seen going on.' Her glare darted towards dark-blonde and denimed Cally as if *she* were a prime example of what had been going on.

'Uh, Sammy's not here.' Creed half grinned and did his utmost to keep his gaze perfectly straight and entirely on Evelyn.

'Why are you staring like a zombie? Are you on something? Good God, at this time of day. I knew I hadn't come a moment too soon.'

'Don't be silly, Ev—'

'And who's this?' She flicked her head in Cally's direction. 'No, don't tell me, I really don't want to know. All I want is my son presented to me right here and now. Watch my lips, Joe – right *here* and *now.*'

'I'll let myself out,' said Cally, moving towards the door.

'*No!* I mean – no. We still have to talk.' Creed blocked her path.

'I'm waiting,' Evelyn said ominously.

The phone rang.

'I gotta answer the phone.' Creed made as if to leave the room.

'Stay,' Evelyn told him. 'This is more important. One more time now before I really get cross: Where is Samuel?'

The ringing was silenced by the answerphone.

'Excuse me,' said Cally as she slid past Creed.

'No, wait.' He caught her by the arm.

'*Joseph!*' Evelyn all but stamped her foot.

'I'll do what I can and call you later.' Cally slipped from his grasp and disappeared down the stairs.

'Cally!' Creed moved to go after, but now his own arm was caught. Evelyn's fingers were like a vice.

'I'm losing patience,' she warned in an even but deadly voice.

Cally had reached the frontdoor and she glanced back up at him before opening it. 'Stay by the phone,' she said, and then she was gone, the door closing quietly behind her.

Creed opened his mouth to call her back, but clamped it shut when he felt his own arm squeezed even harder. He looked deep into his ex-wife's dark, blazing, harridan eyes and realised he had two choices: he could either faint or tell lies. Fainting, he decided, would only provide brief respite and ultimately would dump him in stormier waters anyway – *what made you faint, what have you done, what's happened to Samuel?* No, telling lies was much easier.

'Sammy's gone on a school trip,' he said.

That stymied her. Momentarily, that is. She released his arm. 'A school trip,' she repeated slowly. 'But he's not at school. He's here with you.'

'Ah, no. Not *that* school, not *his* school.' *Oh shit shit shit, why the hell had he said that?* 'Uh, let's sit down? Would you like a cup of tea? You've had a long journey, Evelyn, you must be dry. How about a G and T? Bet you could use one.'

'Cut the crap. What are you talking about, a school trip?'

'Boy, I'm bushed, y'know? Looking after a ten-year-old takes it out of you.'

'What would you know about it? You've only had a couple of days. So what school did he go with and what time is he getting back?'

'Well, not tonight,' he said quickly. 'Oh no, not tonight. Overnight stay, y'see. He was really looking forward to it.'

'Samuel? Looking forward to something like that? I don't believe you.'

'You'd be surprised how he's changed the last coupla days. You know, come out of himself. Let's sit down, eh?'

She allowed herself to be led back into the lounge where Creed almost pushed her into the armchair. 'Frankly, you look as if you need to sit down,' she said. 'What on earth have you been up to? No, please, I don't want to hear about your life. I made that clear years ago.'

He lowered himself on to the sofa. Evelyn's long deep-red hair framed a face that was once pretty, but which had now matured to handsome, if somewhat shrewish. Permanent tenseness had also withered her neck slightly, creating ridges that no cream would ever erase. The long coat and skirt she wore were of a sombre maroon, as were her knee-length boots. Either her breasts had shrunk, he thought, or she had taken to wearing bras that restrained rather than uplifted; her beige blouse hardly swelled at the appropriate places. He swiftly got his mind back on the problem at hand.

'Well, you're looking –'

'I told you, cut the crap. What school?'

'It's, uh, not actually a school. I mean, it's a scout troop from a local school. The Boy Scouts.'

'The Boy Scouts.' It came as a drone. 'Samuel has joined the Boy Scouts? My Samuel?'

'Not actually joined. I thought he might like to try it, just for one day. Er, one night too. Camping, and all that. Maybe a few days and nights depending on how he gets on.'

'And he *agreed*?'

'Couldn't wait.'

She regarded him suspiciously. 'What the hell do *you* know about Boy Scouts and local schools?'

'Oh no, the Scouts from the school are round here all the time, collecting jumble for charity, odd jobs for a few bob. Nice bunch of kids.'

'And exactly what did Samuel wear for this great outdoor adventure? Surely to God you didn't send him off in his school uniform.'

'Are you kidding? And let him catch his death of cold? No way. I bought him a whole new outfit – boots, thick corduroys, woollen shirt, anorak. He looked the part, I can tell you.' Creed gave a shake of his head and smiled at the centre of the room as though his son were standing there all togged up and raring to go. 'I've never seen him so keen.'

'Samuel?'

He nodded. 'Yeah. I thought some time in the open air and getting physical might do him good.'

'So where were they off to? In which wilderness have they pitched their tents? Not too far out of town, I hope.'

'Where? Where? Epping Forest. Not far at all.'

'What's the school?'

'You know the one. Two blocks away.' Oh shit, he'd passed it enough times. 'St . . . St Andrew's. I'm pretty pleased with the idea, actually.'

She studied him for a full thirty seconds before saying anything more. Then: 'Well, I suppose I could take his other clothes home and give them a scrub. Get them for me, will you, Joe?'

'Uh. Uh, all taken care of. Took them off to the cleaners this morning on my way back from dropping him off. He made me promise to give you a call, incidentally, tell you how much fun he's having. Misses you, of course.'

'Maybe I should go out and see him at the campsite; he probably thinks I'm still mad at him. I could get a taxi easily enough, or perhaps you'd care to drive me. It's been a long time since we took a drive together.'

For one brief, but not very compelling moment, Creed was tempted to make a clean breast of everything, to confess that their son had been kidnapped by crazies who worshipped demons and who could hypnotise you so you saw impossible things and who could frighten you so much your heart hurt your throat when you swallowed; he could have told Evelyn the truth, but that would have meant – leaving aside his own castration – hysterics, accusations, the police, and probably the worst for their son. It wasn't worth the risk; nor the pain.

'I don't think that'd be a good idea. Imagine how he'd feel in front of the other kids if Mummy and Daddy showed up to see how their little precious was coping. He'd die.' Creed regretted adding the last remark.

She thought on it. 'Perhaps you're right,' she reluctantly agreed. 'I'd hate the other boys to think he was a sissy. I've missed him so much, though. I didn't intend to, I thought a few days without him would give me a break – God knows I needed one. But he's my son and he's all I've got.'

At that moment she looked so forlorn and lonely that Creed was almost tempted to hug her, almost tempted to pat her back sympathetically, *almost* tempted to bed her right there and then. She was still a good-looking woman, slack-breasted or not.

Evelyn caught his look and said, 'Don't even think about it.' She rose from the armchair, brisk and bitch-faced once more. 'I want Samuel home by tomorrow evening, Boy Scouts or not. Camping in cold weather like this will bring on his bronchitis and I don't relish the prospect of waiting hand and foot on an invalid for the next few weeks. It was a bad move letting him come here in the first place – God only knows what bad habits he's already picked up.'

'You sent him here, Evelyn.'

'Yes, you're absolutely right – it was the last place he wanted to come to. I suppose I'm allowed one mistake though. Pick him up tomorrow and bring him straight home.'

If he's still . . . all right. It was a thought he didn't care to voice.

'Are you okay? You just swayed as if you were about to faint.' Her expression was one of curiosity, not concern.

'Tired, that's all. Too many late hours standing on cold pavements.'

'You look as if someone you snapped gave you more than you bargained for. What happened – you get thrown through a window? And that bruise on your forehead!' She seemed annoyed more than anything else. 'Isn't it time you considered a change in career? Something more adult, maybe? To be frank, you're not wearing too well.'

'Yeah, I think about it every day. It'd be nice to be an accountant. Or I could sell double-glazing, how 'bout that? You always wanted something respectable for me, didn't you, Evelyn?'

'I wanted you to assume some responsibility, that was all. The trouble was – and still is – you could never think beyond what was good for Joseph Creed.'

'That isn't true.'

'Isn't it? Where were all the sacrifices you're supposed to make for your kid? Ask yourself when you ever let Samuel's wellbeing – or mine, for that matter – interfere with your lifestyle.'

'I brought home the bread.'

She laughed, but she might as well have slapped his face. 'You really think that that was all there was to it? My God, no wonder we didn't last long. Did you ever take Samuel to the park to play, or to show him the ducks when he was a toddler? When did you ever sit down with him and read him stories? When did you ever wipe his little bottom, for Christ's sake? That's what being a father is about – those small things, some unpleasant, but mostly delightful. Tiny little moments that show you care.'

'I'm not in the mood for this, Evelyn.'

'When did you ever do those things for me?'

'Wipe your arse?'

'You *know* what I mean. You know exactly what I'm talking about, you uncaring bastard.'

'I did lots.'

'Make a list one day. See if you can fill the back of a postage stamp.'

He ran a hand through his hair and scowled frustratedly at the floor. 'Evelyn, I got things to do.'

'Of course you have. When didn't you?' She strode to the door. 'I've half a mind to go and fetch Samuel now, just so that he doesn't have further contact with you for a while; but no, I won't embarrass him in front of his new friends. I want him home tomorrow though, is that understood? I'll allow him one more day away from his proper school, then it's back –'

'He told me he's been suspended for a week, Evelyn.'

She stopped in the doorway and wheeled round. 'I warned him not to tell you that. Oh, I can see you're as thick as thieves already. Well I'm not surprised, not surprised at all, considering you both lie, steal and bully. Two of a kind made from the same mould. I can promise you this: Samuel is going to change. No way is he going to grow up like his father. Do you understand me? No bloody way.'

He heard the frontdoor being opened followed by muffled voices. Evelyn's voice reigned terror up the stairway once more. *'There's another bimbo on the doorstep. Have you got the energy?'*

The door slammed.

25

Enter Prunella this time, looking nothing like a bimbo.

'Joe, can I come up?'

'What makes you think I have a say in it?' He went through to the kitchen and opened the booze cupboard, ignoring the brandy bottle that Cally had left on the table.

'Joe?'

'In here looking for the hemlock.'

'Bad day?' She stopped at the threshold as if too timid to enter.

'So far. And there's every chance it's gonna get worse. D'you want to join me?' He held up a tumbler.

'Hemlock?'

'Or whiskey. Gin if you want.'

'No, I don't think so. Why haven't you returned my calls?'

'You've been ringing me?'

'For the past couple of hours. I've left messages on your answerphone. Freddy Squires has been trying to get hold of you, too.'

'Any particular reason?' He poured a stiff measure of Bushmills.

'Freddy? None other than you haven't reported in today and he's got an assignment lined up.'

'I'm not a staffy. I don't have to "report" in.'

'That's fine with me, Joe. It's Freddy who needs reminding. Have you been in an accident of some kind?' She wandered into the kitchen, her eyes wide at his condition. 'Every time I see you, you look worse.'

Creed waved a dismissive hand. 'You wouldn't believe me if I told you. You got a cigarette on you?'

She shook her head. 'I don't smoke.'

'No, you wouldn't.' He reached for his tobacco tin and makings and took them, along with the whiskey, to the table. 'So are you here to add to my woes?'

'I'm sorry if you've got problems, Joe.'

He looked at her in surprise. Judas, she'd said that as if she'd really meant it.

Prunella took a seat opposite him. 'Was that woman who just left one of them?'

'The red-haired shrew? Yeah, she's one of them, but the least of them.' He ran the rolled cigarette paper along the tip of his tongue, then sealed the tobacco inside. 'Why are you here, Prunella?'

'We appear to have lost our star diarist.'

'Blythe?'

'He's the only one we've got. Unfortunately our ulcerated editor doesn't like the idea that he's been mislaid. Seriously though, it's not like Antony to go off without letting anyone know where. He usually rings in three or four times a day with items or to check what's happening.'

'What makes you think I know where he is?'

'We thought you might have passed him on your rounds. Besides, the last thing he was looking into had something to do with Lily Neverless, and as you were at the funeral the other . . . day . . . Joe, is something wrong? Why are you staring at me like that? We just thought – obviously very stupidly – that you might be working on something together. As I'm general dogsbody, I was nominated to try and contact either Antony or you. I drew a total blank on Antony, so when you wouldn't return my calls I jumped in a cab and came over. I dropped by Antony's place first,' she hastened to add, then blushed for some reason. (If Creed hadn't been so preoccupied he might have realised that Prunella had relished the thought of stepping inside his 'den of iniquity'. They'll surprise you every time, these quiet ones.)

'What was he looking into exactly?'

She was puzzled by the gravity of Creed's tone. 'Something to do with Lily Neverless' will. Apparently he asked our own legal department to find out who her solicitors were.'

'And did they?'

'Yes, I rang the solicitors and they told me they'd had an enquiry about their late client's estate from Antony this morning. Quite honestly, I don't know what all the fuss is about. He'll turn up when he feels like it.'

Sure he will. Prunella was right – why the fuss just because Blythe had gone walkabout? So what if he did usually call in? He was probably lying under a table somewhere dozing the afternoon away after one champagne cocktail too many. Okay, so perhaps he wasn't known as a big drinker, but what the hell? For once he'd let what hair he had down. Maybe he was even lying somewhere else with a male or female of his choice. Who knows? Who cares?

Prunella interrupted his thoughts. 'I don't think that stuff is doing you any good.'

'Hmn?'

'The Scotch. You keep losing colour.'

'It's whiskey, and it's doing me a power of good. When it hits my gut it feels real – about the only thing that does today.'

'Are you in trouble, Joe? Is there anything I can do to help?'

He could have laughed, but the mood wasn't on him.

'Will you go to bed with me, Prunella?'

He couldn't believe he'd said it, but he had. What was *wrong* with him? His son was in terrible danger and here he was as horny as a goat. And it wasn't only with Prunella: he had wanted to get it on with Evelyn – Evelyn the Untouchable, for Christ's sake! Not just those two, either. When Cally had bathed his wounds in the bathroom he'd become aroused, only the combination of exhaustion, fear and anger quelling the uprising. Of course it wasn't unusual for him to get lechy in the company of an attractive or semi-attractive female, but under these dire circumstances? What *was* wrong with him?

Then he understood, for (and not for the first time in the last couple of hours or so) a vision flashed into his mind. It was of the woman, Laura, kneeling before him, clothes disarrayed, her body ripe and lush, her hands moving erotically over herself. He couldn't shake it; the image kept returning. As horrifically bizarre as it had turned out (and maybe because it was also so *indecently* bizarre) it was the most sexually intoxicating experience he'd ever had. At the time and in retrospect. Especially, it seemed, in retrospect. Christ, what *was* wrong with him?

His throat was dry. 'Prunella, I . . . please?'

Whatever he was giving off, whatever frisson he had aroused between them, it was obviously not ineffective. She didn't appear shocked, nor did she give him a definite no. 'I came over to find out about Antony,' she said, looking down at her lap.

'You didn't need to do that. You wanted to see me, didn't you?' Oh boy, the old ramrod was threatening to lift the table. How could you, you bastard? How could you get it on at a time like this? *White thighs, milky smooth, long tapering fingers delicately touching, beautifully curved breasts so enticing . . .* He closed his eyes, but the mental picture only became sharper.

A redness flushed her neck. 'You know I like you, Joe . . .'

He swallowed. 'I like you too, Prunella.' *Deep red lips, glistening in the gloomy light, nipples taut and pink, so erect, so thrusting, cold, marble flesh spread on the floor before him . . .*

'You did say you'd share the champagne with me . . .'

'I did promise that, didn't I?' Champagne? Where was the champagne Blythe had awarded him? Probably still in the back of the jeep.

She drew in a shallow breath, her small lips parting. There was a heaviness about her eyes. 'I do like you, Joe,' she repeated.

Other images tumbling inside his head. The terrible phlegmy thing that had collapsed over him, the tiny-headed phantoms skiting about the room, the darkness that contained nothing at all, the storm, the hurricane that had exploded from the room . . . *her white hands feeling herself, reaching into the soft hair between her thighs, spreading her wetness on him . . .*

'Laur – Prunella . . .'

'Yes, Joe.'

A question, or acquiescence? 'Let's –'

'Yes, Joe.'

Creed rose from the table, leaving the unlit cigarette lying there, and walked – hobbled – around to her. His hand was shaky when he held her cheek and tilted her face towards him. The tension between them was so tightly sensuous that the very air seemed charged. He leaned forward and kissed her pale prim lips . . .

. . . deep red, full lips . . .

Prunella responded, her arms reaching around his neck, drawing him down so that their mouths were hard against each other's. He felt her tongue dart between his lips, then retreat so that his own had to give chase . . .

. . . firm breasts, hips so voluptuously curved, legs so superbly long . . .

He brought her to her feet, the chair scraping back, their lips never losing touch, their bodies suddenly clenched together so that she felt his hardness, his huge incredible bursting hardness, against her stomach, and her fingers descended his spine so that she could hug him even tighter, pull him even closer, press her hips against him with firmer pressure.

His hand explored, found the small mound of one breast under her coat, ventured further, lifting the jumper she wore, tugging at the skirt beneath, feeling soft skin . . .

. . . lush flesh, so firm yet so soft . . .

'The bedroom . . .' he managed to gasp between frantic kisses.

She moved with him, but they only got as far as the hallway. He groaned aloud when he lifted her long pleated skirt and found instant access to Prunella's naked thighs . . .

. . . white thighs white thighs white thighs . . .

. . . for she was wearing – Prunella, this demure, prim and proper Sloane-type – stockings and suspenders. Creed sank delightedly to his knees so that he could see what he felt, kiss what he saw. A shudder ran through Prunella as his tongue moistened her skin. She slipped off her coat and rested against the wall while Creed busied himself beneath her skirt. She felt the probing of his tongue through the flimsy fabric of her panties and was so glad that that very morning, and for no apparent reason, she had decided to wear her newest La Perla (how had she known, how *had* she known?). She squirmed at the delicate touch and even the wall at her back felt sensuous. Oh Joe, I know you're a swine, everyone says you are, and I know you don't honestly give a damn about me and you'd screw any female who has two legs and two breasts, but I don't care, just do it to me, just do it to me . . .

Her knees were giving way and she was sinking down the wall, and when he slid the silky underwear down her legs she almost collapsed completely.

He let her come to him, encircling her waist with one arm and easing her passage to the floor; then she was lying beside him and his free hand had slipped the panties over her ankles so that she was free, naked, and open to him. He ducked his head again and the tip of his tongue resumed its exploration, this time with no barrier in the way. The hair between her legs was less dense, her skin less white and less rounded . . .

. . . *than Laura's* . . .

. . . but it was glorious nonetheless and Creed buried himself in her so that Prunella cried out and dug her fingers into his shoulders and moved against him and clenched his head with her thighs and pleaded that he shouldn't stop, he mustn't stop . . .

But he needed more than just that. Creed raised his head, ignoring her moan of disappointment and pushing at her clothing, exposing her belly and then her breasts, loving the sight of those breasts as small as they were under their thin lacy wrapping. He groped behind her, found the catch and unfastened it so that the bra loosened enough to be pulled aside. His lips smothered the tiny nipples . . .

. . . *those big, taut nipples, so hard and so hot* . . .

. . . drawing on each one in turn so that they stood proud and eventually firm.

Prunella fumbled at his jeans, struggling for desperate seconds to press the stud button through its eye, the expansion of his own body making it more difficult; but soon it was free and the zip was sliding down so easily, and quickly he was in her hands, warm and soft-hard, and seemingly pulsating with urgent demand.

It was Creed's turn to shudder and it ran through him in a warm wave. Now he was thinking of Prunella and nobody else; it was her body beneath his own and her body alone that filled his mind.

'Oh yes, Joe, please . . .'

Please? Please what? Did she think he was going to stop? Did she really imagine she had to plead with him? He fell upon her and her legs spread around him. Although she was wet, she was not that easy to enter. The initial thrust caused a little shriek from her and he withdrew slightly before making his way more gently, passing the point of resistance more steadily so that the rest of the passage was smooth and easy. She gasped, gave another little shriek; but this was one of delight. Her hands clasped his bare buttocks and pulled him in further. Creed sucked on her neck and she tried to twist away (Prunella was still prim enough not to want *those* kind of bruises visible the next day). The tweed of her rumpled skirt scratched and tickled his stomach and upper legs, adding another, albeit slight, element of joy to the proceedings.

He felt the warm bubbling begin deep inside his loins, a frenzy looking for release, and his motion became more languid, more stretched, and more powerful.

'No,' she said, 'not yet. Please not yet, Joe.' Her limbs tensed solid.

'Babe . . .' His turn to plead.

'Wait,' she insisted. 'This way, this way . . .'

What the hell was she doing? Hey no, she was pulling away, turning over.

'Prunella . . . ?'

'This 'ay . . .' She was having trouble speaking. Prunella crouched on elbows and knees, offering herself to him again.

He went in from behind with no problem at all, hoping he hadn't misunderstood and was taking the right route – anal sex wasn't his thing at all.

'Bedroom,' she murmured. ''ere's bedroom?'

''own a hall,' he replied, having difficulty with words himself now.

She began to crawl and he almost lost her. He quickly shuffled forward on his knees to keep up. Daft as he felt, he wasn't going to spoil the fun at this stage. Besides, who could see him? Grin, solemnly watching as they passed by the lounge, didn't count.

He fondled her pendent breasts on the way, resisting the urge to pull down on the left one for direction as they reached the bedroom door.

'Through . . . there . . .' he managed to say, almost out of breath.

They crawled in, Creed crouched over her, Prunella taking most of his weight. They made it to the bed and her upper body sprawled over it; she bit the duvet as though to muffle her own cries. It was easier for him now and he moved backwards and forwards in regular rhythm.

'That's *so* good,' she sighed.

As his hands massaged her back, then her buttocks and the back of her thighs, he mentally agreed with her: it was *soooo* good!

'Wait!'

He groaned.

'This way, Joe, this way.'

She dragged herself on to the bed.

'Prunella . . .' he complained.

But her legs were apart and she was waiting for him again, and she was so different, so alluring as she rested on one elbow, her hair tangled down over her face, a sleepy kind of lust in her eyes, her lips no longer prim but pouting and shiny, her breasts revealed, exquisite rather than small, and . . . and . . .

He lunged at her and was inside without even aiming. Her legs rose around him and he was racing to his climax and she was in the race with him and they hadn't far to go and she was squealing in his ear and they were in perfect time and he was squealing too and everything was flowing . . .

And suddenly in his mind it was the woman, Laura, he was spilling himself into . . . and then it was Cally . . .

And finally, when he was almost through, it was Prunella once more.

26

They made love twice more after that – if that's the right term.
'Went at each other' might be more appropriate, for there was
no finesse and certainly no fondness in these mutual acts of
self-gratification. They followed on in quick succession (much to
Creed's amazement) and without diminishing vigour (much to Creed's
and Prunella's amazement); there was very little dignity to the
proceedings. Creed wondered at himself and it was the second
coming, if you'll pardon that expression, that he realised the stimulant
was not the woman on the bed with him (although Prunella certainly
played her part) but rather the bizarre episode in the disused office
earlier in the day. To be more precise, the memory of Laura's
tantalisingly sexual display and the subsequent interrupted but erotic
coupling; even the horror that followed immediately after – the slimy
smothering by that membranous substance, which he'd had to tear
and step through to the other side (could it be the ultimate rupturing
of the maiden's hymen by the entire male form as the excessive and
unified penis? Dr Ruth might know) to escape suffocation – had
added a perverse yet undeniably thrilling (in retrospect, of course)

dimension to the carnality of it all. What had happened up there on the seventh floor had left lingering sexual images in his mind; the terror had not been forgotten, but oddly was less accessible to his thoughts than the dubious pleasure.

Finally, thoroughly depleted, they lay naked on the bed, Prunella snuggling her head under his chin, one hand resting on his hip. She was thin and small, her body like a nymphet's and surprisingly pleasing in the fading light.

It was then that Creed told her everything – well, almost everything; he left out the bit about demons, and vampires, phantoms, office tornadoes, black voids, etc., as any sane person (as any person wanting to be considered sane) would. So what was left? Plenty. Threats, violence, kidnapping; enough to leave Prunella aghast and anxious. Mentioning the man who should be dead didn't improve her disposition.

Her hand, which before had strayed occasionally to tinker with his wearied genitals, became affixed to his hip, its grip tightening as the story progressed. When he had finished, her reaction was fairly predictable. 'You've got to tell the police.'

'I can't do that.'

'It's the only thing you can do.'

'If it was your son would you take the risk?'

She paused before saying, 'Yes.'

'I've been warned not to.'

'Well they would do that, wouldn't they? Joe, what do you expect to do on your own? What can you do? You've already given them what they wanted and yet they still haven't returned Sammy to you.'

'Cally will be in touch.'

'How do you know that? They might just be giving themselves time.'

'For what?'

Kill the boy and teach Creed a lesson, then disappear. She didn't say that to him. 'Organise a ransom demand?'

'I don't think they take me for an eccentric millionaire.'

'All right. Perhaps they'll hold Sammy as a permanent threat to keep you quiet.'

'You mean just keep him? For ever? That's crazy.'

222

'According to you they're crazy people.' She looked up from beneath his chin. 'Tell me more about this girl Cally.'

'I've told you all I know.'

'Yes, she's Lily Neverless' granddaughter and somehow she's involved with this sect. But why is she helping you? If that really *is* what she's doing.'

'She might not be involved in that way – I mean, not as a cult member. Maybe because of her grandmother she feels some kind of loyalty towards them.'

'What loyalty could she have towards someone who's supposed to be dead? I'm talking about Nicholas Mallik, not granny. Then again, how can you really believe this person is still alive? You've read those old newspaper reports of the hanging yourself, so how could Mallik be around still to terrorise you? It's not credible.'

'Who the hell knows what's credible? Look, a war was beginning, so maybe the government, the War Office – I don't fucking know who or what – maybe they realised they needed someone like Mallik. He was a foreigner, wasn't he? Could be he had valuable information about the other side. Or they wanted to use him as a spy for England. He had important connections, we know that. But they couldn't pardon him, for Christ's sake, not with the crimes he'd committed – the public would have gone wild, war or no war.'

Creed sat up in bed, excited by his own reasoning. 'Maybe it was better that everyone thought Mallik was dead – what better cover for a spy. That's it! It's gotta be it.'

'You're getting carried away, Joe. What you're suggesting isn't possible.'

'Isn't it? You're a journalist, you know the score. Would you trust a politician, let alone a government, who knew its country was about to enter one of the bloodiest wars in history? They'd use any means and anyone to get an edge. It makes sense, it makes perfect sense. That's the only possible way Mallik could have escaped the noose.' By now Creed was elated with his own theory, even though it hardly helped his cause.

'It's too far-fetched,' was Prunella's view.

'But not that unbelievable. Come on, think about it. The big one's coming, the war to end all wars. Hitler's might is on the move, storming through Europe, heading our way. We know we're in deep shit. We're not ready – we don't have the weapons, we don't have the trained manpower. So any advantage we can rake up, no matter what, is something we're gonna use. It has to be the answer, don't you see? Whatever else Nicholas Mallik might have been, he could still be useful to our side in some way. That's why he was spared. He was more useful alive than dead no matter what public expectations demanded. News of his execution lasted one day, didn't it? There was nothing else in those copies you gave me.'

'I couldn't find any more.'

'Exactly. It was totally forgotten. The authorities wanted it that way. And now he's turned up again and that's an embarrassment for all concerned.'

'After all these years? What does it matter?'

'It's another example of devious government – doesn't matter how far it goes back and who was in power at the time. A known killer – a child killer at that – is still free. But worse than that, the man was sentenced to death and was in custody! They let him walk!'

'But you said the man you've dealt with doesn't look old enough.'

'What do I know? I've seen him at a distance, I've seen him in bad light. I've never been close. He's no spring chicken, I know that.'

Prunella bit into her lip. 'It would be a great story, if it were true.'

'Yeah, wouldn't it just. But I couldn't use it, I couldn't risk Sammy's life.'

She pulled away from him, laying her head back on the pillow. 'I could write it for you.'

He frowned. 'I told you, I couldn't use it.'

'Yes, you're right, you couldn't take the risk. But it might give you something to bargain with. If it turned out to be right.' She gave a small huffing sound. 'I still think the whole thing is too fantastic for words, though.'

'But you'd write the story.'

'Only if there was no other choice. And providing you came up with some proper evidence, of course.'

'Like what? What could I prove? Where would I start?'

'First you'd have to show that Nicholas Mallik is still alive.'

'And how would I do that?' He was quickly losing patience with her.

'Find out whether or not he was really hanged.'

'Sure. Any ideas how?'

She nodded her head on the pillow. 'Ask the hangman.'

That wasn't as silly as it seemed – or so Creed was to discover much later.

He hadn't wanted to leave the house in case Cally called (he also hadn't wanted to face Freddy Squires and explain where he'd been all day for, although he may have been independent of the newspaper, he was still contractually obliged to it). Prunella had returned to the *Dispatch* while he had dressed, drunk coffee, smoked, and generally fretted. It seemed like hours before the telephone rang. It *was* hours before the telephone rang.

'Yeah?'

'Joe? It's Prunella.'

'I know that. What the hell have you been doing all this time?'

'Digging for you, as I said I would. It hasn't been that easy.'

'Okay, so tell me.'

'Antony hasn't turned up yet.'

'I'm not interested in Blythe.'

'Everyone's a bit mystified here. It's not like him.'

'Prunella . . .'

'We've got a deadline and no star diarist.'

'Make something up. That's what he usually does.'

'That's not quite true.'

'You're making me unhappy, Prunella.'

'Sorry. I know how anxious you are.'

'Just tell me what you've learned.'

He heard her take a breath. 'I spoke to features first and they put me on to the right department of the Home Office. They have the list of qualified executioners on record, you know.'

'We don't have executioners any more.'

'I mean the old list. They're still all on file.'

'They told you who hanged Mallik?'

'Of course not. That's not allowed. But remember those old newspaper clippings mentioning that he'd been hanged by the Home Office's principal Official Executioner? I asked them to verify that.

They wouldn't, but neither did they deny it. They probably couldn't be bothered to look it up even if they were permitted to tell. But I think it's fairly safe to assume that in a crime so grievous and with such public interest they would have used the top man. And if what you suspect is true, then all the more reason to assign someone they could trust implicitly.'

'Did they tell you who the Official Executioner was at that time?'

'They got huffy at first and wanted to know what it was all about. I told them the *Dispatch* was doing a feature on the hanging debate; unfortunately that made them even more huffy. But they couldn't withhold the information, so I got the name eventually. It's one that hardly goes with the job, although I suppose it was rather silly to expect something macabre.'

'Who was it?'

'A man called Henry Pink.'

'I don't know why, but it sounds familiar.'

'He was quite famous for a while, especially just before the abolition of hanging. He wrote his memoirs in the 'seventies.'

'Is he . . . is he still alive?'

'Just about. He's old though.'

'Of course he's bloody old. Did you find out where he is?'

'I've done my best, Joe. There's no need to snap.'

'I'm sorry, I'm sorry. You know what I'm going through.'

'Yes, I'm sorry too. I made a few phone calls. Not too difficult – one led to another – but they took time. First was the Booktrust, who gave me the title of Pink's book and publisher. Then I spoke to someone in the publisher's publicity department. The girl there remembered the book, but wasn't sure where the author was now. She checked back for me though and the address they had on file was of a pub in Yorkshire. Seems that was a popular sideline for public executioners; they could run the business and still have time to pop off when the call came. Real servants of the people, these characters. Anyway, I phoned the pub, and no joy. The landlord there hadn't a clue where Pink was now, nor even if he were still alive.'

'Prunella, can you just get to it?'

'Only demonstrating how clever I've been, Joe. Indulge me. I enquired which brewery owned the pub and he told me it was a

Tadcaster Brewery house, so next stop was their head office.' She hesitated then, but not to catch her breath. 'Joe, I . . . I enjoyed today.'

'You rang the brewery's head office . . .'

'It did mean something to you, didn't it? It wasn't just . . .' she lowered her voice, as if suddenly conscious of the office around her '. . . you know.'

'Of course it meant something, Prunella. I've never been so turned on in my life.'

'Not just that. Didn't you feel something . . . more?'

If you only knew the something more I felt. 'It was special, very special. We'll talk about it later, okay? Right now I've got all this other stuff on my mind.'

'Yes. I'm sorry, Joe. I only wanted to make sure you felt the same as I did.'

'What did the brewery tell you, Prunella?'

'I spoke to a very helpful chap there, who said the brewery would still have the address Henry Pink moved to after giving up the tenancy because they liked to keep in touch with their old and valued landlords – apparently they send Christmas and anniversary cards, that sort of thing. Unfortunately they hadn't been in contact with Henry Pink for some time – ten years at least, he seemed to think – so frankly he didn't know if old Henry was alive or dead. Anyway, I took down the address, but the brewery man wouldn't give me the telephone number – against company policy apparently. That was no problem though; I called Directory.'

'You got it?'

'I got it and I rang it.'

Creed waited.

'Joe?'

'You spoke to him.' Not a question.

'No, I spoke to his niece. Pink is a widower with no children of his own and she moved in to take care of the old man when her own husband died. But her uncle has been poorly for some time, which is hardly surprising since he's eighty-one. She told me she hadn't visited him for years, and she was quite guilty about that. She must be getting on a bit herself, poor thing.'

'Visited him? You mean he's not with her any more?'

'He was taken into a rest home several years ago, somewhere too far away for his niece to make regular visits. In fact, she admitted she'd only been there once, and he'd been too far gone in the head to talk sensibly to her. She decided he'd be much better off there with trained staff to look after him, though she said he was a very lucky man to have been accepted by such a fine place. Conveniently enough, if you want to see him yourself, Joe, it's down here in the south. A place called the Mountjoy Retreat.'

27

Basically Creed had three fairly simple philosophies in life (there were others, but they were minor and usually varied when occasion dictated). The main ones were these: 1) Do unto others before they do unto you; 2) Never trust anyone in authority, ex-wives/lovers, helpful strangers, priests (of any variety); 3) Bend with the wind, and snap back hard in the lulls.

He had never actually defined these philosophies in such definitive terms, had never carved them in stone, but they had certainly served as a kind of tacit guide through the last ten or so years of his life. Call him hardbitten, if you like, call him a cynic, call him a fool; what you can't call him is gullible (not entirely, anyway).

Although he was attracted to the girl named Cally – who wouldn't be? – there was no way he would believe she had his best intentions at heart. As far as he was concerned she was up to her gorgeous neck in this unholy mess. She'd drugged him, had kidnapped Sammy, had lied to him – so why *should* he trust her? Even so, to give her a minor benefit of doubt (she had, after all, saved his life too) he'd waited for her call all evening and all night.

Earlier, when Prunella had arrived back on his doorstep, he had turned her away, telling her that he needed time on his own to think, and that he'd take no further action anyway until he was quite sure Cally wasn't going to make contact. Prunella clearly had been disappointed, for the lustre in her eyes was not only because of the exciting story she had become involved in, but was also because she was keen to repeat some of the previous action of the day. Mistakenly, she'd been impressed by Creed's prowess.

She had gone away slightly miffed, even though she'd understood the pressure he was under.

Creed hadn't eaten, hadn't touched the booze, but had smoked and drunk coffee before eventually drifting into a fitful sleep on the lounge sofa, one ear remaining wide awake in case the telephone should ring. It hadn't.

He had risen early the next day and, with a further smoke and coffee, searched through his roadmap book, the address Prunella had given him by his side on the kitchen table. He hadn't found mention in the book of the Retreat itself, naturally enough, but he did trace the village that the address claimed the place was near.

Now he was on his way, through the morning traffic, heading out of the city, going west towards Berkshire, on his way to talk to a retired and, for all he knew, totally senile ex-hangman. He could feel in his water that it was going to be another strange kind of day.

28

The Mountjoy Retreat was impressive, like one of those mansions for sale you often see full-page, full-colour, in *Country Life*; the kind that aren't priced, but for which 'substantial offers are invited'. For all its glory, however, it hadn't been easy to find. One local that Creed had stopped to ask had heard of the place, but was blowed if he knew where the bugger was 'xactly. Another sent him off in a totally wrong direction. Finally he managed a reliable route instruction from the village post office.

The home was several miles from the village itself, tucked away down a tree-lined country lane with only an insignificant and weather-worn sign proclaiming its existence. Creed had steered the Suzuki between the unimposing brick pillars of the gateway and driven along the winding drive until the trees and foliage on each side opened out and the mansion was there in the distance across the sweeping lawns. He brought the jeep to a halt.

If Creed had had any knowledge of old architecture, he'd have noted that the building appeared to be a combination of sixteenth-, seventeenth- and eighteenth-century styles, but basically Tudor

231

in origin. The rose-coloured brickwork was patterned with soft unobtrusive diapering, and tall windows were symmetrically arranged on either side of an early classical portico whose white columns rose almost to roof-height. There were higher turrets at both ends of the main facing, and plain lawns, made sullen by winter, stretched before and around the broad, gravelled forecourt. To Creed it was just a wealthy person's paradise.

He drove on, studying the house as it loomed larger in the windscreen, and brought the jeep round to the wide steps of the portico entrance. He parked alongside a capacious delivery van from which covered trays and cartons were being unloaded. Creed climbed out and followed one of the men who was carrying six narrow cartons balanced precariously on top of one another.

A portly figure in a black suit and shiny grey tie appeared in the doorway ahead. 'Adrian, if you drop those I'll personally strangle you,' he said, his expression one of outraged alarm. 'Chef would *die* if he saw his gateaux in such mortal danger.' His glance flicked briefly towards Creed before he turned and flounced back inside the building.

Creed overtook Adrian, who seemed suddenly to have lost confidence and was testing each unseen step with a probing foot first before committing himself, and entered the Retreat's high-ceilinged hall. Its stark whiteness was almost dazzling.

The portly man in the black suit and grey tie was talking to an even more portly, not to say gross, woman seated at a large oak desk. She wore a fluffy pink cardigan over a uniform of pale blue.

'Final delivery will be around three or four this afternoon, dear, is that all right?' The man's voice rose in a sing-song way at the end of the sentence.

The fat woman made a face.

'Well I did tell you the times when you ordered,' the man said, somewhat piqued. 'If only Mr Parmount would allow Chef to cook on the premises we wouldn't have these problems.'

'It will have to do, Mr Greenaway.' She had a child's squeaky voice. 'But please no later than three for the last load.'

'Load? I hardly think that's an appropriate description. I think you'll find Chef has excelled himself for this little festivity of yours. I'm sure he could show your own chef – or should I say "cook" – a thing or two. As it is we'll have to trust your man to warm up Chef's preparations as best he can. Not the best way to do things, my dear. Extremely *gauche*, if I might say.'

'I'm sure your bill will excel itself too, Mr Greenaway.'

'If you want the finest, you have to pay the price. I believe Mr Parmount does require the finest? I've never known him to settle for anything less in the past. I'll be along later to make sure everything is laid out correctly.' Another quick, and this time disapproving, glance at Creed and the portly man pranced to the entrance door in time to meet the carrier coming through. 'That lot to the kitchen also, and be sharp. There's a lot more to do today.' Then he was gone.

Creed approached the desk.

Miss Piggy-in-Blue regarded him as disapprovingly as had Mr Greenaway. She waited for him to speak.

'Uh, my name's Joseph Pink. I'm here to see Henry Pink,' said Creed.

Her small eyes enlarged a little. 'I beg your pardon?'

'My name's Joseph Pink. I'm here to see Henry Pink.'

She resembled a malformed ten-year-old who'd been asked the square root of 56,843.05.

'My uncle,' Creed explained. 'My great-uncle. My mother is his niece. His niece-in-law,' he quickly added, realising his own name wouldn't be Pink had his mother been a niece by blood. Christ, he should have checked that out with Prunella.

Her lips – thin lips for such a large lady – puckered as though she were about to speak, but instead she cocked her head to one side, examining the oddity before her.

'I've come down from Yorkshire to see him.' He didn't make a fool of himself by trying a Yorkshire accent.

At last she spoke. 'Mr Pink doesn't have visitors.'

'No, not as a rule. It's a long way to come, you see. Mother's not too good on her pins – on her legs – nowadays, and I'm abroad a lot. It's difficult to get a chance to visit old Uncle Henry.'

Her munchkin voice attempted authority. 'I'm afraid it's impossible for you to see him. As I told you, Mr Pink doesn't have visitors. He's much too unwell for that kind of thing.'

'That's exactly why I'm here. Mother and I are worried about his health and, well, frankly I'd hate not to have seen him one last time before he, you know, pops off. I'm due back in Dubai tomorrow. My company doesn't give me much leave, so I have to make the best of it. It'll be another three months at least before I get the chance to return. Still, that's the engineering business for you. Can't complain about the money though.'

By the disdainful way she inspected his unshaven, battered face and rumpled clothing he realised mention of money might have been a mistake in this context; he must have looked like a refugee from Cardboard City. With an inward groan he also realised that if he worked abroad so much, particularly in places like Dubai, then he would have been a little less pallid. The receptionist may have looked dumb, but nobody was *that* dumb.

'Do you have any form of identification?' she asked witheringly.

'The thing is, you see, I'm away so much I rarely carry my UK driving licence with me.'

'Didn't you drive here?'

'Yeah, but I didn't think to bring the licence. Came over to England as a last-minute idea, wanted to see the old boy before he snuffed – before he became too unwell. Let's see if I got my Amex with me.' He patted his pockets, even rummaged through one or two. 'Can you beat that?' he said, giving her the full Mickey Rourke smile. 'I've even forgotten my wallet. I'm such a klutz sometimes, no, a lot of the time, actually, I'm always –'

'Are you a journalist?'

'Pardon me?'

'I said, are you a journalist?'

'Huh, what gives you that idea?'

'People have tried to contact Mr Pink in the past. Writing people.'

'Because of his old job, I suppose. Personally, I think it was a mistake to write his memoirs, should have kept his profession a family secret. Even Mother has been pestered by nosy . . .'

His words petered out. Her face, fleshy though it was, had set rock-solid.

'I think you'd better leave,' she piped.

'I think you're right,' he replied. Years of gatecrashing told him his bluff had failed here; argument, persuasion, insistence, charm, and even a bribe would only be a waste of time and energy with this one. It didn't mean he'd given up, though.

234

She nodded towards the door as if to remind him where it was.

'Might be better if I get Mother to make a proper appointment for me.' He backed away while he talked. 'Go through the right channels, that sort of thing. Bring some proper identification next time, right? I'm so stupid sometimes. Who *is* in charge here, by the way? Mr Parmount, isn't it? You don't want to say? State secret? Well, give my love to Uncle Henry, won't you? Tell him I'll bring him a food parcel. Only joking – I can see you eat well here. Thanks for your cooperation. You've been a peach.'

The rest of her froze to monolithic hardness, but Creed was scanning the hall and the stairway as he backed off towards the entrance. He gave her a wave before ducking out.

Shit! he mentally cursed outside on the step. *Shoulda planned it better, shoulda phoned beforehand, made up a decent story.* In the forecourt, the portly caterer was at the wheel of a Volvo, checking through a list of some kind. Creed descended the short flight of steps and walked over to the car. He tapped on the window.

Greenaway glanced up from the piece of paper, startled. He wound down the driver's window. 'Yes?'

Creed leaned over, resting an elbow on the roof. 'Something going on here today?' he enquired amiably.

'I don't see that it's anything to do with you,' the unamiable reply came back.

'Excuse me, dear,' said Creed straightening. He hadn't needed to ask, for he'd already seen and heard enough to make the question rhetorical. With a sniff, Greenaway wound his window up and switched on the Volvo's engine. Creed stepped aside as the car reversed and swung round to head down the long drive.

Footsteps caught Creed's attention. Adrian, the youth who had carried the cartons into the house, was returning to his van. He slid back the door and was about to climb in when Creed sauntered over.

'Having a big one, are they?' the paparazzo asked.

'Eh?' Adrian turned his head, one foot remaining on the van's step. He had straw-coloured hair, long and straggly on top, cut short at the back and sides. His face was ruddy, not from exertion, but naturally so.

Creed indicated the house with a thumb. 'They having a party or something? That's a lot of food you took in there.'

'Oh. No, a costume ball, so Mr Greenaway says.'

'Don't they have their own people to handle things like that? I mean, they must have a chef and proper staff to cater for all the inmates.'

Adrian grinned. 'Rich bleedin' inmates. 'Course they have their own cooks, but we do the specials. We don't get a look-in tonight though, we just deliver.'

'How many have you catered for?'

'Don't know. A fair amount.'

'You want a cigarette?'

'Yeah.'

Creed produced one of his brown roll-ups.

'No thanks,' the youth said.

Creed stuck it in his own mouth while Adrian produced a packet of Silk Cut. The photographer lit him.

'Cheers. What you doing here then?'

'Trying to visit a sick uncle. Roseanne there wouldn't let me in.'

'Mr Greenaway says they're not allowed visitors. Wealthy lunatics and geriatrics, he says. That's why we can't stay, and I'm bloody glad of it.'

'Lunatics? Here?'

'According to Mr Greenaway. It's not a mental home though, nothing like. Mr Greenaway almost slapped my wrist when I called it one. Very sensitive, the people who run this place.'

'It's private enough.'

'Yeah, never know it was here, would ya? Oh-oh, the circus lady's got her eye on us. I'd better be going.' He hoisted himself up into the van.

Creed turned and saw the blue-uniformed receptionist watching them from the entrance. As the van pulled out he went to his jeep and climbed in. He sat behind the wheel for a few moments staring at the figure blocking the Mountjoy's wide doorway before switching on and driving off. In his rearview mirror he saw that his departure was being watched all the way.

29

Creed crouched in the bushes, studying each car as it went by, a bright moon that was still low in the sky helping the observation. This was what he was good at. It was cold, he was shivering, but he knew how to hide and wait; he'd had years of practice. He ignored the numbness in his big toes.

The best time to gain access anywhere was when there were plenty of bodies around, visitors arriving or leaving (preferably arriving) in a constant flow with everyone and everything busy and half the time nobody knowing who was who. Those were the best conditions. In this case, the guest list was probably specially chosen, so he wouldn't be able to saunter into the house as one of the crowd, particularly in his present dishevelled state. No, a fair amount of subterfuge would have to be used here. Or at least, a back entrance.

Bentleys, Rollers and Jaguars seemed to be the order of the night, with an occasional Mercedes thrown in. BMWs were most definitely out, so it had to be a class affair.

Although he couldn't take suitable snaps in that light and at that distance – about thirty yards from the drive itself – he used the zoom lens of the Nikon to get a closer look at the guests as they sped past. Some of those faces, the ones he managed to get a reasonable look at, surprised him, for they were either famous or at least 'known' to the public. But the face that surprised him most was Cally McNally's.

He had risen to his feet for a moment to ease his aching and frozen limbs when headlights had swung into the drive at a speed that had almost caught him out. He had just managed to duck behind a tree before being caught in the full glare.

He blinked against the dazzle, then, as the XJS drew almost level, he risked a quick peek. Her face was turned towards him, but she was looking at the driver of the coupé, talking to him. Creed didn't have time to check through the camera's viewfinder, but he was sure it was her. The driver briefly blocked his view until he caught a last glimpse of Cally's profile as the car sped onwards towards the manor house. He leaned against the tree, his mouth open, agog, for he'd had a further surprise. The driver had been Lidwit, Lidrip, LidTRAP.

Creed's hands tightened around the tree. *Lidtrap had said he didn't know her! She'd admitted she didn't actually know him! What were they playing at? And what were they doing here at the Mountjoy Retreat?*

Another car drove by, its headlights catching the Jaguar in front, but Creed was too stunned to try and see who was in this one.

Why should Cally be here? The question burned in his brain. *There had to be a good reason, no way could it be a coincidence, no bloody way!*

He moved away from the tree, pushing through the undergrowth and putting distance between himself and the drive; he'd seen enough anyway. So far about forty or fifty cars had passed by, all going towards the rest home, most containing two or three occupants, only occasionally one alone.

Trudging under cover in the direction of the manor house, Creed wondered what Cally was doing in such company. Over and over again he kept asking himself, *Why was she here?* He paused where the trees and bushes gave out to broad lawns. In the distance the guests were alighting from their vehicles and climbing the few steps to the entrance, their gowns and clothing lit by lights from the house itself. His clicker-finger had developed an itch and he had to remind himself that he was there for more important reasons. If he kept to the treeline he'd be able to make his way round to the back of the place without being seen, and experience told him that doors and windows were invariably left open at these kinds of functions; staff were always popping outside for a quick smoke or a breather, while guests often felt in need of fresh air or a swift fondle of a good friend. Creed had stolen into many a private party because of such toings and froings. Once inside, the difficult part would be locating Henry Pink. Knocking on every door and enquiring after him was impractical. So was asking a member of staff. However, there had to be a register of names somewhere, so if he could find the home's offices, and they were unlocked and unmanned at that time of evening, then it should be no problem, no problem at all. Face it, Creed, you don't have a hope in hell.

But there was another method. The place was full of old people, and most old people love to gabble. Find one, or some, try not to frighten them, and merely ask. Providing they hadn't all been packed off to bed early, and if he wasn't discovered loitering in the corridors by a member of staff, it might work out. Anyway, it was the only plan he had.

Adrenaline beginning to pump – he couldn't help enjoying this sort of thing, even though the present circumstances were somewhat dire – Creed crept through the trees towards the rear of the house. He stumbled over so many roots and fell over so much low under-growth that soon he decided it would be easier and faster if he left the cover of the trees and skirted around the lawns. As long as he kept the trees as a backdrop, he should be okay.

Within minutes he was looking up at the building from the back. A terrace ran the whole of its length, with two central staircases leading down to the gardens. There were plenty of hedges and topiary in those gardens to provide cover while approaching the house.

Creed made a crouching dash across a flat lawn towards the first hedge. He ducked behind it and stayed there awhile on all fours, waiting to see if he had been spotted. No one called out. He lingered a little longer, catching his breath, allowing his heartbeat to slow down. Onwards again, keeping low, one hand tucked inside his coat pocket to hold the Nikon steady. He thought he heard a door open above on the terrace and he slid to a halt, cursing himself for the noise he'd made on the gravel path. He hid behind a garden plinth.

Nothing happened. No footsteps, no challenge. He breathed a sigh of relief and ventured onwards, this time not so hastily, making the shadow of the terrace in no time at all. He squatted there, his back against the stone, and did his best to relax his breathing as well as his skittish nerves.

All was quiet. The house itself might have been empty for all the noise that came from it on this side. There were clouds above, but for reasons of their own, they were avoiding the moon; its eerie light reigned supreme. Creed shivered.

'Joe?'

It was almost a whisper in his ear.

He jumped, almost cracking his head on the wall behind.

'Is that you, Joe?'

He turned and looked up and the moon was strong enough for him to gasp at what peered over the balcony at him. It was the head of a silver jackal, and Creed felt very weak.

'It's me, Joe – Cally. Wait there, I'll come down.'

Cally? Cally in a mask? Of course. A ball. A costumed ball. She was wearing a costume. But how could she know he was there? Not just there under the terrace, but at the Mountjoy Retreat itself? *How?*

He was shaking as she descended the steps to his left, the white, long-snouted mask cast silver by the moonlight. He was too shocked to rise.

'It's all right to stand, Joe,' she said in a hushed voice. 'No one can see you from the house.' To his relief, she removed the mask, and now it was her hair that was made silver by the moonlight.

He got to his feet. 'How . . . ?'

'I saw you as we drove past.'

'That's not possible.'

'I saw you in the headlights before you hid behind a tree. You were lit up like a frightened rabbit.'

'So why didn't you stop?'

'I didn't want Daniel to know you were there.'

'Ah,' Creed said. He paused. 'Ah. Daniel. You mean your director friend, the guy you said you worked for, only he told me he didn't have a clue about you and you yourself admitted later you'd lied about that, and here you both are, together, guests at the same bash, arriving in the same car, but you –'

'*Will you be quiet for a moment,*' she hissed. 'I've warned you about these people. They're evil, they're dangerous, and I'm trying to protect you, as well as your son.'

'It doesn't explain anything. Who is this creep Lidtrap, and what's he to you?'

'Daniel is my brother.'

Creed made a sound that was somewhere between a whine and a sigh.

'Our grandmother left everything she had to the Mountjoy Retreat. We were invited here tonight, along with some of her oldest friends and acquaintances, to pay tribute to her.'

'A fancy dress ball? That's a funny kind of tribute.'

'A *masque*. Lily loved such things. It was her last wish that she be celebrated in this way.'

He was thinking hard. 'Wait . . . wait a minute . . .'

'Keep your voice down.'

'Your mother's here, isn't she? Lily Neverless's daughter, Grace. This place is a mental institution.'

'Both the elderly and the mentally unwell are cared for at the Mountjoy. It's a rest home more than anything else though.'

'The *senile* and the mentally unwell, you mean. A bunch of loonies living in a grand style.' Creed shook his head in dismay. 'Oh Christ. That's it, isn't it? That freak you say is Nicholas Mallik is here too. The stupid bastards who run this place allowed him and his bony sidekick to break out to create merry hell.' He banged the wall with the heel of his fist. 'It's all too much, too much of a coincidence. Even Henry Pink, the man who was supposed to have hanged Mallik, is here too. And now you tell me Lily Neverless left her fortune to this place. It's all connected somehow, they're all pieces of the same puzzle.'

He leaned one shoulder against the stone and studied Cally. She was pallidly beautiful in the moonlight, the dark gown she wore, sequins sparkling where they caught the light, moulding itself to her curves; her shoulders were bare, icy . . . For all his doubts, all his distrust, he wanted to draw her close, to sink into her, to warm her shoulders, her back, with his hands.

'Joe, is that why you're here – to see the old executioner?'

'That's right. Henry Pink. I figured he was the one person who could tell me whether or not you were lying about Mallik.'

'But I can help you.'

'Like you were going to help me get Sammy back? Why didn't you call me?'

'I couldn't reach you this afternoon, but I knew Sammy would be safe until this affair tonight was over.'

He gripped her arms. 'Are you telling me he's here, Sammy's *here*?'

'I thought that was why you came. I didn't know how you'd found out, but –'

'*Sammy's here?*'

'Keep your voice down. We can get him away. We can get them both away.'

'Both? Henry Pink as well? He's some kind of prisoner?'

She shook her head impatiently. 'Not him. My mother, Joe. We can take them out of this place. Don't you understand, don't you know why I've had to help them? They've had my mother locked up for all these years and once I was old enough to realise what was going on, they threatened me with her life. I've had to do what they ask.'

'I don't get it. You could have gone to the police, the medical authorities. Your own grandmother could have arranged it for you.'

'No, no. She was part of it. My brother, too. You don't understand what they're like. They're involved in things you'll never understand. My mother isn't . . . she isn't quite right, but she's not like them, she isn't evil. Lily committed her when my brother and I were babies. Our grandmother raised us, she took care of us, made sure we wanted for nothing. But she corrupted us to her ways. Hers and Mallik's.'

She moved into him, and then his hands really were on her shoulders, on her back, warming her icy flesh.

'If you only knew what I've been through. I'm part of them, Joe, but it has to end, it has to stop now. They're insane, they think they can regain past glories –'

'Hold it, hold it. Who are you talking about now? Mallik?'

'Yes. And others. They're aged, some of them are crippled, but they want what they had before. They think they can be powerful again.' She pulled her head away from his shoulder so that she could look into his eyes. 'You've got to help me, Joe. We need each other.'

'Right. Let's go.' He made to move towards the gardens, but she held him back.

'Where are you going?'

'Out of here. We'll tell the police all we know and they can do the rest.'

'Didn't you listen to me?' She sounded angry, although her voice wasn't raised. 'The police don't have the authority to have my mother released.'

'Lily committed her, and now the old hag's dead. Somebody else has to take on that responsibility.'

'Somebody already has. Daniel has agreed my mother stays locked away. He's with them, Joe, he's part of them.'

'All that may be so, but we can tell them about Sammy's kidnapping. At least the police can help me get him back.'

She shook her head vigorously. 'They would never find him. He wouldn't . . . there wouldn't be enough left of him to find.'

The nausea Creed felt made him unsteady.

'I'm sorry,' she said, holding on to him, 'but you have to know how inhuman they are. We have to do this on our own.'

This wasn't Creed's territory at all. 'We can't . . . we can't . . .' he began to say, but he couldn't assemble the rest of the sentence.

'There's no other way, believe me. This is something more than a mere celebration of my grandmother, so they're going to be very busy. It's our only chance, right here and now. There'll be no other opportunity after tonight.' She grabbed his lapels. 'Let me find out where Henry Pink is first . . .'

'He doesn't matter any more.'

'He does,' she stated firmly. 'It's important that you know I'm telling the truth about Mallik. If you're convinced by what Pink says, then you'll be more willing to help me. And I do need your help, Joe, I can't do this alone. Besides, think of the story you'll have for your newspaper.'

There was that. 'We'll get Sammy too?'

'If it's possible. I can't make promises. You have to trust me to do my best.'

Trust her? Trust anybody? That wasn't really in Creed's nature. She had, however, touched a nerve. This story if it were true, could earn him a small fortune. It wasn't *the* shot he'd been searching for all his career, the big one that would have put his name among the photographers' hall of fame; no, this was even better, this would be (if the retired executioner was coherent enough to verify what Cally claimed) the scandal of the century, a revelation of skulduggery in high places from way back, nostalgia with a horrible twist. Imagine the movie rights on such a story! If, if, *if* it were true. Bring it up to date with kidnap, incarceration, and weird devil worship stuff. It was mind-blowing. It was awesome. Of course, he would have gone in to save Sammy anyway, but in all honesty he couldn't deny that the rest of it was an added incentive.

'Answer me two questions first,' he said, feeling a familiar tingling in his nerve-ends.

Her face was close to his own. He could feel her warm breath on his cheeks.

'Why all the different names? McNally, Lidtrap, Buchan . . .'

'Buchanan. My mother's married name was Buchanan, and mine used to be Calmeira Buchanan. I didn't lie to you before – I changed my name by deed poll. Grandmother urged both Daniel and me to shed the Buchanan name legally as soon as we were old enough to do so. She despised my father, you see, she considered him weak and the ruination of my mother. I believe she also despised my mother for her particular weakness until the day she died. So one very drunken evening, Daniel and I stuck needles in a phone directory and came up with our present names.'

'Your brother should have had another go.'

'No. The rule was that we stuck with whatever the pin struck. Silly, I suppose, but as I said, it was a drunken evening. What was your other question?'

'How did you find me here?'

'Use your head, Joe. When I saw you near the estate's entrance, I guessed you'd try to get into the building somehow. This was the only way you could, so five minutes after Daniel and I arrived I slipped away and came out here. I saw you dash from the trees quite clearly in the moonlight and all I had to do was wait until you got close. Can we go now before I'm missed? Besides, I'm freezing.'

Creed could think of nothing else that might delay them. 'I'll break your neck if you're lying to me,' he said grimly. It was a threat without substance, but it made him feel just a mite more bullish.

Unfortunately, when they had climbed the steps and crept across the terrace, lonely, insane laughter from somewhere inside the house set his limbs to shaking again.

30

I f you've ever paid a visit to a lunatic asylum (perhaps been a
resident at some time?), you'll know the stale heaviness that
hangs in the air like floating decay. For some peculiar reason it clings
more stagnantly at night than in the daytime. Possibly it's sick brain
cells crumbling from their hosts to permeate the atmosphere in the
way skin flakes from flesh. At least, that was the fanciful thought
Creed had as he hid inside the small room filled with muddied boots
on the ground floor of the Mountjoy Retreat.

The girl had led him around to the side of the house, away from
the terrace and its large french windows and doors. Even as they
stole past, lights in those windows began to come on behind them
like stalking spotlights so that they had to hurry lest they be exposed
in a sudden glare. The sidedoor they entered was shut but unlocked,
and was the one Cally had used earlier. Holding his hand, she took
him along a narrow corridor. Music and muted conversation from
somewhere in another part of the house came to them, but it seemed
a long way off.

She had found the boxroom quickly enough (perhaps she had

already planned to hide him there). Its window was small, the glass thick and mottled so that moonlight barely scraped through. She had told him to wait for her there. 'I have to get back before they realise how long I've been away. I'll find out which is Henry Pink's room, then I'll come and get you.' Unexpectedly she had kissed his cheek before slipping outside into the corridor again. Given the chance, Creed would have held her tight and returned the gesture with considerably more passion, but she was gone, the door quietly closed behind her, and he was all alone, cold and nervous and wondering if he wasn't the world's biggest fool for entering the lion's den like this.

For twenty minutes at least he waited, listening to the creaking of the building, the faint strains of chamber music and muffled voices. Mercifully he did not hear that empty, manic laughter again, but this sombre cubby-hole, with its smell of dirt and dinginess, had an eeriness all its own. Twice he opened the door a fraction, not so much to investigate the ill-lit corridor beyond, but more to disperse his own rising claustrophobia. It didn't really work, for as soon as he closed the door again, the shadows and the walls crept in a few more inches. It was funny (funny in the *peculiar* sense) how some of those shadows, when he looked away and then quickly back, seemed much darker than before and somehow took on slightly (you'd only notice if you concentrated hard) different shapes. And the shifts in air inside there were surely unnatural; the coldness that regularly brushed by his legs was more like the ephemeral touch of icy fingers than the passing of draughts from the window or the crack beneath the skirting. He should have gone with her, taken his chances, found a friendly broom closet in a bright hallway to hide in until she got the information he needed; this was bloody daft, waiting here in the dark, scrutinising the shadows, his own imagination taking the piss. Creed felt the wall next to the door for a switch, the palm of his hand sweeping wider and with more urgency when he failed to make contact with anything.

For the third time he inched open the door to allow in a lick of light from the corridor. He leapt back, jolting his spine against the stone sink behind him and almost twisting his ankle on a carelessly discarded boot, when fingers curled through the gap and pushed from the other side.

'What are you doing, Joe?' Cally whispered. 'You should have kept this door shut. My God, we'd both be in terrible trouble if you were discovered inside the house.'

She came in breathlessly, closing the door for safety. Her scent was stronger within the confines of the room, but hardly a match for the other smells present. She carried the jackal mask in one hand.

'Cally, can you give me a warning before you creep up on me again? You know, whistle a tune or something.' Creed held a hand against his chest to pacify his wildly beating heart.

'I didn't mean to startle you.'

'It's something you're becoming very good at. Did you find out where the old boy is?'

'Yes. All the residents have their own labelled pigeon-holes in the main office. I suppose they're for mail and messages. They also have hooks with individual keys.'

'This place is more like a hotel than a nuthouse.'

'I think the keys are to lock them in.'

'Not Pink, surely? As far as I know, he's not mentally ill, just ancient.'

'Perhaps so. But there was no key with his name on it. Just these . . .' She held up a metal ring on which hung two large keys. 'They were on a hook marked "Basement".'

'You think he's down there?'

'Room 8. I checked it with a register they keep in the office.'

'Clever girl. You're sure one of these will open Pink's room?'

'There were no others. One might open the basement itself, the other his room.' She handed the keyring to Creed.

'Maybe that's where they keep the poor folk. Listen, I've been reconsidering our position. I think it might be better if we get out of here and bring in –'

'We've been through all that.'

He flinched from her anger.

'Let's just get on with it, Joe.'

His hands dropped from her shoulders. 'Did you manage to find out where Sammy is?' he asked sullenly.

'Not yet. But I will. I'll take you downstairs first, then I'll start hunting. Don't worry, I'll find him.'

Cally turned away and peeped out into the corridor. 'All clear,' she whispered. She squeezed through the narrow gap as though that were the discreet thing to do; Creed followed suit.

The corridor joined a wider hallway, and this was much better lit. Conversations and laughter could be heard from the far end, all perfectly natural, sane and sociable.

'There's a reception room near the front of the house. That's where all the guests are gathered at the moment. Fortunately for us, most of the Retreat's staff are being kept busy because of tonight's celebration.'

'Don't they have nurses or wardens patrolling?' asked Creed, taking a furtive look into the hallway.

'There are only ever two on duty at night, and they'll be upstairs somewhere. They tend to keep the worse cases sedated once it gets dark.'

'You seem to know a lot about the place.'

'I should. My mother has been a patient for a long time. You could say it's almost a second home to me.'

'That's rough. You didn't try to forget her?'

'I could never do that.' Although she spoke quietly, Cally said this with passion.

She suddenly grabbed him and pushed him further back into the corridor. He looked at her in surprise and she put a finger to her lips. He heard footsteps in the hallway, but they were walking in the opposite direction.

'Somebody came out of a door halfway down,' Cally whispered. She peeked round the corner and Creed jerked her back.

'How do we get to Pink?' he demanded to know. 'I don't want to stay in this place one second longer than necessary, so let's get on with it.'

'I think there's a way down over there.' She pointed to a door almost opposite them.

'Why didn't you say?' He gritted his teeth, exasperated.

'Because I'm not sure. There's a proper staircase near the front of the house, but on my way back to you I looked in some of the doors in this corridor. I knew there had to be another way down, and I think that's it. There's an old iron staircase, and it should take you to the main basement area.'

'Aren't you coming with me?' He really didn't feel like investigating alone.

'I have to get back to the reception for a while. I'll get away again as soon as I can.'

'Then we find Sammy and leave, right?'

'Mother, too. I'm not leaving without her.'

'Okay. Mother, too. But don't leave me on my own in the crypt too long.'

'It's a basement, that's all. And it was your idea to see the hangman in the first place. You don't believe me about Mallik.'

'Let's not argue over it now. Just come and get me soon as you can.'

He went over to the door and gripped the handle. Before he opened it, he looked back over his shoulder at Cally.

But Cally had already gone.

It was dusty and even more smelly down there, obviously the neglected part of the mansion (unless the upper floors were in a similar state). At the bottom of the creaky stairway, he found a passageway whose walls were of crumbly brickwork and where cobwebs draped from cracks and rafters. The lightswitch had been at the top of the stairs, but the two bare lightbulbs along the passageway's length cast scant light, probably because they were covered in thick dust. The concrete floor was damp, as though water freely flowed through on occasion. Here and there were clods of mud where dust had collected and congealed. In all probability there was an underground spring beneath the foundations that swelled and flooded when rainfall was particularly heavy. Creed half expected a rat or two to scurry by; fortunately, that didn't happen, although he did hear scraping and scratching noises from behind the walls at certain points.

It was a relief when he finally came to the end of the passage, even though the next one was only a minor improvement. This was wider, paralleling the one above, but when he found a lightswitch, it was almost as dingy as the one behind. A heavy, dull thrumming meant there was a boiler room nearby. There were doorless doorways on either side of the passageway and when he poked his head into one or two he saw rooms filled with bric-à-brac – odd bits of furniture, stacked pictures, some with frames, others without, as well as unidentifiable pieces of machinery. A veritable basement junkyard.

He noticed there were other doorways leading off to other rooms, but had no inclination to explore them. Instead he moved on, coming next to a chamber with a padlocked iron door. The family vault? he wondered. Was this where they kept heirlooms and treasures? But no, this was a 'rest' home, not a family mansion.

He tried both keys on the ring, but neither one fitted the lock. He moved onwards, choosing one of the few corridors that led off from the chamber, hurrying his steps now. He couldn't deny it: the whole place gave him the creeps. Even the fat receptionist, with her piggy little eyes set deep in rolls of swollen flesh and her tinkly, child's voice, gave him the creeps. And skulking down here in this dirty inner sanctum definitely gave him the creeps, not to mention that lonely loony laughter he'd heard outside. That gave him the creeps in abundance.

He spotted a rough, but strong-looking door ahead. Maybe that would lead to a more sanitised area. He would expect so, if they kept patients there. He went to the door and found a sturdy bar across it that fitted into an equally sturdy slot mounted on the surrounding frame. Below this was a lock. Creed pulled back the bar, then used one of the keys. It turned stiffly at first, but soon yielded under pressure. The door moaned open.

The stink that wafted through was of a different kind: it was of things gone bad, cream that had curdled, meat that had moulded. He wrinkled his nose. He shivered. He wasn't happy at all.

Dim, caged lights lit the passage ahead, the kind of lights you get in prisons (and asylums, of course), themselves incarcerated behind metal grilles to prevent human incarcerates from getting at the glass. There were narrow, shadowy doors on either side, low doors, the kind that, if you were just over normal height, you'd have to stoop to enter. They were shadowy because they were deep-set into the walls. From where he stood, he could see that the first few were numbered.

'Ready or not,' he muttered to himself, 'here I come.' He entered the passage of cells.

Number 8 was about a third of the way down and he stopped and listened outside the door before trying the keys. There were no sounds from within. There had been no sounds from any of the other rooms he'd passed either. He wasn't sure if he should knock, but then thought, what the hell, let's surprise him. The second key did the trick. He took a breath and pushed the door open.

'Hello?' he said, peering in.

He withdrew his head quickly. The air outside was nasty, but this was *foul*. The geriatric must have messed himself and nobody had bothered to clean him up. Or there was a slop bucket in there which hadn't been emptied for some time.

Creed stiffened his resolve, narrowed his nostrils.

'Hello?' he said again.

There was no answer. And there was no light either. Swinging the door wide, Creed used what light there was from the passage behind to search for a switch, which he found all right, but which didn't work. Standing to one side so that more light might come through, he studied what he could of the room. Which wasn't much: one narrow bed, no more than a cot, and that was all; apart from the figure beneath the sheet on the bed.

Creed went in and was surprised it wasn't colder inside. It wasn't terrifically warm, either, but he'd expected it to be as chilly as the rest of the basement area. He saw that there was a cast-iron radiator behind the door and surmised that although this Parmount character obviously wasn't concerned about the unhygienic conditions his subterranean patients lived in, he at least wasn't going to let them die from hypothermia. Handkerchief to his nose, Creed approached the bed.

A withered head, the only part of the body under the sheet that was visible, considered him.

'Get away,' a quavery voice.

Creed raised what he hoped would be taken as a reassuring hand. 'It's okay,' he said. 'I've just come to see how you are.'

'Nay, I don't know you. You're a stranger t'me.' Feeble though the voice was, neither its feistiness nor its Yorkshire accent was entirely lost.

'It is Mr Pink, isn't it? Your daughter . . .' what the fuck *was* her name? '. . . sent me to see how you were getting along. She worries about you . . .'

'Sheila? Worries about me? Don't make me laff, lad.' His snort of disgust was more like a throaty hiccup. 'Who are yer? What d'yer want with me?' Shakily, he raised his head and strands of white hair still touched the pillowless mattress beneath him. 'Is it time for m'feed?'

'Uh not yet. Soon.' Creed ventured closer and even in that poor light he could see the sheet covering the frail old man was stained and soiled. 'Are you all right, Mr Pink?'

The figure was silent for a while, the face still towards Creed, studying him. With a rasping sigh, the shrivelled head settled back, the eyes closed as if claimed by sleep.

'Sir . . . ?' Creed said after a moment or two, for he thought the old man really had gone to sleep.

'Am I all right?' the old man asked himself. 'Am I *all right*?' What started as a tiny snigger finished as a body-racking cough.

Creed waited for him to settle. 'Your daughter . . . Sheila . . . wants you to know she can't get down to see you so often nowadays because –'

'Daughter-in-*law*,' came the correction. 'She's no blood-kin of mine. If my lad were alive today he'd never 'ave seen me put away in this cesspit. He'd never let those bastids torment me the way they do.' The last word was punctuated by a half-suppressed sob.

Trying to ignore the malodour rising from the bed, Creed leaned forward. 'Who's tormenting you, Mr Pink?'

'I told you. Them bastids.' The head creaked towards Creed again, the tired rheumy eyes wide open. 'You're joost another one of 'em, aren't yer? Y'ere to spite me.'

'No, I'm a friend. Honest. If you've been treated badly, maybe I can do something about it.'

Pink's voice took on a self-pitying whine that was childish yet ancient at the same time. 'They won't let me be, mister, they won't let me go. I'm old and I'm tired and I've seen enough of life. I don't want any more, I've 'ad enough. But they won't let me go.' Another sob spasmed his body, and this was followed by a quieter weeping.

'Who's doing this to you, can you tell me that?'

'Let me be. I don't know who you are.'

'I can help.'

' 'Ow can you help? 'Ow can you undo what's been done to me?'

252

Creed knelt next to the bed. 'I'm here to investigate these people, Mr Pink,' he whispered close to the old man's ear.

'Eh?' The weeping stopped and the head lifted from the pillow again.

Creed cleared his throat. 'I'm really from the Ministry of Health – I only used your daughter-in-law's name to get inside as a regular visitor rather than an official. We've had our eyes on this place for some time. We've had one or two complaints.'

Those watery eyes narrowed to a squint. Then the thin, buzzard-like head supported by its scrawny, buzzard-like neck flopped back on to the mattress. He mumbled something to himself.

Creed wasn't sure if the geriatric believed him or was too weary to argue. 'Just, er, just for my notes, to make sure they're accurate, you are Henry Pink, retired executioner for the government?'

'Get it right, lad – Official Executioner to the Home Office.' There seemed to be an even greater tiredness to his words. 'Hundreds I did fer. So many I lost count in the end. I tell yer, though, only a few disgraced themselves on the gallows. Most of 'em went off with some dignity, and I did my best to help them with that. Womenfolk went off best. Sort of resigned themselves to it. Mind, most of those 'ad thick ankles with brains to match. Understand me, lad?'

Creed nodded, but Pink didn't notice; he was staring at the black ceiling as if seeing his past up there.

'Did for all kinds, from Nazi war criminals to silly buggers who strangled their wives in fits of temper. From mass murderers to poor fools who made but one mistake in their miserable lives. I treated them all with the same dignity, made no difference to me what their crime were. Gave each one the respect due to those about to die. It were all about doing it right, and respect towards another was part of that. And quickness, that was another part of it. Know 'ow long it took me to hang someone, from the moment they entered the execution chamber 'til they were danglin' in space? Know 'ow long, lad? Thirty seconds. 'S'all it took if yer did it right. Even if they struggled to the end, made no difference, none at all. Thirty seconds.' He sighed again, a long rattling breath that conveyed satisfaction.

Creed felt sick again and it was not only because of the smell, the location, and the decrepit bundle of bones he was so close to. Hangman's tales were not to his liking. 'Mr Pink . . . Henry . . .'

'Mr Pink.'

'Mr Pink, do you recall someone –'

'Now they've come back to haunt me . . .'

'. . . er . . .'

'Even those I don't rightly remember. Every night they're 'ere, outside the door, sniggerin', callin' out my name, scratchin' on the wood. They remind me, who they were, what they did. The worst of 'em, the devils, they come inside. They taunt me and spit at me and sometimes they lay the noose round my neck. And when they're gone I cry, I can't stop m'self, and they know I cry, because I 'ear them laff, I can 'ear their mockin'. They think they've driven me mad, they think they've done that to me, but I've seen and I've hanged more devils that were 'uman than them that weren't. D'yer think I'm crazy, lad? D'yer think that?'

A thin, almost skeletal hand shot with surprising speed from the bedsheet and gripped Creed's wrist. The executioner's hand had all the strength and brittleness of a bird's claw, but the photographer had to steel himself not to yank his own arm away.

'No, I don't think you're crazy,' he forced himself to reply.

'Then that might be your mistake, lad.'

The old man lifted himself and the covering slipped from his shoulders to reveal a body so loose-fleshed and emaciated that Creed turned away, thankful that at least the shadows obscured the worst of it.

Pink chuckled quietly, his bony shoulders jerking as if on strings.

'I was going to ask you, Mr Pink,' Creed began again, 'if you recall hanging someone named Nicholas Mallik? Just before the last World War, it would've been.'

The chuckling, and the jerky movement ceased. A high-pitched keening sound came from the back of Pink's throat, the kind a smallish animal that was in pain might make. He lay down, turning on to his side so that he faced the wall, away from Creed; he pulled the bedsheet up around his ears.

Creed reached over, intending to reassure the ex-hangman, but the thought of touching that scraggy old body, let alone the dirty sheet he lay beneath, stayed his hand. It hovered an inch or so above the knobbly shoulder and only strong effort of will eventually forced it down. Pink's body flinched at the touch.

'It's all right, Mr Pink. Mallik can't hurt you. He's dead now, isn't he? You hanged him yourself.'

'He's the worst, the very worst.' This was said with a great bitterness. 'He dances on me and it's my grave he dances on, only I'm not dead, and he likes that, he don't want me dead, he wants me where he can hurt me, where he can punish me . . .'

'Don't you remember hanging Nicholas Mallik? About fifty years or so ago, before the big war? Don't you remember that?'

Pink swung round with such agile ferocity that Creed nearly toppled backwards.

The old man peered over the edge of the cot, his face only inches away from Creed's. 'He won't let me forget, that one won't. He haunts me, does Count Nikolai Mallik. Haunts and taunts, taunts and haunts. Devils enjoy that. It's what gives 'em life.'

'You hanged him,' Creed persisted.

'Oh, there were a big fuss. All them little ones he'd murdered. Cut 'em up. Worse.' He looked at Creed slyly. 'Worse 'n that. Ate 'em. They said.' He nodded slowly. 'Home Office wanted best man, that's why they called in Henry Pink. There were none better'n me in those days, plenty who thought they were, but the governors of them prisons knew who were best. You know, they were frightened of him, this bastid Mallik. The authorities were frightened of the man. So cut-and-dried wicked, y'see. Never knew anyone as bad as him, not before, not after. He shone Evil, it came out of his eyes and flesh.' Pink gave an exaggerated shudder. 'It was in his very stink.'

He fell silent, remembering this distant past.

While Creed's thoughts were racing. Was Mallik alive, or was he dead? Had Cally told the truth, or had she lied? The executioner had said Mallik was still punishing him, so had a deal been struck and the child-murderer not been hanged at all? Or was this merely the dream-ramblings of senile dementia?

'Tell me what happened that day, Mr Pink,' he urged as gently as he could.

Pink looked at him sharply. 'What day would that be?'

'The, uh, the day of Mallik's execution.'

'Why d'yer want to know?' The thin line of his crinkled mouth set firm.

'Just interested. You had quite a reputation in your day, Mr Pink.'

'Best there were. Everyone knew it. Wrote a book about it once.' He leaned forward again and Creed held himself rigid, for foul air travelled with the old man. 'The Home Office could count on me.' Pink touched the side of his nose with a skinny finger and winked. 'They knew they could trust me.'

Trust you to do what? Creed wondered. To do the job well, or to conceal the truth from the public?

'Knew he was the Devil soon as I set eyes on him.'

'Mallik?'

'That's who yer want to know about, i'nt it? That's the real reason you're 'ere. I'm not afraid of talkin', lad.' He lay back in the bed, drawing the sheet up to his chin so that only his head was visible again. 'Aye, I remember the first time I set eyes on him. Day before execution, it were, and I'd come to size him up. I watched him through the Judas Hole and he had his back to me, just lookin' out the bars of his cell window. Pentonville, that were the prison. I'd already checked the execution chamber, made sure everything were right. I'd chosen the rope – always preferred the old 'un, never the new – tested the drop and left the sandbag to hang overnight t'stretch rope. Next job was to examine the condemned man himself to decide the length of the drop – didn't want him stranglin', y'see, nor his head torn off. Y'ave to get the drop perfect so the neck's broke outright. Like I say, I peeped through the Judas Hole and the Count was standin' there, lookin' t'other way. He seemed to sense me and he turned round to look me in the eye. I'd never seen such malicious evil in all me life before, and never did since – 'til they got me 'ere, that's t'say.' For a reason best known to himself, he sniggered. ' 'Til they got me 'ere,' he repeated. 'That look he gave me preyed on me mind all night. Usually I gets a good night's sleep before a hangin', sound as yer like . . .' (he said this as if still in occupation) '. . . but that night I 'ardly slept a wink. I think I was a-feared t'fall asleep.'

He shook his head, as though still dismayed by this rare loss of sleep. 'Next mornin', just before nine o'clock it would 'ave been, a group of us went to condemned cell. Sheriff, prison governor, a doctor and one or two senior prison officers. They went into execution chamber while me and my assistant went t'fetch prisoner. Waitin' for us calm as you like, were Nikolai Mallik. Calm as you like.

Never said a word, though, not one blessed word. I told him to turn about and he did that without fuss. I strapped his wrists, fast like. There were no priest present in that cell – Mallik didn't want one. We took him through, and he didn't bide his time, I'll say that for him. No stumblin', no resistin'. He walked like he were takin' stroll through park. Mallik didn't even flinch when he were confronted by the noose hangin' there. He stepped right up to it like he didn't give a monkey's doodah. He stood on the T, escortin' officers on either side of him in case of trouble. Then he looked me right in the eye and you know what the bastid did?' Pink took a deep, unsteady breath. 'He smiled at me, pleasant as yer like. Not a grin, nor a laff. Just a smile, an "I'll see you some time tomorrow" type of thing. That nearly unhinged me, I'll tell you that for nowt. I took the white cap from me breast pocket and was glad to cover them over, them evil smilin' eyes. My assistant strapped his ankles at same time, then I went through routine: noose over Mallik's head tightened towards t'right shoulder, fixed rubber washer, pulled the pin holdin' trapdoor and pushed lever. He was gone and rope were straight. It were a clean kill, clean as you like.'

'You hanged him?'

' 'Course I bloody hanged him. What d'yer think I was there fer? I went down below with doctor and he confirmed what I already knew. In those days it was my job to measure corpse, and the Count was a little bit longer than before, I can tell you that. But there weren't a twitch and nary a murmur. He was gone all right and a good job an' all, I thought at time.' He uttered a long, whining moan and closed his eyes. 'I wish he'd bloody well leave me alone now, though.'

31

'J*oe.*'

It was more of a hiss than a whisper.

Creed wheeled round and Henry Pink ducked beneath the sheet.

Cally entered the chamber, first glancing back down the passage, presumably to check that she hadn't been followed. Pink went foetal, pushing himself close to the stone wall, his back to his visitors.

'It's okay,' Creed reassured him. 'She's a good guy.'

A muffled kind of wheeze-grunt came from under the soiled sheet; the old man remained hidden.

'I don't know what the bastards who run this place have been doing to him, but he's terrified,' Creed said to the girl. 'He may be difficult, but nobody deserves this.'

Cally came close and her tone was low and urgent. 'Don't worry about him now, I want you to see something I've just discovered.'

Creed rose to his feet, not liking the sound of her voice at all. Even in the dimness he could see she was badly shaken.

She held on to him. 'I had no idea such things were going on here.'

He thought she was referring to poor Henry Pink and his living

258

conditions at that moment. 'Yeah, well, I think we can get this place closed down easily enough once we expose what's happening. All we need is the evidence.' He dug into his pocket, indicating the huddled figure with a nod of his head. 'This'll make a great shot.'

She tugged at his arm. 'There's no time for that. Come with me, I'll show you something much worse.'

'You kidding?' Creed whispered excitedly. 'I can't miss out on this. England's greatest and probably last executioner ending up like this, in an underground cell, sleeping in his own shit, haunted by his own past. It's wonderful.' He drew out the Nikon, switching on the flash recharger with easy speed. 'Hey, Mr Pink. Come out of there and look this way, will you? Won't take a second.'

The shape beneath the sheet hugged itself tight.

'Leave it, Joe. There are more important things to do.'

'Listen, Cally, grab the sheet and whip it back when I tell you. He's bound to look round. You should see the state he's in – it'll make a fantastic shot.'

'I don't believe this. How can you act this way? The poor man's frightened out of his wits and you want to take his photograph?'

'You should see his eyes. It's like they've seen the ghost of every person he's ever hanged.'

'Did he tell you about Nicholas Mallik?'

'Sure. But he's round the bend, mad as a hatter. He thinks his victims have come back to haunt him.'

'Mallik, too?'

'Especially Mallik. Move aside so I get some more light from the door.'

'Didn't you *listen* to him?'

Creed took his eye from the viewfinder. 'What's wrong with you? The man's crazy.'

'Nicholas Mallik is here.'

'Pink told me he hanged him.'

'He did.'

'Christ, make up your mind. Mallik either escaped the noose or he didn't. You can't have it both ways.'

Cally vented her frustration with an angry groan and a clawing at the air. 'Have it your own way, but come with me now.'

'A coupla quick shots. Hey, Mr Pink . . .' He stepped forward and, with much distaste, grabbed the edge of the bedsheet. 'Henry . . .' He tugged hard.

The old man rolled over with the covering as the photographer almost pulled it from the cot. Creed moved back a pace or two and swiftly lined up the shot. The small room flooded with blinding light and Pink's scream rang round the walls so piercingly that both Creed and the girl cringed.

'You really are a bastard, aren't you?' Cally said when the echoes had died away.

He shrugged acceptance and was about to reel off some more shots when a long, rising wail came through the wall from next door. Creed literally as well as metaphorically freeze-framed, finger poised, body motionless, as other cries filtered through from the passage outside. His look went from the bony, naked figure on the bed to Cally, and then to the open door. The combined wails and moans from out there steadily grew to a cacophony of misery.

'Judas,' Creed whispered. 'Showtime . . .'

Pink joined in the wailing.

'Can we go now?' Cally demanded rather than asked.

All he would get from the old executioner was a bare-arsed shot, so Creed nodded agreement and ducked out of the door ahead of the girl. The wretched ululation was even more alarming out there in the wide passage, for it seemed that every room had its own voice, and every voice encouraged its neighbour.

'They must keep the worst cases down here,' Creed said over the hubbub of woe. 'Or maybe they're the charity cases.' He glanced from left to right. 'We'd better make tracks before somebody comes to check it out.'

'The whole basement area is soundproofed from upstairs. Nobody will hear.'

'I don't suppose they'd want to spoil the Mountjoy's tranquillity with the clacking of the cuckoos, right? Did you say you'd discovered something else?'

Now, although still nervous – well, bowel-clenching witless, actually – and desiring nothing more than to be back in the warm, cosy world of sex, scandal, booze and smoke-filled rooms, Creed could feel the familiar buzz all good newsmen and paparazzi get when a unique or, at least, newsworthy story is there for the taking (or making). Creed, as we know, was a *good* paparazzo – one of the best, in fact – and his senses were being titillated to the full, so much so that all other dreads at that moment were being overridden. The contrast between the gracious manor house above, obviously where richer 'clients' were cared for, and the squalid dungeons below where the less sane and no doubt less wealthy 'clients' were interned, was fantastic. He wondered if the celebrity guests who had arrived that evening to pay tribute to the late Lily Neverless were aware of conditions belowstairs? The tabloid newspapers and the Sundays would love it, especially if he got some decent shots of the more distinguished guests to run alongside the picture of Henry Pink, a frightened skeleton of a man, forced to live in a perpetual twilight world, driven crazy by nightmares of his own past . . . Great stuff!

'I can show you if we hurry.'

'What?'

'You asked me what else I'd discovered,' said Cally. 'It's not far from here, but I'm expected back, so we'll have to be quick. I hope you've got a strong stomach.'

He looked at her quizzically. The wailing around them rose in pitch.

'Come on, Joe, I can't stand this noise.'

He allowed himself to be led away, although he regretted not having taken more snaps of poor Henry Pink. Something thudded against the inner side of a door to their left, but Cally dragged him onwards, not giving him time to investigate. Someone pummelled on another door and Creed wanted to stop and enquire who was in there; still the girl pulled and pushed him further along the passage. As he went he managed to turn and snap off a couple of shots of the almost mediaeval passageway behind them. Cally tugged at him impatiently.

They reached a corner and there in front of them was a solid and mean-looking iron door. Without hesitation the girl turned the wheel-handle and swung the door open. The brightness that poured through from the other side hurt Creed's eyes.

Cally hastened him into the passage beyond, and he found himself in a place that was in total contrast to the dreary nether region they'd just left. The walls here were spotlessly white, the floor grey-tiled and equally pristine. Neon tubes, like pointers, lit the way ahead.

'This is more like it,' Creed remarked. 'But why the Inner Sanctum back there? It's as if whoever runs this place wants those loonies to live in misery.'

'Perhaps that's it.'

'Huh?'

'A punishment of some kind?'

'For what?'

Cally shrugged. 'Who knows? Perhaps they upset someone at some time or other.'

He stared hard at her. 'You know more than you're saying.'

'Now's neither the time, nor the place. We have to move on, Joe.' She swung the door shut behind them, then started off down the passage.

Creed took a swift shot of the iron door before hurrying after her. She stopped halfway down and waited for him to catch up. 'In there . . .' she whispered when he drew close.

'What's in there?' he whispered back.

'You'll have to see for yourself.'

He examined the double-door that she indicated. It was made of overlapping plastic, much like the push-through doors used in hospitals. Already, as if by instinct, he felt queasy, and the paleness of Cally's features told him he had a right to feel that way.

'Can't you just tell me?' he said.

'You need to find out for yourself. Then perhaps you'll believe me about these people.'

'I believe, I believe.'

'Go in.'

Resignedly, and with much trepidation, he pushed one side of the door. It opened a little.

'Inside,' Cally insisted.

'You first.'

With a sigh, she pushed by him. He kept close behind.

They were in a small ante-chamber with a door opposite similar to the one they'd just come through.

'An airlock?' he suggested.

'The doors are sealed to keep the room beyond as sterile as possible. You'll find it's very cold in there.'

The coldness rushed out at them as though in flight when Cally opened the second set of doors. She held one side back for him and, drawing a chilly breath, Creed entered.

It was like stepping into a giant refrigerator, for it was cool enough inside . . . he froze, but not because of the low temperature . . . cool enough inside to store dead meat . . .

There stood, in the room's centre, a stainless steel table, the kind you might find in a morgue, with channels grooved in its surface for fluids to drain away. On the surface lay a naked grey-white body. There was a long gaping hole in the belly of that body.

The head was turned towards Creed and the girl, its mouth forming an immaculately toothsome grin of welcome. However, the welcome might have been more convincing had there not been a darkly-red hole where one of the head's eyes should have been. The remaining blue eye seemed friendly enough, if a little glazed.

Creed thought he recognised the grin, with all its capped perfection, but it was the silver-fringed bald head, gleaming as though recently Mr Sheened, that confirmed the recognition. Even then he had to make sure; whether out of morbid curiosity or simply because of shock he did not know, but closer he moved. He bent down to look the mutilated corpse in the eye.

Creed stepped away so quickly that he stumbled and fell against one of the white-tiled walls. He slid to the floor, retching along with the descent. He wanted to be sick, for the heaving mess that rose from stomach to chest would have been better out than in, but it wouldn't come; the bile just churned and lifted without making the full journey.

'Someone you know?' Cally asked from across the room.

He couldn't take his eyes off the corpse. 'Blythe. Antony Blythe. He writes the gossip column for my newspaper. I don't get it. What's . . . what was he doing here?'

'Why don't you take his picture?'

It was several moments before her remark registered, and several more moments before he could shift his gaze to her. 'Are . . . are you taking the piss?' he managed to say between gulps of purified air.

She had moved over to the stiffened body. 'You want interesting photographs. It's what you do, isn't it?'

'Leave it, Cally. Now's not the time.'

'I thought it was always time for a good shot, a great story. That's why you're here, isn't it? You thought you might be on to something hot.'

'I came here . . .'

'To see if I was telling the truth. And if I was, then you had quite a story on your hands.'

He pushed himself erect against the wall, but his knees were not ready to bear his weight. He held them rigid. 'I don't understand this,' he said desperately. 'I don't know why he came here and I don't know why you're talking this way.'

Cally hugged her bare shoulders against the cold and her face was angry, her eyes glaring. 'I wish I could trust you,' she said, but her voice softened, became quieter when she added: 'Were you in this together, Joe? Were you both working on the story you thought you had?'

'Cally, I swear I don't know why Blythe came here. We couldn't stand the sight of each other . . .' His words tailed off when he glanced towards the open cadaver. 'I don't know how he found out about this place,' he said lamely.

'You haven't told *any*one else?'

'I didn't know about it myself until last night.' Last night? It felt like half a century ago. He forced himself to look at the corpse again. Oh God, why had they gutted him? 'How did you know he was here, Cally?' he asked.

'I came down this way when I was looking for you. I looked into some of the rooms along this corridor – don't ask me why. Curiosity, I suppose. I wondered what they kept behind these doors.'

'Still you came and found me. Most women would have got the hell out.'

'You're forgetting my mother is here. I'll do anything to get her away.'

He couldn't be sure, he just couldn't be bloody sure if he could really depend on her. Too many things had happened, her involvement was too deep. And she kept showing up at the oddest times, even if she always had good reasons for doing so. But what else could he do? He had to find Sammy and get him out, and she was the only one who could help him do that.

'What now?' he asked grimly.

'The other rooms . . .'

'I don't want to see 'em.'

'They keep large jars in one . . .'

'I'm not interested.'

'In the jars . . .'

'Don't tell me, I don't want to know.'

'Parts of bodies . . . organs . . .'

He moaned.

'They preserve them . . .'

He walked towards the plastic doors. 'Are you coming?' he said over his shoulder.

'You'll still help me?'

'Like you keep telling me – I've no choice.' He turned at the doorway and raised the camera. 'Rest in peace, Antony. You were a bitch, but nobody deserves what they did to you.'

He took the shot.

32

ow you might think that the sight of Antony Blythe's eviscerated corpse would have been the last straw for Creed, the occasion that finally sent him over the edge; but then, blinded by his many faults so diligently recounted thus far, you might have forgotten how much stubbornness and dogged determination, not to mention sheer nerve, it takes to reach the top of the ignoble paparazzo tree. He'd had doors slammed in his face for years, and suffered threats, even physical violence against his person; yet in general he'd managed to overcome most of these setbacks and adversities, so much so that he was acknowledged as *pap supreme* by his peers, albeit grudgingly. The point being, there had to be some strong inner drive within Joe Creed's nature that endowed him with resilience, resolve against all odds (most odds, anyway). So far, two emotional concerns have prevailed over this evening's substantial disincentives to proceed: firstly (in correct order, that is), the sensing of a great – a truly great – news story and all the allure that went with that; and secondly, paternal instinct to protect his son. As of this moment, a third emotion has been aroused, and that is anger. Creed is bloody livid. Scared too, no denying that, but the outrage perpetrated upon a colleague (he'd had no liking for Blythe, far from it, but the man was a member of the NUJ, for God's sake!) has not only fired the other two motives already mentioned: the story is HUGE and the danger to Sammy has been proved beyond doubt. No Sir Galahad he, no defender of righteousness, but charge on does Creed . . .

'Joe – wait!'

Cally let the plastic door flap back and hurried after the photographer, who was by now some distance down the corridor. She caught up with him and pulled at his sleeve to bring him to a halt.

'What are you going to do?' she asked, gripping his arm tightly in case he tried to run off again.

'I'm gonna find my son and get him out of here. Then we're going straight to the police.'

(You didn't imagine, in all his anger, he was going to apprehend these vile villains himself, did you?)

'My moth—'

'She can wait! After I blow the lid off this place you'll get her back anyway.' Now he gripped her arm. 'You had a name for these people. What was it? Fallen Angels? Demon worshippers, didn't you say? Well, after seeing what they did to Blythe, I believe you. Oh yeah, I believe everything you've told me. What I don't believe, though, is those things I saw for myself – the woman, Laura, changing shape, becoming that disgusting glob of slime, and Dracula's double drilling a hole in me with a finger and watching me through a window that he couldn't possibly reach. Those, and more. A bed full of spiders making a meal of my blood, trees that go hiking, lifts that have a will of their own – you know, little things that don't happen every day of the week. I want to know, Cally, I want to know how they happened. They were all illusions, weren't they? But how did I think those things, how did they do it to me? I know you fed me something the other night that sent me a little crazy, but that was the only time you had the chance to. How did they make me *think* all those other things?'

'You didn't "think" them. They happened.'

He thrust her away. 'Go screw yourself.'

They faced each other, Creed white with rage and a big quota of fear, Cally in earnest, desperate to convince him.

'Look,' she said, moving in closer again and laying a soft hand on his chest, 'I know it all seems impossible, but there's a way you can prove it to yourself.'

Oh God, he thought, *she's sincere, she really means it.*

'The camera never lies, does it?' she persisted.

'Of course it bloody lies. The camera can say whatever you want it to say if you're clever enough.'

'But not to the person who's in control.'

'So what are you getting at?'

'Can you take pictures without using a flash?'

'In here? Sure, if the light's good enough. I've got the film for it and I can open up the camera setting. The shots won't be the greatest, but they should be usable.'

'Something will happen at the ball tonight that you'll see with your own eyes, but still you won't believe. Make the camera a witness too.' She tugged gently at his lapel. 'I can find a place to conceal you. No one will notice you if you're careful.'

Excitement began to hold sway over anger and fear. This sounded like an offer that was hard to refuse.

'You'll get a photograph that will make world news, Joe.'

Impossible to refuse.

'Give me a clue,' he said.

'I can't. You'll have to see for yourself. Even then you're going to doubt, which is why you'll need the camera.'

'Okay, you got me, I'm hooked. But what about Sammy? I've got to find him.'

'I'll do that while you're taking the photographs. Everyone will be intent on what's happening in the ballroom, so I won't be missed. It'll give me an opportunity to search the whole place if I move fast. I'll bring him to you and we'll leave.' She was nodding as if reassuring herself. 'You're right about my mother – nothing will happen to her now. I'll have her back as soon as the people who run this place are exposed for what they are. And you're going to help me do that.'

He drew in a deep breath. 'All right. One other thing while we're down here, though – where do they keep those pickled organs?'

*   *   *

It was a good place to observe while unobserved.

Cally had brought him to a shadowy balcony overlooking the long ballroom and although the floor below where the costumed guests were gathered was brightly lit by crystal wall lights, the upper regions were in gloom, as though hovering darkness over a gaiety of colour was a designed effect. Further along from the pillar behind which Creed knelt, his camera pointing through the fancy balustrade, was a minstrels' gallery; even there the musicians were cast in shadow, the only illumination being soft lights over their music sheets. A harpsichordist led the quartet through a lively High Baroque piece, music that was in keeping with the general choice of early eighteenth-century dress worn by the assembled company. Handel, Creed guessed, although for all he knew of the difference between classical and Baroque, it could have been Mozart or Bach. Whoever, the composer would have rolled over along with Beethoven had he known the sinister kind of establishment in which his jolly tunes were being aired.

He watched the dancers cavort or gavotte, whatever it was they did to this sort of thing, and cursed silently because they were all wearing masks – and some pretty bizarre ones at that. The shots he had taken so far were interesting enough, but worthless without the identities. He could only hope there would be a mass unmasking later on.

The musical piece came to an end and the dance (it seemed like nothing more than a sedate barn dance to Creed) concluded with it. Chatter and subdued laughter filled the gap until the orchestra began a minuet. As the dancers paired up again and the pale colours – golds, blues, pinks – of hooped gowns and flared coats genteelly swirled and dipped, Creed indifferently reeled off a few more frames, this time concentrating on the more preposterous masks among the crowd.

Although in a minority, a number of guests were in costumes other than the period most in evidence, some of the men even in normal black tie and dinner jackets, their partners wearing fashions you'd find in today's *Tatler*; yet no one was without a mask, be it half-face, full-face, or covering the head completely. And these, even the simplest, had one common theme: they were all grotesque. Like Cally's jackal head, many were caricatures of animals, several of the more exotic kind such as griffins, serpents, dragons and rukhs. One person wore the giant head of a rat.

And then there were the demons among them.

These came in all shapes and sizes and all manner of images. With the Nikon's zoom lens, Creed was able to pull in close and he had to admit that the make-up and disguise of some of the guests was quite incredible, if somewhat over the top.

Creed thought they must be hired masqueraders, there to lend fantastical atmosphere to the revelry, for they were treated with almost mock reverence as they wandered through the crowd. Oddly, their clothes – robes, tunics, or loincloths in some cases – seemed lacklustre and shabby, like well-worn jumble from a village sale, and the creatures themselves (difficult to think of them as people, so professional were their disguises) appeared weary, as if the evening was a little too much for them. They shuffled rather than walked, their bodies stooped and uncertain. In truth, they looked dreary rather than exotic.

One was almost naked, a fat-bellied thing with the beak and crest of a rooster; a faded crown adorned his head and a tail in the form of a snake dragged behind him. He wore dulled metal amulets, carried a whip, and appeared to be walking on serpents rather than legs (how did he *do* that?). Another resembled a peacock, tail feathers spread in dingy splendour, his face elongated like a donkey's. Yet another sported limp, tattered wings and a long gown whose ragged edges dragged along the floor; he would have looked like a downtrodden angel had not his countenance been so disgustingly ugly and had he not carried a mock viper that wriggled and squirmed as if real (clever stuff, this). Creed wondered if this was the idiot's crass idea of a Fallen Angel. His attention was drawn to someone wearing a crown over long horns. Huge thick-haired ears protruded from this one's skull, and the goatish face was enhanced by a straggly beard. Fingers and toes tapered impossibly and on his wrist was perched an unhooded goshawk. A white-haired woman – he *assumed* it was a woman – hobbled past the dancers, her face so haggard and severe it seemed she bore the world's ills upon her crooked shoulders. She was strange enough in herself, but what was even stranger was that one half of her body was painted blue. An individual who Creed couldn't figure out at all was a man who had a single eye in the centre of his face, a hand that emerged from his chest, and an extra leg that came out of his backside (how *did* he do that?). His skin was covered in metallic feathers.

Creed shook his head in scorn. Maybe *they* thought they looked like demons, but to him they were merely a bunch of badly designed freaks. There were others down there – some even more bizarre – but by now Creed was bored by them. *If you've seen one devil, you've seen 'em all*, he told himself as he sank into a more comfortable position on the balcony floor. He rested his back against the pillar, taking care he couldn't be seen by the musicians further along.

Was this what Cally wanted him to witness? Christ, there were better weirdos at the annual Alternative Miss World, when the more extravagant drags went on parade.

He wondered if she had found Sammy yet. The journey from the basement had been easy enough, although once they'd had to duck out of sight when they heard voices around the corner ahead. By this time they were on the ground floor and the room they'd hidden in was an office filled with filing cabinets. He'd recognised the high piping voice of the fat receptionist as footsteps passed by the closed door. Creed had taken the opportunity to change the film in his camera, and then had wanted to snoop into some of those files; but Cally wouldn't allow it, telling him it was too dangerous to loiter.

Avoiding the main reception area, they had moved towards the rear of the house, into the quieter regions. Cally found a narrow staircase (she seemed to know the place like the back of her hand, and Creed was uneasy about that; still, her mother *had* been locked up there a long time, so maybe it was almost a second home to Cally) which led them to a side entrance to the balcony overlooking the grand ballroom. Behind the minstrels' gallery was another, much wider, staircase which he assumed descended to the ballroom itself. She had left him there to observe proceedings, warning him to stay hidden and to keep very, very quiet; she promised to return as quickly as possible. That had been over an hour ago, perhaps a bit longer.

At first the spectacle downstairs had dazzled and even excited him, although he soon sensed that the atmosphere wasn't quite as convivial as it appeared. The mood of the revellers(?) seemed strained, anxious somehow, rather than cheerful. There was a tension in the air, a brittle kind of expectancy that was almost tangible.

He decided he wasn't going to wait around much longer. Another ten minutes and he'd go in search of Sammy himself. He'd find him even if it meant checking every room in the goddamn place and kicking down doors to do so! Enough was enough.

He checked how much film was left in the camera, which wasn't easy in that dim light. Plenty more for the main event, he assured himself. *If* there was to be a main event. He glanced down at the ballroom again.

Well, there was one he hadn't noticed before. God, this guy was an ugly brute. Big and pretty clumsy too (unless he was very drunk). The other guests were quickly stepping out of his path as he clomped through them. Those who failed to notice his approach in time were rudely nudged aside. Every so often the tall man would come to a halt and stand there looking around, his whole upper torso moving with his head as though he were wearing a neck and back brace of some kind beneath his baggy jacket. Creed tried to think who he reminded him of.

His fancy dress was pretty crummy compared to most of the other guests' and the mask he wore, with its ridiculously high forehead and scar-stitched face, was neither extreme enough nor subtle enough to win any prizes. Oh yeah, that's who he looked like: a cheapo edition of the old Frankenstein monster. This was a *weird* way of honouring the late Lily Neverless; but then maybe it was exactly what the old girl had wanted. The movie world loved eccentrics, didn't it?

Whoops! Frankie had bumped into one of the dancers, and the other guy didn't seem too pleased. This one was a snazzier dresser in his velvet frock coat, embroidered waistcoat and knee breeches. A powdered wig would have been more in keeping with the costume though, rather than the mangy-haired mask that made him look like an oversized Yorkshire terrier. A ferocious one at that, for he snarled at the big man and swiped at the air between them with an equally hairy paw – sorry, hand. Creed zoomed in and took a snap.

His hope that something worthy might develop from this incident was dashed when the big man turned and lumbered away, treading on a lady guest's delicate foot as he went. She howled, but her partner, who was wearing a threatening Scaramouche mask, bowed an apology at the broad back and timidly led her hobbling away. Terrier Man – or Wolf Man, as he undoubtedly thought of himself – resumed the dance, and very graceful he was too.

Creed lost patience and began to tuck the Nikon back into his coat. He was too agitated to sit there any longer; too agitated and too bloody scared for Sammy and himself! Time to move out, find the boy and run. And if he *couldn't* find his son, then the police would have to. That was their job, that's what they were paid for.

The music stopped abruptly as he was pushing himself to his feet, and a peculiar hush fell over the assembly. There was no more chatter, although whispers passed through the crowd like a rustling breeze; there was no more laughter, and no one dared even to cough. Creed peered through the ornamental balustrade, puzzled by the intensified atmosphere. He saw one man grab his partner to hold her upright as she swooned. Everyone was perfectly still. They were all looking in the same direction.

At the far end of the room was a short but broad semi-circular staircase leading up to a curtained set of arched doors. A lone, gaunt figure was standing before the doors.

The man Cally claimed was Nicholas Mallik wore the same eighteenth-century attire chosen by so many of the guests that night, except that his costume had none of the soft shades of those others. His was black. Jet black with thin gold braid edging the tunic and swirling through the waistcoat. Even the muslin scarf around his neck and tied in a bow over a white wig at the back was black, as were the stockings rising from buckled shoes.

Had it not been for his deeply lined face and thin frame he might have looked wickedly elegant. As it was, he merely looked wicked.

But why no mask? Creed wondered. True, with a kisser like that a funny mask wasn't entirely necessary to keep faith with the company of grotesques down there, but why should he be the only one to flout the party spirit?

An extraordinary thing happened then. Someone in the crowd whispered a name, and so still was the room that the sound carried to every part. Somebody else repeated the name, louder this time, although still in a whisper. Now another person spoke it, and yet another joined in. Soon it was chorused around the ballroom, but quietly as though there was something awesome in its very sound.

'*Belial.*'

Everyone present sank to their knees and bowed their heads.

Creed blinked. Even the women were grovelling on the floor. He shook his head in surprise. Who *was* this guy? Did these people kneel in reverence or in fear? And why were they calling him Belial? Well, at least they weren't calling him Mallik, so that scotched the idea that the mass murderer had risen from the dead! Creed smiled grimly. He had almost – *almost* – come to the point of believing it himself. Despite his own ridicule, he had started to have doubts! Schmuck.

But this was great. As he'd suspected all along, this was some freaky kind of quasi-religious set-up. Or its opposite, more likely. Judging by many of those disguises, plus what was going on in the Retreat's cellars, *definitely* the latter. Creed retrieved the Nikon from his pocket, hoping desperately that a grand unmasking was about to take place and he could snap some well-known faces. Oh the fame, the glory. The lovely filthy lucre! He'd be able to name his own price.

He zoomed in for a close-up of the man they were calling Belial (had a strangely familiar ring to it, that name) and shuddered. Christ, he was an evil-looking mother. This was only the second time Creed had got a really good look at those deep-set eyes and he realised they were as black as sin itself. (Hadn't they been a pale grey the first time he'd seen them?) Their dark gaze drifted over the masqueraders as if demanding complete supplication and woe betide anyone who wasn't offering it.

Creed jerked back as those thunderous eyes seemed to meet his own.

He held his breath and bit into his lip as he crouched as low as he could possibly get. Surely he couldn't have been seen – it was too gloomy up there, the thick balustrade he hid behind too concealing. Yet for a split-second – not even that; an infinitesimal fraction of time – Creed had experienced that same jolt, that same stab-into-the-mind sensation as when they had first locked eyes in the cemetery.

This time it had been sharp, like an instant electric shock; it left him momentarily stunned.

Nothing else happened however, at least, not as far as he was concerned. There was no shout of alarm from below, no denouncing finger pointing his way.

Cautiously, Creed aimed the camera again and took a quick shot.

Through the viewfinder he noticed the low light reading and realised that the ballroom had become perceptibly dimmer; he quickly adjusted the setting and took another couple of shots.

Belial (*Belial?*) had begun to speak and, although his voice was low, his words were perfectly audible even to Creed up on the balcony.

'There are doubters among you,' the man said, seeming to challenge everyone in the room, including Creed himself. 'There are those who, despite all they have witnessed, all they have been given, are still unsure of the old powers. There are those among you who have been corrupted by the age in which you live, your minds jaded by the mundanity of materialistic realism and values, your faith dwindled by the atheism of your own intellect, your senses pathetically satiated by bogus and vulgar imageries of celluloid fantasy and the false word.'

Prat, Creed thought.

'Should your hearts and minds be so shallow that you perceive the mysteries and ancient ideologies as mere divertissements, indulgent abstractions eventually to be scorned, there is no place here for you. I will also remind you of this: if you do not believe in the God, you cannot believe in the anti-God.

'Each of you has been touched by the powers and gained from their influences, yet even so there are those who are not satisfied, and others who fear that the forces of the outcast Angels, the Archangels and the Virtues, are waning, that anarchic scepticism towards all things nether-worldly has dissipated their spiritual potency.'

Creed quietly clucked his tongue. If he'd got it right, this guy was bemoaning the fact that nobody believed in the boogeyman any more, that it was all entertainment as far as the great unwashed public was concerned. Maybe he had a point.

'Tonight your faith will be renewed and your beliefs strengthened for the new millennium, when once more disorder shall reign and the dark hierarchies shall roam the earth. You, the disciples of the diablerie, shall follow in our paths and be awash with our glory.'

Someone applauded, hesitantly at first, and Creed wondered if it was out of embarrassment. But no – others joined in and soon the whole room was in appreciative uproar. The speaker held up his hand to stay the noise and Creed aimed the camera again. The raised hand, in Hitleresque salute, would please the caption writers.

The speaker continued, his voice low and as dark as the clothes he wore. 'Tonight the Power will also be witnessed by an outsider . . .'

Uneasy murmurs spread around the ballroom.

'. . . an outsider who epitomises the cancerous cynicism of this secular and creedless age. Someone who has joined us willingly and who will provide impartial testimony to our omnipotence.'

Creed looked up from the viewfinder for a moment and stared. His eye went back to the camera.

Ravage-face appeared in the lens again, an ugly smile on his thin, line-ridged lips. His gaze roved over the audience before him as Creed fiddled with the focus. Judas, this face was pure unadulterated evil. Fantastic. Creed clicked the shutter.

And as he did so, and as if on cue, the man he was photographing looked directly into the lens.

Pain as well as shock caused Creed to close his eyes. It was as though the delicate walls of his brain had been scraped crudely with an artist's pallette knife. His whole body cringed into itself and his sudden cry brought spittle to his lips.

He blinked, forced himself to look down into the ballroom once again.

All the masked faces were turned in his direction and the man in black, the one they called Belial, was pointing up at him.

Creed rose awkwardly, the Nikon falling to his chest to hang there, forgotten, no longer important. He wanted out, *right now*, out of this hell-hole. The dread in him outweighed anything else, even the thought of rescuing Sammy. *Out, out, out . . .*

He whirled around. And stopped dead.

The jackal mask was grinning at him.

Cally was holding Sammy's hand.

Creed's jaw sagged. He tried to say his son's name.

But Cally was removing the jackal mask.

And it wasn't Cally at all.

It was the dark-haired woman, the one called Laura.

And she was smiling too, just like the maniac below.

And Creed realised for the first time that her teeth were slightly crooked, crooked like Cally's.

33

The tight, sequinned gown was like the one Cally had been
wearing too, although the cleavage was under considerably
more pressure from Laura's brimming breasts. Her bitter/musky
odour came at him in a wave and he knew he'd sniffed something
like it earlier that evening, although it had been more subtle, an
underlying fragrance, a bouquet rather than a heavy scent. He'd
noticed it when Cally had returned to the boxroom where he'd been
hiding while she searched for Henry Pink.

As if to mock him with the truth, Laura shimmered her image so
that for an instant her features transmuted to Cally's.

Creed felt dizzy. His body sagged.

With great effort, he steadied himself; he was in *too* much trouble
to faint.

He switched his attention to Sammy. His son seemed out of it, his
eyes glazed, unfocused. He was still wearing his school uniform, the
tie askew, shirt collar unbuttoned. But he didn't appear to be harmed;
doped up, maybe, but otherwise untouched.

'Sam . . . ?'

The boy blinked, but did not answer. A tiny frown shadowed his
pale forehead.

The woman was frowning too, but with hers went a grin. 'They're waiting for you downstairs,' she informed Creed.

One of her hands reached behind for the boy's coat collar and, with no effort at all, she raised him from the floor. Sammy hung limply, still no recognition in his gaze. Slowly, and still watching Creed, Laura turned her head and 'breathed' the boy.

Creed reacted instantly, possibly faster than he'd reacted to anything in his life before. He lunged for his son, rising into the air and taking him on the jump like a basketball player collecting a high pass, the impetus wrenching the boy from the woman's grasp. Creed stumbled on, Sammy clutched to his chest. He shifted his burden on to his shoulder as he gathered pace.

Unfortunately, in his panic Creed ran straight into the quartet of musicians grouped together in the semi-darkness. Cello, violin and viola clattered to the floor, arms and legs intertwined like Kerplunk sticks. Creed struck out, kicked out, yelled out, and generally made a nuisance of himself among the fallen bodies. As he rose, bringing Sammy up with him, one of the musicians (a man so emaciated he made Mother Teresa look a glutton) raked at Creed's chest with twiggy fingers. A hard-driven knee under the musician's pointed chin put paid to that nonsense; he fell away with a plaintive squeal and a badly bitten tongue.

Creed cradled Sammy in his arms, carrying him like a baby, one arm around his shoulders, the other beneath his knees. Toppling music stands and kicking aside obstructing limbs, he staggered towards the central staircase. The descent wasn't easy – Sammy really had to cut down on shakes and burgers – and twice Creed's heel slipped off the steps, only good fortune and desperation preventing disaster. He reached the turn and realised too late that the stairs only led to the ballroom itself. Worse still, lumbering up towards him was the crazy fuck made up to look like Frankenstein's monster.

All in all, the evening was turning out badly.

'Keep away!' Creed warned, taking a step backwards, and then another. This was a bad dream, his – *anybody's* – worst nightmare. Although the make-up didn't have quite the same scare factor as Boris Karloff's original, this one was big and frightening enough in his own right. 'I'll kick your teeth in, you come any closer,' Creed warned again. And he meant it, he really did.

Unperturbed, the monster climbed.

Creed took a threatening step towards him, changed his mind and turned to run back upstairs. He stopped, almost overbalancing, for Laura was coming down to him.

But she wasn't walking, not in the real sense; she was sort of floating and shape-changing at the same time, her edges wavering, becoming messy, bits of her dripping on to the steps, smearing one of the walls. What was left of her face leered rather than smiled.

'Oh . . .' Creed couldn't help but say.

He turned again and stood at the centre of the bend where he could view both staircases. Sammy stirred. 'No school today, Mum,' the boy pleaded in his sleep. He snuggled his head into his father's chest.

Creed had two choices, neither of which was particularly attractive. If they ascended, the quick-growing glutinous mess would engulf them; if they descended, the brute would flatten them.

Oh shit.

He took two fast paces down, then leapt feet first at the climbing figure, Sammy held tight in his arms. With luck (and it was about time some of *that* came his way) the 'goliath' would break their fall.

As it turned out the fall broke the goliath's neck; however, that didn't hamper him as much as it should have.

When all three had tumbled to the bottom of the stairs Creed heard the snap – an awfully *loud* snap – of breaking bones and as he slithered himself and Sammy off the floundering giant, he fervently hoped the damage was mortal. Imagine his surprise when he pushed himself into a sitting position to find the other man also starting to sit up, albeit very clumsily and with a lot of arm-waving and nonsensical roaring. The monster's neck was at a ridiculous angle, the head flopping loosely on to his chest. He used a big, scarred hand to push his forehead upwards so that he could look accusingly at Creed. His other hand swiped angrily in the photographer's direction.

But now others grabbed at Creed and his son. Sammy was wrenched from his arms as Creed was dragged to his feet. Resistance was useless, but he did his best. After some tussling and a lot of cursing, he was confronted by the roly-poly receptionist, who (obviously not having being invited to the ball) still wore her pale blue uniform and fluffy pink cardigan. She also wore a very serious expression. Two muscly men, the kind you see in those High 'n'

Mighty catalogues, in the male equivalent of the blue uniform (without pink cardy), held his arms.

'Let go of me!' Creed demanded. 'You people don't realise how much trouble you're in.'

The receptionist smirked. 'You're the one who's in trouble,' she said in her squeaky voice. 'We knew you'd come back. You're even more stupid than you look.'

Inwardly, Creed agreed. He was, he really was, stupid. Why hadn't he cut and run when he'd had the chance? He looked around for Sammy.

The boy was awake again and on his feet, although still doddery. He was being held by one of the costumed guests, someone dressed in a white silk Armani dinner jacket and paisley waistcoat. He also sported a jackal head.

Sammy blinked his eyes several times, the lids remaining heavy as though sleep was not fully conquered. 'Dad . . . ?' he said when he saw Creed in the grip of the two male nurses, attendants, warders, whatever they were.

'It's okay, Sam. The police will be here soon to give us a ride home.'

That assurance set off a drone of murmuring through the crowd gathered around them.

'I think not.' The voice came from the far end of the ballroom, but it was as clear and as menacing as ever. The crowd parted like the Red Sea to reveal the dark-clothed man who claimed to be (or whom others claimed to be) Nicholas Mallik. 'Bring them to me,' he said.

Creed was reluctant to go, but had little say in the matter. The two attendants (or warders, etc.) propelled him forward, while Jackal Head brought along the sleepy boy.

'A lot of people know where I am!' Creed shouted, resisting still. 'My newspaper for a start!'

'Nobody knows you're here.' Mallik's low voice carried such conviction that Creed quaked. Someone in the crowd tittered; someone else laughed aloud.

Odd, fantastical faces peered into his as he was hustled along, some of them so credible (lifelike would be the wrong word in this context), so skilfully made, that it was difficult to consider them as masks. The fat man with the beak for a nose and a rooster's crest on his head prodded Creed with his whip. The photographer flinched and kicked out at the blubber belly, but the attendants kept him in check. As he was manhandled onwards he wondered if he hadn't hurt himself more than he'd thought in the fall down the stairs: the fat weirdo hadn't been quite in focus when he'd aimed a kick at him.

Eyes behind masks stared as he passed; other eyes, patently false, for they bulged from the masks themselves, inexplicably gleamed with malicious pleasure at his predicament. The two-tone hag, one side of her painted blue, stood on tiptoe to cackle into his face. He jerked his head aside at the terrible stench that was discharged.

Creed managed to look over his shoulder for his son and saw he was right behind, the dopey expression still there, his mouth half-open, not in fear but in dulled bewilderment.

'Don't worry, Sammy,' Creed called back, his bravado not quite up to scratch by now, 'we'll –'

Something had bumped into him. Creed turned to look into the shaggy face of the masquerader with the head and paws of an unkempt dog. Canine teeth were bared only inches from Creed's nose and he almost gagged at the foul breath – this one hadn't seen his dental hygienist for a long time either. For a terrifying moment, he thought the wolfman was going to bite him – those teeth were *wicked* – but suddenly the attendant on Creed's left gave the pest's snub nose a sharp smack. The wolfman yelped and loped away whimpering like – well, yes, like a chastised dog.

Creed looked from one attendant to the other and said, 'You gotta be kidding.'

They forced him to walk, no emotion in their expression, just two regular guys doing their jobs like Heinrich and Hermann did theirs in the old days. They threw him at the foot of the short staircase where Nicholas Mallik had been waiting patiently.

Creed landed heavily on hands and knees, but angrily, fearfully, pushed himself to his feet.

'I'm gonna sue for this!' he shouted. 'You're making a very big mistake!'

'No, you're the one who has made the mistake,' came the soft-spoken reply.

Yeah, Creed thought, I trusted the girl. Or at least, went along with her.

'Unfortunately you have interfered in matters that are well beyond your very limited perception.' Mallik took a step towards him and

Creed took two steps back. The pale blue wall of muscle behind prevented further retreat.

He grimaced at the close sight of that withered and worn countenance, a face so saturnine, with so much evil written in those deeply trowelled lines, and so infinitely aged, that this man could have been a *thousand* years old.

'Look, I don't care what you're into,' Creed insisted, trying not to wilt under the intimidating inspection. 'I've already handed over the photographs, so what more do you want from me? I just take snaps, you know, I'm not interested in anything else. I mean, what did I have anyway? A picture of a grief-stricken mourner at the graveside of a dear, departed actress. Big deal. Who gives a – who gives a damn?'

'But you've witnessed so much more. And your presence here tonight would eventually cause further problems.'

Creed didn't like the way Mallik was smiling.

'All I've seen tonight is a high-class fancy dress party. What's so special about that?'

'Oh, but you've had a grand tour, you've discovered much more than you should have. You have visited the secret chambers below this house, for instance. Tell me, what impressions do you have?'

The décor could have been a little brighter, Creed thought of quipping, but somehow the humour wasn't in him; his mouth was too dry, his throat was too tight and – oh God, he was too scared. What were they going to do with him and Sammy?

'No comment? Too tongue-tied? Now there's a refreshing change.' Mallik raised his head and addressed the assembled guests. 'This person . . .' even the finger he pointed was rutted with lines '. . . this fool, this unbeliever, represents – no, is the *embodiment* – of today's vulgarian society, a society that denies the traditions, and the truths, of the ancient faiths, a society that mocks the subversive dynasties and substitutes its own shallow mythic creations.'

He glared, he spat out the words. 'The infernal deities are ignored in favour of false devils, the kind who have blades for fingers, or wear foolish masks, or are physically deformed, imposters who create havoc with nothing more than knives or cleavers. Mundane demi-demons who possess chainsaws rather than diabolic powers. While we . . .' he roared the word '. . . WE . . . are passed over for these new fashions in evil.'

282

Creed shook his head in disbelief. This guy was pissed off with Freddy Krueger and his pals.

Mallik's voice quietened again. 'Even our own creations have been stolen and adulterated into spurious visual fallacies that serve as entertainment, unworthy thrills for the masses. This feckless insensibility has wearied us. Our primacy in the order of chaos is diminished by public capriciousness and social cynicism. Our sovereignty over the iniquitous courses is threatened by glib, deceitful metaphors. But this rot will end, and it will end tonight. This one . . .' he stabbed the wrinkled finger at Creed again '. . . will bear witness to our resurgence, this cynic will *believe* in the rebirth.'

Everyone in the ballroom appeared pleased at the idea. They applauded, they cheered. One or two even gave game-show whoops.

'If it's all the same to you . . .' Creed began to say, but Mallik didn't even have to ask him to be quiet; his look stung the photographer hard enough to make his body sag. If the two attendants had not held him he would have collapsed completely.

Creed wrenched himself away and shook his head to clear it. 'Who . . . who are you?' he stammered. 'Who are you really?'

'You know my identity,' the man in black replied. 'It was Nicholas Mallik in my last existence. Now I'm called Parmount. In this world, that is.'

'So they didn't hang you. You got away with it, you did a deal.'

'Don't be ridiculous. Naturally I was hanged, and very unpleasant it was too.' He reached for the silk scarf at his neck and loosened it. 'See for yourself,' he invited.

Creed took in the shrivelled throat and flinched at the ugly scars there, scars that looked as though they had been caused by rope-burn. Although they were undoubtedly old, they were still a vivid mauve mottled with red, the flesh itself indented.

'You survived *that*?'

The other man became impatient. 'Of course I didn't survive. But I survived afterwards.'

Creed nodded as if he understood. Then he said, 'I don't understand.'

'You will . . . presently.'

Mallik aka Belial aka Parmount half-turned towards the arched door at the top of the staircase and the assembled guests became hushed once more. He called a name: 'Bliss.'

The curtained door opened slowly. The Nosferatu doppelgänger emerged.

Creed stared. Bliss? *Bliss?* This freak was called fucking *Bliss?*

Bliss was leading someone by the hand.

She was in pink, but pretty by no means. The ballgown's skirt was hooped and foamy with lace, and white gloves rose over her elbows. Her shoulders were covered, but the neckline plunged obscenely for one of her age and condition; her chest was rutted and liver-spotted. The skin of her neck and upper arms hung in loose folds from the bones as if meat inside had wasted away.

Helped by her thin escort, she tottered out to the top of the stairs and looked around in a jerky parody of regality. Creed heard the masqueraders behind him gasp in awe.

Her descent was precarious and twice she lurched, only the swift attention of Bliss (*Bliss?*) preventing her from falling.

The one attractive thing about Lily Neverless was the wig she wore, the same outdated but shiny trademark bob she'd used in most of her movies and for public appearances.

Clasped in her free hand – the other was held grimly by her hunchbacked aid – was a cigarette in a long black holder, another trademark of Lily's, and several times during her unsteady descent she attempted to place the end between her heavily rouged lips. Unfortunately she seemed incapable of coordinating her actions and all she achieved was a continual poking of her cheek and chin.

Oddly (an understatement if ever there was one) a vividly blue eye, along with her other natural brown one, was staring fixedly at Creed.

He cringed, he shuddered. He guessed where that alien blue eye had come from. Again his body sagged and this time it was nausea as well as fright that weakened him.

Lily, or the thing that once had been Lily, leered crookedly as she drew near.

She uttered something, cleared her scraggy throat and tried again. 'He . . . ooks . . .'

A dry tongue flicked across her glossy lips. 'He . . . looks . . .'

She passed by Mallik on the stairs and his eyes were hooded, thoughtful. She reached the bottom, wobbled a little, then extended the cigarette holder towards Creed.

'He . . . looks . . . ike . . . Mi . . . ickey . . . Rourke,' she said.

34

C reed was too shocked to speak, too petrified to move.
Lily Neverless – the *dead* Lily Neverless – was standing
before him, swaying a little, a nerve twitching in one cheek, but
standing there, impossibly breathing and smiling and watching him
with one rheumy brown eye and one dazzlingly blue eye, the blue
eye not hers at all but winkled out of Antony Blythe's lifeless skull
(*had* he been lifeless when they stole it from him?) and stitched into
this . . . this zombie's. And there was no doubt in his mind that this
was her, this *was* Lily Neverless, for he'd been this close to her on
other occasions, on *normal* occasions, when he'd reeled off shots as
she'd arrived at theatres or left restaurants, and she'd either smiled
or scowled, depending on her mood, so he knew, he was sure, that
it was her, that Lily Neverless had returned from the grave . . .

He *believed*.

He suddenly *believed* everything he had been told about these
people, about Nicholas Mallik defying the noose, about demons and
monsters and power over life and death. He *believed* . . .

Lily lurched a step nearer.

Oh God, *this* was her *coming-out* ball.

Her other hand worked loose from her macabre escort's grasp and reached to touch Creed's face.

She made a burbling noise, a word of some kind that had no sense. Pale yellow liquid ran from one nostril.

Creed's chest expanded, gathering strength for his scream.

But before he could, all hell broke loose.

35

The catalyst was white lightning, brilliant, instant flashes that filled the ballroom and blinded vision. But there was no following thunder, only continuous and silent fulgurations that were so swift they were almost one long outburst of light.

The masqueraders searched around and blinked, and blinked again, bewildered for the moment and totally hushed. Creed, who was used to the glare of flashbulbs, automatically shielded his eyes.

Nicholas Mallik was frozen on the steps, those dark eyes uncomprehending. Lily Neverless moved in this strobe effect in the manner of her earliest silent movies. Bliss wheeled this way and that, a giant white-headed spider ensnared in a net of fluctuating luminance.

This only lasted seconds. Then somebody screamed, and it wasn't Creed.

There was pandemonium when others took up the scream, everyone in the ballroom suddenly galvanised by the sound. There were shouts, confusion and a lot of rushing about.

Only Creed knew exactly what was happening. He turned towards the tall french windows that graced one side of the long room and from where the camera flashes were emanating. He thanked God, he very nearly went down on his knees and raised his hands to the Lord right there and then. The boys were all here.

One of the window-doors burst inwards under the combined weight of the excited paparazzi outside. The breeze fluttered the heavy drapes on either side as the cameramen tumbled through, more following, stepping over their colleagues, camera motors whirring, lenses pointed at the old shrivelled actress who danced an ungainly solitary waltz, smiling for the crowds, a star again, her blue eye twinkling in the light, the brown one curiously dull and flat. Although mystified, amazed and perplexed, the photographers never ceased their busy work, the veterans among them realising they were getting the shots of a lifetime, the younger paps, who perhaps didn't quite appreciate the legend they were shooting, nevertheless carried away by the news value of the subject. This once-great star had fooled the world into believing she was dead.

Creed could have kissed every ugly one of them – he could have *French*-kissed every one of them – including Bluto who, as usual, was well to the fore, shuffling around on his knees like some stunted troll, trying to steady his Leica whilst being nudged and elbowed by his equally enthusiastic chums. Unembarrassed by conscience, not giving a toss about invasion of privacy, trespass, or hooliganism, they advanced on Lily Neverless, calling her name and pleading for her to *stand still for a moment*!

'Is she the real Lily?' one of them shouted to Creed.

He nodded and couldn't stop nodding as he backed away from them all, his blue-uniformed minders rushing past him to get at the paparazzi pack. He bumped into masqueraders who seemed at a loss to know what to do with themselves. Several held their masks in place with their hands as if to secure their identities.

A roar carried over the general babble and everyone in the vicinity looked towards the staircase where Nicholas Mallik stood rooted, his shoulders hunched, a quivering finger pointed at the intruders. His face, thunderous at the best of times, was dark – literally *blackened* – with rage. To Creed's astonishment (further astonishment, given everything that had gone on before) the man seemed to be breathing steam (it *had* to be cold air coming through from the open window misting the warmer draughts of wrath from Mallik's nostrils, *had* to be).

'*How dare you!*' he screeched, his usual sombre tones not much in evidence now. '*How dare you enter these premises!*'

The photographers gawped.

Someone took a snap.

'*Get out!*'

They looked at each other, eyebrows raised. One of them shrugged and took another picture.

Mallik's chest and shoulders began to heave. The vaporous air from his nose blew in a steady stream. His image began to falter.

Creed saw the gradual, wavering transformation and almost sank to the floor in an overload of terror. He watched and thought of storybooks and horror-movie devils, although this was more subtle, far less extreme than those man-conceived visions, yet all the more horrific – and *real* – for that. The manifestation wasn't clear, for it quivered, throbbed, became a kind of shifting hologram, ebbing but returning with added force, growing bolder until it was firm and unmoving. Those around Creed sunk low, whether in fear or homage he had no idea.

'Who is that guy?' one of the paparazzi asked.

'Nobody,' another replied.

They turned back to Lily Neverless, who was by now staggering around like a grotesque marionette, most of whose strings had been cut.

'Over here, Lil.'

'This way.'

'How 'bout a smile?'

'Why'd you pretend to be dead, Lil?'

Creed wiped his palms over his face. He looked incredulously from the glowering demon to the ratpack. They didn't see what he and others in the ballroom did. The hideous metamorphosis had had no effect on them whatsoever, *they saw nothing unusual at all.*

He went back to the demon again and saw only a tired and stooped old man on the stairway, someone who contemplated the pack of photographers with weary despair. Mallik's body seemed to shrink into itself with the defeat.

Pandemonium started up all over again.

'Dad!'

Creed whirled around. Sammy evidently was no longer so sleepy; he was twisting in the arms of the man wearing the jackal mask, trying to get away. Creed pushed his way through costumed figures to get to them.

Grabbing hold of the boy's arm, he tugged hard, but the masked man pulled from the other side. Someone ran past in panic, bumping the photographer and almost knocking him over; but he kept his hold on Sammy, refusing to give him up. He tugged again, but the other man clung on grimly. In desperation Creed finally let go of the boy and went for the man, grabbing the mask's long snout and jerking it aside so that he could smash a fist into the exposed face. The jackal head fell to the floor.

'Lidcrap!'

The grimace of pure hatred Lidtrap wore was infinitely more ugly than the fancy dress mask. He tossed his dampened blond curls from his eyes and hurled himself at Creed.

The photographer had dodged people as angry as this one many times in the past though, and was, in fact, master of the cunning duck. Lidtrap went sailing past and Creed used a sharp elbow in the back to help him on his way. The expensive Armani jacket ripped nicely as Lidtrap slid along the ballroom floor.

Creed grasped the boy's hand and glanced around wildly, not sure of which way to run. He wasn't the only one in this dilemma, for figures dashed here and there in total disorder, colliding with each other, shoving, pushing. It appeared that nobody wanted to be photographed.

The open french window was the best bet, Creed decided. Get among the paps and worm through to the outside. Taking Sammy with him, he made his way in their direction. A few of them were arguing with the two attendants who were jumping up and down in front of the pack, waving their arms to spoil the shots. One of them made the mistake of trying to snatch Bluto's Leica. Now Bluto got upset very easily when anybody touched his camera – even Sean Penn had learned never to get too obstreperous with this particular paparazzi – and he smacked the offending hand; then, to show how serious he was, he smacked the attendant's cheek. All three, both attendants and Bluto himself, went down in a struggling heap after that, which left the other paparazzi happily free to get on with the job in hand.

'Come on, Sam,' Creed urged, moving swiftly, 'we're getting out.'

But something snagged his collar, spinning him round. The man made up as a pug-nosed wolf uttered a low growling sound that Creed would have thought ridiculous had he not seen and heard too much that defied reason that evening. He turned his head aside from the awful breath as canine teeth snapped at his throat.

'Don't be bloody stupid!' he said, grabbing at the shaggy mane to push the head and its slavering jaw away from him. He quickly realised that this was no mask he was holding on to, for there was warm flesh beneath the hair. Sharp claws raked his clothes, tearing through his coat and shirt, and the beast snarled and growled and gave a very decent impression of being a blood-crazed werewolf and Creed, whose disbelief had, by now, been suspended totally, kicked and screamed to get away. It was all insane and it was all very real.

The only weapon he had, the only hard object at hand, was his trusty Nikon, and it was with some regret, but without second thoughts, that he lifted it from his chest and jammed it into the great slobbering mouth before him. His assailant yowled when three jagged teeth broke off and he leapt away to twirl around on the dance floor in agony, scattering guests in all directions. Unfortunately, Lily Neverless happened to wander by at that moment, a hand imperiously stretched out before her, the long cigarette holder at last in its proper place between her rouged (and now smeared) lips. She was unsteady, but she smiled a benign if crooked smile, and as she passed the agonised wolfman she patted his head. That particular condescension enraged it even more; it leapt upon her and tore at her throat, drawing blood that was too oozingly thick to be natural (or healthy).

Lily squawked and gurgled blood and the paparazzi stopped what they were doing in shocked horror, their cameras dropping away from their faces. The horror may have lingered, but the shock didn't: viewfinders returned to eyes and shutters clicked and motors whirred with renewed frenzy at this fresh spectacle. 'Help her!' one of them cried, but no one wanted to miss this unique photo opportunity, least of all the photographer who had shouted.

Another figure, this time a woman in pale gold, her powdered hair coiffured high, barged into Creed, the knock bringing him to his senses. He ceased watching the old actress dying all over again and turned to grab hold of his son.

But the boy was gone.

He wheeled this way and that in panic. By this time, most of the masqueraders were making their way towards the main doors at the far end of the room, their intention obviously to get out, find their transport and flee the Mountjoy Retreat as swiftly as possible, no doubt grateful that it had been a masked ball and their identities would be safe from tomorrow's newspapers. He was halfway down the ballroom before he realised Sammy wasn't among them. He caught a glimpse of the two-tone hag, and that's all it was, merely a glimpse, for she was fading fast like a movie-dissolve, becoming nothing, an empty space. Then another blur, this one closer to him, a quick impression of the beak-nosed blubber-belly before he, too, vanished. The thing with the donkey face and peacock tail was standing alone, glaring resentfully until it popped out like a spent lightbulb, leaving behind a small cluster of drab feathers which drifted lazily to the floor before they, too, disappeared.

Creed's search became even more frantic. Maybe Sammy was lost somewhere in the crush around the main doors, too small to be seen among the tightly packed throng. Or maybe he wasn't down that end at all. He turned back to where Mallik was standing – *had* been standing, for he was gone also – and was just in time to see the spidery figure of Bliss (what a misnomer) slipping through the narrow gap of the partially opened doors at the top of the short staircase. He had his back to Creed, but it was obvious that he had something clutched to his bent body. Creed caught sight of a small shoe and a grey sock protruding from beneath Bliss' elbow.

'*Sammy!*'

Creed chased after them, skirting round the hairy beast that was hunched over the dead rag that had once been Lily Neverless, and had been Lily Neverless again for a short time, worrying the limp form, tearing off slivers of stale meat and swallowing. With the flashing lights, running figures and other fallen bodies, it was almost like crossing a war zone. Creed mounted the stairs two at a time and burst through the door.

Beyond was a wide corridor brightened by a central chandelier, with several doors leading off it. Gilt-framed portraits decorated the walls, faces from history judging by the style and their garb; some of them he vaguely recognised, although he took no time to make a study. At one end was a staircase, its balustrade elegantly curving to the floor above. He heard footsteps and made towards the sound. He paused at the staircase. He could still hear the hurrying footsteps, but they were going down, not up.

Creed went past the stairs and discovered there was another set behind them, these descending to the Retreat's cellars. It was dark and uninviting down there, but when a door slammed below he knew that that was where the creature had taken his son.

He took a little time to think it over. He really didn't want to go down there, he didn't want to follow that wretched thing into the sinister depths of the Mountjoy Retreat. But Sammy was there and who knew what malicious intent Mallik and his creepy henchman had in mind? He remembered the crime for which Nicholas Mallik had been hanged; would he do the same to Sammy, would he dismember the boy out of spite, revenge, maybe even for old times' sake? He had to go after them.

He hesitated on the top step and thought, *on the other hand . . .*

The arched curtained doors further along the hall crashed open and the big man with the broken neck lurched through to smash into the wall opposite. He staggered back a step or two and stood there breathing heavily, his loose, scarred head surveying the floor. His right eye moved round to regard Creed, then he used one of his huge hands to tilt his head for a better view. A low grunt that might have been satisfaction came from him and he swivelled his whole body towards the mesmerised photographer. He lumbered forward, arms waving, head lolling.

Creed descended rapidly and the unhealthy smell of dinginess and dementia welcomed his return. Whether or not he would have entered this dark catacombed sanctum without the added incentive of this maddened monster coming after him he would never truly know, and right then wasn't the time to contemplate the question. He jumped the last couple of steps and fell against a door at the bottom.

He felt for the handle and prayed that the door wouldn't be locked. It wasn't, but once on the other side he looked for a key. There wasn't one, but there was a centre bolt (strange that one should be fitted on *that* side – to keep people out, perhaps?) and he quickly shot it, then leaned back against the wood to catch his breath. A heavy, rolling clatter came from the other side as his pursuer fell down most of the stairs, and Creed smiled with grim satisfaction in the silence that followed.

The smile was wiped away when something slammed against the panel close to his head. The door rattled in its frame and the wood bowed outwards. He leapt away from it as though propelled.

An inadequate naked lightbulb lit the way to another inadequate naked lightbulb along the low ceiling and Creed followed them, having no desire to linger by the increasingly swelling door. He was obviously in the more slummy part of the basement area again, probably close to the rear of the house and perhaps somewhere near where he and Cally (*was she* really *Laura, was she another one of these degenerate fuck-ups pretending to be human?*) had entered originally. There were stone steps now, a short flight, and another passage. He thought he could hear voices in the distance, but had no idea of where they were coming from. He sniffed, catching the faint odour of smoke.

From behind there came the splintering of wood, then a rending and finally a crashing, this followed by the *clomp clomp* of heavy boots.

Creed quickened his pace, breaking into a run when he reached a wider area. The place looked familiar with its various openings and corridors, and he knew he'd been here before when he spotted the big vault-like door set in the opposite wall.

The iron door was open this time. And it was at its entrance that Bliss and Sammy were waiting for him.

36

The spindly creature's wickedly-pointed fingernails were digging into the boy's throat.

'Take it easy,' Creed appealed, holding up a restraining hand, but keeping his distance.

Bliss bared his outrageously long and jagged teeth and hissed.

Creed shivered. 'Tell you what,' he said, doing his utmost to remain calm and reasonable, 'you let the boy go and I'll give you a head start. You could be long gone before the police get here. The place is finished, you know that, but you don't need to take the rap. Cut out now while you've got the chance . . .'

Voices drifted from one of the corridors and Bliss' bug-eyes shot left and right, searching for the source. Creed was delighted to note the confusion in them.

'Come on, give it up,' he said, taking a pace forward.

Bliss lifted Sammy and dipped his bony head to the boy's angled neck, those sharp teeth poised.

'Daaadd . . .' Sammy wailed.

'Don't be stupid!' Creed snapped. 'You're not a fucking vampire, you're just a skinny guy with a diet deficiency. But if you really want to suck blood, here, have some of mine.' *Humour the bastard,* he thought as he pulled up a sleeve and offered his bare arm. 'Come on, forget the virgin stuff – his'd be too sweet for you, anyway. This has been around awhile, matured in the cask you might say, like fine old Scotch.' *When you're dealing with a crazy, you gotta think like a crazy,* he told himself, moving closer all the time. *And this crazy is interested, he might just go for it . . .*

'No!' Creed screamed.

Bliss had jerked back his head to plunge.

Creed held out the camera as if it were a crucifix on a chain. He pressed the shutter release, hoping to use the Hitchcockian trick as before in the park. If he could momentarily blind him with the flash he might be able to snatch Sammy back. But nothing happened this time. He tried again. Still nothing. He moaned aloud, realising he must have broken the mechanism when he'd smashed the camera into the wolfman's jaw earlier.

Was that malicious glee in those horrible staring eyes, Bliss at last betraying some human emotion? Creed attempted to speak, to protest at least, but couldn't. Bliss's mouth opened wider, the fangs glistened wetly.

Two things happened at once.

The broken-necked monster who had been *clomping* the corridors arrived on the scene and threw a clumsy arm over the photographer's shoulder, while on the other side of the chamber a horde of hooting, yelling banshees poured through (at least to Creed they looked like banshees, not that he'd ever seen or even heard banshees in his life before but if he had he was sure they would look exactly like this motley crew). Many were naked, others wearing tattered rags that might have been bedsheets; all were painfully emaciated, resembling refugees from Belsen, and there were women among them, their hair bedraggled and long, breasts like envelope flaps, bodies caked with filth; some of the men, those who wore sheets like robes, could have been auditioning for the part of 'ranting ancient prophet of doom' in a Greek tragedy. Henry Pink, his grimy and stained bedsheet wrapped around his lower body like a huge nappy, feebly waved the keys that had been left in his unlocked cell door. *Les* gleeful *Misérables* crowded into the chamber and stopped dead when they spotted the other occupants. All parties were transfixed, staring in surprise at each other.

It was Creed, needless to say, who reacted first.

He dropped like a stone, slipping under the big restraining arm and made a half-crouched dash for his son.

When he reached him the proceedings became enlivened once more. The mob surged forward and swamped the trio. Creed, Bliss, and Sammy went down under the crush of bodies, falling through the vault-like doorway and sprawling on to a concrete platform inside.

Creed felt a sharp pain in his chest as he pushed himself away, lifting his body and dislodging whoever it was clinging to him from his back. He cried out as the pain became intense and he looked down, thinking he had been stabbed; in a sense, he had, for the vampire wannabe was up to his old tricks again and boring a hole through Creed's torn coat and shirt with his home-grown lethal weapon, i.e. one bony finger.

Creed shook his head and looked directly into the protruding eyes beneath him. 'That's not really happening,' he informed Bliss, but when he examined himself again to make sure, blood was beginning to trickle down the creature's hand.

Creed screamed and pain and fear and aversion to seeing his own red stuff drove him to almost superhuman efforts. He heaved himself further upwards, easily throwing off two more scrawny bodies that had leapt up on him, and grabbed his assailant by the lapels to lift his head and shoulders from the floor. At the same time he brought down his own head in a short but extremely hard movement, executing a perfect head-butt.

His hands let go and shot to his own forehead as he yowled at the new pain. He fell away from his stunned victim and rolled on to his back on the stone floor.

'Dad, Dad . . .' Sammy was kneeling over him and shaking his shoulders.

'Yeah . . .' Creed struggled to sit up. 'Yeah . . . I'm okay. Christ, is that the time?'

He massaged his forehead, forcing his eyes to open, not quite sure of where he was or what he was doing.

'Dad . . .' Sammy urged, shaking him some more.

Creed winced, promising himself he'd never try a head-butt again.

He became aware that the smell of smoke was much stronger and when he focused his eyes he saw why.

The first thing was the gold-amber reflections flickering on the faces and bodies of those gaunt, naked and half-naked ravers assembled around the doorway; the second was the dancing flames shining in his own son's eyes. He turned in the direction they were all looking.

The platform that they were on was, in fact, the landing to a concrete stairway, and below them was a vast room, one that must have been built around the very foundations of the house itself. Its floor was low rather than its ceiling high and there was not a cobweb or damp stain in sight, for this was a protected treasure house of antique furniture, paintings and precious paraphernalia. There were clocks, both small and tall, there were statues, some damaged, some perfect; there were gold and silver boxes and large trunks that might have contained jewellery, or documents, or anything at all. There were also several big safes in the room, every one of them open, their paper contents scattered and feeding the spreading fire.

And at the centre of all this, surrounded by beautiful things that would soon be destroyed by avaricious flames, was a sturdy though intricately-carved chair, a throne of oak, on which sat the slumped form of Nicholas Mallik.

So aged, so incredibly ancient, did he appear, his skin so rutted and dry, the joints of his hands so gnarled, that he might have been sculptured from old oak himself. He sat there without life, unmoving even though fire licked at his ankles. He remained still even when the flames caught the black costume, and unflinching when his flesh began to rupture and sizzle. He seemed too tired to move.

It was almost fascinating to watch, perversely enthralling in its way, and Creed wondered why the man didn't writhe, didn't scream in agony. How could anyone stand such pain? His legs were ablaze, and then his torso, whatever fatty parts there were on that lean frame flaring brightly, infernos within the grand inferno. The fire swallowed his arms, smothering them completely so that his hands blistered and punctured before becoming a deep reddened brown.

The smell of roasting became as strong as the smell of smoke.

Creed hugged Sammy to his chest so that he couldn't see. He held him firm, even though the boy squirmed.

Only when the conflagration reached the gruesomely desiccated face did Mallik begin to move.

His head came up slowly as his thin hair smouldered and his cheeks began to pucker and split. Perhaps it was the sight of the onlookers that changed his expression, or perhaps it was the intense heat shrivelling the stringy meat of his face that forced his lipless mouth into a smile. And Creed, himself, might only have imagined that those dark contemptuous eyes singled him out before they began to bubble and soon cloud over with an opaque whiteness. The fire took hold of the head and Nicholas Mallik shifted for the last time.

He rested back in the blazing chair as though it had been a long tiresome day and now he was going to sleep.

The fire crackled and raged over him, sending out sparks that spiralled to the beamed ceiling.

A high keening sound close by turned Creed's attention from the funeral pyre. Bliss was frantically struggling to free himself of the tangle of bodies at the top of the stairs, his shining eyes never leaving the dreadful sight below. The photographer slid himself and Sammy aside as the creature broke loose and darted past with that peculiar spiderish gait, descending the stairs and running straight into the rapidly spreading blaze, oblivious to the heat, unconcerned, it seemed, with the flames that instantly caught his clothes.

Creed watched horrified as Bliss threw himself on to the shrunken thing inside the inferno. A great plume of flame engulfed him as if he were no more than fresh kindling and the fire shot upwards to torch the ceiling. It spread outwards on the overhead surface, rolling and billowing in a searing wave and the lunatics near Creed and Sammy cheered and pointed.

Sammy clutched his father tightly and hid his face again, this time voluntarily. His voice was muffled when he said, 'Take me home now, Dad. *Please.*'

Keeping his back to the wall, Creed eased past the jubilant banshees, his son clinging to his waist, an arm held up to protect his face from the fierce heat. Together they slipped through the doorway, Creed still keeping his back to the wall and trying to remain unnoticed, ready to run the instant anyone took an undue interest. Fortunately most of the attention in there was on the broken-necked monster, who was beating the air with his enormous fists, roaring his wrath at the unkempt lunatics who were tormenting him. With his unsupported head rolling from one shoulder to the other it was difficult for him to aim effectively. Someone appeared in the doorway behind Creed carrying a burning piece of furniture – it might have been an arm or a leg from a chair – and he waved it over his head, almost setting light to his own long hair. He whooped as he ran at the monster with his firebrand and others present thought it wonderful when he pushed it into the big man's face; they danced around the chamber, mimicking the monster's bellow of pain. Others ran from the burning vault-room with more fire torches and began taunting the Frankenstein thing, surrounding him, poking and lighting his clothes.

I've seen this movie, thought Creed.

An explosion of fire swept through the doorway, hurling several bodies before it. More figures followed, screeching fireballs that bounced off walls or disappeared into corridors, lighting their own way.

'Can you run, Sammy?' Creed asked his son, raising his voice over the bedlam.

The pudgy face jerked itself off Creed's stomach and looked up at him, eyes wide and fearful. 'Will you hold my hand, Daddy?'

He hugged him close again and blinked. God, the smoke was making his eyes water. ''Course I will. Let's give 'em all a race.'

Clasping each other's hands tightly, they took off.

Through the gloomy passageways they went, with Creed praying they were heading towards the back of the house and, hopefully, to the narrow staircase which would lead them to the sidedoor he'd used earlier. No such luck though. He soon realised they were deep within the Retreat's underground labyrinth and when they arrived at the passageway housing the open cells, he considered turning back. Kerfuffles approaching from behind told him that might be a bad idea: the crazy inmates were blocking any retreat.

He led Sammy onwards, once again putting a hand over the boy's eyes as they passed a blackened, still-smouldering heap that was sprawled against a wall. The smell of the charred corpse (Creed was astounded that the poor wretch had got this far) was terrible, but then so was the general stink from the open doorways on either side.

As they passed further along the dimly lit passage they met something crawling towards them. At first Creed had thought it was only a bundle of rags, possibly dumped there by an escapee, but as they drew closer he observed that it was moving – very slowly, but moving nonetheless. The whole of this one's body was swathed in filthy bandages; even one eye was covered (there was just the faintest glitter coming from the other that might have been a reflection of an eyeball). Even more disconcerting was the sight of bandages trailing along the ground where this mummified thing's lower leg should have been. In fact, the lower leg was several yards behind, a black stump with just two toes, and it was trying to catch up.

Creed squirmed at the sight of the remaining big toe, thin and almost fleshless, wriggling in conjunction with the heel in an effort to move itself along, while Sammy was merely absorbed. The bandaged thing raised an arm as if for assistance as they side-stepped by, but it soon flopped to the floor shedding dust (and perhaps a little more rotten flesh) when it was ignored.

There were other things moving in one or two of those open cells, shapes, *lumps*, that bore scant resemblance to anything human, but Creed's curiosity had been more than adequately satiated for one night and he made no attempt whatsoever to discover what these were. He hurried Sammy along and was relieved to leave the dingy chamber of horrors behind and enter the brighter – although, in its way, equally as sinister – corridors of the 'medical' area where the plundered body of Antony Blythe lay on its cold metal slab and where the storeroom of spare parts, organs and eyeballs, limbs and livers, spleens and larynxes was housed.

He would not allow Sammy to rest, even though they were both puffing and panting, the boy's footsteps becoming sluggish. Creed dragged him along, slowing his own pace only slightly. 'Not . . . far, Sam. Only . . . a little . . . way . . . to go,' he encouraged between breaths.

Sammy began to cry.

'Okay . . . okay.' Creed stopped and knelt in front of his son. 'Fireman's lift. Remember how we did it when you were little?'

The boy nodded, his lower lip trembling. 'I don't like it here,' he said miserably.

'Did they do anything to you, Sam?'

He shook his head. 'Don't think so. I've been asleep.'

Creed closed his eyes in relief. With luck his son had been too doped up to take in any of the weird goings-on in this place. 'Over my shoulder you go.'

Sammy leaned forward and allowed his father to rise with him on his shoulder. Creed patted the plump rump. 'Back to the diet after this, Sam,' he called out.

'Yes, Dad,' the meek reply came back.

Onwards again, Creed's legs not too steady under the load, and quite soon they found themselves in another corridor at the end of which was a broad concertina door. Creed remembered it from earlier, when he and Cally had been making their way up to the ballroom; it was a lift used for goods, patients (presumably when they were brought down to receive transplants from unconsenting donors) and geriatric invalids on the Retreat's upper levels. He and the girl had avoided using it then, figuring it might be more discreet to sneak up the staircase; however, now was not the time for sneaking and climbing stairs.

Footsteps and demented hollering from behind sent him on his way again. By the time he reached the lift it felt as if he had a sack of coal over his shoulder. He pulled at the handle and the door slowly, awkwardly, folded open. He bundled Sammy inside and dumped him unceremoniously into a corner, quickly spinning round to shut the door again.

The lunatics were already halfway down the corridor, a terrifying sub-human rabble who lurched and reeled after him, their skin black with dirt and smoke, their faces alight with madness. He couldn't see old Henry Pink among them, but then he didn't stop to look too long. He heaved at the door.

It slid along, then stuck.

Creed pulled harder and the door moved again, then stopped again, leaving a six-inch gap. He smacked it and added a kick for good measure. 'Bastard,' he accused.

Changing position, he pushed at the handle rather than pulled and the concertina straightened a little more. Four inches to go, now three . . .

Grubby fingers, nails chewed to the quick, crept round the opening and stopped the door.

Creed didn't hesitate. He bent down to the grimy digits and bit as hard as he could. A shriek from the other side and the fingers disappeared. He slammed the door shut and held it there.

The pounding from the other side was fearsome, but the door was solid enough. Someone out there started tugging at the handle and it took all of Creed's strength to hold it steady. He had to take the risk of letting go for a moment to reach for the level buttons and of the three, he punched the middle one. He swung back against the elevator wall as the metal door sank away. Perspiration trickled into his eyes and it was difficult to wipe away, so shaky was his hand. His chest was heaving as he tried to catch his breath.

Sammy watched from the corner, his knees tucked under his chin, his round face deathly pale, mouth agog. Creed was too anxious himself to reassure the boy convincingly.

The ride was brief and the door that came into view was straight and made of rich mahogany. 'Beds and garden furniture,' Creed announced with forced humour when the lift bumped to a halt. He leaned forward and hauled Sammy to his feet. 'We'll soon be out, Sam. Wait 'til you tell the kids at school, huh? They won't believe it.' Judas, who would?

He wrenched back the door (which ran more smoothly than the one below) and they stepped out into further mayhem.

The hallway was filled with agitated masqueraders, milling around, jabbering excitedly, all of them trying to make for the Retreat's main doors. Creed was surprised at how many there were, for surely the majority of them should have been well away by this time; then he saw that their numbers had been swollen by others clad in nightwear. It seemed that everyone in the home, geriatrics as well as lunatics, was on the loose.

He and Sammy joined the throng, Creed leading with the boy close behind, shoving their way through the crowd, not caring who they nudged aside, be it male, female, young or old. Some of the guests' masks had gone, no doubt knocked off in the jostle, and he mentally whistled when he recognised a few faces here and there. Wasn't that the silly old bishop who was forever upsetting his Synod with his stubborn repudiation of all things miraculous? And that definitely was a member of the Shadow Cabinet, a man they said was on the shortlist of those in line for premiership should the current government lose the next election. Christ! And that woman over there looked like the wife of the American tycoon whose multinational companies virtually dominated world trade. There were other, lesser mortals that he recognised or half-recognised and he couldn't help but wonder what the Devil's going rate was for souls. Had he known where to apply he might have struck a deal himself some years ago when young and even more desperate for wealth and fame.

He kept moving, elbowing aside a frail old lady in a dressing gown who wouldn't hobble out of his way fast enough. She wished him joy in catching cancer, but he was too busy with escape to respond. A silver-haired gentleman in a deep-green quilted smoking jacket turned to admonish him for shoving (he was an old theatre queen Creed had thought long-dead) but somebody else pushed by with such ferocity that they both nearly went down.

This is getting ridiculous, Creed told himself, dragging Sammy on. What the hell was the hold-up? By now they were almost in the reception area near the frontdoors and the crowd had grown too thick for anyone to move. He stood on tiptoe to see what was causing the blockage, using his son's shoulder to steady himself. He caught sight of several blue-uniformed attendants by the doors and it was they who were holding back the crowd; he couldn't see her but he could hear the familiar voice of the fat receptionist, squealing at the people to remain calm and to move away, to return to the ballroom until it was safe to leave. Creed guessed that the paparazzi had been thrown out of the side entrance and had gathered out front with freshly loaded cameras, waiting for the guests to make their hasty departures.

He realised that he and Sammy would never get out this way. Okay, find another exit.

'No problem, Sam,' he told his son. 'We'll use the back way.'

But right then there erupted a scream so shrill that everyone was stunned for a second or two. It was followed by a word that was equally piercing:

'*Fire!*'

This time everyone screamed.

Creed was just able to lift Sammy before they were swept forward in a tidal wave of bodies, the surge heading directly for the big double-doors. Nothing – certainly not the obese woman and her burly cohorts – could stem that tide. The guests and residents, newly joined by the basement lunatics, who had found their way upstairs bringing bits of the fire with them, burst out into the cold night air, trampling those who wouldn't go with the flow (like the fat lady) underfoot, smoke already beginning to pour through with them.

Creed and Sammy were spun around, bumped this way and that, flashlights blinding them, yells and screams of panic almost deafening them. But they were *free*, and Creed shut his eyes and whooped with delight. He kissed his startled son and rumpled his hair, then from sheer elation he whipped off the mask of the nearest person to him, turning swiftly to do the same to the fleeing masquerader on his other side.

'*Get 'em, boys!*' he shouted to the busy paparazzi, laughing as he was carried along. '*Get the fuckers!*'

The crowds thinned as people headed for their cars, others among them sprinting across the lawns and into the darkness.

'*Joe! Joe!*'

Creed paused at the sound of his name. He looked around, steadying himself against the knocks and shoves. Someone was running across the drive towards him and he held up a hand against the popping lights, squinting to see who it was.

'*Joe, what's happening here?*'

Prunella threw herself at him, knocking him back a step or two. Sammy, who had been watching the house and the lovely orange glow that was spreading along its lower windows, twisted in his father's arms to see what had hit them. He returned his attention to the house when he realised it was only a girl.

'*You did it!*' Creed shouted at Prunella, holding her tight and making a sandwich of the boy.

'But I still don't understand what's going on here, Joe. You didn't explain when you rang this afternoon, so tell me now. What kind of party was this and who are the big names you said would be here? One of the paps told me Lily Neverless was inside, but that's impossible, isn't it, Joe?'

'Yeah, it's impossible. But they got the shots.'

'I don't understand. Why did you want me to spread the word that something big was happening here tonight? Didn't you want it just for yourself? I don't get it, Joe, I don't *understand*! Tell me *why*!'

'Insurance,' he said, still grinning from ear to ear. He kissed her and Sammy said, '*Yuk.*'

'Insurance,' Creed repeated.

37

That's it, more or less.

Creed, our not-so-lovable hero, has come through. He's saved his son from a fate as bad as death and, as he's soon to find out, discouraged a great evil from rearing its ugly head once more – for the time being, anyway. He has managed this without much mettle, with very few scruples (if any at all), and a great deal of self-interest. That might be a lesson to us all.

Having fought the great fight (fought it by running away mostly) and won, Creed has shown that it's not only the bold, the brave, and the noble, who can achieve a result; sometimes a little rottenness can too.

The future for Joe Creed? Well the present isn't quite over for him just yet. The finale is still to come . . .

Another day, another dollar, he thought as he wearily turned the frontdoor key.

A rooftop bird trilled in the dawn and Creed peered up at the sky, grateful for the creeping greyness. He'd had enough of the night.

He stepped over the threshold and closed the door behind him, then sat on the bottom step, giving himself a moment of quiet contemplation, a catching up of his thoughts.

Sammy was back home with his mother and Creed expected the phone to start ringing at any second. Evelyn had probably been phoning since their son's return, and he pictured her at that moment, fast asleep, receiver still in hand, exhausted by her own persistence. Well, she'd have to wait for the full story.

It had taken over two hours to get Sammy back to his mother's house, and the boy had slept all the way, his eyes closing as soon as Creed had laid him in the Suzuki's passenger seat and wrapped him in a rug. Creed had stopped the jeep just around the corner from home and had woken him, anxious to find out what the boy understood of his big adventure. Thankfully it turned out to be not too much. Sammy remembered sort of waking up in a big house, then sleeping again, then seeing all the funny dressed-up people, then being chased by a lot of other funny people, and that was about it, and was it tea-time, because he was starving and thirsty too and could we go home now, Dad?

Relieved, Creed had started up the jeep again and driven round to Evelyn's house. The boy might remember more later when the effects of the drugs they'd kept him on wore off, but half of it would still seem like a dream, and thank Christ for that. The worst Evelyn would hear of was a short-term kidnapping.

He parked the jeep, then carried Sammy up the short garden path to stand him on the doorstep. After ringing the bell, Creed bent down and kissed his son on the forehead. Sammy didn't respond, he didn't throw his arms around his father and tell him he was the best dad in the world and he wanted to be just like him when he grew up and when could he visit again? Sammy yawned.

The hall light came on and Creed was back down the garden path and climbing into the Suzuki even as his ex-wife's voice came complaining through the letterbox. He heard Sammy reply and waited only for the sound of the door being unlocked before gunning the engine and burning rubber. No way could he face Evelyn tonight.

Besides, there was still too much to do.

When he got back to London the word had spread for, although the Fleet Street ghetto was no longer in existence, the telepathy between newspapers still flourished. The buzz was on about the great fire at the country mansion and the paps were busy selling shots to the various journals and syndicates of a dancing woman who bore a remarkable resemblance to the recently departed actress, Lily Neverless. Some of them even had snaps of the woman being savaged by what appeared to be a very large dog in fancy dress, but none of these had turned out very well. Unfortunately the whole place – it was later discovered to be some kind of upmarket old folks' home – had gone up in smoke, apparently taking the old girl and many others with it. To make matters worse, there had been a grand masked ball that night and the guests had been involved in the fire too; just how many had been burned alive had not yet been ascertained. Still, there were good pictures of masqueraders – with some well-known faces among them – fleeing in wonderful costumes. Great stuff for the breakfast table.

When Creed arrived at the *Dispatch*, he refused to make any comment until he had developed the film from his damaged camera himself. The shots taken at the Mountjoy Retreat were okay, not a frame lost. In fact, the shots were terrific. He had evidence on film of the awful things going on at the so-called rest home: the dungeons, poor Henry Pink, the operating theatre with Antony Blythe's mutilated body lying on the metal slab, the storeroom full of spare body parts. It was sensational and Creed knew he had finally made the big one.

But of course when he went to the night editor with the story he kept the unbelievable bits – the ones about demons and resurrections and monsters and shape-changers – to himself. No way was he going to kill his story (and its value) with such supernatural nonsense. No way.

Kidnap, murder, illegal transplants, cruelty, arson and lunatics taking over the asylum – plus the suggestion that a notorious child-murderer had escaped the hangman's noose before the last World War with full knowledge of the authorities concerned – was good enough. Who could want anything more? Not he, oh no.

He insisted, being in the bargaining seat for the first time in his life, that Prunella, who had been waiting for him at the *Dispatch*, write the whole story (so, not such a bad guy after all and besides, he'd enjoyed the afternoon romp with her and hoped to repeat it in the near future).

It took time to tell and to answer the thousand-and-one questions afterwards, which was why it was dawn when Creed finally reached home.

He might well have fallen asleep right there on the stairs had not a sound from above (oh God, how he'd grown used to that over the past few days) roused him.

He was aware of who it was with him in the house and he didn't bolt for the door. No, he was too tired for that and besides, most of his fear had been drained by now. Perhaps instinctively he knew the worst was over; perhaps the atmosphere itself held no hint of danger. Or it could simply have been that there had to be a conclusion to this whole bizarre affair and he knew it was waiting for him up there somewhere.

The slightest aroma of musk on the stairs had already hinted at her presence.

With heavy legs, Creed climbed the stairs. He found Cally in the bedroom.

38

S he was wrapped in deep-red, a cloak or cape of some kind that covered most of her body, and she sat on the bed, her knees drawn up, back against the wall. The early-dawn light through the partially drawn curtains offered shadows rather than brightness.

'No point in asking how you got in,' he said from the doorway.

She said nothing.

'I thought not. You can come and go as you please, right?' He loitered by the door, no longer afraid of her, but not so foolish as to lessen the chance of a quick exit.

'I had to talk to you,' she said, her voice heavy with tiredness, as if she were as exhausted as Creed himself. 'I wanted to . . . explain.' The last word was spoken limply, as if it were inadequate.

'Why? What do you care?'

He heard her sigh, a rough-edged sound.

'I want it to end here, Joe. If you keep wondering you'll never be content, you'll try to find out more for yourself, and that might upset things again.'

'You think I'm that interested? Listen, I've had enough, I want to forget the whole thing.'

'Perhaps you feel that way now. But eventually you'll get curious again, you'll start delving into matters that could be harmful to you and to those around you. Unanswered questions never quite go away, do they?'

He shrugged. 'Maybe you're right. Too many unbelievable things have happened to me to think straight.'

'Yet you did begin to believe. Finally you lost your scepticism.'

'Wasn't that the idea?'

A pause, then: 'You're not always so dumb as you appear, are you? You knew we were breaking you down, showing you things that no normal person would ever accept, priming you for the time we needed you to believe in everything we presented to you.'

'No, I didn't know. It occurred to me driving back here this morning. You could have dealt with me easily enough right at the beginning. Christ, he had the power to do that.'

'Belial?'

'Nicholas Mallik.'

'The same.'

'Whatever. So I figured you terrorised me for a specific purpose. Sure, the original idea was to get the shots I took of Mallik at Lily's funeral, but then it became more than that. It developed into a kind of game, didn't it?'

'In a way. He had the notion that if you, a true cynic of this sceptical age, could be convinced that the Fallen Angels existed and were not merely figments of mythology or fable, then it would help them regain their dwindling powers.'

'Wonderful thing, faith.'

'It works for God.'

'I still don't understand why me.'

'You happened along.'

'No, I mean there were plenty of believers at the masquerade last night.'

'They had good cause to believe. Every one of them has gained from their homage to Belial. You were an outsider, a materialistic non-believer, and as such you became the test.'

'Lucky me.'

'I tried to warn you.'

'That I couldn't figure.'

She remained silent for a while. 'Will you come closer?' she said at last.

'Uh, I don't think so.'

'You're safe, Joe, I won't harm you.'

'Oh yeah?'

'Sit at the end of the bed while I tell you more.'

What the hell, he thought. He could be through the door and down the stairs before she raised a hand or started a shimmer. He sat on the corner of the bed, poised to take flight at the slightest provocation.

'So why did you try to warn me?' he asked.

'I'm not one of them, part of me is different. There's a conflict inside me that as yet has not been resolved. It's possible to become tired of evil, you know.'

'Too much of anything can become tedious.'

'Yes, I suppose even for them.'

'Tell me who "they" really are, Cally.'

'I already have. The Fallen Angels, cohorts of the Archangel who fell from grace. You saw some of them for yourself last night – Abraxas, Hel, Fomors, Adramelech, Loki, and others. They manifest themselves when the faith is strong.'

'Wait a minute. You mean those moth-eaten freaks with snake tails and peacock feathers and God-knows-what-else were these *Angels*?'

'You would rather call them demons. But no, that isn't how they are, it's how mankind sees them or, I should say, imagines them. They appear as they are perceived.'

'I saw Mallik become one of them.'

'You saw Belial, but only as a concept. Very few have the potential to observe the real demon of lies, and the sight has always taken their sanity, if not their life.'

'Mallik and Aleister Crowley . . .'

'Crowley had both the ability and the yearning to see. Belial revealed himself to the master magician and his son in Paris many years ago. Crowley was driven mad and his son died from the trauma of what they witnessed.'

She noticed Creed's thin smile. 'Ah, your doubt is returning so soon. For you, that's good. It'll help you cope.'

312

Her hair had no lustre in the weak dawn light and her eyes seemed heavy, her shoulders slumped. He thought she might fall asleep at any moment. 'Tell me about the Mountjoy Retreat,' he prompted. 'What was it used for?'

'I think Belial meant it to be destroyed when its purpose had been fulfilled. It was a place to rest, Joe, a place to recuperate. A refuge, you might say, as well as a treasure house for all the possessions he had gathered through the centuries.'

'It was more than that. It was a bloody asylum.'

'And even more than that. A home for rejuvenation.'

'For resurrection, you mean.'

'That too.'

'Lily Neverless . . .'

'She didn't turn out too well, did she? The new organs they gave her failed to help in the end. And her brain had deteriorated too much. Belial blamed you for interrupting the ritual at the cemetery.'

'When I photographed Mallik?'

'As he spilt his seed into the earth for the rebirth.'

'And I thought he was just a dirty old pervert.'

'Joke if you want, Joe. It's probably better that you do.'

'No, none of it's funny.' He gave a shake of his head. 'That's the pity of it. Lily wasn't the only one, was she? You kept your own supply of goodies down in the basement for instant use. Mallik was doing it back in the 'thirties.'

'They've always . . . collected.'

He leaned forward, one hand resting by her foot. 'Tell me, what would have happened to old Lil afterwards? You know, if things hadn't turned out so badly last night. What would they – you – have done with her?'

'She would have continued to live at the Retreat, that was her bargain with Belial. She would have lived on, like so many others.'

'Other failures?'

'The failures are few, and the worst of those were kept in the lower chambers.'

'The dungeons, you mean. I thought they were for loonies like Henry Pink, a place to torment anyone who had ever upset Mallik in the past.'

'Certain people had to be punished.'

'Pink was a professional hangman, for Christ's sake. He didn't get any pleasure out of it.'

'You think not? And you the cynic.'

That silenced Creed for a moment. 'Who else was kept down there?'

'The experimentals, and others who had been kept alive too long.'

'I saw someone covered from head to foot – one foot, anyway – in bandages.'

'He was centuries old. There was hardly anything left of him.'

'He was like a . . . like a mummified thing.'

'Where do you think your own legends spring from? Do you honestly believe in vampires, mummies . . .'

'Werewolves? And the other goon who looked like Frankenstein . . .'

'Frankenstein's monster. Prometheus, to be precise. And, of course, the walking dead. All these imaginations created by yourselves from rumours, even subconscious knowledge, of our ways, exaggerations realised to abate your deeper fears.'

'Are you saying that Nos – Bliss – wasn't a vampire?'

'Of course he wasn't, but eventually even he wasn't too certain. You might say Bliss had begun to believe his own publicity.'

'But he did things, he floated outside my window . . .'

'An illusion, as you originally suspected. We *wanted* you to believe these things, we *helped* you to.'

'He stabbed me with his finger. He drew blood. I didn't imagine that.'

'Show me the wound.'

Without hesitation, Creed opened his coat. 'There, look, bloodstains.'

'Show me the wound,' she repeated.

He pulled at his shirt and stared at his own chest. He touched his skin, then turned towards the light from the window. 'It's gone. Not a mark.'

'Already you're beginning to distrust what you know.'

'It's only genuine if you believe?'

'No. It's real enough. But if you don't accept it, the effect is minimal. And it works both ways, Joe – the powers of Light are as diminished as the powers of Darkness if they're not accepted.'

'A coupla days ago I'd be rolling on the floor listening to this. Even now I'm telling myself I should at least be chuckling.'

'Tomorrow you might. You'll start to ask yourself if you didn't dream half the things you witnessed. You'll be protecting yourself.'

'I *know* what happened.'

'We'll see.'

She moved on the bed and Creed edged away, almost rising. Cally settled once more. 'Don't be nervous, Joe. I told you, it's over. Belial has left this place for the time being.'

'That's something else I don't understand. Why *did* Mallik kill himself last night?'

'Belial was never alive – at least never in the sense that we've been conditioned to believe in. He destroyed the shell he'd been using for so many, many years, along with the secrets and the prizes he had gathered during that time. Quite simply, he had wearied of the game.'

'Is that all it is, a game?'

'More or less. It's always been such.'

'And it's finished?'

'Oh no. There'll be a fresh start, but I don't know when or where it will originate. Perhaps in a place where the old beliefs are still strong. South America, India – who knows? The Middle East is already being used by others. But there are still scores of dark zones on this earth, countries, even continents, where the demons can thrive.'

'That's it, though? He's packed his bags and left here for good?'

'He took nothing with him. He needs nothing, not even his loyal servant, Bliss. He grew weary of him, too.'

'Has everything been destroyed at the Retreat?'

'Everything of importance.'

'And you let your mother die there.'

Her head snapped up as though he had surprised her. 'I keep forgetting how little you understand,' she said. 'Lily Neverless was my mother. Nicholas Mallik, Belial incarnate, was my father.'

It took a while for that to sink in. Creed rubbed his forehead, then the back of his neck. He opened his mouth to speak and closed it when he realised his thoughts were not quite there yet. He tried again. 'There is no Grace Buchanan?'

'Joe, everyone knew Lily had a daughter, and they naturally assumed that Edgar Buchanan was the father. Haven't you realised by now? I *am* Grace Buchanan.'

His voice was even, but very grim. 'She'd be old, she'd be at least –'

'You've witnessed so much, yet still you doubt the Delphian forces. We can control the ageing process just as some of us can control our shape. I chose to remain of a certain age, although it meant I could not be known as Lily's daughter after a time. That was why Grace was kept away from the public eye, why stories of mental illness were deliberately rumoured.'

'But your brother . . .'

'Daniel? Not my brother, Joe – my son. Sired by someone not unlike yourself, and with no demonic powers because of it.' She spoke in a whisper: 'But then all our powers are waning more rapidly now that Belial has forsaken us.'

Something dredged the lower regions of Creed's stomach. Cally was still in shadow, although the light shining through the gap in the curtains had grown stronger since he'd entered the bedroom. He could see her eyes, but there might have been a thin veil over the rest of her face so indistinct was it. He rose from the bed and went to the window; he drew back the curtains and allowed the grey dawn full incursion. Creed turned back to the figure sitting on his bed.

He (and possibly you, too) expected to find an elderly woman there, maybe even a wrinkled hag, given the physical trauma of a young body ageing overnight. But Cally was no Ayesha: she had hardly changed at all.

She smiled at him. 'It'll come, Joe. But not for a while.'

He was relieved and, perhaps naturally enough, far less wary of her. He went back to the bed and sat closer to her. He frowned.

There was a difference. Cally's skin was still clear, her features fine and unsagging. It was her eyes that revealed the passing of years, for they were not just tired, they were dispirited.

He reached to touch her hand, but she swiftly withdrew.

'Please don't, Joe. For your sake, don't.'

'Laura . . . you . . . ?'

She nodded. 'God knows why, but I had some feelings for you at the beginning, I really did want to help you. I'm afraid the human condition has always been one of my failings. I wanted you, but those desires changed to something more, an unholy kind of lust. I became something else, something basely carnal so that I could take full pleasure in you, and even that mutated to something more, something worse . . .'

'But you saved me that day at . . .' He stopped, thinking hard. 'Liable and Co.' He clucked his tongue. 'I thought there was something about that name. A simple anagram of Belial, right? Not very smart, but then who would know, who would care? You did come and rescue me, though.'

'The game had to go on. It was only your friends who saved you last night.'

'My pals the paparazzi.'

'How did they know Lily would be there?'

'They didn't, and neither did I. I just felt I was getting into something way over my head so I arranged a little insurance. I asked someone at my newspaper to put the word around that something big was going down at the Mountjoy Retreat last night. I figured there might be safety in numbers, and I wasn't wrong. You didn't see me hiding near the drive, did you? You just knew I'd be along at any time, that's why you were waiting for me. That fat receptionist knew who I was when I spoke to her in the afternoon. You had me half-suckered, Cally, I'll give you that.'

'Will you tell everything, Joe?'

'You mean will I sell the *whole* story to the highest bidder? I'd be crazy to. I've got enough without the demon stuff, anyway.'

'You've no evidence of Nicholas Mallik's existence. No photographs, no negatives. I'm glad of that.'

He shrugged. 'It would have added a little spice. A child murderer and mutilator who supposedly was hanged back there in the 'thirties, assuming a new identity and still plying his old trade behind the harmless façade of a rest home for gentlefolk. Even after all these years his mug shots compared pretty well with the old newspaper copies.' He sounded regretful.

She managed a weak smile. 'You won't change, Joe. Perhaps it was your low-life nature that ultimately got you through all this.'

'I like to think so.'

The smile stayed and she lifted a hand towards him. 'You're not so different from us,' she said.

A softness melted into his mind, a seductive and pleasing infiltration that slurred his thoughts. Cally was breathing deeply, watching him with hooded eyes. He remembered the changeling, the one who had called herself Laura, and he thought of her pale skin, the deepness between those albescent thighs . . .

Cally breathed him and he pressed forward to –

He froze. Her image had become less defined, had begun to waver. *'Noooo,'* he heard her moan.

But he was sinking into her, his senses aroused both through memory and the allure of Cally herself. The musky smell of her sexual desire was strong, intoxicating. He was close, so close, his lips an inch away from hers . . . from Cally's . . . from Laura's . . .

'No!' This time it was a sharp cry and she pushed at his chest, sending him toppling to the floor.

And she was Cally again, her eyes clear, yet somehow distant. For a fleeting second she seemed to shrink within herself.

'It's over,' she said, her voice dry and passionless.

Creed steadied himself. Yeah, it was over, he knew that, but for a moment there . . .

He stood up and went back to the window, blocking half its light. 'You'd better go, Cally,' he told her, unsure of himself.

She nodded, and did not move. Maybe she was getting control of herself. Finally she rose from the bed and she seemed smaller, somehow less vital, less forceful. She moved to the door.

'Where will you go?' he asked, not wanting her to leave, yet desperate for her to.

'I'll wait. And then I'll find him again.'

'D'you have to do that? Can't you just live a normal life?'

Even her laughter was worn.

'I'm his daughter,' she said.

She pulled the dark red garment around herself and went through the door.

Creed followed, but not right away; the 'impulse' required a few seconds' thought.

'Cally!' he called, but when he reached the landing only Grin was waiting for him there, the dead mouse in its mouth spoiling its smug expression somewhat.

'Not now, you bloody fool,' Creed muttered, stepping over the cat, who swished its crooked tail in exasperation.

The frontdoor was open and Cally had gone. Creed ran downstairs and out into the cobbled mews. '*Cally!*' he called again, but even when he reached the corner she was nowhere to be seen. He looked this way and that, wildly at first and then more moderately. 'Cally.' This time he spoke the name.

Creed shivered – with the cold, he thought – and took one last look towards the mews entrance. Was that it? Had she really gone for good? A part of him hoped so. A smaller part, tucked down somewhere on a level between the conscious and subconscious, the place where all kinds of perversities like to skulk, hoped not. He groped in his pockct for a cigarette.

Shit, he didn't need her kind of aggravation.

He strolled back to his frontdoor, pausing on the step to light the crumpled roll-up. It was going to be a heavy day. An hour or so of sleep, phone off the hook. Evelyn would be burning wire before very long and he wanted a good story ready for her when he finally took the call, something that would make him the hero. Hell, he *was* the hero; his son had been kidnapped and he had rescued him single-handedly. No knight in shining armour could have been bolder and no father more courageous. The media would be beating a path to his doorstep as soon as the first edition of the *Dispatch* hit the street, but they wouldn't get much from him. The cheque-book deal had already been struck with his own newspaper, God bless the wealthy proprietor and all his forefathers, so after a short rest it was back to the office to fill in some more of the story. But first, when the hour was a shade more civilised, a little detour to Fix Features where a contact sheet was waiting to be examined, the shots from the second roll of film he'd used in the cemetery on that fateful day. The roll that had a clear shot of Nicholas Mallik approaching Lily Neverless' grave. Wouldn't prove anything, might not amount to much; but it would just add that little extra spice.

Yeah.

Creed went into the house and closed the door behind him. This time he bolted it, top and bottom.